9/08

THE DAY BEFORE MIDNIGHT

THE
DAY
BEFORE
MIDNIGHT

Stephen Hunter

BANTAM BOOKS
TORONTO · NEW YORK · LONDON · SYDNEY · AUCKLAND

THE DAY BEFORE MIDNIGHT
A Bantam Book / February 1989

All rights reserved.
Copyright © 1989 by Stephen Hunter.

Book design by Richard Oriolo.

No part of this book may be reproduced or transmitted in any form or by any means, electronic or mechanical, including photocopying, recording, or by any information storage and retrieval system, without permission in writing from the publisher.
For information address: Bantam Books.

Library of Congress Cataloging-in-Publication Data

Hunter, Stephen, 1946–
  The day before midnight.

  I. Title.
PS3558.U494D39 1989   813'.54   88–22177
ISBN 0-553-05327-2

Published simultaneously in the United States and Canada

Bantam Books are published by Bantam Books, a division of Bantam Doubleday Dell Publishing Group, Inc. Its trademark, consisting of the words ''Bantam Books'' and the portrayal of a rooster, is Registered in U.S. Patent and Trademark Office and in other countries. Marca Registrada. Bantam Books, 666 Fifth Avenue, New York, New York 10103.

PRINTED IN THE UNITED STATES OF AMERICA

DH   0   9   8   7   6   5   4   3   2   1

If you were at Waterloo,
If you were at Waterloo,
  Makes no difference what you do,
If you were at Waterloo.

—*British schoolboys' rhyme,*
nineteenth century

AUTHOR'S NOTE

Close observers of Maryland geography will immediately recognize that the author has allowed himself to manipulate the landforms of the state to suit his dramatic purposes. To note two such obvious alterations in reality, South Mountain, though it exists exactly where I have placed it, is not nearly so high and formidable a peak as I have pretended. And the relationship of Burkittsville to South Mountain has likewise been adjusted a few miles to fit the story together more conveniently.

I've allowed myself a similar latitude in depicting the performance of certain military units. Though in fact the Army's Special Operation Group/Delta, the Rangers, and the 1st Battalion (Reinf), Third Infantry, as well as light infantry and tactical air support units of the Maryland National Guard and the Maryland Air Guard do exist, the author hopes that readers understand this is a work of fiction, and although it aspires to accuracy in its portrayal of procedure, its depiction of the performance of these units during a national security crisis is wholly a fabrication.

Finally, the author would like to thank all who gave so generously of time and energy in his researches. These include colleagues Michael Hill, Randi Henderson, Matt Seiden, Pat McGuire, Weyman Swagger, and Fred Rasmussen; friends Lenne P. Miller, Jr.; Joe Fanzone, Jr.; Gerard F. "Buzz" Busnuk; T. Craig Taylor, Jr.; David Petzal; Ernest Volkman; my father-in-law, Richard C. Hageman; my brother-in-law and medical adviser, John D. Bullock, M.D.; my brother, Tim Hunter; and my two children, Jake and Amy, who cooperated (more or less) on a long Sunday drive out to South Mountain. And lastly let me issue special thanks to four believers without whose support I could not have endured: my indefatigable agent, Victoria Gould Pryor; my editors, Peter Guzzardi and Ann Harris of Bantam Books; and most especially, my hardworking, ever cheerful, and forgiving wife, Lucy Hageman Hunter.

0700

It snowed that night, and sometime after three, Beth Hummel awoke, as she always did, to the sound of small bare feet padding urgently across the hard wood of the floor.

"Mommy?"

It was the voice of her older daughter. Bean—derived somehow from Elizabeth—was seven, a careful, grave second-grader who wrote her numbers and her name with exaggerated precision and had filled out her Christmas list from the Sears catalogue as if it were a college application.

Beth rolled gently, hoping not to awaken Jack next to her, and turned to face the child in the darkness. Her daughter was very close, and Beth could smell her, warm and fresh like a loaf hot from the oven.

"Yes, honey?"

"Mommy, it's snowing."

"I know. They said it would on the TV."

"The world is all white. Jesus loves the world, he made it all white."

"I'm sure he does, honey," said Beth.

Jack snorted in his sleep, came from unconsciousness with a loggy lurch, half rose, then whispered gruffly, "Shhhhhh, girls."

He fell back, inert in seconds.

"Mommy, can I get in?"

"Of course, honey," said Beth, scooting over and lifting the covers so that there was room for Bean, who climbed in and snuggled against her mother. The child was still in a second. Beth could feel her daughter's heart pumping and the rise and fall of her fragile chest. Her little nose was full; she breathed with a vaguely ragged sound, and Beth worried that it would bother Jack, but behind her he continued to sleep heavily.

Beth drifted off herself then. She was dreaming of tropical beaches. But only an hour or two later another soft tread, slightly swifter, slightly lighter, nudged her from her shallow sleep. Poo—from Phyllis—had discovered the snow.

"Mommy!" Poo whispered in a gleeful rush of excitement, touching her mother with taut fingers. "Mommy, it's white outside."

"Shhh, I know," whispered Beth. Poo was five, a kindergartner, whose blond hair had not yet begun to darken, like Bean's. She was impossibly beautiful, and as lively as Bean was grave. She was a bossy, feisty child who tormented her older sister, and occasionally her mother. You couldn't tell her a thing, like Jack.

"Mommy, Jesus loves us."

"Yes, he does," said Beth again. The connection between Jesus's love and the snow dated from an obscure remark made by a Sunday-school teacher a few weeks back to Poo, in November, on the occasion of the season's first snowfall. Beth had never been too sure what to make of it.

"Mommy, I'm cold. I had a bad dream. Can I come in too?"

Jack sometimes joked that all his life he'd wanted to sleep with two women at the same time and now he sometimes woke up with *three* of 'em in the same bed.

"Yes, but be careful," Beth whispered. "Don't wake Bean or Daddy."

But Poo hadn't waited for the answer. That wasn't her style. She climbed aboard and scuttled like a little commando up the gully between her mother and her father, and slid in between them.

Beth felt the brush of her younger daughter's toes, cold from the long race across the bare floor. Then Poo seemed to merge with her mother, to simply become one with her, their breaths and rhythms joined. Beth pulled the covers up to her neck, felt the embrace of the warmth, its sluggish, numbing power.

But she could not get back to sleep. She lay in the silence, feeling the ease and sighs of her daughters. Now and then something ticked in the house, or a draft of uncommonly cold air came through the door. She lay, waiting for unconsciousness, which did not come. Finally, she looked over at the clock. It was almost six. The alarm would go off at six-thirty, and Jack had to be out of the house and in his pickup by seven for a drive to a new job in Boonsboro; the girls had to be fed and dressed for the bus by eight. So finally, Beth decided to get out of bed.

Crossing the floor, she pulled her slippers on and then her robe, a red polyester thing from Monkey Ward that had seen better days. She hoped

Jack would get her a new one for Christmas in a few weeks, but since he usually did his shopping at the drugstore on Christmas Eve, she knew it to be unlikely. She looked back at the three heads sunk into and embraced by the pillows. Her husband, an athletic and muscular man three years older than her twenty-nine, slept heavily. He looked like an animal in a den, lost in dreamless mammal sleep as the seasons changed. And her two daughters, facing the other direction, out toward the shaded windows, were delicate and lyrical in the dim light beginning to stream in at the margins of the shades. They were tiny and perfect, their nostrils fragile as lace, their lips like candy slices, the whisper of their breaths soft and persistent. But she was aware that it was sometimes far easier to love them when they were in repose, as now, than when they were at each other like wildcats in the backseat of the station wagon. She smiled at them—her three charges in the world—and felt something profoundly satisfactory move through her. Her family. Hers. Then she crept into the bathroom, quickly squirted some Crest on her toothbrush, and cleaned her teeth. She headed downstairs to start breakfast.

Beth walked around the house, pulling up the shades. The morning light was just beginning to show over the trees. Yes, it had snowed; a light powder, unmarked as yet by human traces, lay across everything. Maybe Jesus did love them. The world looked freshly minted. It was radiant as far as she could see. The clouds had cleared overnight. From the kitchen window, over the sink, she could see the white roofs of Burkittsville, a collection of sloping rectangles against the white netting of the snow on the trees. Beyond them was the mountain.

It wasn't much of a mountain, almost more of a large hill in the feckless Blue Ridge chain, which had itself seen better days. But to Beth, who was born and raised in Florida, it was a real mountain, a huge hump, crusted with pines, that rose two thousand or so feet above the town. She knew it had been mined for coal back in the thirties, and some of the old people in the town talked about the great Burkittsville cave-in of thirty-four, which had ended the mining operations, and almost ended Burkittsville until Borg-Warner opened its big plant in Williamsport twenty miles away, where most of the men worked. Up top she could see the red and white towers of the phone company's micro-wave processing station, or whatever it was.

The mountain was something she liked, and in the spring she and the girls would drive to the park and go for long walks along the trails at its base. You got about one thousand feet up it, and there was even an overlook, where you could sit on a little bench and look across the valley, see Burkittsville spread out like a collection of dollhouses, and beyond that the undulating farmland of Maryland. To the left, a dark blur, was Middletown, and farther out was Frederick, the big city. It was a lovely view. The girls adored it. Even Jack liked it, though he wasn't much on views.

Beth shook her eyes from the mountain, and returned to reality. She took out the Honey Nut Cheerios, shook the box, and got the bad news. There was enough for only two bowls—this meant that the third person down the stairs would have to make do with corn flakes. Beth tried to work out the political permutations. If Bean came down last, it wouldn't matter. Bean liked Honey Nuts, but if she couldn't have them, she'd smile and get on with things. Jack and Poo, however, loved Honey Nut Cheerios with the frenzy of zealots. If Poo or Jack came down to see the other finishing the cereal, there'd be trouble. The Jack-Poo relationship was the volatile one in the family because Poo was such a replica of her father—stubborn, selfish, vain, charming. The whole morning could come apart.

Upstairs, Beth heard the shower come on. He was up, that meant, which was a good start to the day, because she didn't want to have to rouse him, a task you wouldn't want to wish on a Russian soldier.

But her heart fell.

Bean walked in.

"Honey, what are you doing up? You don't have to get up yet."

"Mommy," said Bean, one small finger rubbing one sleepy eye, her hair a mess, her little body swaddled in its purple pajamas, "I heard something. It scared me."

"Oh, honey," said Beth, bending to her daughter, "there's nothing to be scared of." At that moment a man in black with a large black pistol stepped into the kitchen. She looked up at him, stunned. She heard the steps of other men moving speedily through the house.

"Mommy, I'm scared," said Bean.

Two more black-clad men with huge black guns rushed into the kitchen. They seemed so huge and she felt powerless. It seemed the world was full of men with guns.

"Please, Mrs. Hummel," said the first man, a blunt, suntanned fellow with shiny white teeth and blank eyes. "Don't make any noise. Don't make any problems."

Beth panicked, started to scream, but a hand came over her mouth roughly, locking it in her throat.

Gregor Arbatov spoke the name "Tata," shook a terrible dream of caves and mountains from his head, and came awake. He found himself where he should be, in the bedroom of Molly Shroyer in a high-rise apartment in Alexandria, Virginia. The time on the clock radio was approximately seven A.M., and already Gregor was late. He was always late.

Gregor still shivered from the dream—he'd been having it more and more lately, the same damn thing. In it, he'd wrestled someone; it was cold and dark, a memory of iron fingers around his throat and hot breath in his face. He had a sense of his strength ebbing. He took a deep breath, trying to clear his head, and touched his temples, contemplating the white ceiling above him. He tried to lose himself in its blankness.

Next to him, Molly Shroyer made a wet noise. He turned to study her torpid form. She was somewhat less than beautiful. With a great deal of effort, Molly was able to transform herself into a reasonably attractive woman by encasing herself in some kind of elastic device to supply to her body the kind of discipline that her own mind lacked. A muumuu also worked. Molly breathed heavily under the covers, and when she breathed, the image of mountain ranges trembling under a mantle of snow came to Gregor, which is perhaps why he'd been having his cave dream so frequently; the girl, so big on the outside, was tiny on the inside. He knew her to be a delicate, vulnerable, tragically neurotic creature, wretchedly unhappy in her loneliness underneath the excess flesh.

This was Gregor's specialty. In his own small way he was a legend. Gregor, nominally second assistant commercial attaché in the Soviet Embassy in Washington, an old D.C. fixture who drank with Western newsmen, followed the Redskins, filled in at bridge, knew the difference between a Big Mac and a Whopper, was in actuality an illegal operative of the GRU, as Red Army Intelligence is called to distinguish it from the swankier, civilian-run and deeply loathed KGB. His undercover job consisted of agent running, and as he had worked it out, this primarily entailed wooing, then seducing, then turning lonely American women who worked in secretarial or clerical positions in the security or military establishment. Molly, for example, was a secretary to a staff assistant of the Senate Select Intelligence Committee. But Gregor had a few others, all equally enslaved to him, all equally imperfect, all equally rich in self-loathing and impoverished in self-esteem. Yet Gregor's talent and perhaps his most impressive grace was that he loved them all: he really did.

He was not, despite embassy gossip which he did not discourage, a particularly gifted sexual athlete. As a technician, he was irredeemably proletarian: He just got on and plowed until he couldn't plow anymore. Nor was he unusually endowed in the physical sense. But he had the gift of conviction, and the patience to listen, and a slightly romantic tendency. He was kind, considerate, gentle, flirtatious, indefatigible. He remembered birthdays and anniversaries and special restaurants. He always brought little gifts. He gave flowers. He nursed his girls slowly toward friendship and then intimacy and then compromise. It was a good system, carefully wrought, the result of much experimentation.

But on this morning Gregor awoke with a nightmare and a headache, late. Molly preferred him to get up before the sun and slip out, a sensible precaution. He concurred. There were so many foolish ways you could be tripped up by the FBI, turned out and ejected, and the one place on earth this GRU agent did not care to see again was Russia.

He headed into the bathroom and caught a quick shower. A thickish man with exceedingly strong, broad hands, forty-three years old, his body was extravagantly hairy and he left a trail of fur wherever he went; Molly said he could turn a bathtub into a national emergency faster than any man she'd ever known.

You're a whale, he told himself, and it was true. He was easily twenty-five pounds overweight. You need to exercise, be careful what you eat and drink. You'll drop dead in bed one night, and then what?

Gregor dried off, squirted on some cologne (he always tried to smell good), brushed his teeth, pushed the hair he had left on his head into some semblance of wet order, and quickly climbed into his baggy blue suit. It would need pressing again before the end of the century or the end of the world, whichever came first. He tied his black shoes, thinking how nice it would be to shine them someday. He had owned them for seven years. A little cracked, perhaps, but extremely comfortable.

Molly snorted like a large African game animal wallowing in the mud. Without makeup she was quite appalling to look at. In the dark, when he was riding her like a buffalo, yelping and plunging, it was quite another thing. Now, in the harsh morning, she was the perfect symbol of his imperfect life.

Melancholy seeped through him.

He faced an unpleasant day. To begin with, the boy genius Klimov, Deputy *Rezident*, had called a meeting for the morning, and Klimov had lately been somewhat unpleasant. Then Gregor had to service his most important source, the mysterious Pork Chop, at a shopping mall out in Maryland, a tiresome, dreadful prospect, very tense, very exhausting. Then, far worse, he had communications duty that night, which meant sleeping on a cot in a basement cell that embassy tradition called the Wine Cellar, attending encryption equipment in case a hot eyes-only zapped over from Moscow. In truth, the Americans at the National Security Agency out at Fort Meade, in Maryland, would have it unbuttoned before he could; perhaps he could simply call them and request the message. But the duty, which came about once a month, was the worst thing in his life: It would upset his entire system, which depended on a solid ten hours' sleep, plus a little nap in the afternoon.

And then the other thing gnawing at him, not yet put into words by anyone, but clearly expressed nevertheless. For the truth was, he was now in trouble in the embassy. Of late, the gleanings had gotten thinner and thinner. Where once he'd had nine girls and his life had been a phenomenon of scheduling, an athletic extravaganza, the action was now slow. He was losing his touch. Younger men had been brought in, and they treated him with contempt. Only Pork Chop seemed to please them, and Gregor was only a cutout to Pork Chop, who worked for bigger fish.

Klimov, the awful Klimov, was twenty-eight. Twenty-eight! With shrewd, furious eyes and the energy to work like a beaver, tirelessly. A true believer. A lover of the system, and no wonder. He had a vastly important uncle who could see that things always came to him. Arbatov hated Klimov almost as much as he feared him. And he felt exposed, vulnerable, a target, since he was the only man in the section who was over forty. And because he'd lasted so much longer than the others.

My time, he thought, is almost over.

Molly's left lid crept open, then her right.

"Are you still here, Gregor? God, you're so late."

"I'm sorry, darling," Gregor said.

She laughed, but then turned petulant.

"Who's Tata?" she demanded. "I heard you say her name. Is she a new girlfriend, Gregor?"

"No, no, my love," said Gregor. "Tata's a prince. Prince Tatashkin. A hero from an old story in my childhood. A great knight who saves the world. He came to me in a dream, that's all."

"It's so hard to be mad at you," she said babyishly, scrunching up her features into the mask of an infant. "You're so cute. Mowwy wubs her Gweggy-weggy."

She offered a mouth to kiss. He did, gently.

"I love you, too, my love," he said, and left.

Jack Hummel had seen the movie *Psycho* at an impressionable age, and for that reason—Beth never could fully understand it—he had ordered her never to come in while he was showering.

"Honey," he'd say to her, "if you saw that movie, you'd know. This guy comes in when this girl is showering. All you can see is his *shape* through the curtain, and then—"

"I don't want to hear," she'd say, covering her ears.

So when the door of the bathroom opened and he saw a black shape through the torrent of water and through the steam and through the translucent plastic of the curtain, he jumped, of course, feeling the lingering imprint of the movie. A second later his anger burst out, on the presumption that Beth had, once again, forgotten.

"Beth, honey, how many *times* have I got to—"

But the shower curtain suddenly exploded in a clatter of ripping plastic and popping rings. Jack's mouth fell open dumbly. In the steam he saw that it wasn't Beth at all, but some figure out of a terrible dream.

The man stood there in black boots, black combat fatigues, and a black face mask. He had a gun, too, and it was black. Jack, who knew a little about such things, recognized it as an Uzi with about half-a-yard of silencer hooding its short snout.

Jack felt himself pissing in the stall. The water continued to spray down on him. The man gestured with the gun.

"My children," Jack begged, raising a feeble hand against the surrealism of the moment.

"Oh, God," he begged again, "please don't hurt my children. Please, please, don't hurt my children."

Another gunman, this one unmasked, popped into the door. He was deeply tanned with the white teeth of a toothpaste commercial and the air of command. He held a black automatic, also silenced.

"Come on, now, Mr. Hummel. You can't stand there all day." He leaned into the stall and with his free hand turned the water off.

"I hate waste," he said almost conversationally. "Now, come on. Dry off and get dressed. We've got a job for you. Herman, if he's slow, you might prod him a little."

He looked at his watch, a fancy black scuba number which he wore inverted on his wrist.

"We have a schedule to keep."

Jack dressed quickly with shaking knees and trembling fingers, while the man with the Uzi watched him. He couldn't get the buttons on the fly to work, and it bothered him that the leader hadn't bothered to wear a mask. Jack wondered if that meant they'd have to kill them all because they'd seen his face.

And it was the kind of face you wouldn't forget. He had a pro linebacker's battered mug with a nose that had been broken dramatically into a crooked hawk's bill. He had almost expressionless eyes, and his hair had been cropped close, almost into blond stubble. His cheekbones were wide and the skin had been tanned until it was almost leathery. He looked like Jack's old football coach, who'd been one tough son of a bitch.

"Hurry," said the man with the Uzi.

"Okay, okay," Jack complained, pulling on his work boots.

Downstairs he found his two girls sitting stiffly in their chairs, eating Honey Nut Cheerios. For once they were quiet at breakfast. His wife stood at the stove. There was a total of five men in black, four of them with an assortment of exotic weapons vaguely familiar from the movies, and the leader with his pistol.

Jack's problem now was shock. The image didn't make any sense at all to him. It was as if guys out of the TV news had crawled out of the box and taken over. He stood there trying to put it together.

"You see, Mr. Hummel. No harm done. Breakfast as usual. No problems."

"What do you want?" stammered Beth. The color had drained from her face, and her gestures were mechanical. He could see her shaking; she had wrapped her arms tightly around herself, as if the fear had made her cold. Her eyes were unfocused. Jack longed to touch her and to make the men go away.

"We don't have a lot of money," he said through a clog of phlegm in his throat, though he was certain it wasn't money the men wanted. But he couldn't begin to guess what they were after. What could *he*—?

"Come this way, please," said the leader.

They went into the living room.

"Now, it's very simple, Mr. Hummel. We have a job to be done. That is, we *may* have a job to be done. We can't do it. You can. Therefore, you'll have to come along."

There was something remote in his voice—not an accent so much as the effort to pronounce each word perfectly. It had an odd, disconnected sound to it.

"And if—I'm just asking—if I don't?"

"Best to come, Mr. Hummel. We'll be leaving some people here. Best to come, Mr. Hummel, and avoid unpleasantness."

"Oh, Jesus," said Jack. "Please don't hurt them. Please, I'll do anything. Just don't—"

"Mr. Hummel, if you do what you're told, no harm at all will come to your wife and children. Do you understand?"

"Yes."

"You may say good-bye. If all goes well, you'll be back by noon. If not, it may be a day or so. Your children, however, and your wife, will be perfectly all right."

"Yeah, yeah," said Jack, wishing he sounded a little less terrified. "I'll do it. No problem, I'll do it."

"Fine. Then we are off."

"I suppose I'm an idiot for asking. But where are we going?"

"To meet the general, Mr. Hummel."

0800

H

apgood had tendencies toward comedy which he could not suppress. In his third grade class picture, for example, amid all the still, grave faces, his is the only blur; he is laughing at something private, his face gone in the smear of movement.

"Donny," his mother had said, "Donny, I declare, what *are* we going to do with you?"

As it turned out, very little could be done with Donny. He laughed his way through high school and college and got extremely high grades. He laughed his way into a marriage and nearly out of it. In his profession, his humorous impulses continued subversively, for he made his living amid men who laughed at very little because there was very little to laugh at. But he could not resist: In his infantile scrawl he had crayoned a large sign on a piece of shirt cardboard and taped it above the heavy steel blast door to the launch control center, where its orange childishness fluttered against the rows and rows of switches, the bright red NO LONE ZONE imperatives from SAC stamped everywhere in sans serif—forbidding solitude in proximity to nuclear weapons systems—the constellations of red and green status lights, the big twenty-four hour clock, and the dizzying mesh of wires, cables, and solid-state units that comprised a communications bank comparable to that of a small midwestern top-forty radio station.

WELCOME, the cardboard sign said, TO THE MIRV GRIFFIN SHOW.

Then, just today, on the console panel itself, above the launch enabling keyhole, the famous little metal slot which would, if penetrated, set in motion the probable end of the world in fire, he had added, in ball-point, on an index card, AND HEEEEERE'S MIRV. . . .

The star of the show, MIRV, was the Multiple Independently Targeted Reentry Vehicle, perched in a cluster atop the bird nested at the center of Hapgood's command. The ten MIRVs and their second bananas, the W87/Mk-21 thirty-five-kiloton fissionable warhead, sat atop a tube of black titanium dubbed, with a sense of humor that the great Hapgood could only aim for, Peacekeeper.

This was more famous in the lexicon as MX, Missile Experimental. No longer an experiment, it stood now in its super-hard silo not one hundred feet from Hapgood, long, silent, and enigmatic. A large-payload solid-fuel cold-launch four-stage intercontinental ballistic missile, it was seventy-one feet long and ninety-two inches wide and at launch weight 193,000 pounds. It was fired by three solid-propellant booster motors, with storable liquid hypergolic propellant in the fourth-stage post-boost vehicle. It was guided by an advanced inertial reference sphere and delivered a payload of 7,200 pounds. Its targets included all Soviet "super-hard" control centers, fourth generation ICBM silos, and "very hard leadership bunkers." It was, in short, a head hunter, a Kremlin buster, a leader killer, an assassin.

"If anybody from Squadron sees that," his partner Romano informed him, pointing at the new bit of comedy taped to the launch board, "your ass is history. This is a no-laugh zone."

"Squadron," replied Hapgood with a snicker, "is two thousand miles away. Out in Wy-fucking-oming, if memory serves, where the deer and the antelope roam. We are all by our lonesomes in Burkittsville, Maryland, the ultimate lone zone of the entire universe. Moreover," he continued in his grand voice, aching to get a smile out of the dour but focused Romano, "if I am going to unload thirty-five megatons of nuclear doom on top of the Soviet Union and face my maker as one-half of the greatest mass-murder team in history, I'd prefer to do it with a smile on my face and a song in my heart. You're too fucking *Air Force*, man. Lighten up."

Romano, a captain to Hapgood's first lieutenant, two years older and maybe ten years wiser, simply made the unhappy face of a man sucking a ReaLemon bottle. Still, Romano would go easy on the kid: whatever his excesses, Hapgood was the best, the sharpest, the smartest missile officer Romano had ever seen. He knew the procedures and he knew the boards as if he'd invented them.

Besides, Hapgood was largely correct. He and his friend and superior officer occupied the only strategic missile silo east of the Mississippi. Originally a Titan prototype silo, from the late fifties when the liquid-fuel Titan seemed to be The Answer, it had never been completely developed and was left fallow after Air Force enthusiasm had shifted in favor of the western-states-based solid-fuel Minuteman in 1962. Now the installation, on a bit of government real estate in central Maryland, had been hastened into operational condition because it was available and obscure, being located halfway between the Pentagon in Washington and the National Alternate Military Command Center at Fort Richie, and also because the Titan configuration called for basing bird and LCC in the same hole rather than remote from each other, as was Minuteman doctrine.

"Rick, I just had a flash from God," Hapgood suddenly blurted out. "He wants us to redecorate! Think about it, Rick! A launch control center done over in—*knotty pine!*"

In spite of himself, Romano smiled.

"God, Donny, what the fuck are we going to do with you?"

"Pray I turn my key, if turn it I must," said Hapgood, touching the red titanium key he wore around his neck on a chain and tucked into his white jump suit's breast pocket.

"But who knows," Hapgood continued, "I might, like, not be in the right mood, you dig?"

Romano laughed at the kid again. If the word came, Donny would turn, on cue, and send the bird on its flight.

It was another day in the hole. They would pass it as they had passed so many others, one day in three, one hundred feet underground in the hardened command capsule of a missile launch site, aware that if World War III were fought, they were the ones who would fight it, at exactly the same time they were convinced that their very presence guaranteed that it would never be fought.

The chamber of their drama was a one-piece capsule sunk deep into the earth so that its interior curved at the ceiling line, increasing the sense of claustrophobia; at forty-one by twenty-six feet, it looked like some kind of meditation chamber. The steel floor actually floated above the surface of the capsule, suspended from the roof of the vault by four hydraulic jacks, to better absorb the impact of a nuclear near-miss. The men sat at right angles to each other, twelve feet apart, in cushy swivel chairs complete with seat belts, quite comfortable, quite adjustable, very jet-age. Before each was the console, that is, a panel of switches, ten rows of labeled lights, red or green, each a checkoff to a certain missile function. All these lights were green, meaning the status was go. It looked like a fuse box in a large apartment building or the control room of a television station. There was a computer keyboard by which one entered the daily twelve-digit Permissive Action Link code, or PAL, freeing the machinery for terminal countdown and launch. There was a radio telephone mounted at the base of the console, and it also had a few rows of switches, which could zip the caller all around the installation on various lines. A huge clock hung between the two units. And, of course, the keyholes, marked LAUNCH ENABLER at each console, hinged red metal flaps encasing them. Assuming doomsday has been decreed, the launch siren is wailing, the proper Emergency Action Message has arrived to the encrypted uplink ("Let's hope our EAM is true," Hapgood once joked, squinting like a musical-comedy marksman) from any one of several command sources, and the proper PAL twelve-digit code has been entered in the security system, one has to yank the flap up, insert the key, then turn smoothly a quarter turn to the right, this within the same two-second time envelope as one's pal down the console. One man may not start World War III; it takes brotherhood, the true meaning of SAC's mandatory NO LONE ZONE signs. One minute after that—during which Peacekeeper gets a last go-over from its computer baby-sitters—the launch enabling circuits get a short blip of energy, the silo doors are blown, and off the bird flies, its ten warheads, like ten kings of hell, primed for deployment.

Against another section of wall there sat quite a bit of communications equipment, including several teletypes, a satellite communications terminal, and both high and low frequency radios; and at another, racks of metal-covered notebooks which contained hundreds of standing orders and regulations for silo procedure, and at still another, a cot, where either guy could grab a nap if necessary. There was one peculiarity to this capsule distinguishing it from the hundreds like it in the missile fields of the West: a small black glass window mounted to the left of Hapgood's console, mounted in the very wall of the chamber itself. It was about a foot square and looked almost like a computer screen. Two words were stenciled across it in red paint: KEY VAULT.

The command capsule was reached by elevator, but not directly. Due to the configuration of the mountain, there was a long corridor between it and the elevator. Beyond the capsule the corridor continued, arriving eventually at a huge safety door, electrically controlled, by which technicians could access the missile itself. The whole thing was constructed of concrete doubly reinforced with steel rods and coated with a special polymer to discourage penetration by the electromagnetic pulse generated by an airborne nuclear explosion, or by the effects of a blast itself, that is, anything less than a direct hit by a Soviet SS-18, carrying a throwload in the twenty-five-megaton range. And sealing the capsule off from the rest of the installation was a huge blast door like a door on a bank vault, usually kept closed tight.

"Junie says we ought to have you guys over," said Romano.

"Uh, not a good idea," said Hapgood. "I think we're in terminal countdown. She spends a lot of time on the phone to her mother. And she's not exactly nuts about the trailer. And look at *this*."

He made a fishy face, and held up the object of his contempt. It was a paper lunch sack with grease spots on it.

"Jeez, I remember when she made bacon, lettuce, and tomato sandwiches, or Reubens, or hot turkey, that you could zap up in the microwave. Now look. The sad reality of my marriage."

He pulled out a Baggie with a wilted sandwich in it.

"Peanut butter," he announced.

There was a buzz on the installation phone.

"Oh, hell, now what?" Romano said. Their twenty-four-hour shift had another ten hours to run. Relief wasn't due until 1800.

He picked up the phone.

"Security Alpha, this is Oscar-one-niner," he said.

"Oscar-one-niner, just a security warning, SOP. Be advised I have some kind of disabled vehicle just beyond the gate. It looks to be a van of some sort, off the highway. Looks like some kids in it. Advise SAC or National Command?"

Romano looked swiftly to the console for his indicators for Outer Zone Security and saw no blinking lights, then glanced at Inner Zone Security and confirmed the status freeze. These lights were keyed to the installation's low-level Doppler Ground Radar networks, which picked up intruders beyond the perimeter. Occasionally they'd go off if a small animal rushed through the zone, and a security team would be dispatched to investigate. But now he saw nothing.

"Security Alpha, what's your security status? I have no OZ or IZ indicators showing."

"Affirmative, Oscar-one-niner, I don't either."

"Have you notified Primary and Reserve Security Alert Teams?"

"Primary is suiting up, sir, and we woke Reserve, affirmative, sir. Still, I'd like to put a message through to Command—"

"Uh, let's hold off, Security Alpha. It's only a van, for crissakes. Keep it under observation, and let your PSAT do the walking. Report back in five."

"Yessir," said the security NCO topside.

"I'm surprised he didn't shoot," said Hapgood.

The Air Force Combat Security Policemen who maintained the defensive perimeters of the installation were traditionally not much loved by the missile officers. The missile guys viewed them as cops, the technologically uninitiated. Besides, the security people were known to have sent complaints to Missile Command if Capsule personnel showed up with unshined shoes or uncreased uniforms.

"Jesus," Hapgood, a notorious security baiter, said, "those guys must think they're in the *military* or something. I mean, what is this, the *Air Force*, for Christ's sake?"

He went back to his homework, part of his program to get an MBA. It was a case study of difficulties encountered by a fictitious bicycle manufacturer in Dayton, Ohio. Now, with assets of $5 million, operating costs of $4.5 million, a decline in sales projected at 1.9 percent over the next five years, what should CEO Smith do? Buy a motorcycle, thought Hapgood.

"I wish he'd call back," said Romano ten minutes later.

Dad was struggling with the spare tire. He crouched next to the vehicle just off the snowy roadway beyond the gate of the installation. The voices of impatient children lashed out from within the interior of the van.

"Dammit, settle *down* in there," he bellowed. "This isn't *easy*."

Master Sergeant O'Malley of the Air Force Combat Security Police watched him from the guardhouse. Even from where he stood he could hear the children inside the van.

"This guy is making me nervous," he said to the two policemen with him. All were dressed in the uniforms of a private security service, in keeping with the sign that stood above the gate house: SOUTH MOUNTAIN MICROWAVE PROCESSING STATION/ AT&T/ PRIVATE PROPERTY/ NO ADMITTANCE.

"You want us to frisk him?"

O'Malley vacillated. He looked again at his Alert Status board, and saw no change in the OZ and IZ lights. He gave a quick visual sweep of the mountain slope below him, and saw nothing but white snow and black stubble. He blinked, swallowed. He looked around. Where was his three-man Primary Security Alert Team? Jesus, those guys were slow!

Finally, he said, "No. We're supposed to keep a low profile. I'll just go help him along. I don't want him spending the morning here."

O'Malley drew his parka on and stepped out into the roadway, wincing at the brightness even through his aviator sunglasses. He walked across the hard, cold road.

"Sir, I have to ask you to move on," he said. "This is private property. You aren't even supposed to be back on this road."

The dad looked up. He was a suntanned man with very white teeth. He looked, to the sergeant at any rate, like some kind of athlete, a boxer maybe. He had a broken nose.

It was a vivid morning, just a little after eight. The sun spread through the valley. The sky was flawless, dense blue. The chill in the air rubbed on O'Malley's skin; he could feel the mucus in his nose freezing.

"I'm sorry," the dad said. "I thought there was a McDonald's up this way. I must have taken a wrong turn, and now I've got a flat. Just let me get this tire fixed and I'm gone."

"Sir," said O'Malley, "if you like, I can call a garage and they can send a tow truck up here."

"I think I can get it," said the man. "If I can just find the lug wrench in the toolbox." He reached into the box, which was old and battered. In the background the kids began to cry.

The young sergeant was by nature suspicious—his profession demanded it—but when the dad brought out a silenced Heckler & Koch P9 in 9mm, his first impulse was not to reach for the Smith & Wesson .38 he carried on his belt, or to cry out. Rather, he was stunned at the incongruity of it, the sheer, appalling absurdity of such a weapon, here and now, in the man's hand. But he had no time to react.

The major dropped to one knee, and, aiming from a two-handed isosceles position, shot O'Malley twice through the center chest from a range of seven feet, firing 115-grain Silvertips, which blossomed like spring tulips as they tumbled crazily through the young man's chest, knocking him to the earth inside a second.

The major stepped back from the van and its rear double doors sprang open. Inside, two men fired a long burst from a bipod-mounted M-60 into the guardhouse, which shivered, its glass splintering with the impact of the 7.62-mm rounds. Inside, the two air policemen died almost instantly amid a spray of glass chips and wood bits.

The major jumped onto the running board of the van, whacked it with his gun butt, and the driver gunned it. It slithered, kicking up the dust, and whipped through a ninety-degree turn and smashed through the gate. Before him, the major could see three nondescript corrugated tin buildings inside the complex, one of which boasted a red and white radio tower of perhaps fifty feet.

According to plan, they had thirty seconds from the first shot until they took out the above-ground communications center.

Romano called back Security Alpha. There was no answer.

"I wonder what that guy is doing?" he said.

"Those cops. You never know."

"Donny, take your key off your neck."

"Huh?"

"Do what I say, Donny." He dialed Communications. There was no answer. He went to the teletype. No messages had come through on their watch.

"Shit," he said. "I wonder if—"

"Hey, Rick, ease off, man. So the guys haven't answered the phone. What does that mean, nuclear war? You know as well as I do nobody's getting down here unless we say so. We control the elevator."

The post's entire defensive response to the attack consisted of an air security man from the Primary Security Alert Team with a Winchester twelve-gauge pump. The man with the shotgun fired one shot from behind the Commo building at the major, who clung to the van as it rushed through the compound, but he hurried, missed him, spattering his burst against the van door. Then the van disappeared in a swirl of dust as it reached and slammed into the communications building.

The air security man rethrew his pump and waited for a target to emerge from the confusion. He had a queer sense, however, of being watched, and turned to peer at the Cyclone fence to the left of the gate. He had an impression of someone scurrying away, but as he brought his weapon to bear—it would have been a long shot, anyway, for a shotgun—

five charges went off under the fence. It lifted and twisted in the concussions. The explosive was plastique, French-manufactured, detonated by a U.S. Army M-1 Delay Firing Device with a fifteen-second delay.

The young man was blown backward and down by the blasts. When he regained his senses, he could see troopers in snow smocks with automatic weapons moving very fast up the hill and through the gaps in the fence. He was amazed at how many there were, and with what precision they moved. He wondered where the hell they'd come from, how they'd gotten so fucking close. He understood, too, that he was probably doomed, that the post was overwhelmed, that unless the guys in Commo got an emergency message out to SAC that it was all over. His own inclination was to run, but he realized he couldn't. A piece of shrapnel from the fence burst had torn into his knee. Then he realized he'd been hit in the chest too. There was blood all over the snow, flooding down around his combat boot. The shotgun slipped from his grip. He wished he'd killed one of the bastards.

There were three strong points in the compound. The first was the barracks, where the installation's complement of air policemen was headquartered. One unit of the assault team broke off from the general rush and dashed toward it. Fifty yards out, the four men dropped prone as they deployed their chief weapon, a Heckler & Koch HK-21. The gunner pumped a three-hundred-round tracer belt into the building. The tracers flicked out and kicked through the corrugated tin walls. As the gunner was changing belts and his loader and one other man were supplying suppressing fire, the fourth member of the team dashed forward with a three-pound plastique package with a four-second time-delay mechanism. He primed it and hurled it through the window. The detonation was tremendous, blowing out three of the four walls and collapsing the roof. The barracks team moved through the wreckage of the building, shooting everything whether it moved or not.

The second strong point was the launch-control facility itself, with its elevator to the capsule beneath. Generally staffed by three men, it was this day staffed by only two: They died in the first seconds after the fence burst, when one superbly trained raider kicked the door open and fired a long burst from his Uzi.

The third strong point was Commo, the communications center, which the van team hit, led by the major, carrying an Uzi. There was smoke everywhere, and as the major kicked his way through the haze, he fired a burst into the shapes he encountered. Each went down.

He pushed his way back to the teletype machines and the computer encrypters and the hardened cables that fed into them.

"There," he commanded.

A man came forward with a huge pair of industrial wire cutters.

"The red ones," the major said. The man with the clippers was well trained. He knelt, and adroitly began to cut the post's contact to the outside world, leaving only a single cable.

The major pushed his way through the rubble to the security officer's office, off the main room. The man himself had already been killed with a machine pistol burst. He lay across the threshold of his office, having been the first of the major's victims. A satiny pool of blood lapped across the linoleum.

The major stepped over him and went swiftly to the wall safe, where his demolitions man already crouched.

"Any problem?"

"It's not titanium. You'd expect better stuff."

"You can blow it?"

"No problem."

"I've almost got it rigged," the demo man said. Swiftly, he pinched a latticework of plastique into the crannies of the safe. He worked like a sculptor, trying to build a cross current of pressure that would, upon detonation, spring the box. Then he pressed a small device called a time-pencil into one corner of the glop.

"Are we clear?" he asked.

The major, in the doorway, gestured his men out.

"Do it," he said.

The demolitions man squeezed the bulb at the end of the pencil, which released a droplet of acid. As he raced from the building, his gear and weapons slapping against his body in his sprint, the acid began to eat through a restraining piece inside the time-pencil. It took seven seconds. When the wire yielded, a coiled spring snapped a striker down to a primer cap, which in turn detonated the explosive. The metal tore in the burst, and the safe was ripped from its moorings in the wall.

The major was the first in, rushing through the smoke. He rifled through the papers until he found what he wanted. Outside came the intermittent sounds of gunshots from the mop-up.

He beckoned to his radioman, took the microphone off the man's backpack of gear.

"Alex to Landlord," he said, "Alex to Landlord, are you there?"

"This is Landlord, affirmative."

"Get the general."

"He's here."

"Yes, I'm here, Alex," came a new voice on the net.

"Sir, we've got it. We're going down below."

"Good." The voice was cheerful. "I'll meet you at the LCF elevator."

Even the major was impressed. In the middle of the smoking battle-field the general still looked magnificent and unruffled. But then that was the general's gift. Beyond the force of his intelligence and the depth of his vision, he radiated confidence, beauty, and supreme knowledge. He had a way of drawing you to him and making you his absolutely.

"Report, Major?" the general asked.

"Seizure procedure complete, General. We control the compound."

The general nodded, then smiled. His features lit up; his eyes warmed. His sleek hair was gray, almost white, and had been expensively trimmed. He wore a Burberry trench coat over a well-cut jump suit. He seemed, somehow, more like an executive vice-president than a military officer.

"Casualties?"

"None, sir. The surprise was complete."

"Good. No boys hurt. You planned well. Communications out?"

"Yessir."

"Enemy casualties?"

"Sixteen, sir. Their entire complement."

"The specs called for twenty-four. You'd think in an independent-launch-capable facility they'd be at full strength."

"Yes, sir."

"They had no idea anybody even knew they were here. Still, it wouldn't have mattered, would it, Alex? Superb."

"We try, sir," said Alex. "I guess we were lucky. We got through the radar all right, and caught them asleep."

"The elevator code?"

"Yessir."

The major went to a computer terminal installed in the wall next to the double titanium blastproof doors that led to the launch command capsule; it was configured like a television screen over a typewriter keyboard and looked a little like a bank machine. He bent to it and typed in the twelve integers of that day's Permissive Action Link, which he had just gained from the safe in the security officer's room.

ACCESS OK, the machine responded.

The elevator doors opened.

"Final assault team forward," said the major.

"Time to talk to the boys downstairs," the general said with a smile.

"I'm going to call Command," said Romano. He typed a quick message on the teletype, then hit the send button.

Nothing happened.

"Goddammit," said Romano. "Get your pistol out."

Both men carried Smith & Wesson .38s, not for defense but to execute the other in the event, however unlikely given the screening procedures, of some kind of psychotic attack.

"Mine's not loaded," said Hapgood. "I never—hey, come on. They aren't going to—"

The phone buzzed.

"Jesus." Romano jumped. Then he snatched the phone.

"Hello, this is Oscar-one-niner," he said.

"Oscar-one-niner, Christ! You won't believe it. We had a goddamn power failure up here. Emergency generators are on and we should have full power back in a sec."

"What about that vehicle?"

"Sir, PSAT got his tire changed. He's outta here. All clear, affirmative, and PSAT back inside the perimeter."

"That's a big hip hooray. Is this O'Malley?"

"Sir, no, it's Greenberg, code authenticated Sierra-four, Delta-niner, Hotel-six—"

"That's okay, Alpha Security, I have you authenticated."

"Sir, just to remind you, SOP on power failures is for you to open the blast door. You wouldn't want to be caught in there, sir, if we lose power again and the generators go."

"Affirmative, Security Alpha, will do. Jesus, you guys had us scared," Romano blurted out.

"Sorry about that, sir. Couldn't be helped."

Romano spun the cylinder on the door, and with a whoosh, the big thing opened. He leaned out into the corridor and took a deep breath.

"Jesus," said Hapgood. "You were really sweating there."

"Boy, I—"

But a woman's voice suddenly filled the air. Her name was Betty and she was the voice of the computer.

"Warning," she cooed, "access has been achieved."

At that moment, at the end of the corridor the elevator doors burst open. A trooper with a laser-sighted Uzi put a beam of red light into Romano's center chest and fired a burst. As Hapgood watched, his friend's uniform exploded; Romano's eyes went blank as he pitched forward, his head askew.

Hapgood knew he was going to die. He could hear them coming down the corridor, the swift, slapping pound of their boots, driven on by the shouts of their officer.

"The other one. Quick, the other one."

Panic scampered through the young man's mind and he felt his joints melt, his will scatter. He knew he could never get the blast door closed in time.

They're coming for the bird, he thought.

And at that moment he remembered procedure. He turned and sprinted for the far wall. His one advantage came from Romano. "Take your key off, Donny." It was a small thing. That was all, but it was enough.

For as Hapgood dashed to the wall, the major ducked forward into the capsule, and put three Silvertips from a range of ten feet through the young officer's lungs; but the impact of the bullets only hurried him those last few feet. Before him he saw the black window set in the wall, the one that admitted no light and was the latest wrinkle in installation security. KEY VAULT.

And because Hapgood did not have to get the key off his neck, because he had it in his hand, he was able to punch through the glass—

"Nooo!" screamed the major, firing twice more; the man with the laser-guided Uzi fired the rest of his clip, the bullets slamming into Hapgood, who slid in bloody splendor down the wall. But he had already dropped the key into the key vault and, one second later a half-ton titanium block slammed down, sealing the key off from reach.

*   *   *

The general wasted no time.

"It couldn't be helped," he said cheerily. "We've made contingency plans. We'll get what we want. We just won't get it right away."

The general looked at the two combat missile officers soaking in their own blood. The young one, the boy, had been shot dozens of times. The back of his jump suit was a spatter of bullet holes and burned fabric. The general betrayed no surprise or regret. He simply passed on from the bodies to other issues.

"Get them out of here," said the major. "And get the blood mopped up."

The general turned.

"Commence our occupation phase, Alex," he commanded. "We'll be having visitors soon, and we've got much work to do."

"Of course, sir."

Alex issued orders quickly. "Get the trucks up here with Hummel and send the demolition team down to blow the road. Roll out the wire for the field telephones. Get the canvas strung out. And get the boys started digging in."

The general turned to the teletype machines against the wall. Five of them—marked SAC, ERCS, UHF Satellite, Looking Glass, and SLFCS—were still, as if dead. The sixth—marked National Command—suddenly began to clatter away insanely.

The general touched Alex on the arm.

"Look, Alex," he said. "They know. The key vault must be rigged to send a robot signal to Command when it's deployed."

He looked at his watch, a gold Rolex.

"About three minutes. Not bad. Not outstanding, but not bad."

He pulled the message off the platen.

FLASH OVERRIDE
FROM: NMCC WASHINGTON D.C.//J3 NMCC//
TO: SOUTH MOUNTAIN MISSILE OPERATIONS OFFICER
AIG 6843
SECRET
FJO//001//02183Z 17 DEC 88
IMPERATIVE YOU CONTACT THIS HQ ASAP. REPEAT. IMPERATIVE
YOU CONTACT THIS HQ ASAP.

The machine spurted again. It was the same message.

"They must really be going crazy in the Pentagon about now," the general said with something like a chuckle. "Lord, I wish I could see their faces."

Alex nodded, and hustled out.

The general had two things to do now.

First, he went to the shortwave radio transmitter nestled between two of the teletypes. It was the Collins 32S-3 model, an older machine that had been installed in the capsule purely as an emergency backup method of communication. He flicked it on, bent to the band selector, and turned it to the 21.2 megahertz setting, then dialed in a more specific frequency on the tuner. That done, he simply twisted the emission dial to the CW setting and held it for five seconds exactly, sending out a burst of raw noise across the airwaves on his frequency. Then he turned it off.

All right, he thought, very good, according to plan. And now . . .

He pulled one of the chairs from the console over to the operative teletype. He pushed the red send button. Immediately, it stopped clattering.

He bent to the keys.

In one swift burst he typed out his message. He had no need to pause to think. He knew the words by memory, and it was in the spirit of memory that he delivered them.

Speak, Memory, he thought, as he hit the send button, and the lessons of the past reached out to twist the present into the future.

0900

"Imbecile," yelled the excited Klimov. "Fool. Idiot. Do you know how much we spend on you? I mean, can you guess?"

Gregor Arbatov said, "No, comrade."

It was useless to resist. Klimov was making an example of him before all the others. To defy Klimov in public circumstances such as these was to risk more than disaster, it was to risk humiliation. Christ in heaven, it was to risk recall to Russia! Klimov was ruthless. Klimov was tyrannical. Klimov was perhaps psychotic. But worst of all, Klimov was young.

"Well, let me tell you, comrade. I was up half the night going over budgets while you were rooting around under the sheets with your fat friend. It costs us over thirty thousand dollars a year to support you. We pay for the apartment, we give you a food and clothing allowance, we lease your automobile. And how do you repay us, to say nothing of fulfilling your duties? With drivel! With nonsense! With hearsay, gossip, and rumor! Some agent runner you've become in your old age, Arbatov. I remember once you were a hero. And now this. What the senator really thinks of SALT II. Where the senator stands on Peacekeeper. What the committee will do when next the Director of Central Intelligence requests a fund increase. I can read all this in *The New York Times*, where it's much better written. Thirty thousand buys a lot of subscriptions to *The New York Times*, Comrade Arbatov."

Arbatov mewled an explanation, head down, contrite, his eyes riveted on his bleak black shoes.

"In some cases, Comrade Klimov, it takes time before a source can be cajoled into producing high-grade product. It takes much patience and manipulation. I am working diligently to—"

But as he spoke, he sneaked a peek at his tormentor and saw the interest drain from Klimov's eyes. Klimov was not much on listening.

Klimov was a great talker, a lecturer, a young man extraordinarily fascinated with his own life and career; his interest in the human race seemed to stop at the tip of his own nose.

Klimov had ugly eyes, a short temper, and a quick mind. He was what everyone in Washington feared and hated, regardless of political inclination or global loyalty. He was very young, very bright, and very connected.

It was this last that so filled Arbatov with terror. Klimov was the son of the sister of the great Arkady Pashin, GRU's Chief of Fifth Directorate (Operational Intelligence), the man next in line to be first deputy. And this rotten little Klimov was his nephew!

With Uncle Arkady's kind intercession, young Klimov had shot through the ranks. To be a deputy *rezident* at twenty-eight, unheard of in the old days! Poor Arbatov would never make *rezident* rank. He had no relatives, no supporters in high places.

"Do you think," said Klimov, "that when Comrade Pashin assumes full operational responsibilities for the organization he will tolerate such foolishness?"

Of course poor Arbatov had no idea what Pashin would or would not tolerate. How could he?

"Do you think because you service a special asset you are invulnerable to criticism and beyond self-improvement?"

Klimov must be feeling especially bold today to even mention the agent Pork Chop, on whom, as much as anything, Arbatov had staked his chances of survival. Was even Pork Chop to be taken from him?

"I—I—" he began to blubber.

"Your special source can easily be serviced by another," roared Klimov. "You are merely a technician. You can be replaced as simply as one changes a light bulb, comrade."

Arbatov saw that he was lost. There was but one course left open to him.

"But, comrade," whined Arbatov, "it's true I've become sloppy in my ways. Perhaps I take too much for granted. I've let the *Amerikanskis* penetrate my inner being. I have allowed myself the vanity of pride in the way I service my primary asset. Let me confess my crimes. I ask the comrade only for a chance to repair the harm I've done. Perhaps he'll give me enough time to prove that I'm not utterly beyond reform. If I fail, I'd gladly return to our motherland, or to any less comfortable post it prefers for me."

Lick his boots, he told himself. *Lick them. He'll like that.*

"Ah!" Young Klimov made a snort of disgust. "These aren't the old days. No bullets in the neck for such as Gregor Ivanovich Arbatov! We require only that he rededicate himself, as he says he shall."

"I shall," squeaked Arbatov as radiant relief beamed from his face. Then he looked down in expiation, aware that in sniveling he had once again survived. The young officers of the embassy *apparat*, which Klimov ran, looked at him with unconcealed contempt; he could feel their eyes harsh against his fat form. He didn't care. He could have wept for joy. He had more time.

The meeting turned from Arbatov's weaknesses to other concerns. Arbatov appeared to be listening intently, a new man. He even took notes eagerly, quite a change from the insolent, lazy old Arbatov. What he was writing down in his little notebook was, This little fucker should burn from the toes up. Over and over.

As he was walking from the meeting, someone came flying after him.

"Tata! Tata, stop!"

He turned to see the stout form of his one true friend, Magda Goshagarian, bearing down upon him.

"Tata, darling, don't you think you laid it on a bit thick?"

Magda was another of the old ones. She had an uncle who was a general of artillery and was thus safe from Klimov's predations, at least for now. She was a rumpled, plain woman who wore too much makeup, drank too much, and danced too much in the Western idiom for her own good. She even went to discos in Georgetown when she thought she wasn't being watched. She was perhaps his only remaining friend, now that Klimov had exiled Daniel Issovich to Krakow and old Pasha Vlietnakov to Ethiopia.

"Darling, you have no idea how abject I can be in the service of survival," said Gregor. "These young bastards were disgusted? They haven't seen anything yet. I won't stop at licking his boots. I'll eat them too. I'll butter them and eat them if it buys me one more day in the West."

"You are a sorry Communist, Tata."

"No, I'm an excellent Communist. I'm merely a sorry spy."

"Any new fat American girls, Tata?"

Tata was her pet name for him. As he had told Molly Shroyer, it was derived from the hero of the fourteenth-century folk tale, Prince Tatashkin of the noble heart. Prince Tatashkin, lean and golden, had gone into the Caves of the Urals, there to fight the Witch of Night Forever, or so the story went. He was still fighting her all these years later, losing in the early hours of evening but regaining his strength in the morning. As long as he fought her each night, there'd be a morning. It was a wonderful story, never failing to bring tears to Gregor's eyes, though he was aware that he was Tata to Magda only in the ironic sense.

"Yes," Gregor said with a sigh. "I've a nice one going now, though she talks like a baby sometimes. But say, what are you doing here? Didn't you have Coding Station last night? Why aren't you home in bed?"

"I was in the Wine Cellar, yes, Tata. But the meeting was so early, I thought I could score a few points with young Klimov by hanging around. There's a new bitch in the apparatus who may have her eye on my apartment."

"The blond one? I'd like to set her on fire. I hate the young ones. Especially the beautiful young ones."

"I hate them too. Gorbachev's dreadful children. Little rats, squandering all our labors. But, Tata, you must promise to be careful. Who will fight the Witch of Night Forever if they send you back? Worse, who will I talk to if they send you back? The walls?"

But Gregor wasn't listening; he was thinking only of himself.

"Do you know, Magda, I had my dream about you last night. I heard you say my name, and it jolted me awake."

"A dirty one, Tata? Filthy with Western perversions, I hope."

"No, I've told you. A nightmare. Scary. Caves, the like. Quite awful. As if I really *were* that damn prince. I remember fingers on my throat, someone's hot breath. Troubling. The Witch of Night Forever."

She laughed.

"Gregor, you fool. It's a fairy tale. Look around you, at your dreary reality and the little snail Klimov hungrily sniffing after you. Is that the stuff of fairy tales?"

"No," confessed Gregor. "You're right. The age of fairy tales is gone forever. I believe only in love. Do you love me still?"

"I'll always love you, Tata, love you most of all. You know that."

"Thank God," said Gregor, "that someone does."

*   *   *

It was called the situation room, on the B level, the second sub-basement level beneath the White House. It wasn't much architecturally: a conference room, roughly fifteen by twenty feet, painted a grim institutional green, in which there was one large conference table and several comfortable chairs. It could have been located in any ambitious motel chain in America. There weren't even any maps.

The President of the United States sat in a sweat suit with his eyes narrowed in extraordinary concentration as a lieutenant colonel in the Air Force read aloud from a document he held before him.

" 'No man sent us here,' " the lieutenant colonel read, " 'it was by our own prompting and that of our maker, or that of the devil, whichever you ascribe it to. The cry of distress of the oppressed is my reason and the only thing that has prompted me to come here. I wish to say furthermore that you had better prepare yourselves for a settlement of that question that must come up for settlement sooner than you are prepared for it. The sooner you are prepared, the better.' "

"All right, when did this come over?" the President demanded. He looked around the room. The Chairman of the Joint Chiefs was there, as were the Chiefs of Staff of the Services, impressive men in their well-tended uniforms ablaze with decorations. Each was served by an aide of no less than field grade rank who sat behind him, against the wall. The Secretary of State and the Secretary of Defense had arrived, as had the Deputy Director of the Central Intelligence Agency filling in for the Director, who was in Phoenix this morning for a speech; the Director of the FBI was there, too. Finally, the National Security Adviser. Yet among the fifteen or so of them, there was not the slightest tick of sound beyond the rise and fall of breaths and the occasional rattle of paper.

"Sir," the lieutenant colonel responded, "we received that over the National Command teletype link from the South Mountain installation at 0823. It followed by three minutes and fourteen seconds a clear-channel robot signal from the launch command center that the key vault had been deployed."

"And that means one of our silo officers deposited the key in the key vault. The significance, Mr. President, is that our officers are instructed to utilize the key vault only in the last stages of a seizure operation," said the Air Force Chief of Staff.

"Then let me get this straight. Whoever sent this message—he's in the silo?"

"Yes, sir."

The President looked again at the peculiar message. Then, to nobody in particular, he said, "A madman is in a missile silo. That's the situation?"

There was silence from the military men and civilian security officials who shared the room with him.

"It's signed 'Commanding Officer, Provisional Army of the United States,' " said the Air Force Chief of Staff.

"I assume you have staff psychiatrists at CIA examining it?" the President said.

"Yes, sir," came the response.

The President shook his head. Then he turned and said, "Would someone please be so kind as to explain how the hell someone could take over a missile silo. Especially *this* missile silo."

His rage turned his skin the color of an old penny and his eyes into even older dimes. Yet the anger did not dent the laconic voice of the officer who responded.

"Sir, as you know, the primary defense of a silo is its Doppler low-level radar, which marks the approach of any moving object. However, in the last year or so, it's been technically feasible to defeat radar with some kind of stealth, that is, radar-absorbing material, as some of our new bombers now have. In other words, it's at least possible that men approaching on the ground, very carefully, could have shielded themselves under some kind of stealth material and gotten through the radar, close enough to rush the installation in force. That's our reading."

"So how do they get down below? Don't the officers—"

"Sir, since South Mountain is independent launch capable, its elevator access is keyed into the PAL mechanism. This enables us to get down, say, in the event of an emergency, by using the SAC daily PAL code. If, say, by some freak of nature, both men in the LCC should come down with disabling stomach problems or heart attacks. But the men in the capsule don't know this. At least they're not supposed to."

"But whoever assaulted this installation *did* know this?"

"Evidently, sir."

"It's frighteningly clear that this man knew an awful lot. And there's nothing else? No offers to negotiate, no hostages, no demands for television coverage or cash? Nothing conventional for a terrorist event?"

"No, sir. We don't even have a reading yet on their unit size. The only thing we have is an awareness of their impressive level of technical sophistication as manifested by the seizure, indicating great resources and resolve, and that document, sent by teletype. Then silence. No answer to any of our messages."

The President looked again at the message from the mountain. He read the lines aloud. " 'You had better prepare yourselves for settlement of that question that must come up for settlement sooner than you are prepared for it.' "

He paused a second, then looked up to them all.

"Well, let's face it. He's going to launch. Without demands, without preparations, without anything. He's simply going to fire that missile if and when he gets that key out. What's our time frame?"

"Sir, the key vault is designed of high-grade titanium with some strengthening alloys added. It's very, very hard to get into, designed to delay any kind of implementation of the launch system for at least eighteen hours. With the right kind of tools, they could get into that block, say, by midnight."

"What kind of tools? Saws, drills? Would you be thinking of a safecracker, something like that?"

"Well, sir, no, not a safecracker. You'd have to burn your way in with a very powerful plasma arc torch. It would take a skilled man, a man with lots of experience."

"Where would they find such a man?"

"Well, sir, you can find them just about anywhere. He'd be a welder."

"Sir," someone said, "if they didn't find out about this until quite late, there's a chance they might not know about the key vault and they might not have a welder with them."

The President paused.

Then he said, "Oh, hell. They have a welder. You can bet on it."

Jack Hummel shivered, blew a hiss of breath from his chilled lips.

"Pretty damn cold," he said to the fellow across from him.

"Cold here," the man said. "Pretty damn hot up there."

They sat in the back of Jack's van. He was sure he had been brought with his equipment through town and then he had had the illusion of climbing over bumpy roads. Soon it got very cold. Then the truck waited for a time, and Jack had heard some kind of weird commotion up top. Fourth of July stuff, cracks and pops and snaps. Occasionally, an extra-loud noise would reach him, thumping on his eardrums. He guessed they were to be parked halfway up South Mountain.

These guys were taking over the phone company?

The man had some kind of strange gun. It looked big enough to start World War III. It was black and complicated. Jack couldn't tear his eyes off of it. He'd never seen anything like it.

"Say, pal, what kind of gun is that?"

The man smiled. His teeth were so blindingly white.

"It's the kind of gun shoot you dead if you don't shut up."

Jack smiled dryly. Some joke.

A few minutes later they drove on. Jack had the sense of gravel under the tires. Then again they sat and waited.

Jack was squirmy, curious. He was also bored. Jack's problem with life was that once upon a time he had been quite a good athlete. He had been quarterback of the Burkittsville Demons and, senior year, taken the squad to a 9–2 record; then he'd been a rangy, good-shooting forward for the cagers, averaging thirteen points a game; and finally, he'd hit .321 as a good-fielding third baseman. Yet his senior year had more or less been the climax of his life; it had been one long skid ever since. He was one of those guys good enough to be a star in high school but not quite good enough to perform at the next level, and when Maryland moved him from QB—his arm wasn't quite college material—to defensive halfback his sophomore year, he quit the team and the university.

Now he found himself at thirty-two married to a girl he'd been pinned to when he quit school. He had two great kids and a profession which, if it offered steady income and a reasonable standard of living, offered very little in the glory department.

Jack was used to making some kind of difference. He wasn't at all pleased at becoming one of life's little guys, workingmen of obscure skill who keep the country going without attracting much notice.

So there was a little bit of him—beyond, of course, his horror and his fear for his children—that was somehow slightly tickled by all this. Whoever these guys were, they had *studied* him, he realized. They knew his house and how to get in it, and when he'd be in the shower, and how best to make him compliant.

His athlete's vanity was pricked: he counted again. He was important.

The door opened.

"Time to go, Mr. Hummel," said the major.

"Sir, there's another development you should be aware of. South Mountain may be only a part of the problem."

"Jesus Christ," said the President. He began to crunch his molars together.

"Sir, we monitored a five-second LF radio transmission at 0819 from within the installation. It was a burst of raw noise sent out on a frequency of 28.92 megahertz, receivable by anyone pretuned to that frequency within a radius of, say, two hundred miles. We read it as a signal from whoever is in there. That means there may be another part to their operation."

The President shook his head.

Then he said, "I assume that you'll take every precaution, General. And I assume we've got our security agencies operating at maximum effort to try to figure out who they are?"

"Mr. President," said the Director of the FBI, "upon receiving the red flash from Defense, I instigated a crack task force investigation; right now I've got men working at Defense and in coordination with—"

"All right, all right," said the President.

Then, leaning forward, he said, "General, I order you to target a short-range missile with a low-yield, maximally clean nuclear warhead aboard for that mountaintop. If it becomes apparent that whoever is in that base is about to launch a preemptory mission against the Soviet Union, then I want you to take the base out. Meanwhile, I want the proper civil defense authorities to begin an evacuation of the area. I'm prepared to accept some casualties, but if we move swiftly, we may be able to limit them. In the meantime, I want—"

"Sir," the Air Force general said, "I wish it were possible."

Jack stepped out of the van into bright, cold light. An odd tang hung in the air; he sniffed hard. Familiar, but still difficult to place. Then he realized it was gunpowder.

Jack saw that he was inside the perimeter of the phone company's microwave transmission station for long distance calls.

It looked as though a battle had just been fought up here. All about him, fit-looking young men in snow smocks bustled about with automatic weapons and crates of equipment. Some were digging, some were unspooling barbed wire, some were working on weapons. And there was something else that Jack noticed instantly: a sense of wild excitement. Whatever the hell these kids were up to was going well; they were proud. It was the locker room at half-time, they were up twenty-one–zip.

"This way, please, Mr. Hummel. You three, bring Hummel's equipment. Corporal, park his van out of sight and cover it with the tarpaulin."

"What's going on?" Jack asked.

"No questions, Mr. Hummel. Time is of the essence. Come, please."

Then Jack noticed a weird thing. Over to one side of the place there was a bunch of young soldiers spreading large sheets of canvas all over the place. Still others were digging postholes in the ground about every twenty-five feet or so, and there seemed to be a lot of rope around. It looked as though the circus was coming to town; they were putting up the big top or something and—and then he noticed the bodies.

There were a dozen or maybe more, he couldn't be sure, in the rag-doll postures of the fallen, inert as stones. He could not tear his eyes away for a second, and yet did not want to be caught staring. And then he noticed the buildings in the compound; one had been knocked down by explosives, and others were tattered by gunfire.

"Who *are* you guys?"

"This way, please."

They led him to a small building, badly shot up. Inside he was surprised to find what appeared to be a sophisticated elevator door with its name stenciled on it. SHAFT ACCESS—RESTRICTED ENTRY—SECURITY-CLEARED PERSONNEL ONLY.

"This way," said the major.

The door opened with a dull pneumatic sound, and he stepped in with the major and the men carrying and pushing his equipment. He felt the elevator begin to sink through the earth.

The Air Force Chief of Staff paused, thinking about the man in the mountain, whoever he was. *The fucker!* he thought. Whoever he was, he knew just where we were weakest.

Though the general was in his private life a flamboyant man, a warrior king of the old style, in this room he kept his voice steady, professorial, reedy, thin.

"At the installation in question, the Peacekeeper is *in* a mountain. It's what we call deep under-mountain basing mode, conceived by Peter Thiokol's MX-Basing Modes Group out at Hopkins Applied Physics under a grant from the Air Force Research and Development Division. The thing is one hundred feet down, surrounded by hard rock. The missile is suspended by a special shock isolation system that will provide protection from nuclear attack and induced ground shock. It's the hardest missile silo in the world, and it would take an enormously powerful bomb—a bomb so powerful we don't have it in inventory—to destroy the silo inside that mountain. We haven't built bombs that big in some time, not since we had B-36s to deliver them back in the fifties. Today, our missiles are so accurate we can get by with small bombs, and we can mount ten warheads on a single missile. But we couldn't de-mothball a bomb that big and get it delivered for seventy-two hours at the minimum. That's the brutal truth, Mr. President."

The President said, "What are the odds on a missile intercept if they get a launch?"

"I'm afraid the news is bad there too, Mr. President," said the Air Force general. "If you recall, after SALT One we decided against developing an antiballistic force because we felt it would involve billions for something that was technically unfeasible. We simply don't have a bird capable of tracking a Peacekeeper in the boost phase and destroying it. Maybe if and when SDI becomes operational—"

"General, what is the megatonnage in the silo?"

"Sir, you have one missile with ten Mark 21 reentry vehicles, the very latest. Each warhead is the W87 in the 3.5 kiloton range with extreme hard target-busting capabilities. The total package is in the thirty-five-kiloton range."

"Targeting?"

"All for the Soviet Union, sir. The headquarters of the PVO Strany, the Soviet defense command about thirty miles outside Moscow; the main long-range transmitters that talk to their subs at Petropavlovsk, Vladivostok, Dikson Ostrov, Kalingrad, Matochin Shar, and Arkhangelsk; the ground control stations for Soviet satellites; their missile command center at Yevpatoriya in the Crimea; assorted ICBM launch sites spread throughout the central region; their early warning radars near Minsk and Novogrod."

"Jesus, their command system. What's the probable Soviet response?"

"If the bird flies, they'll launch on warning, you can bet on it."

"Could we detonate the bombs in the silo?"

"No, sir."

"What about a command disable system?"

"Only from within the launch command capsule. The reality is that there's no scenario for stopping the launch if they get the key."

"Why? With the Minutemen, it takes *four* keys, two sets of two officers in two separate launch control centers, and any of the three other launch control centers can inhibit launch."

"Yes, sir. But we felt that made launch control centers vulnerable, especially to the new SS-24s with their capacity to take out a hardened silo. If you take out the command capsule, none of the remote silos could launch. You could hit ten launch control centers and disable one hundred missiles. It was too tempting a target for the 24s. Therefore we built South Mountain as an independent-launch-capable installation. Even if Washington, SAC, Cheyenne Mountain, the airborne launch control center, and the ERCS missile are out of the picture, our command and control system totally fried, the boys in the silo could still launch. It was Peter Thiokol's idea. The guy at Hopkins who also created up the key vault."

"Yes, Thiokol," said the President. He'd had lunch with Peter once. An impressive young man, very smart, though almost totally bloodless where nuclear war was concerned. But somehow immature in other ways. The disparity had scared him a little. But then his mind moved quickly on.

"Then we'll have to use conventional bombs. Drench the place in napalm."

"No, sir," said the Air Force general. "The key to accessing this installation is getting down the elevator shaft. And accessing that elevator shaft is by means of a mainframe computer mounted directly adjacent to it, a Hewlett-Packard LC5400. The machine is sheathed in titanium. We feel that it's pretty invulnerable to small-arms fire, but any kind of heavy round—above a grenade, say—could damage the circuits. And if you damage the circuits, you lock the doors shut. Sir, you'd never cut through those doors. Never. They weigh eleven tons. So you've got to limit your applications of high explosive and napalm to the immediate site area, or you'll seal things up and we'd never get down there."

"Nerve gas," the President said. "Soak the mountain in nerve gas. Kill them all. If we have some civilian casualties, then—"

"Mr. President, Peter Thiokol was a step ahead of you there. He reckoned someone might try to nerve-gas his way in, so he had a filter system built into the computer. One whiff of bad odor, and the computer locks the mountain off. Not to mention that if these troops are as professional as we suspect, they'll be trained in chemical warfare. They'd just slap on their gas masks."

Damn Peter Thiokol, the President thought.

He looked at his watch. So, this was it. Here we are. And what do we do now?

"Sir, I think the solution is simple," came a new voice.

"It takes a bit of time, Mr. Hummel. We descend a full hundred feet."

Jack felt the pull on his knees as the chamber plunged down and down. Jack didn't like it. He had the sense of sinking forever beneath the waves, a sense of *submerging* somehow. You could get so far down you never got out again. You were buried.

At last the descent ended and the doors opened.

Beyond, Jack could see a corridor spilling away, lit by the odd bare bulb. But he also saw the man waiting for him: a trim fellow in his late fifties, well-cut white-blond hair, a slick, handsome face lit with charm.

"Welcome, Mr. Hummel," said the man. "Welcome to our little crusade."

Jack just stared at him dumbly. He felt a little as if he were in the presence of a TV anchorman, or a governor, or a talk show host. Something about the guy made him swallow hard. Jack felt as if he ought to ask for an autograph.

"This way now, Mr. Hummel. Come on, can't be slow. I know it's all new to you, but we are *depending* on you."

This queerly pleased Jack's ego. A big guy like this depending on him.

"Well, whyn't ya just *hire* me and leave my wife and kids out of it?"

"Security, Mr. Hummel."

They walked down the corridor, at last came to what appeared to be some kind of hatch door. Jack ducked his head to enter and still again he thought of subs: two chairs catercorner from each other, facing dozens of switches. NO LONE ZONE the walls said. Jesus, who'd want to be alone in *this* creepy place? The only human-scaled thing he could see in the small room was a crude, hand-lettered index card which read AND HEEEERE'S MIRV taped above an odd keyhole garlanded with an uptilted red flap in the control panel. Jack noticed then that there were *two* keyholes but that only one of them had keys in it.

"Say, what the hell is this?" he asked.

"It's a kind of computer facility," said the white-haired man. Jack didn't buy this at all. Computers, yeah, computers, but something *more*, too.

The man took him to a wall. There, before him, stood a broken window; shards of glass lay on the floor. But behind the window was not a view but simply a shinier grade of metal.

"Touch it, please, Mr. Hummel."

Jack's fingers flew to the metal.

"Do you recognize it?"

"It's not steel. It's not iron. It's some kind of alloy, something super-hard." He plunked his finger against it; the metal was dull to the touch. It didn't retain heat; it didn't scratch; it looked mute and lifeless. And yet it felt to his touch oddly light, almost like a plastic.

"Titanium," he guessed.

"Very good. You know your business. Actually, it's a titanium-carbon alloy. Very tough, very hard. There's probably not another block of metal like it in the world."

"So?"

"So. This block of titanium has descended into a second block of titanium. When it fell, thousands of pounds of rock above it locked it into place. It cannot be lifted. We need a welder to cut into the center of the titanium as fast as possible. You are a welder."

"Jesus," said Jack. "Titanium's the toughest stuff there is. They build missile nose cones out of it, for crissakes."

"The melting point of titanium is 3,263 degrees Fahrenheit. Add the carbon, which has a melting temperature of over 6,500 degrees, and you are dealing with a piece of material that has been designed to be impenetrable. Can you penetrate it?"

"Shit," said Jack. "I can get into anything. I cut metal. That's what I do. Yeah, I can cut it. I have a portable plasma-arc torch that should get hot enough. Heat isn't the problem: You can make a puddle out of anything. You can make a puddle of the whole world. The problem is how much I'm going to have to melt away to get inside. It takes time. You cut in circles, narrower and narrower. You cut a cone into its heart. You dig a tunnel, I guess. So what's at the end of the tunnel? A light?"

"A little chamber. And in the chamber, a key. The key to all our futures."

Jack looked at him, trying to connect the dots.

A feeling of intense strangeness came over him.

"You're going to all this trouble for a key? That must be one hell of a key."

"It is one hell of a key, Mr. Hummel. Now let's get going."

Jack thought about keys. Car keys, house keys, trunk keys, lock keys.

Then, with a woozy rush, it hit him.

"A key, huh? I read a little, Mister. I know the key you need. It's the key that'll shoot off a rocket and start a war."

The man looked at him.

"You're going to start World War Three?" Jack asked.

"No. I'm going to finish it. It started some time ago. Now, Mr. Hummel. If you please: light your torch."

A boy rolled out the portable Linde Model 100 plasma-arc cutting control unit. The coiled tubes and the torch itself were atop it. Another boy wheeled in the cylinder of argon gas.

"I suppose if I—"

"Mr. Hummel, look at it this way. I'm willing to burn millions of unnamed Russian babies in their cradles. I would have no compunctions whatever about ordering that two American babies—called Bean and Poo—join them. After the first million babies, it's easy, Mr. Hummel."

"The torch," Jack Hummel said, swallowing.

The President looked into the eyes of the Army Chief of Staff, a blunt-looking man who bore a remarkable resemblance to a .45 Colt automatic pistol bullet. On his chest he wore enough decorations to stop just such a round. "It couldn't be simpler," the general said. "It's straight infantry work, bayonet work. We have to get our people into that hole and kill everybody in it before they dig out that key. Say, by midnight. Or else the bird flies."

"What's the recommendation?"

"Sir, Delta Force is already gearing up for deployment," said the army general with a small, harsh smile. "Best small-unit men we've got. Our computer tells us there's also a company of Maryland National Guard infantry in training not two hours away from the site. That's two hundred more men, although you'd have to federalize them. I'm sure the Governor of Maryland would agree. We can truck out elements of the 1st Battalion, Third Infantry, from Fort Meyer, a good infantry unit, your ceremonial troops, hopefully by 1300 hours. I've already put them on alert. Then, I can get you a Ranger battalion air-dropped into the zone from its home base at Fort Eustis, Washington, by mid-afternoon, weather permitting. I can throw together a makeshift chopper assault company from Fort Dix and I can get you air support from a Wart Hog unit of the Maryland Air National Guard. With Delta, Third Infantry, and the Rangers, you'll have the best professional soldiers this country has produced."

"And armor, General. Could we just blow them out?"

"There's only one road up, and the latest information is that they've destroyed it."

There was silence in the room for a time.

"We're back to rifles and balls," said the Army Chief of Staff.

"Can you do it in time?" the President said to the army general.

"I don't know, Mr. President. We can solve the logistics of it. We can get the men there in time, and we can send them up the mountain."

"It's going to be a long and bloody day," somebody said.

"But it's a very hard assault. First, you've got to get to the elevator shaft, and you can only attack on a very narrow front because the mountaintop is surrounded by cliffs. Once you get to the LCF and its elevator," the general explained, "you've got to rappel down the shaft, and fight your way to the LCC, where they're trying to launch the bird."

"Sir," said one of the President's advisers, "you'll have to declare a phase four nuclear emergency, which empowers federal authorities to literally take over a given district, and turns all civil authority over to federal command. You're going to have to turn Frederick County into a war zone. I think maybe you'd also better raise the defense condition to a Defcon 4."

"No to that," said the President. "I don't want the Soviets thinking we're ready to launch. Increase security at all our missile sites and our satellite receiving stations."

"It's been done, sir," said the Air Force Chief of Staff.

"Okay, go to the phase four. Put out some kind of cover story about a military exercise to keep the goddamn press out of it. Now it's the Army's baby, with all due respect to the Air Force. I don't want a lot of different services falling all over each other's toes. Set up the roadblocks, seal off the area. Go to war if that's what it takes. But get those people out of there, or kill them all."

"Yes, sir," said the general. "Now, as for the command—"

"For the commanding officer out there, General, I want the best combat man you've got. And I don't care if he's a PFC in Louisiana."

"No, sir," said the general. "He's a full bird colonel, retired. But he's one mean son of a bitch."

Jack Hummel pulled his goggles down over his eyes and the world darkened. He held the cutting torch in one hand, and reached back to the control panel to switch the device on. The current flowed and the electrode in the tip began to glow from red on through the hues of orange. He watched it heat and grow within the nozzle, and then when it became almost white, he released a slow, steady stream of nitrogen. The gas ignited with a pop. In the crucible of the nozzle it became ionized—that is, electrified. Jack turned the temperature dial on the Linde control unit up to the top so the flame would reach the plasma temperature range, almost fifty thousand degrees.

The flame was a white killer's tongue, as hot as the center of any nuclear blast, but controlled there at the end of his torch. The men around him, reacting to the power of flame, drew back instinctively. He increased the pressure so that the flame was almost a needle that darted out two inches beyond the nozzle.

"I'm going to cut up into it," he told the general. "That way, the molten metal will run out via gravity."

The general looked at him.

"It's going to take a long time," said Jack. "Jeez, I don't know, maybe ten or twelve hours."

The general bent over.

"You know what's at stake. Your own children," he said. "Do you understand?"

Jack said nothing. Jack knew he could do it: if he could launch missiles against the Russians, he could murder his own children.

But a part of Jack said, Your children will die anyway if this rocket is launched.

Yeah, that's tonight. Today it's this fucking block I have to crack. I'll face tonight when it comes. I got to get them through today first.

"Okay," said Jack.

He bent, holding the plasma-arc torch in one hand, and with his other touched the smooth, burnished surface of the block of metal. Somewhere inside was a key.

He touched the torch to the metal. He watched its bright needle attack and liquify the metal; at fifty thousand degrees the ionized plasma-arc gas first seemed to define a bubble on the surface of the block, and then a dimple, and then an indentation, and finally, something very like a little tunnel. Jack cut deeper; the molten metal ran from the kerf, the gap gouged by the flame, and down its face like tears.

"The colonel," said the Army Chief of Staff, "did time in SAS in Malaysia on an exchange officer program. He was Special Forces from the start and had a brilliant Vietnam. He had seven years there, spent a lot of time in places we never officially went. He was stuck in a siege under heavy fire for thirty-eight days, and held out."

"Oh, God, Jim," said the Chief of Naval Operations.

"And, most important," said the general, "he invented Delta. He fought the Army and the Pentagon to get a Delta Force created when nobody cared. He trained Delta, he knows Delta, he lives and breathes Delta. He *is* Delta."

"Except," said the Chief of Naval Operations, "Dick Puller led Delta into Iran in 1979, in the operation we called Eagle Claw, and at Eagle One he panicked. And he canceled the mission when he came up one chopper short at the staging site."

"At Desert One," said the Army Chief of Staff, "he had to make the most difficult decision any American soldier has had to make since six June 1944, when Eisen—"

"He failed. He lost his nerve. And retired in disgrace, Jim. Dick Puller failed. He was a man who trained his whole life for a single moment, and when it came, he failed."

"I say that when it was decision time, everybody backed away from him. We all did. The president of the United States did. They hung a poor colonel who'd bled himself empty for this country for the best part of thirty years out to dry."

"He's a walking Greek tragedy," said the Naval Chief of Staff, "who blew the one—"

"Mr. President, if you asked me to name one man who could get you up that mountain and into that silo before midnight, I'd name Dick Puller. Dick Puller is the bravest officer I ever served with, and the smartest. He knows more about combat than any man alive. He's done his share of the planning and his share of the killing. He's a great soldier. He's the best."

"I never heard any man say Dick Puller was a coward," said the Air Force Chief of Staff. "But I never heard any man deny that he was an obstreperous, willful, self-indulgent, sometime psychot—"

"Jim, this isn't just an old protégé you're trying to help out?" asked the Chief of Naval Ops.

"*All right!*" said the President. "Goddammit, enough is enough."

He turned to the Army Chief of Staff.

"Then get me this Puller," he said finally. "Call him. I don't care what it takes, tell him to do it. To get it done."

"If it can be done," said the Army Chief, "Dick Puller will do it."

1100

From a cold start, Delta Force would arrive on site not in three hours, as the Chief of Staff had promised, but in two and a half. It took a miracle of logistical planning, most of it thrown together while the unit—the one hundred twenty men of Special Forces Operational Detachment/Delta—was in the air, being hauled up from Fort Bragg by two C-130s of the first Special Operations Wing of the 23d Air Force. The initial plan was to have them HALO onto the site—to parachute from a high altitude, then open at a low one—in case Aggressor Force, as the occupiers of the complex were now called, had mounted a watch for the approach of airborne troops. But Dick Puller's first decision, made eleven minutes after his arrival, was no.

He stood in the ramshackle office of the Misty Mount Girl Scout Camp, about a half mile from the mountain, across a flat, snowy meadow that lay at the mountain's foot.

"I don't want 'em spread out all over the goddamned landscape," he snapped, his face set in a glare, "with broken legs and dirty weapons and love affairs with farmer's daughters. We don't need it. I won't begin my assault until I get my tac air, and that's a good four hours. Land 'em in Hagerstown under battle conditions. I want airfield perimeter security from the state police, I want advance parties on the convoy into us as well as route security, and I want perimeter security set up ASAP upon arrival. Those guys on the mountain sent out a radio transmission; maybe there's a column of unfriendlies waiting to bounce Delta on the way in. I want the men locked and loaded from minute one. I don't want any screwing around. Get 'em in here fast, and tell 'em to get working on their assault plan as soon as they get here. First briefing is at 1200 hours and I'll expect complete terrain familiarity."

Puller turned from the young man who took this order, a mild-looking twenty-eight-year-old FBI agent of no special ability named

James Uckley who had been appointed Dick's No. 1 guy because he was the first to show up, having been ordered onto the site by a special Bureau flash from his Hagerstown office, where he'd been investigating a bank embezzlement. Dick chose Uckley because he believed that enthusiasm was far more important than intelligence, and Uckley seemed enthusiastic, if bewildered. Moreover, Dick didn't want smart guys around him to argue with him. Dick liked dumb people who did what they were told, and he liked telling them what to do.

Uckley put this decision out on the emergency teletype which clattered back to the Situation Room, where it was put on to the troops.

"They get those recon shots yet?" Puller demanded.

"Not yet," said Uckley, looking at the staggering amount of communications equipment that had been set up with surprising speed against one corner of the rickety old wall of the place. Several technicians bent over the stuff, but for some reason Puller refused to acknowledge them, preferring instead to deal with the world through Uckley.

"I'll sing out if they come over," Uckley said uncomfortably. In truth, he was a little afraid of Puller. In truth, *everybody* was a little afraid of Puller. He wasn't even sure whether he should call him sir, or colonel, or what.

Puller went back to his binoculars. Above him the mountain loomed, white and pristine. The red aerial stood out like a candy cane. He could see no movement.

There was one road up, through rough ground. Halfway up it just stopped, where Aggressor Force had blown it. Smart. No armor would come their way, at least not today.

He looked at his watch—1124. A little more than twelve hours to go. And Delta still wasn't on the damned ground, this sorry-dick Maryland Guard unit was trying to get its act together, 3rd Infantry was fucking around somewhere on the road, and the only good news was that his Ranger battalion was at least airborne for its cross-country flight and now had an ETA of 1600 hours.

Twelve hours, he thought again. His expression was grim, but this was nothing new: Dick Puller's expression was *always* grim. He was born grim. Whatever thoughts he had he kept to himself, although the tension in his face and the way it drew the color from his skin and pulled his muscles taut and his mouth flat suggested something.

At last he asked, "Any word on those locals yet?"

"State police still knocking on doors," Uckley said.

Puller's first move was to send state policemen into the town of Burkittsville on a fast canvass of old-timers. Who knew that mountain? What was there? How did you get up it? What was inside it? Dick didn't trust maps. It was an old 'Nam habit, where a bad map had once almost killed him. It was one of the few mistakes he'd made in his career.

Richard W. Puller was a stern, rangy man of fifty-eight with a gunmetal-gray crew cut that revealed a patch of scalp up top. He had remarkably forceful dark eyes and a way of moving and walking that suggested if you weren't part of the solution, you were part of the problem. Someone—not an admirer—once said of Dick Puller, "You'd have to put a full magazine into the bastard to stop him from coming at you, and then his shadow would cut your throat." He was not a well-liked man and he did not like many people: a wife, his two daughters, a soldier or two along the way, mainly the tough old master sergeant types that got the killing done in the hairy moments and a few guys in elite units the world over, such as SAS, where he'd done a tour of exchange-officer duty.

He also had a talent for the truth. He would tell it, regardless, a gift that did him little political good in the Army, where you had to go along to get along. He was hated by all manner of people for all manner of rudenesses, but particularly for his willingness to look anybody straight in the eye and tell them they were full of shit. He was, in short, exactly the sort of man made for war, not peace, and when a war came, he had a great one.

He was in-country from 1963 to 1970; he did two tours with the 101st Airborne but spent most of his time leading A-team detachments way out off the maps, interdicting North Vietnamese supply routes in Cambodia or training indigenous troops—Nungs and Montagnards—to fight against the hated North Vietnamese. He got stuck in a long siege in a big A-camp up near the DMZ and with a twenty-four-man team and three hundred indigs he held off a North Vietnamese Division for thirty-eight days. When an airborne unit finally fought its way through to relieve them, he had seven Americans and one hundred ten Nungs left alive.

He also worked for MACV's Special Observation Group, the mysterious, still-classified intelligence unit that sent ops all over 'Nam, some said even up north. Puller then had a long and flashy career running a

Mike Force battalion, a quick reaction team that helicoptered to the relief of A-team detachments in the soup and proceeded to do maximum damage in minimum time. He was an exceedingly aggressive officer, but not a sloppy one. He'd been hit three times, once with a big-ass Chinese .51, the shock of which would have killed most men. It didn't matter. If you were professional, you got hit, that was all.

But he came back from the war with a special vision, a Mike Force for the world. His idea was that the United States should have at its disposal a group of swift, deadly raiders. He had a dream of a commando group, superbly trained, fast-striking, brilliantly equipped, that could react swiftly to any major incident.

And he had gotten it, too, though as he fought for his project through the tortuous labyrinth of army politics, his personality had assumed the unlovely contours of a zealot. Somewhere in the Pentagon's D-ring he lost the capacity to laugh; somewhere at some meeting or other he lost his perspective. He won, and Delta Force was the prize: Delta Force, which he had defined and trained and led: which he had, in the final analysis, fathered. And which he had, in the popular view, failed.

A bell rang.

"Sir, the recon photos are coming in," Uckley shouted as the photos began to roll off the computer transmission platen.

Puller nodded grimly, not really seeing Uckley until the boy handed them over.

Dick looked at the pictures. They were in color, but they were like no pictures Uckley had ever seen. It seemed to be some kind of white-gray blur; in the murk there were little red flashes.

Dick was counting.

"Thirty-eight, thirty-nine, forty . . ."

Then he went silent.

"Sixty. Sixty of the fucks above ground. These are men, son. Aggressor Force as seen from outer space, a million miles up, portraits courtesy of an Itech infrared floating up there in the sky somewhere. Now, why is that number significant, Uckley?"

Uckley swallowed. He'd never been in the military. He made a guess.

"It's the size of an infantry platoon?"

"No," said Puller. "You just guessed, right?"

"Yes, sir," said Uckley.

"Good. If you ever guess again around me, I'll end your career. You'll be history. Do you understand?"

"Yes, sir."

"If you don't know, that's fine. But things go freaky when junior officers try to guess their way through. Is that understood?"

Uckley gulped. The older man's stare was like a truck pressing on his sternum.

"Yes, sir," he said.

Instantly, the transgression was forgotten.

"An infantry platoon is thirty-two, a company about one twenty-eight. No, the significance of the number is twofold. First, it's so large that it's clearly a holding operation. It's not an in-out job; these guys mean to stay up there until we find the guts to push them off that hill. And secondly, it's so large that it means these people couldn't come in private cars. We'd see a caravan. So there's got to be a staging area around here, maybe a rented farm. Find the farm and maybe you find out who they are."

"Yes, sir."

"Get on that thing, and have the Sit Room send out your pals in the Hoover building to go through the rentals in this area over the last year or so. The state cops could help on that too."

"Yes, sir," said Uckley.

As the young man hurried over to the communications room, Puller studied the picture. Yes, he was good. Whoever was running Aggressor Force had been on a few special ops in his own time.

He had at least half of his men on the perimeter and the other half on some kind of work detail up near the launch control facility. Reading the signature of the men and the operation, Puller swiftly concluded that he was up against a well-trained elite unit. Israelis? The Israeli airborne were the best special ops people in the world. South Africans? There were some ass kickers in that fucked-up country, too, you could bet on it. What about Brit SAS? With a regiment of SAS boys, Dick often said to American generals, I could take over any country in the free world, with the exception of the State of California, which I wouldn't want.

Or maybe they were our own guys.

That thought had gone unspoken so far, and even now no one really wanted to face it. But the truth was, Americans could easily be doing this. Maybe some hotshot in Special Forces got tired of waiting for the balloon to go up. He thought he'd help it, rid the world of commies, and to hell with the two hundred million babies that got burned in the process. "Provisional Army of the United States!"

Dick looked at the picture again.

Who are you, you bastard? When I know who you are, I'll know how to beat you.

"Sir!"

It was Uckley.

"Sir, Delta's on the ground at Hagerstown. They're on their way."

Puller looked at his watch. Three and a half hours had elapsed since the seizure. Skazy had Delta on the ground now, and moving to the staging area. The choppers for the air assault would be in inside the hour. The A-10 crews were getting their ships gunned up at Martin Airport outside of Baltimore, that was one hangup. Some kind of new weapons pod had to be mounted, 20mm instead of their usual 30-mil cannons, because the big 30s with their depleted uranium shells had too much kinetic energy for the computer in the LCF at the top of the elevator shaft; they'd cut through it and seal the silo off forever. Puller hated what he couldn't control, and he couldn't control this. But there wouldn't be a party until he had his Tac Air, because you don't send boys in without Tac Air.

They could go soon now.

But Dick didn't want to move until he knew more. Patience, he thought, patience was the answer. Already Washington was on the horn wanting results. That was shaping up as the hardest battle. But he would wait. There had to be another angle, and he would find it.

He lit a cigarette, one of his beloved Marlboros, felt it cut deep into his lungs. He coughed.

"Sir," it was one of the Commo specialists, overexcited as usual. "Sir, look."

Someone else came running into the room, too, a state policeman, and then one of the army Commo teams.

"Look, Colonel Puller. Jesus, look."

Puller raised his glasses to his eyes and saw that a dark blur had suddenly obscured the mountaintop.

"What is it?" someone yelled. Other men were fumbling with binoculars.

Puller concentrated on the dark stain that now lay draped over the mountain. He gauged it to be about five hundred square feet, undulating slightly, black and blank.

It made no sense at all.

And then he had it.

"It's a goddamned tarpaulin," he said. "They're covering up. They don't want us to see what they're doing up there."

God damn them, he thought.

In the uproar he almost missed Uckley telling him softly that someone had tracked down the man who'd created South Mountain, a guy named Peter Thiokol.

Poo Hummel was at an age where she liked everybody, even men in her bedroom with guns. She liked Herman. And Herman seemed to like her right back. Herman was big and blond and all dressed in black, from his boots to his shirt. His gun was black too. Despite his size, he had gentle eyes—and the bumbling mannerisms of a well-trained circus bear. Not an atom of his body radiated anything except an awesome desire to please. He loved her pink room and especially her toys, which were displayed on shelving her daddy had built. One by one, he took her animals down and studied them with massive concentration. He liked Care Bear and Pound Puppy and all her Pretty Ponies (she had almost a dozen). He liked Rainbow Brite and Rub-A-Dub Doggy and Peanut Butter too. He liked them all.

"This one is very pretty," he said. It was her favorite, too, a unicorn with a bright pink polyester mane.

Poo was no longer upset that her mother would not stop crying down in the kitchen and that Bean was so quiet. For Poo, it was a great big adventure to have new friends, especially like Herman.

"Will you ever go away?" she asked, squinching up her nose and making a face.

"Sure," he said. "Soon. I gotta go. I gotta job."

"You're a nice man," she said. "I like you."

"I like you, too, nice little girl," he said, smiling.

She liked his teeth especially. He had the whitest, friendliest smile she'd ever seen.

"I want to go out," she said.

"Oh, no, Poo," he said. "Just for a little while longer you have to be inside with Herman. We can be chums. Best buddies. Pals. Okay? Then you can go out and play and it will be all fun. You'll have a good time, you'll see. It'll be great fun for everybody. And Herman will bring you a present. I'll bring you a new Pretty Pony, all right? A pink one. A pink unicorn, just like the one you have there, all right, little girl?"

"C'n I have a drink of water?" Poo asked.

"Of course," he said. "Then I'll tell you a story."

Peter Thiokol was rambling.

He could feel his sentence trail off in a bramble of unrelated clauses, imprecise thoughts, and hopelessly mixed metaphors until it lost its way altogether and surrendered to incoherence.

"Um, so, um, it's the decapitation theory that holds, you see, that a surgical strike aimed at leadership bunkers, if it should come, and of course we all hope it won't, anyway, um . . ."

The note card before him was no help.

It simply said, in his almost incomprehensible scrawl, "Decapitation theory—explain."

Their faces were so bored. One girl chewed gum and focused on the lights. A boy looked angrily into space. Someone was reading the feature section of *The Sun.*

It wasn't a great day in 101, the big lecture room in the basement of Shaffer Hall on the campus of the Johns Hopkins University in Baltimore, where Peter Thiokol convened Strategic Theory, an Introduction three times a week for an ever-shrinking group of undergrads, most of whom wanted to be M.D.s anyway. How do you reach these damned kids?

Just make it interesting, one of his new colleagues had suggested.

But it *is* interesting, Peter had said.

He struggled to find his focus, a problem he'd been having ever since the problems with Megan.

"Decapitation, of course, is from head cutting-off of, that is, it's the idea that you could paralyze a whole society by sort of removing, like in the French Revolution, with the, um, the guillotine, the—"

"Uh, Dr. Thiokol?"

Ah! A question! Peter Thiokol *loved* it when someone in his class asked a question, because it got him off the hook, even if for just a minute or two. But there were hardly ever any questions.

"Yes?" he said eagerly. He couldn't see who had spoken.

"Uh," an attractive girl asked, "are we going to get our midterms back before we have the final?"

Peter sighed, seeing the pile of exams, ragged blue booklets smeared with incomprehensible chickentracks in ballpoint, sitting on the table next to his bed. He'd read a few, then lost interest. They were so boring.

"Well, I'm almost done with them," he lied. "And yes, you will get them back before the final. But maybe nuclear war will break out and we'll have to cancel the final."

There was some laughter, but not much. Peter lurched onward, trying to relocate his direction. He had expected to be so much better at this, because he loved to show off so for Megan.

"You show off *very* well, I must admit," Megan Wilder, his ex-wife, had once said. "It's your second greatest talent, after thinking up ways to end the world."

The teaching had seemed to offer so much after his breakdown—a new start, a sense of freedom from the pressures of the past, a new city, new opportunities, a discipline he loved. But the kids turned out not to be very interesting to him, nor he to them. They just sat there. Their faces blurred after a while. They were so passive. And this performing took so much out of him. He went home at night bleached out, too tired to think or remember.

He'd just stare at the phone, trying to figure out if he should call Megan or not, and praying that she'd call him.

The memory was still brittle. He'd even seen her two weeks ago, in a wretched, maybe heroic, attempt at reconciliation. She'd simply showed up after months of staying out of touch. For a night it had been spectacular, a greedy carnival of flesh and wanting; but in the morning the old business was there, his guilt, her guilt, the various deceits, the betrayals, his narcissism, her vanity, his bomb, his fucking bomb, as she called it, the whole ugly pyramid of it.

"Anyway," he said, still scattered, "um, on decapitation stuff, um— look, let's be frank here." He had this sudden weary urge to cut through to the truth.

"Write this down. Decapitation is about killing a few thousand people to save a few million or billion people. The idea is that Soviet society is so centralized and authority-crazed that if you kill the top few, you wreck them. So you build a missile that's really an intercontinental sniper rifle. You become the guy in *Day of the Jackal*. The only problem is, they can do it to us, too."

They looked at him dumbly. Not even murder touched them.

He sighed again.

And so the mighty have fallen. The great Peter Thiokol, magna cum laude, Harvard, a Rhodes scholar, a master's in nuclear engineering from M.I.T., a Ph.D. in international relations from Yale, golden boy of the Defense Department, prime denizen of the inside-the-beltway Strategic Community, author of the famous essay in *Foreign Affairs*, "And Why Not Missile Superiority?: Rethinking MAD," was drowning.

Peter was a tall, reedy looking man of forty-one who looked thirty-five; he had thinning blond hair that exposed a good stretch of forehead, which made him look intelligent. He was also rather handsome in an academic sort of way, but he had a disorganized quality to him, an alarming vagueness that put many people off. Outside his area of expertise, he cheerfully admitted, he was a complete moron.

In a no doubt desperate attempt to camouflage his discomfort, he was dressed as he imagined a professor should dress, that is, as he had remembered them dressing from twenty years before: He wore a tweed jacket so dense it looked like a map of a heather Milky Way, and a Brooks Brothers blue oxford-cloth shirt, that deeper, stormier blue that only Brooks offers, with a striped rep tie, a pair of pleated khakis from Britches of Georgetown, and a pair of beat-up, nearly blackened Bass Weejuns.

The student tried again.

"Uh, Dr. Thiokol? Could you at least tell us if it'll be an essay exam or a multiple choice? I mean, the test is next week."

The girl looked a little like Megan. She was dark and beautiful and very slender and intense. He stared at her neurotically, then struggled with the question. Reading more of their essays would just about kill him. But he knew he didn't have the energy to go back through his chaotic notes to develop some kind of objective thing. He'd probably just give them all B's, and go back to staring at the phone.

"Well, why don't we take a *vote* on it?" he finally said.

But he was suddenly drowned out in the hammering of a huge roar. The class turned from their lecturer to the window, and watched in amazement as a scene from a fifties monster movie began to unreel. A large insect appeared to be attacking the parking lot. As it got closer, the bug became an Army UH-1B Huey helicopter, a great olive drab creature with a huge Plexiglas eye, a bloated thorax, and an almost delicate tail, and as it floated down out of the sky, adroitly sliding through a gap in the trees, its howl caused all the fixtures in the lecture hall to vibrate. Preposterously, it landed in the parking lot, whirling up a windstorm of dust and snow and girls' skirts.

Peter could hear the giggles and the gossip as two officers in dappled combat fatigues came loping out of the hull of the craft, grabbed a kid, spoke to him, and then headed toward his building. But he himself did not smile. He understood that they were here for him and that something was terribly wrong. He felt the blood drain from his face.

It took them about thirty seconds to reach Shaffer.

And in the next second the doors flew open, and a lean middle-aged officer walked with utter lack of self-consciousness to the front of the room.

"Dr. Thiokol," he said without a smile, "we need to talk."

Their eyes met; the fellow looked focused and excited at the same time. Peter knew many career military types; they were okay, a little literal-minded, perhaps. And generally quite conformist. But this guy had something a little extra: He looked like a young dragoon officer racing toward Waterloo in 1815. Peter had seen it in a few bomber pilots, usually the wilder kinds, the ones who wanted to go thermonuclear three times a week.

"Okay," Peter said to his students, "you guys get out of here now."

The students trundled out, gossiping among themselves.

Then the officer held up *Nuclear Endgames, Prospects for Armageddon* by Peter Thiokol, Ph.D.

"In this book you talk about what you call the John Brown scenario, where a paramilitary group takes over a silo."

"Yes," said Peter. "I was told by a very high-ranking officer that it was the stupidest thing he'd ever read. It hadn't happened since 1858 at Harpers Ferry and it couldn't happen now."

"Well, it seems to have happened."

"Oh, shit," said Peter, who didn't like to swear. He found his breath suddenly ragged. Somebody took over a bird? "Where?" But he knew.

"South Mountain. High-force threshold. Very professional take-down."

The major sketched in the details of the seizure operation as they were known and it was clear he had been thoroughly briefed.

"How long ago did this happen?" Peter wanted to know.

"Going on three hours now, Dr. Thiokol. We have people there now, setting up an assault."

"Three hours! Jesus Christ! Who did it?"

"We don't know," said the major. "But whoever, they know exactly what they're doing. There's been some kind of massive intelligence penetration. Anyway, the commanding officer/ground wants you along to advise. All the signs are that they're going for a launch. We have to get in there and stop them."

So it had started. It was close to the final midnight, and he thought of all the things he had meant to say to Megan but never had. He could think of only one thing to say, but it was the sad truth, and he said it to this soldier.

"You won't make it. You won't get in there. It's too tight. And then—"

"Our specialty is getting into places," the officer said. "It's what we do."

Peter saw his name stenciled above his heart against the mud-and-slime pattern of the camouflage.

SKAZY, it said.

The officer looked at him. They were about the same age, but the officer had that athlete's grace and certitude to him. His eyes looked controlled, as if he had mastery even over the dilation of his pupils. It suddenly occurred to Peter that this would be an elite guy. What did they call them? Alpha? Beta? No, Delta Force, that was it, a Green Beret with an advanced degree in homicide. The guy looked like some kind of intellectual weight lifter. He had incredibly dense biceps under his combat fatigues. He'd be one of those self-created Nietzschean monsters who'd willed himself toward supermanhood by throwing a bar with iron bolted to the end up and down in some smelly gym for thirty or so years. Peter felt a sudden sadness for the deluded fool. He had half a mind to argue, out of sheer perversity. For if the idea that they could get in was this Skazy's vanity, Delta would be disappointed tonight.

Peter had a sudden sense he was in somebody's bad movie. The world should end in grace, not Hollywood melodrama. It couldn't even destroy itself well. He almost had to laugh at earnest Skazy here, the Delta Viking. It's not an airliner you're trying to crack, he wanted to say, it's a missile silo, with the best security system in the world. I ought to know; I designed it.

"Let's go," said Peter. He reckoned the world didn't have much longer to live, and he wanted to be there for the last act. After all, he'd predicted it.

And then he thought he ought to call Megan, just in case, but decided, she's on her own now, let her *be* on her own.

One of the chief curiosities of modern life, Peter often reflected, was the acceleration of change.

For he had gone, in the space of a twenty-two-minute helicopter ride, during which time his thoughts had remained jangled and painfully abstract, from Hopkins to the middle of a battle zone. He felt as though he'd flown back through time into the Vietnam War, a conflict whose intricacies he had studiously avoided in his lengthy stay in graduate school. It was like a TV show from his childhood: He heard the young Walter Cronkite intoning, "Everything is as it was, except *You Are There*."

And so he found himself among military killer types all clustered around a dilapidated girl scout camp in rural Maryland. All these lean young combat jocks with crew cuts and war paint on, festooned with a bewildering variety of automatic weapons, as well as ropes, explosive packs, radio gear, exotic knives taped upside down on various parts of their bodies and, worst of all (and Peter could sense it, palpable as the smell of kerosene in the air), an ineffable *glee*.

He shivered. He liked his wars abstract and intellectualized; he liked the theory of destruction at the global level and the excitement of thinking in awesome geopolitical terms. This closeness to the actual tools of small-unit warfare—the wet, greasy guns, the snicking, clicking bullets, the *klaklaklakklak!* of bolts being jimmied, the clank of magazines being locked and unlocked (the guys were going crazy playing with their weapons) left him more than a little nervous. The guns especially scared him; guns could kill you, he knew. He shivered again, as some supernumerary, an FBI guy whose name he didn't quite catch, took him into the cabin proper, and there he got his second massive shock.

He expected on the inside just more of what was on the outside: more special ops pros all talking in hushed tones over detailed maps, discussing their "assault," or whatever their term was. What he got was something out of Mark Twain: two country cronies sitting hunched together, their faces lost in shadow, swapping tall tales amid the clouds of weed gas and the smell of stale tobacco that brought a pain to your forehead. The butts, in fact, heaped like a funeral pyre in the cheap ashtray between the men. This was Mission Central? This was HQ? It felt like the general store.

"I remember," he heard one of them saying, "I remember. The world ran on coal in those days."

"Yep, by golly, and a sight it was, them days. We had over two hundred boys working in the Number Six hole, and, by damn, this was the center of civilization. Not likes he be now, with just a few hangers-on scruffin' by. Everybody had a big black car and everybody had a job, Depression or no. Burkittsville was coal and coal was Burkittsville, by damn. I remember it like it was yesterday, not fifty years ago."

Then one of the fogies looked up, and Peter caught a quick glimpse of his face in the light, even as he felt himself being appraised and then dispensed with rather magisterially. Involuntarily, he swallowed. He recognized the guy.

It had to be the famous or infamous Dick Puller, exactly the kind of nut case you could trust Defense to pull out of the files to take over in an unconventional situation. Even Peter knew of Dick Puller, his many moments of glory in far-off paddies and glades, and his one moment of frozen terror at Desert One.

What Peter saw was a sinewy man in his late fifties with a face that looked as if it were hacked from ancient cotton canvas. He had a tight sheen of short iron-gray hair, almost stubble. He had a flat little hyphen of a mouth. Peter saw also that he had large, veiny hands—strong hands, worker's hands—and ropy arms. He had a linebacker's body, lacking the vanity of precisely engineered muscles but possessing—radiating, in fact—a sense of extraordinary strength. He had eyes like an ayatollah: hard, black little stones that glittered. He was in old jungle fatigues, and had a montagnard bracelet around his wrist. He wore jungle boots. Yes, goddammit, the faded stencil on his ample chest bore the legend PULLER.

" 'Course that damn cave-in closed it all down," said the geezer. "A black day for Frederick County, Mr. Puller, if I do say so. The women-folk wore widder's weeds for a year 'fore they moved away."

"Dr. Thiokol," Dick Puller suddenly said, not ever having been introduced formally to Peter, "Mr. Brady here tells me something very interesting about your installation. Something I doubt you even know."

Peter was ready for this.

"That it's built a thousand feet above the ruins of an old coal mine? I knew that. We had all the old documents. We took test borings. The mine has been sealed since 'thirty-four, when it collapsed. Our tests indicated no presence of geological instability. That mine is history,

Colonel Puller, in case you had some delusion of going in there as a way of getting into the installation."

Dick's eyes stayed flat and dark as he answered Peter. "But our reports say that original old undeveloped Titan hole was left open to the elements since the late fifties. Lots of rain in thirty years, right, Mr. Brady?"

"Rains a lot in these parts, sometimes like a son of a bitch," said Mr. Brady. He turned, his leathery old face locking on Peter's. "Son, you must know about a mess of things, but I have to wonder what you know about coal. You open a coal seam to a mess of rainwater over a period of years, you get some damned interesting formations down through a mountain. Coal is *soft*, boy. Soft as butter."

Peter looked at him.

Then he looked at Dick Puller.

"You get tunnels, Dr. Thiokol," said Dick Puller. "You get tunnels."

Gregor beat a hasty retreat from the embassy to the nearest source of booze, which was Capitol Liquors, three blocks away at L and Vermont, a harshly lit joint with a pretentious wine display for yuppie Washington, as if yuppies wandered into such a place. He went in, fought through the listless crowd of unemployed Negroes who passed the time here, and bought a pint of American vodka (he could not afford Russian) for $3.95. Outside, he opened it quickly, threw down a quick hit.

Ah! His oldest and dearest friend, the one who never let him down. It tasted of wood smoke and fire and bracing winter snows. It belted him like a two by four between the eyes. He filled with instant love. The cars whirling up the street, the American automobiles, endless and gaudy, he loved them. Klimov, little rat Klimov, he loved him. Pashin, Klimov's powerful sponsor, he loved him.

"To Pashin," Gregor announced to a man standing next to him, "a hero for our times."

"You said it, Jack," said the man, bringing the muzzle of a bottle of Ripple in a paper bag up to his lips, drinking. "Git *all* our asses in trouble."

Fortified, Gregor lurched ahead. The sun was bright. It hurt his eyes. He put on his sunglasses, cheap things from the drugstore designed to look expensive. He felt much better now. He felt in control. He looked at his watch. He still had some time before his little job.

Gregor wandered around for a few minutes before he finally found what he was looking for, a public phone. You always call from a public phone. That was the oldest rule. In Russia you may be sure the public phones are tapped, but in America you were sure they were not.

Gregor found a quarter, called the number. A woman answered, a new voice, but he asked for Miss Shroyer. There was some fumbling, and finally she came on the phone.

"This is the Sears computer," he said. "Your order is ready. It's"—he squinted, reading the number of the phone—"it's 555-0233. Have a nice day. This is the Sears—"

The phone went dead. He stood, talking into it anyway, holding the button down, seeing her leave her desk in the Crowell Office Building, pick up her coat, nonchalantly mosey down to the drinking fountain, take a long drink, duck into the ladies room, her fatness imposing, her huge back and bent shoulders like a cape, her personality bright and phony, to the pay phone in the next corridor.

The instrument against which he leaned produced a squawk surprising Gregor in his reverie, but he freed the receiver button.

"Gregor, good God! The chances you take! Suppose they are watching you? I told you, Gregor, never, *never* call me at—"

"Molly, oh, Molly!" sobbed Gregor. "God, darling, your voice, it sounds so wonderful."

"You fat bastard, you've been drinking already, I can tell. Your words are all mushed together."

"Molly, listen, please, yes, I had a little taste, that's all—"

"Gregor, don't be sloppy, you know how I detest it when you're sloppy!"

"Molly, please, I had no other place to turn. This Klimov, he's really after me this time. He wants me. It's worse than ever. God, darling, they are going to send me back."

"Gregor, you pulled this routine months back. It's where we started."

Gregor sobbed. The sound of his pain and his fright must have been amplified by the wires of the phone, for it seemed to release in Molly something his implorings had failed to touch: her pity. He sensed her compassion suddenly: he sensed her coming to him. He pressed on.

"Please, please, darling. Don't fail me. You've got to get me something. Something soon. Something big. Something I can give them. Not just your chicken-shit minutes and the gossip. They can get that from the *Post*. No, Molly, if you love me, if you fear for me, if in the smallest, tenderest part of your baby toe you feel for poor Gregor Arbatov, please, please, oh, my Molly, please help me."

"Jesus, you bastard," she said. There was almost a laugh in her voice. "You're so far beyond shame, you're into squalor."

"Please," he begged again.

"Call me in a few days."

"In a few days I'll be on my way to Latvia or some awful place."

"There is no Latvia, Gweggy."

"That's what I mean. Please, Molly. Oh, please, by tonight. I'll call you at four."

"You're really pushing your luck."

"Oh, Molly, I knew I could count on you."

"I can't—what? Oh, yes, sure." This last was mumbled to an intruder. In seconds she was back, breathless. "Christ, I have to go, baby doll, they're calling all of us for something."

"My sweet, I—"

But she had hung up. Strange, no? he thought. But he felt much better now. He looked at his watch. It was almost eleven. Time for his drive out to Columbia and his little job for the agent Pork Chop.

"Colonel Puller?" It was the FBI agent, Uckley.

"Yes?" asked Puller.

"It's an eyes-only from White House Operations. They want to know what's happening."

"What's happening?" A quick, angry glance. It was said that Puller had talked to Carter himself from the ground at Desert One. "Tell 'em Delta's in, we're working out our assault details, we're waiting for Air and the Third Infantry and have high hopes for the Rangers. Make something up."

"They sound mad," said Uckley, a little unsure at Puller's lack of interest in Washington.

"I don't give a fuck what they are," said Dick sharply. He looked over at Peter. "They'll want action. What they don't know, of course, is that the wrong action is worse than no action. *Much* worse. See, I have to fight *them* just as hard as I have to fight what's-his-face up in the mountain. Now, Dr. Thiokol. Peter, is it? Okay if I call you Peter?"

"Sure," said Peter.

"Now, Peter, I checked your file. Very smart guy. Great record. A-plus on the report card, all the way through." His cold little eyes gazed at Peter with regret. "But what's this shit about Taylor Manor? Some bin in Ellicott City. You had a problem?"

"I had some difficulties when my marriage broke up. But that's all taken care of now."

"You flipped, huh? Let me ask you straight out: How's your head? Screwed on tight and outstanding? Are you crazy anymore?"

"I'm feeling fine," said Peter evenly, wondering why this bastard hated him so much. Then he concluded that Puller hated everyone. The man was sheer aggression.

"What I need from you is a lot of hard work. I need a genius. I need a guy who knows that mountain who can figure things out for me. See, maybe I can crack that hole if I can figure out how. But I need a genius along to whisper in my ear. Can you give me the help I need, no bullshit games, no little sullen pouts, no prima donna shit. I don't have time for the star system."

"I'm fine," said Peter again. "You can count on me. I guarantee it."

"Excellent. That's all I need to know. Now—who's up there?"

"Search me," said Peter.

"All right. *Why* are they up there?"

"To launch," said Peter. "This is the only strategic installation in the United States with independent launch capability. There's no point to taking it if you weren't going to make the bird fly."

"Why? What would be the point?"

"There isn't one that I can figure," said Peter. "Unless it's sheer nihilism. Somebody just wants the world to end. It doesn't make any kind of strategic sense; when the bird flies, the Sovs launch on warning. Then we all die. The beetles take over."

"Some kind of crazy death wish, like the guy who took the gun into the airliner and shot the pilot?"

"More than that, but I don't know what it is. But I guarantee you, there's more, somehow. There's some other aspect to the plan, some wit, some theory, some long-range aspiration. This is only one part of it, that I can tell you. This is part of some larger scheme."

"Goddammit, I thought you were supposed to be some kind of genius!"

"I am a genius," said Peter. "But maybe that guy up there is too."

"When you figure it out," said Puller, "I want you to tell me first. Right away. It's crucial. If I know what's going on, maybe I can figure out who's doing it. Now, can we get in?"

"No," said Peter.

"Goddammit," said Dick Puller.

"No, I don't think you can. I understand they have people up there."

"Sixty well-armed men."

"Military?"

"The very finest. From what I've been able to tell, their seizure op was very crisply handled. Very neat, very impressive. Right now they've thrown the goddamned thing under some kind of tarpaulin. We can't see what they're doing up there. Pretty damned smart. We've got zillion-dollar birds in the sky that can see through clouds and rain and tornadoes and tell us whether Gorbachev had his eggs up or over easy. But there isn't a lens alive that'll see through an inch of canvas. What do you suppose they're up to?"

"I don't know," said Peter. "I don't have any idea."

"Worse than that, they sent a radio signal to somebody. Who do you suppose they were talking to, Dr. Thiokol? Another bunch of commandos, getting ready to jump us as we put our assault together, really mess us up? Maybe a group to hit our airfields, stop our goddamned Tac Air? Maybe a part of this other aspect of the plan. What, Dr. Thiokol? Any ideas?"

"I don't know," said Peter bluntly. "The only thing I know about is missiles. And missile basing. And I know this. You're going to have a hell of a time getting up there, whether you get hit by another outfit or not. I had access to a computer survey of small-unit action in Vietnam and it suggests that all the advantages are with the defenders."

"Jesus, you had to get a computer to tell you *that?*"

Peter ignored him, plunging onward to the dark heart of the matter. "But even, say, even if you kill the men on the hill, you've still got to get through that door to the elevator shaft in the LCF to get to the LCC. It's the only way down. And the door is eleven tons of titanium. If you started cutting through last week, you wouldn't get there by midnight."

"What about just opening the door?" Puller asked.

Peter made an involuntary face that communicated the idea that he was talking to a child, then said contemptuously, "The door is controlled by a Category F Permissive Action Link security device. A multiple twelve-digit code with limited try. Three strikes and you're out."

"How did he get it? Inside job?"

"No, they change the code every twenty-four hours. But one of the wrinkles here is that the code is kept up top, too, in the security officer's safe, in case SAC has to get down there. That's the way we planned it. But nobody is supposed to know this. It was a secret. Anyway, they must have blown the safe, got the code, and rode the elevator down and jumped the guys in the hole. Easy."

"Can't we call SAC and get the code?"

Peter made another snotty face. "Come *on*," he said. "This guy—"

"Aggressor-One, we've tagged him."

"Yes, Aggressor-One," Peter said, thinking, they certainly got *that* right, "he can reset his own code from inside."

"Could we blow through it?"

"You'd need so much explosive, you'd blow the mainframe that runs the upper installation, including the door code. The doors would lock shut permanently, you'd *never* get in."

"Hmmm," said Dick Puller.

"Maybe, just maybe they don't know about the key vault. If the guys inside had enough warning to use the key vault, then they're sitting on the most useless piece of real estate in America. Because the key vault was a late modification. If we knew *when* they made their intelligence breakthrough, then we'd know how much they could know. That's the prime question. Do they have a welder?"

"Let's assume they do. They certainly knew everything else. They knew the codes, the procedures. They knew the Commo equipment."

If it were possible, the skin on Puller's face seemed to stretch tighter. He looked like a man with a massive headache. He lit another Marlboro. He turned back to the old man, who had been sitting abstractedly during his conversation with Thiokol, chewing on his dentures.

"Well, Mr. Brady," he said, "you think we could get in from below?"

"No, no," Peter interrupted impatiently. He hated stupidity. "No, the concrete is super-hardened to thirty-two thousand pounds p.s.i. It'll stop everything except one of the old super H-bombs. And it's surrounded by ten million square feet of rock."

"So a man couldn't get in from below? Or get close enough to plant a small-yield nuclear device. I mean, theoretically?"

"In twelve hours?"

"Yes."

"Well, if he could get up there, I suppose . . . this is highly abstract, but theoretically, I guess he could get in through the exhaust vanes, tubes that will blow out if the bird fires. That would get him into the silo, and if he had a device or the knowhow, he could disable the bird that way. Theoretically, at any rate."

"Now, Mr. Brady. These tunnels that may be in this mountain. What sort of shape would they be in?"

"Worse damn shape than you could imagine, Mr. Puller," said the old man, pausing to hawk up a wad of phlegm. "Some of 'em may go nowhere. Some places they may narrow down so small a man couldn't get his fist through 'em. And black, Mr. Puller. So black you can't imagine. You have to be underground for dark like that."

"Could men operate down there?"

"Wooooo, Mr. Puller. You wouldn't want to. It'd have to be a certain kind of man. Down there in the dark, you're always scared. If the ceiling goes, there's no help for you. You can't see, you can hardly move. You've always got shit in your pants, Mr. Puller. A tunnel sits on top of your head something mighty heavy."

Puller sat back. Outside he had one hundred twenty of the most highly trained military specialists in the world. Yet somehow he knew Delta Force wasn't the answer. This called for someone who probably didn't exist; a man who could slither up a hole in a mountain in the fetid shroud of perpetual night, a mile and a half with his fears bouncing around inside his head like a brass cannonball, and come out at the end sane and . . .

"I suppose I could get some volunteers from Delta. Mr. Brady, any coal miners around, men who've been underground?"

"Not in these parts, Mr. Puller. Not anymore. Not since the cave-in."

"Hmmm," Dick Puller said again. Peter watched him. Puller seemed to implode on himself as he thought, his face gray, his eyes locked on nothing. It was old Mr. Brady who spoke.

"Now, my grandson, Tim. Tim, he could get you in there."

Dick looked at him.

"Tim wasn't much good at nothing, but he was your natural-born tunnel man. Wasn't no hole ever made he was afraid of. His daddy, my son Ralph, was a miner and Tim grew up near holes. When Ralph died in a fire in 'fifty-nine, Tim came to me. I was a state mine inspector up in West Virginia by that time, and Tim went into a lot of holes with me. Tim was a tunnel man."

"Where is Tim?" Puller asked, almost fearing the answer.

"Well, you folks had yourself a war few years back. Old Tim, he was asked to go fight it, and fight it he did. Won some medals. Crawled in some holes and did some killing. Tim was what you call your tunnel rat. He was with 25th Infantry, place called Cu Chi. Those little yellow people built some tunnels, too, and Tim and his pals went down into 'em day after day, month after month. Not many of those men left alive. Tim didn't make it back, Mr. Puller. Not outside of a body bag, that is."

Puller looked at Peter Thiokol. He smiled.

"Tunnel rats," he said, turning the phrase over in his mind, absorbed. "Tunnel rats."

The major was deliriously happy. He was an excellent soldier and he loved battle. He loved to think about it, to dream about it, to plan for it, and to fight it. Now he scurried over the hill checking on his men with the boundless energy of a fourteen-year-old boy.

"Any movements?"

"No, sir. It's quiet."

"You know, it might be Marine Recon or Special Forces. Camouflage experts. You wouldn't see them until it was too late."

"No, sir. There's nothing out there yet. Only state policemen, more to keep civilians out than to attack us."

His soldiers were young but well trained and especially eager. The very best. No amateurs here. Men who wanted to be here, who believed. They were wonderful boys, in their dappled uniforms under the snow smocks, their equipment hard and clean, their faces clean-shaven, their eyes keen. They'd gotten the big tent up in two hours and were now digging under it furiously. The tent itself was not an impressive structure, but it had been constructed for a specific purpose and for that purpose it was perfect. The tent rose on poles no more than five feet off the ground and the various sheets of canvas that had been crudely lashed together to form it came, in the end, to about 2,000 square feet. It was meant for only one thing: privacy. Underneath, the major's men labored mightily to create their little surprise for anyone coming up to them. They'd learned about it firsthand, and they were eager to apply it to other new learners.

Meanwhile, at the outer perimeter of the position, breastworks had been constructed around the heavy machine-gun positions and a single firing trench had been dug. The trucks had brought the ammunition, nearly a million rounds. Hold off an army.

He dashed from position to position, checking lanes of fire and, more important, resolve.

"How do we feel? Do we feel strong and brave?"

"Yessir. Strong and brave and well-prepared."

"It's going well, then. It is going as we planned it. It's all on schedule. It's working. We can all be proud. We've worked so hard, and it's all paying off."

He had designed well. Only napalm could get them out, and the Army couldn't use napalm because napalm would melt the big computer. No, they'd have to come up and do it with lead. Close-in, hand-to-hand. A real battle.

At one point, at the crest of the mountain, one of the lookouts told him about the helicopters.

"About twelve of them, sir. To the east. They fell in and landed."

The major looked through his binoculars. He could see quite a little force gathering its strength a mile away, down in the snowy meadow by some jerry-built buildings. The twelve choppers sat in formation; there was some kind of communications trailer, and even as he watched, a convoy of trucks pulled in. Men hustled and bustled. Someone had erected a big tent with a huge red cross on its sloping roof. More and more cars pulled up, and occasionally a helicopter would land or depart.

"They're getting ready, no doubt about it. An air assault. Of course. That's how I'd do it, at any rate."

"When, sir?"

"Actually, I'm impressed. Whoever is running their show knows what he is doing. The general and I assumed their first attack would come in the first three hours, and that it would be badly coordinated and ill planned. A lot of smoke and fire, a lot of casualties, no concrete results. But whoever's down there is waiting. He wants his assault to count. Helicopters—"

"Airplanes high above, sir. We catch the glint in the sun occasionally."

"Yes, an electronic eavesdropper. Be careful what you say, boys. They're listening. And they're taking pictures. Of our beautiful big tent."

His men laughed.

For the major the pleasure was intense. He had hunted guerrillas for years: dreadful scrapes, ranging across the countryside. Occasionally, the enemy would catch a trooper and leave a trail of his guts for miles until you finally came across the gristle and bone that was left of him. It was so hard to close with the bastards: they melted away into an alien landscape. You could torture their women and remove their children, but they were always there, just out of reach.

But not now. Now we're on the mountain, and *they've* got to come up to us. He had a real battle to fight: a hill to hold for a period of time, a real mission.

"Look for planes first," he told them. "We know they have A-10s in the region, in Baltimore. They'll come low over the mountains. They'll soften us up with those. Then the choppers. You'll see the choppers swarm up. The A-10s will hold us down while the choppers ferry men in close. The men will rappel down to the road, because the choppers won't land. It should be Delta Force, very good men, the best. They'll be very aggressive. But they'll be stupid, you'll see." He smiled. "It'll be a great fight, I promise you that. Oh, it'll be a great fight, boys. One they'll talk about for a hundred years."

"We'll win it for you and the general, sir," said one of the boys.

The major went over to the ruins of the launch control facility, and plucked a telephone off one of the standing walls.

The general answered.

"Sir, no sign yet of an assault. I expect it within the hour, however. They've brought in helicopters and a fleet of trucks. But we'll be ready for them."

"Good, Alex. I'm counting on you."

"How are things down there, sir."

"Oh, we're making progress. It goes slowly, but it goes. The flame is bright and hot."

"We'll hold until they have us all."

"You buy me the time I need, Alex. And I'll buy you the future you want."

1200

Walls stared at the door. The door was the worst part of it. There had been other doors, of course, and maybe were still doors to come for him. But this was the motherfucker of all doors. Massive, green, and iron, it looked about a million years old. Its hinges were rusty, and scabby little patches stood out where the years had beaten against it. And someone had scratched two words that Walls recognized onto it in crude, desperate letters a foot high: FUCK NIGGERS it said, and as Walls saw it, that's just what the door did.

Walls lay back. He'd go crazy in here soon enough, and then they'd let him go, and he'd get killed.

Yeah: FUCK NIGGERS, that was it all right.

He tried to think of nothingness to rush the time along. It didn't work. He and the door, they were all that was. He had faced that, because he was by nature a specialist in reality. And his of the moment happened to consist of green walls close around him, and the pot for him to piss in, and the scungy collection of dried snot under his cot, and some faggot's suggestions carved into the walls. And the door. That was it, really, the mighty iron door, with its pins and bolts and massive hinges that sealed him off, and said FUCK NIGGERS.

"Hey, boy."

It was the Pig Watson, calling in from the peephole.

"Hey, boy, get your black ass up, or I give you over to the Aryans, and they turn you into a bone harmonica."

The Pig Watson unlocked the door with the clank of metal on metal, hauled the sucker back, and entered. It was such an easy thing to do if you had a key. Watson was about six four, with acne, his white gut hanging over his wide black belt like a pillowcase full of lead shot. He was basic cracker white, with an art museum of tattoos cut into the skin of his fat arms and his knuckles saying LOVE and HATE. He had two pig eyes and a little pig nose. He carried a nightstick and could expertly dial long distance information on your skull.

"What you doin', boy?"

"I was praying," lied Walls, a gifted liar.

"Don't make me laugh, boy. Yer fuckin' prayers already been answered when you got an extra six weeks solitary before the Aryans get their paws on you."

And so they had been. An Aryan named Hard Papa Pinkham had taken an intense liking to the contours of Walls's rear end and one night in the showers with three of his biker pals had decided to possess it. It was a short-lived triumph, however; Walls caught him in the corridor between wings with a straight razor and made certain Hard Papa would never again have his way in the showers. So much blood. Who would have thought there was so much blood in a dick?

The Aryans were not pleased and had sworn to make Walls sing an equally high falsetto.

"Some shot wants to see you, boy," said the Pig Watson. "Now, you go and be quick or you answer to me. This way."

And so they took Walls from his solitary cell in the B Wing and marched him through the main hall to the cells of the Aryans, the best-organized gang in the Maryland penitentiary. The Aryans had heroin and porn and barbs; they had murder and protection and laundry; they had shivs and thumpers and knuckles. They ran the place.

"Hey, mo-fo, your ass gonna be fuckin' worms for sure," one of them informed him.

"Nigger, you one dead piece of Spam," another decreed.

"Jive, you on the hook," said another.

"You a real popular little songun," said the Pig with a gleeful laugh on his face. "You know, they got a pool going how long your ass going to last once you sprung from the tomb."

"Be round 'long time," said Walls insolently. "Longer than your fat white ass."

The Pig thought this was hysterical.

"Dead guys with smart mouths, I love it," he chuckled.

They checked through Processing—Walls was roughly searched, but his knife had been lodged elsewhere for safekeeping—and he was removed from the main cell block to the warden's office, where he was ushered by the Pig Watson into a roomful of suits. And there were also two soldiers boys. The warden signaled Watson out of the office and he closed the door behind him.

"And here he is," said the warden, "our favorite parishioner, House Guest No. 45667. How are you, Nathan?"

Walls just looked at the white faces which always had for him the look of balloons, smooth and fat and full of gas.

"Specialist four Nathan Walls, goddamn," said the soldier boy, some kind of super sergeant with all kinds of stripes running up and down his arm. "Jesus, what a crime, a guy like you ending up in a place like this. I checked the records. Man, you were a *hero*. There's a hundred men alive today because of you, Mr. Walls."

Walls just put his sullen face on and didn't say anything. He made his eyes see infinity.

"This hero," explained the warden, "was known on the streets as Dr. P. P for, excuse my French, pussy. He had nine girls working for him, all of them beauties. He also specialized in angel dust, uppers, downers, grass, Mexican mud, and just about everything chemical designed to screw up the inside of the human head. To say nothing of two or three assaults with intent, and no end of muggings, breaking and enterings, and felonious assaults various and sundry. But none of it was Nate's fault. It was Vietnam's fault, right, Nate?"

Walls flexed his strong hands and made his face as empty as a bucket with a hole in it. He would not let them get into his head. He was done with that.

"You were also," said soldier boy, "the best tunnel rat 25th Infantry ever had. Let's see, two Hearts, Silver Star, two bronzes. Jesus, you had yourself quite a war down in those holes."

Walls's military exploits had very little meaning to him. He'd put all that far away in the deepest part of his head, and anyhow, a tunnel was just a street with a roof on it.

"Mr. Walls, we're in a mess," said the officer, some kind of stern bird colonel. "And we need a man to help us out of it. At 0700 today, some kind of military unit seized a national security installation out in western Maryland. A very crucial installation. Now, it happens that the only way into this installation may involve a long, dangerous passage in a tunnel. Very scary work. We need a man who's fought in tunnels before to take a team through that tunnel. A tunnel rat. And we need him fast. You're the only one we could find in our timeframe. What do you say?"

Walls didn't even have to think about it. His laugh was rich and merry. "It don't have nothing to do with me. I'm all done with that shit," he said. "I just want to be left alone."

"Oh, I see," said the suit. "Now, Mr. Walls, may I tell you that I believe you're not going to be left alone. In about twenty hours from now the idea of being 'left alone' is going to lose its meaning."

Walls just looked at him.

"Yes, well, what you're going to notice is the warhead of a Soviet SS-18 detonating at about four thousand feet over downtown Baltimore in a fused airburst for maximum destructive potential. That is, about four thousand feet over our heads as we speak today. We figure the throw weight of an 18 to be about fifteen megatons. Now, what you'll sense, Mr. Walls, is one second of incredible light. In the next nanosecond, Mr. Walls, your body will be vaporized into sheer energy. As will the bodies of everybody in the first circle of destruction, which will extend in a circumference of about three miles from the point of detonation. What's that, warden, would you say, about a million and a half people?"

"Yes."

"Yes, and in a wider circle—say, ten miles in diameter—there will be extraordinary blast damage and your usual run-of-the-mill trauma associated with high explosive. You know, Mr. Walls, you saw enough of it in Vietnam: third degree burns, severed limbs, blindness, deep lacerations and contusions, multiple fractures and concussions. I expect it will be worst on the kids trapped in the schools. There won't be any parents around to do much good for them, so they'll just have to do the best they can, and pray for an early death. Now, in a circle out to twenty miles you'll have much less actual damage, but the deaths from radiation poisoning will begin within forty-eight hours. Horrible deaths. Deaths by vomiting, by dehydration, by nausea. Not a pretty picture. I'd say in this immediate area no less than three million dead by the end of the week. Now, Mr. Walls, you project that onto every major city in America and the Soviet Union and you'll see that we're talking about some severe consequences. A full nuclear exchange would involve the deaths of no less than five hundred million people. And, Mr. Walls, if we don't get into that installation, that's what's going to happen."

"If the white man blow his ass up, that's his problem," said Nathan Walls.

"Mr. Walls, the Soviets have some extraordinary hardware at their disposal, but not even they have been able to build a bomb that discriminates between races. Think of the bomb as the greatest equal opportunity employer in history. It will take us all, Mr. Walls, regardless of our race, creed, or political affiliation, and it will make ash or corpses of us. And if you have any illusions of the third world picking up the pieces, I'd advise you against them. A, there will be no pieces, and B, the radiation deaths will girdle the globe. The survivors will be mutant rats and your friends the cockroaches, who will outlast us all."

This had very little impact on Nathan Walls, who had never, by inclination or opportunity, had much chance to cultivate the ability to think in abstract terms. There was, in the entire universe, only one phenomenon worthy of consideration: his ass. Yet he saw how urgent the situation was to the suits, even if he could not quite get with the doom jive offered him by the head suit. And so he decided to play a little game.

"And if I can get you into this place?"

"You'll have the thanks of your government. And the satisfaction of knowing you changed history."

"And I'll throw in another six weeks in solitary," said the warden.

This wasn't quite enough. But Walls reasoned that in the open he might have a shot at a getaway and, failing that, if by chance he brought it off, it might jingle out to some loose change for him.

"Couldn' get Nate Walls a shot at another joint?" he asked. "Say, Allentown, where all the white politicians go? There's a swimming pool and pussy there, or so they tell it."

"Mr. Walls," said the suit, "you give us Burkittsville and we'll give you Allentown."

"I'll give him *Miami,*" said one of the other suits.

Even as the leader of Rat Team Baker was being recruited in the Maryland State Penitentiary in downtown Baltimore, the leader of Rat Team Alpha was being lured out of retirement in the suburbs of Washington, D.C. The key figure in the seduction was a young man from the State Department named Lathrop, who found himself nervous and alone in the front room of a small house off Lee Highway in Arlington, Virginia. It smelled of pork and odd spices and was decorated cheaply, with sparse furniture from Caldor's. Awkwardly, as he waited, he looked out the window. There he saw a young woman wrapped warmly against the chill, playing with three children. He was struck by her beauty: She had one of those delicate, pale Oriental faces, and there was something extraordinarily graceful in her movements.

Someone called his name, and he turned to discover a middle-aged man in a Hawaiian shirt and a pair of polyester trousers.

"Mr. Nhai?" he said.

"Yes, Mr. Lathrop. What have we done wrong? Is something wrong with our papers? All our papers are in order. The church checked them out very specifically, it's—"

"No, no, Mr. Nhai, this has nothing to do with papers. It's something quite unusual, uh—" he paused, sensing the utter despair behind Nhai's obsequiousness. "I have been asked by my government to bring an unusual request to you."

"Yes, Mr. Lathrop?"

"I can tell you only that we have an urgent security problem a hundred miles outside of Washington, and it appears that one of the solutions to this problem may involve a long and dangerous passage through a tunnel. We've set our computers to work to uncover former soldiers who served in a unit in Vietnam we called tunnel rats. That is, soldiers who went into tunnels, such as the ones at Cu Chi, and fought there."

Nhai's eyes yielded no light. They surrendered no meaning. They were dark, opaque, steady.

"It turns out these men are very difficult to find. They tended to be highly aggressive individuals, the sort who don't join veterans' groups. We've found only one."

Mr. Nhai simply looked at him, sealed off and remote.

"But one of our researchers found out from a book a British journalist wrote that there was a single North Vietnamese who had served a decade in the tunnels who had actually immigrated to this country. A man named Tra-dang Phuong."

The little man kept looking at Lathrop. His expression hadn't changed.

"He'd had mental problems after the war, and his government sent him to Paris for treatment. And, by a strange turn of events, he met an American psychiatric resident there who took an interest in the case, and arranged for him to come to this country under the sponsorship of an Arlington Catholic church. We cross-checked our immigration records, and sure enough, Tra-dang Phuong is here. The man is here, in this house. He came over in 'eighty-three. Our records say he lives here."

"I am Phuong's uncle," Mr. Nhai said.

"Then he's here?"

"Phuong is here."

"Can I see him?"

"It will do no good. Phuong spent ten years in the tunnels. The effects were grievous. Phuong believes in nothing and wants merely to be left alone. There's little that makes Phuong happy anymore. Dr. Mayfield felt that to get Phuong away from the country and the memories would be of great help. It turns out he was wrong. Nothing is of help to Phuong. Phuong suffers from endless melancholy and feelings of pointlessness."

"But this Phuong, he knows tunnels?"

"No one knows tunnels like Phuong."

"Sir, would Mr. Phuong be willing to accompany our forces on this most urgent security operation? To go back into tunnels again?"

"Well, Mr. Lathrop, I seriously doubt it."

"Could we please ask Phuong?"

"Phuong doesn't like to talk."

Lathrop was desperate.

"Please," he almost begged. "Please, could we just ask him?"

Mr. Nhai looked at the young man for quite a while, and then with great resignation went to get Phuong.

While he waited, Mr. Nhai came back with the nurse and the children that Lathrop had seen outside in the garden, scrawny, energetic kids, all tangled up in one another. They ran forward to Mr. Nhai. He nuzzled them warmly and cooed into their ears.

The nurse stood to one side, watching.

It seemed to take an awfully long time. Lathrop wondered when Phuong would show.

"Mr. Lathrop," said Mr. Nhai, "may I introduce Tra-dang Phuong, formerly of Formation C3 of the Liberation Army of the People's Republic of Vietnam. She is famous in the north as Phuong of Cu Chi."

Lathrop swallowed. A *girl!* But nobody—still, they wanted a tunnel rat. And she was a tunnel rat.

The girl's dark eyes met his. They were lovely, almond-shaped. She couldn't have been more than thirty, or was it that he didn't read Oriental faces well, and hadn't seen the lines around her eyes, the fatigue pressed deep in the flesh, the immutable sadness.

Mr. Nhai told her what he wanted.

"Tunnels," she said in halting English.

"Yes, ma'am," Lathrop said, "a long, terrible tunnel. The worst tunnel there ever was."

She said something in Vietnamese.

"What did she say?" he asked Mr. Nhai.

"She said she's already died three times in a tunnel, once for her husband and once for her daughter and once for herself."

Lathrop looked at her, and felt curiously shamed. He was thirty-one, a graduate of good schools, and his life had been laborious but pleasant. Here stood a woman—a girl!—who had literally been sunk in a universe of shit and death for a decade and had paid just about all there was to pay—and yet was now a child's nurse, aloof in her beauty. If you saw her in the supermarket, you wouldn't get beyond the beauty of her alienness: she'd be part of another world.

"Will she do it? I mean"—he swallowed, uncomfortable with the break in his voice—"she's *got* to."

Mr. Nhai spoke quickly to the woman in Vietnamese. She replied.

"What did she say?"

"She'd rather not go back to tunnels."

Lathrop was stymied. He wasn't sure how much latitude he had in briefing her.

"It's very important," he said.

The girl would not look at him.

"I am sorry, Mr. Lathrop. I could talk to her. Make her see. But it would take time."

Lathrop turned.

"Please," he said. "It's an emergency. Lives depend on it."

The girl's eyes would not meet his. She spoke quickly to her uncle.

"She says she would be no good in the tunnels. She would do more harm than good in the tunnels. She begs you to understand. In the tunnels, there is great fear for her."

Lathrop mumbled something banal, made a last attempt at eye contact and failed. He searched his orderly mind for inspiration, and could find none. But in admitting defeat, he relaxed, and thereby found the key.

"Tell her it's about bombs," he said suddenly. "The bombs that burned her children. Her daughter. There's more bombs for more children, for millions and millions of children. Now, if she can believe it, we Americans have to go into tunnels not to kill but to stop bombs falling on children and setting them aflame. It's the only way, and the time is very, very short."

The old man began to translate, but Phuong cut him off.

Her eyes looked into Lathrop's and he was unhinged by their bottomlessness; it was like looking down into the deep black water.

Then, almost demurely, she nodded.

1300

It fell to Peter Thiokol to background-brief the Delta officers, the various state police supervisors, and other federal functionaries who had just showed up, and the liaison officer from the Maryland Air National Guard who would talk on the air strike. Peter knew he was not ordinarily an effective communicator, but in this one area he had maximum confidence. Nobody knew more about the subject at hand than he himself; he had created it from the deepest part of his own mind, and from his own terrors of—and deep fascination for—nuclear war. And also from his deepest vanity: that he could play the most dangerous sport of all and win.

"Peacekeeper is radical in two respects: first, it's extremely accurate. We use it to target their ICBM silos. We don't have to neutralize a soft opportunity like a city and kill five million people in order to hurt them."

The officers looked at him mutely. He radiated conviction and kept his neuroses, of which there were many, well hidden. Peacekeeper was the redeemer. He believed in it; he was its John the Baptist.

"And secondly"—he had them, he could feel it—"these warheads bite very, very deep. By that I mean—this is the key to the concept—they give us access to all hardened targets. So we have the capacity not merely to disarm but to perform an activity we call decapitation. We can cut the head off, cleanly and surgically. Do you understand the implications?"

Of course they didn't. The parabola of the grenade was the extent of their strategic imagination.

"It means from now on, when we talk, they listen, because we can put the warheads in their pockets. They hate it, let me tell you, the bastards hate it. It scares them. There are Soviet generals who know they're behind and see Peacekeeper as the beginning of the end. Now," he went on, getting at last to the crux of the matter, "what terrified me as I thought about ways to deploy Peacekeeper was the knowledge that the system itself has tendencies toward destabilization. If those missiles are the best in the world, and if we're a couple of years ahead of the Soviets in our modernization program as we upscale from Minuteman II to Peacekeeper, then, goddammit, the way we install them has to be the best too. Because"—he probed the air, to stress the point—"if the system is vulnerable to anything, then it tempts the other side to first-strike at its vulnerability. Weakness is destiny; strength is security. The secret of strategic thought is the prevention of first-strike temptation. Our other forty-nine Peacekeepers are going in little dinky Minutemen II holes out west, which is craziness! It offers such a premium for a first strike. That's why South Mountain's is the hardest silo basing in the world and that's why it had to be targeted against Soviet command and communication. We call it Deep Under-Mountain Basing. And that's why it's so impossible to get into."

Dick Puller's voice cut at him out of the dark, impatient with the strategic context that had decreed South Mountain into existence, pressing for the hardcore nuts and bolts.

"Dr. Thiokol, let's get to the tac stuff. We don't have to understand it. We just have to shoot our way into it."

"Then what you have to understand is that now that they're in command, it's not only them we're fighting, it's the mountain too. It's the installation. If you bomb, say, or use heavy shells, napalm, that sort of thing, you'll melt down the up-top mainframe and you're out of luck. That's not an accident: it was planned that way." By me, he didn't add. "And I'm telling you, the only possible way to get inside is to pop that door without explosive, get down in that hole. It can't be done any other way."

"Mr. Thiokol"—the voice was familiar, and Peter eventually recognized it as Skazy's—"what do you think they're doing under that tarpaulin they've thrown up?"

"I don't know."

"What could they do?"

"Well, not much. Dig in, I suppose, dig trenches. Perhaps they have some weapon they don't want you to see, like a . . . a—well, I don't know."

"Why would they try to cover up like—"

"I don't know," Peter said, again irritated to be sidetracked at this silly stuff about the tarpaulin or whatever it was. That wasn't the *center* of it, didn't they see?

"Mr. Thiokol, uh, Dr. Thiokol, what are our odds at pulling off a multiple simultaneous?"

Peter stumbled again. The jargon was from some other war culture. He didn't recognize it.

"I'm sorry, I don't—"

"Multiple Simultaneous Entry." It was Puller. "That's the Delta Doctrine. Attackers always outnumber defenders, but that advantage is lost if you can get in through only one entrance. We like to go through several at once. Can we get in more than one place at once?"

"No. Only through that shaft. The silo doors are super hard; the exhaust plugs don't blow until the bird launches. There's no other access."

"What about underground? The mines?" Skazy asked.

"Dr. Thiokol does not see our tunnel rats as the answer to anything," said Dick Puller to the group.

"I think they are a delusion," said Peter Thiokol. "And the more time you waste on it, the less time you have to deal with reality. That door is it. You've got to get through the door."

Puller said, "Dr. Thiokol, now you know why you're here. *You've* got to get us through that door."

And so Peter sat back.

The door. He had to figure the door. The door had just become his problem.

"Can you do it?" asked Puller.

"There's a code," said Peter. "Whoever is running things up there will reset the PAL to his own specifications. So that means I've got to break their code. It's very tricky. There're twelve digits required for an unlock. It's got what's called a limited try capacity. If you—"

"*Can you do it?*"

"You need a cryptanalyst, Colonel Puller."

Dick Puller's voice was hard.

"I know I do. I don't have time to dig one up. I have to fight with what I have. That's you."

Peter said nothing. He had a splitting headache. The irony was almost comic now; Megan, a cultivator of ironies, would have loved it: he had crafted the system to be impenetrable, and now he had to penetrate it.

Delta staff was working out its assault plan when the first chopper arrived; before Puller could pull himself away, the second one pulled in.

His young factotum, Uckley, hustled in.

"They're both here. Jesus, Colonel, you won't believe—"

But Dick merely nodded; he had no time for surprise.

"Dr. Thiokol, you stick with the Delta assault plans team. Uckley, you buzz FBI counterintelligence and get us into their loop. I want all their findings. That's highest priority. Then you get Martin again, and bug 'em on regunning A-10s ASAP. Nobody goes anywhere without air. I'm going to go see the recruits."

Pulling on his coat, he rushed out. The two new Hueys sat out on the softball field, their rotors whirling up a cascade of snow. He looked for his prizes and saw a crowd huddled over in the garage and rushed to it. Entering, he was at first baffled: nothing but state cops and Delta operators and a few National Guardsmen from the first NG trucks that had pulled in. But no, he'd missed them, because they were so small. Yes, they'd be small.

The black man had worn his prison Levi's but had conned a Delta trooper out of a black commando sweater and a blue wool watch cap that was pulled down low to his eyes. He was only about five eight, but Dick recognized certain things immediately: The hands holding a cigarette were surprisingly large. The eyes were narrow and surly. He held himself with an impossible combination of insouciance and discipline. He had some hard sense of self to him, a kind of physical confidence that burned like heat. He had street smarts. He looked at no one: his eyes were fierce and set and dark and glared furiously into space. It all said, don't fuck with me.

As for the woman, it wasn't so much her gender or her unprepossessing size that shocked him, but her youth. She must have gone into the tunnels early in her teens, for now, ten years after her ten years then, she looked just a bit over thirty. And she was beautiful, wouldn't you know it? Dick's wife had never suspected, but Dick had lived with a Vietnamese woman for two years during his long pulls in country. Her name was Chinh; the Communists had finally caught her and killed her. She died in a burst of plastique on Highway 1 moving into Cholon in

THE DAY BEFORE MIDNIGHT

'72. Phuong looked a lot like Chinh: the same dignity, the same sweetness. Or no, not exactly: Dick thought that with study he could see the weight of the war on her. He shook his head.

"My rats," he said.

His rats looked at him. The girl had trouble focusing; the black man looked as if he wanted to fight him.

"You the man?" asked Nathan Walls.

"I am, Mr. Walls."

Walls laughed. "Where's the hole?"

"The hole is at the base of that mountain there," Dick said, pointing to the dramatic white hump out the open door, seeming surprisingly close. "And that"—he pointed out the lumpy, ragged silhouette of the South Mountain installation at the peak—"that is where we want to go. Where we need to go."

"So let's do it," said Walls.

Puller went to the woman.

"*Chao ba*, Phuong?" he asked, meaning Hello, Madame Phuong.

She seemed to relax at the sound of her language, issued a shy smile. He saw that she was scared to death to be among so many large white men.

She said, "*Chao ong*," meaning, Hello, sir.

"I am privileged that you are here," he said. "We are very lucky to have you."

"They said there were bombs for children. Firebombs. It was for us to stop them, sir."

He clung to the formal voice in addressing her, feeling the language, so far buried in his memory over the past fifteen years, work itself free from his brain. "The worst American demon, worse even than the terror bombers. Some men have taken it over. We have to get it back and the only way in is through a tunnel."

"Then I am yours to command," she said vaguely.

"Do you have any English, Madame Phuong?"

"Some," she said. "Little." She smiled shyly.

"If you don't understand, stop me. Ask questions. I will explain in your language."

"Tell me. Just tell me."

He switched to English, addressing them both.

"I want to place you during the assault, which will begin as soon as we get our air support. We have to blow a hole in the mountain and I want it done under the cover of a lot of other fireworks going on. I don't want whoever is up there knowing we've put people in the ground."

"Shit," laughed Walls. "If he smart, he know. If he so smart, he got all you down here sucking your thumbs, he going to know. He going to be waiting. Like they was back in his pretty lady's country. Tunnel going to be hot, let me tell you."

That was part of it, Dick thought. The tunnel rats always knew somebody was awaiting them.

"Are you hungry? Would you care to eat? You should rest, you'll be going in soon. And I'd like you to take people along. You shouldn't be alone in the tunnels."

"In the tunnel," said Walls, "you always alone. But get me a skinny man who don't get too close and listen to orders."

Dick was a bit undone by Walls's directness, and on this next point he proceeded with unusual caution, aware he'd entered delicate territory. "A black man, Mr. Walls? Would you feel more comfortable with another black man?" Several of the Delta troopers were black.

Walls laughed his hard laugh again. "It don't matter," he said. "In the hole, everybody's a nigger."

Phuong sat as if in a trance. She was not quite healthy, and had never been, since the tunnels. Her French psychiatrist had diagnosed her as a fifth-level schizophrenic, as if so many jolts in the tunnels, the loss of so many, the experience of so much horror, had finally, almost mercifully, broken the moorings of her mind, and like a small boat it drifted this way and that just off shore. She did not like bright lights, crowds, or to talk much about herself. She liked children, flowers, the out-of-doors, children especially. She spoke to her daughter at night, when she was alone, carrying her in a place near her heart. She remembered watching her daughter dissolve in a blossom of napalm; the flames had burned her eyebrows and the roar of the explosions had almost deafened her. She had tried to run into the fire, but someone had stopped her.

So now she sat in the barn with the black man whom she understood to be in some queer way her equivalent and at the same time tried to force herself to demonstrate out of politeness interest in the K ration they had put with apologies before her. It was getting close to time now, she could tell, because all the men were grave and drawn and they had at last stopped playing with their weapons; she recognized the symptoms: battle was near. She had been there before.

In the old days, her revolutionary fervor, her nationalism, had sustained her. She believed in her country and in freedom from the hated white men; it was worth dying for and worth killing for. But the killing had finally taken its toll: she was thirteen when she went underground and twenty-three when she came out and had killed over one hundred men, most of them with an M-1 carbine but more than a few with a knife. Her skill was stealth and patience: she could lie in the dark forever, almost still as death. Yet she felt so tired and now she was going back. To stop bombs from burning more children. To stop the world from becoming all fire and darkness everywhere.

A man came before her.

"*Chao chi*," he said, using the familiar, as in, Hello, Sister Phuong.

"*Chao anh*," she replied, out of politeness, feeling awkward in calling him brother.

"My name is Teagarden."

The American names were so hard.

"Dee-gar-dahn," she tried. It hurt her mouth.

"Call me brother. I will be your brother in the tunnel. They asked me to go with you, which is why I call you sister."

She asked her daughter, who still lived in her heart, what do you think of this man?

He seems decent, her daughter said from her heart. But is he strong, Mother? In the tunnel, decency doesn't count, only strength.

"Have you ever been in a tunnel, brother?" she asked.

"No," he admitted.

"Why are you here? Did you volunteer for this?"

"Not exactly," he admitted. "They asked me because of the language, sister."

He is not pleased about it, her daughter told her from her heart. Not good. In the tunnel, faith is important.

Her frank stare encouraged him to confession.

"To be honest, Sister Phuong, I'm scared to death," he said. "I hate the dark, I hate close, dirty places. But they asked me, and in our unit it isn't done to refuse an assignment."

"Can you control your fear?"

"I was in your country for over three years," he said. "I was scared every day and in battle every other day. I learned to control my fear there."

Tell him that underground is different, her daughter said.

"Underground is different," she said. "You'll see, it's different. Control is everything. Iron will, resolve."

"I'll try," he said. He was a healthy, leathery-looking man, about forty.

"In the dark, everybody is scared. The survivor is the man of control."

"I can only try," said Dee-gar-dahn.

"Do you have a family, brother?"

"Yes. Three boys. Great boys. The big one's a hero on a sports team. The other two, well, it's too soon to tell."

She could see his eyes warm at the mention.

See, Mother, he has children. He has love in his heart. He is not alone.

"You are a lucky man, brother," she said, "and I will let you come with me into the tunnel. We still stop the demons from setting the world on fire."

"Sister, we shall, this I swear to you," said Dee-gar-dahn, and thus did Rat Team Alpha begin its career.

Rat Team Baker began under less auspicious circumstances. Delta command selected, for crude and perhaps obvious reasons, another black man to accompany Nathan Walls. He was a short, muscular staff sergeant named Jeff Witherspoon. Witherspoon was a proud, furiously hardworking, and gifted young soldier who had at one time been an excellent boxer. He was every bit what might be called a team man: he believed in committing to the larger issue and therefore transcending the limits of his own rages. His commitment went first to his country, secondly to the Army, and third to Delta Force, which was the first team. He had joined Delta from the 3d Ranger Battalion in Fort Eustis, Washington, just in time to see action in Grenada.

Nate Walls was, by his peculiarities of vision, everything to be despised, everything that hurt the American black: a lazy no-account black-as-black northern jive-ass nigger, a dog. He was poison to the country and to the race.

"Walls?"

"Yo, man."

"Name's Witherspoon. I'll be going with you."

"Man, they pay you for this shit?"

"Yes, they do."

"How much? How much you make?"

"With hazard pay and various allowances, seventeen hundred a month."

A big grin split Nate Walls's face.

"Shit, man," he laughed, "I used to do that kind of change on a Saturday night on Pennsylvania Avenue. You going to risk your motherfucking ass for a seventeen spot." He laughed at the richness of it.

Witherspoon just looked at him, controlling his temper. Then he turned his wrist, looked at his watch, a big Seiko worn upside down.

"You'd better get some food. We go at 1450 hours. That's soon."

"I *like* that watch, man. That's one pretty piece of jewelry, and I *like* jewelry. Let me tell you, in the 'Nam, sergeant named Lopez get himself a new fancy Seiko scuba watch like that, he take it in a hole. Man, you could see numbers a mile away. The gooks used it to read by, and then some gook lady like that pretty girl over there, she put a bullet through it, right through the number twelve, blow off his hand. When he scream, she put a bullet down his throat. I know, 'cause I had to go in and throw some motherfucking wire around his legs, you know, drag his dead ass out of there. So you want to wear your fancy watch, Jack, you stay the fuck away from me." He laughed again.

Witherspoon looked at him.

"I'll take it off before we go and leave it with somebody."

"And, man, that deodorant. I can smell that shit, man, you know. If there's Charlie Gook in that hole, man, he smell that shit too. Then he blow your ass away, and mine too. Man, do us both some good and wipe your arms out, man. Shit, you sending telegrams."

"There isn't supposed to be anybody in the tunnels."

"Man, lemme tell you, just when you think nobody there, that's when they put you in a body bag. You married, my man?"

"Yes," said Witherspoon.

"You get any pussy last night, man?"

"Knock it off."

"Shit, man, only ass I had was when some white biker dude use *my* ass for fun in the showers. I could check out some pussy about now, let me tell you, before this last trip."

"They wanted me to go over weapons," Witherspoon said crisply.

"You can do an M-16, or one of these little German machine guns, the MP-5. Or a .45 or a 9-mm automatic."

"Fuck, man, I could never hit the ground with a pistol. I hate them big automatics too. Machine guns make my ass nervous, bounce around too much. I want a shotgun, a pump, sawed down real good. When you fire that mother, I want a noise louder than hell. Scare Charlie, if it hot down there. You ask that girl. Gooks don't like noise."

"These aren't Asians. This isn't Vietnam," Witherspoon said dully.

"Oh yes it is, my man. Oh yes it is. Now, let's see about a shotgun. You got a shotgun for this nigger?"

Witherspoon said he'd check it out and trotted off.

Walls sat back, smoking a cigarette. The old feeling was beginning deep inside him. It was what you felt when you knew the shit was going down, a kind of loose, trembly buzz in the gut, not really unpleasant, just odd.

Back in a hole.

Hey, Jack, I was done with holes. Man, my life was *golden*, you know.

He thought he was going to die today.

Die in a hole.

I thought I was *done* with that shit, man.

Jack Hummel watched the flame eat into the metal. The world was flame. And as he watched, he fought the temptation to surrender completely to craft, and to think of nothing but the job. He forced himself to think about the general.

Guy was plenty strange. First, he made Jack nervous because he was so sure and calm. And he scared Jack with his magical ways of persuasion and leadership. And he intimidated Jack because he seemed somehow rich, or at least upper class, and Jack was a little unsure of himself around such a customer.

But he also seemed fabulous, somehow, like something out of a movie. Jack remembered when he'd been a kid there'd been a lot of movies about crazy generals who tried to take over the world and Jack tried to place this guy against that context. But it didn't work, because he saw vapidly handsome star faces, remote and eighteen feet tall in black and white. No help here; this guy was flesh and bone and charm. The difference struck Jack as weirdly comical. He laughed in an involuntary spasm.

"You find this amusing, Mr. Hummel?" said the general over the roar of the flame.

"No, it's just that—" But Jack couldn't finish.

"That's all right. Laugh away. I'm used to it. I've been laughed at before."

But Jack's face had locked up. The man's hard eyes, empty of merriment, nailed into him. The torch wavered and slipped in his grip and he lowered it.

"And now you can't laugh. I'm used to that too. When people encounter the strength of my will and understand what I represent, they hardly find it humorous. I represent the memory, Mr. Hummel. The memory of a once-great country, but a country now fallen on terrible times, its way lost, its leaders pathetic, its enemies ravenous with the hunger to rip it to shreds. And I represent the strength to regain that past. And these soldiers feel the rightness of my way and the urgency of my moral mandate. They give themselves to me. It's happened before, only my predecessor lacked my skill. He had my will, but he didn't have my talent. You know him, Mr. Hummel. Remember your history. It all happened right around here. His name was John Brown. John Brown took over a federal armory with nineteen half-wits and idiots, who came unglued when some townspeople took potshots at him. He was captured by a junior Marine officer with a toy sword, which bent when the officer stabbed him. That was less than fifteen miles from here. At Harpers Ferry. Have you been there, Mr. Hummel?"

Jack wasn't sure if the guy really wanted an answer or not. But this was getting crazier by the minute. The guy was a real total screwball. So Jack gave him the earnest response he thought was required.

"Uh, yeah, as a matter of fact. Last year, I think, my wife, she said we ought to, you know, get more out of the *history* of the state and—"

"Mr. Hummel, I mention John Brown because in a peculiar way he's quite important to me. A very bright young man once predicted what I might do, and called it 'The John Brown Scenario.' Since I hold that young man dear, it's important to me that I draw the contrast with John Brown. I've taken over a federal armory that stores missiles instead of muskets. I'm going to do what has to be done. I'm going to launch a strike against the Soviet Union. I'm going to give the world the future it hasn't the guts to get for itself. I'll kill millions, yes, but the outcome will be survival not only for a political system I believe in but survival for the planet. The fools who haven't the guts to face this simply pass it on to future generations, so that when it does happen—and we both know it will—then *everybody* dies. Not just the race but the world. The planet. In my way I'm the most moral man who ever lived. I'm a great man. They'll hate me for a dozen generations and worship me for a thousand."

"Uh, yeah, but—"

Jack decided he didn't have the mental equipment to argue with the guy. Who was he, some dropout from a state university who now made his living with his hands? What power did he have against a guy like this?

"The torch, Mr. Hummel," commanded the general, the power of his brilliant eyes surging into Jack.

Obediently, up came the torch and again it began to lick at the metal.

1400

P

ilots don't work. This is one of the universal laws of aviation culture. Pilots fly. They are special. They only fly.

"Higher, goddammit," said Leo Pell to Rick Tarnower, both of whom were pilots and both of whom were working.

Tarnower, twenty-six, was not happy to be laboring next to ground crew in the goddamned unheated hangar of the 83d Tactical Fighter Wing of the Maryland Air Guard at Glenn L. Martin Air Field just north of Baltimore; he had skinned his knuckles evilly twice already, and he was cold and he was greasy and he was a pilot and pilots don't work.

"Higher, goddammit," cursed Leo Pell again, his eyes squinting. Leo looked a little like a pig, especially when he squinted, collecting his tiny little eyes up in folds of fat. He was a squat, bald man with thick hands and short pistonlike arms. He had the body of a linebacker and the face of a fireplug and right now he was greasier than any mechanic. He smelled of sweat and joy. It was no coincidence that Leo had named his ship *The Green Pig*, and that he liked flying it low and slow and bouncing it off the Chesapeake now and again, getting his nose down in the shit, as his men said. There was something definitely anal compulsive about Leo and his willingness to get in close to the elemental stuff of life. Leo Pell was your natural-born ground-support man.

"Leo, goddammit," Tarnower squealed in response, "I'm not even supposed to be *doing* this! I'm supposed to be putting together a mission assault profile or—"

Above him loomed the massive wing of an A-10 Thunderbolt II ground-support fighter, called *Wart Hog* or *Flying Pig* by its pilot and air crew. It was a big ship with a long bony prow, a single-bubble cockpit, and two high twin rudders, almost like the old B-25 Mitchell of World War II fame. Two gigantic General Electric TF34 GE-100 engines were mounted like spare parts from some surplus airliner halfway back along the fuselage. They looked as if they didn't quite belong; in fact, the whole airplane had the look of having been designed by a bright but evil eleven-year-old boy with a yellow crayon.

"Rick, chum, we don't get these goddamned guns bolted up just right, we ain't got no mission," Leo said with a grin, which showed his yellow stubby teeth. "Now, boy, people depending on us, and goddammit, I'm not going to let 'em down. Besides"—he smiled his most malicious, most charming smile—"we gonna be live shooting. Twenty mike-mike, goddamn, Rick, twenty mike-mike. Life is good!"

Leo loved shooting better than anything.

All up and down the line the pilots and men of the unit scrambled over their big green ships as they tried to speed-mount two SUU-23 gun pods in the five and seven slots in the external stores loading stations under the big wings of the green birds.

Tarnower cranked on his lug wrench, wiped the sweat from his brow, and—goddamn!—skinned his knuckles again.

"Tighter, sir, you almost got it," his chief crewman called. "The 20-mil ammo's just come in."

"Great," said Tarnower, twisting the wrench again.

"Hurry up, Larry," Leo said, and ducked on to the next plane, cackling gleefully.

The assault plan that Delta had worked out was relatively simple. It was now predicted that the ANG A-10s from Martin would be regunned and airborne by 1445 hours. At 1500 the flight would peel through a gap in the Appalachians and hit the South Mountain installation with their external 20-mm cannons, in theory cutting the hell out of Aggressor Force without blowing away the mainframe computer, and at the very least, chopping the hell out of that mysterious tarpaulin that draped the mountain top.

At 1505 hours a flight of fifteen Hueys would deploy to the road moving up the mountain, intersecting it at an altitude of about 1,200 feet, roughly 1,000 feet beneath the installation, but well beyond the point where Aggressor Force had blown the road. To save time, the choppers would not land; they would swoop in in batches of four, and from each, eight Delta Commandos would rappel downward. In less than a minute, Delta felt, one hundred twenty operators could be placed in position for the assault. Divided in two elements, Delta would move up the hill and force the attack against the narrow front of the installation.

Midway during the fight, a sixteenth chopper trailing smoke would break from the formation, career over the crest of the hill, and be seen to wobble, then land hard at the base of the mountain. Thirty seconds later it would seem to detonate. Actually, this was the detonation of over twenty pounds of C-4 already implanted by a probing force that had located the mouth of the collapsed mine shaft. The blast—or so the plan went—would open a hole big enough for Rat Team Alpha and Rat Team Baker to penetrate the mountain and begin the upward climb into the installation itself, a distance of almost half a mile underground, through uncharted and quite possibly nonexistent tunnels. The two teams would be in radio contact with Rat Six—a radio team at the opening of the shaft—which itself was patched into the Delta command network.

Up top, when the elevator shaft was finally taken, a message would be flashed, and Peter Thiokol, now madly trying to figure out a way to beat the door and its twelve-integer code, would be dispatched to the site to get the door open and get the surviving Delta operators down into the hole. The idea was to bring off the vaunted multiple simultaneous entry— from above and below.

The briefing officer, Skazy, stood back, well pleased with the presentation. It had everything: succinctness, economy of force, a certain audacious daring, split-second timing. It was Delta all the way.

"No, no," said Dick Puller quickly, "no, no, it's all wrong."

The disappointment in the room was audible.

"Goddammit, Major, you haven't thought it out. You're willing to spend too much of your own blood on preliminary objectives. You'd waste highly trained specialists taking trees and gullies that are meaningless except as a route to the real objective, which is the shaft to the LCC. And what happens if you make it but you've sustained so many casualties you're effectively out of commission? Who goes down the shaft?"

He stared brutally at Skazy, a former protégé now fallen on hard times in his career. This was classic Dick Puller: he had no qualms about blowing people away. Skazy swallowed.

"We thought it was a very sound plan, sir," he said.

"It's a very sound plan for a different war, but not for today's."

There were a lot of peculiar vibrations in the air. Skazy was popular, hardworking, one of the Delta originals who went all the way back to Eagle Claw. He was a Delta zealot. Nobody liked to see him trashed.

"Colonel Puller," another Delta officer said, "it's a *good* plan. It's stable, it's solid, it's well within our capabilities, it's—"

But Puller wasn't interested.

"Mr. Uckley, what's the latest word on my Ranger battalion?"

"Uh, sir, they're just entering St. Louis air space. They ran into turbulence coming over the Rockies."

"Great, and how about Third Infantry?"

"The trucks are hung up in traffic. Evidently, there's quite a buildup. The state police are trying to hustle them through, but the traffic is a mess. We could divert some helicop—"

"No, we need the choppers for Delta. What's the disposition on that National Guard infantry unit?"

"Colonel, they're the perimeter defense team. You said you were afraid we'd be jumped and that—"

"How many?"

"Uh, they're at company strength now. It's Company B, 123d Light Infantry, Maryland National Guard. Say, a hundred fifty men. They were on winter maneuvers at Fort Richie. They've been trucking in the last few hours."

"Get 'em assembled," said Dick.

He turned to the Delta officers.

"You're grounded. Get Delta on the perimeters, they're now security. I don't want Delta into it until we crack the perimeter and carry the elevator shaft. There's no point in those men dying in the woods like infantrymen. Let 'em die in the shaft, where it'll do some good."

Skazy said through a tide of awkward phlegm clogging his throat and a wretched moment's hesitation, "Colonel Puller, with all due respect, those National Guardsmen are teachers, lawyers, construction workers. They're fat and out of shape. Now, we've got a good, sound plan. These guys can't—"

Dick cut him off, speaking with brutal authority.

"Maryland NG draws preliminary assault responsibility for this operation, working in conjunction with Tac Air. I can't wait for the goddamned Third Infantry or the goddamned Rangers. I want them deploying via their trucks too; no sense wasting our choppers on troops who can't rappel. Get Delta on the perimeter, Major. Call the NG and give 'em the good news. What's the guy's name?"

"Barnard. He's an accountant."

"Well, today he's an infantry officer."

And so Dick Puller made the first of his controversial decisions. It was based on a secret conviction: that the planes would not kill enough of Aggressor Force to suppress its calculated fire. The first assault would be a failure: those who waged it were like the Brits who went over the top at the Somme in 1916, a doomed generation. With their lives they would purchase very little: at best, they would bleed Aggressor Force of enough of its will and its health, so that, as he now saw it, a second assault with Third Infantry and the Rangers sometime after nightfall would carry the perimeter. Then the real drama would start: Could Peter crack the door? Could the Delta specialists get down the shaft and into the capsule? Could the Rat Teams get there from the rear?

"Sir, the CO of the guard wants to talk to you."

"Put him on."

Dick took the radio phone.

"Delta Six, over."

"Delta Six, I'd like a clarification on this order."

"Affirmative."

"You got federal specialists in there, commando types, hardcore pro military. But you want my guys to carry the brunt of this attack?"

"Affirmative, Guard Six."

"Do you have any idea what's up there? They—"

"I heard. I saw the report."

"Sir, I'd like to request that my higher headquarters authenticate the or—"

"Captain, you do any damn thing you like, but at 1500 hours I want your company humping that hill. First, you'll do much better in the light. A night attack's a terrible thing. Second, and more important, I've laid on Tac Air at 1500. You want to hit the Aggressor area just as the Air moves out. Those A-10s are going to make hamburger out of whoever's up there. You have my word. You'll be mopping up, that's all. I'd warn your guys to watch out for unexploded 20-mil shells. Those things can tear a leg off. *That's* what you have to worry about."

Puller's face was bland and sweet as he lied. He was an excellent liar.

"Oh, Air. *Air.*"

"A-10s, affirmative, Guard Six. Ever seen 'em hose something down? Those cannons rip through lumber like a chain saw. You've never seen anything like it!"

"Yessir," said the captain. "I'll get 'em assembled and on the way, sir."

"Real fine, Guard Six. Real fine." He looked at his watch. It was close to 1400 hours. He heard whistles somewhere, and the sound of trucks. It was the Guard, already saddling up.

He felt somebody looking at him. It was the hard, lean face of Skazy, closing in on him.

"What are you looking at?" Puller said.

"I hope you know what you're doing, Dick," said Skazy.

"You're out of line, Major," said Puller, facing him square.

"You wouldn't send us in from Desert One. You've *got* to send us in here."

Puller looked hard at him. Skazy had been combat assault commander seven years ago in Eagle Claw. When Puller made the decision to abort, Skazy had called him, to his face, a cowardly motherfucker and taken a punch at him.

"You'll get your great chance, Frank. Just grow up a little, will you? It's going to be a long day."

Skazy said, "Look, Dick, if you have any trouble because it's me here, and because I took my shot at you at Desert One, that's fine. A commander deserves support from his juniors. I'll step out of my command and go in as a regular trooper. McKenzie can take over, he's a good man. But goddammit, Dick, you've *got* to use us this time."

Puller looked at him.

"Get back to your unit, Major," he said.

Outside, the trucks had begun to move toward the mountain.

Rat Team Baker was suiting up in the barn. In the distance a chopper had landed, its blades beating with a liquid slosh of noise against the wooden walls. The rhythm was insistent, urgent, and through it they could hear the sound of the National Guard trucks rumbling down the muddy road toward the mountain. But the two men, aware that in minutes they'd be airborne, worked hard at getting ready.

"Here," Witherspoon said. "You keep this on your belt."

"Yo, man, thanks," said Walls, taking it. It was a Taurus PT-92 9-mm automatic in black matte finish, with a double-stacked magazine that held fifteen rounds. He popped the magazine, which dropped out, then locked back the slide and looked into the chamber, where everything seemed to gleam with bright highlights. He thumbed the slide release, and the heavy sheath of metal slammed forward. The gun snapped in his hand. He reinserted the mag, and rejacked the slide to chamber a round.

"Safety up or down, man?"

"Up is on. You go to red by snapping it down. That's a double-action piece, so you don't have to carry it cocked and locked."

"Cocked and locked it's gonna be," said Walls, "just like my old .45. Cocked and locked is *best*."

It was a nice piece for backup, but not quite what he wanted for the main work.

"Now, what about Mr. Twelve?" Walls asked, slipping the automatic into an ambidextrous Bianchi holster on his belt.

"Say again?"

"Mr. Twelve *Gauge*. Shotgun, man."

"Yeah, so I found one. Here it is," Witherspoon said, handing the weapon over: a Mossberg 500, with a twenty-inch barrel in a grainy gray Parkerized finish. It had a combat magazine extension beyond the pump reaching out to the muzzle, giving it a chin-heavy, pugnacious profile.

"That piece is very important to the guy that owns it. He didn't want to give it up. It's called a Persuader. Now he didn't want to give it up. It's his life insurance. But I talked him into it."

Walls took the gun and knew at once it was made for him. He held it, touched it, rubbed it, smelled it, clicked it. Damn, it felt good.

He began to thread the heavy red plastic double-ought twelve-gauge shells into it, discovering that it would swallow eight of them. Loaded, it felt heavy; all that buckshot slung out under the barrel. He jammed dozens more into the leg pouches of his camouflage pants until his legs felt as if he were exercising. It would mean he might have to lay on the suckers, but it was better to hurt a little and have the spares when you needed them than to be comfortable and come up dry at party time. He'd found that out in a hole somewhere. He held the loaded gun close to him.

Meanwhile Witherspoon was locking a 30-round 9-mm clip into his Heckler & Koch MP-5. The gun had a foolish look to it, a sci-fi look: its ribbed silencer threw it out of proportion.

"Is that a toy, man? It looks like some kind of plastic kid toy."

"It works great," said Witherspoon, "a great close-in weapon."

Then Witherspoon put on his AN/PVS-5C night vision goggles. They looked like a set of binoculars mounted in some kind of scuba-diving mask, which was held on Witherspoon's head by a harness of elastic straps; they drew their power from a 1.3V DC battery pack he wore at his belt. The glasses responded to heat, and in the cool blackness of a tunnel a man would radiate an orange glow as if he were on fire, making him easy to track and kill.

"You could have used this stuff in 'Nam," Witherspoon said.

Walls snorted.

"Man, I'm so bad I can *see* in the dark without help, you know. That's what kept me alive."

Then Witherspoon pulled on his flak jacket, which had already been mounted with an AN-PRC-88 radio receiver. A pair of headphones, with a hands-free mike on a pylon out in front of his lips completed the outfit. He stuffed a book-sized mass of gray clay into one bellows pocket. Walls knew it to be C-4; he'd blown up a few things in his time in the tunnels.

Witherspoon stood, staggered for just a second under the weight of the gear. Walls couldn't help a little laugh.

"Man, you look like a ghostbuster," said Walls, "and you talk like an ofay. Man, how long you study, learn to talk that white bullshit? 'It's a great close-in weapon,' " Walls mocked through his nose with a cruel grin on his face. "Be natural, my man. Be a nigger. You a nigger, *be* a nigger."

"I don't care how I sound if it keeps me alive and gives me the edge," said Witherspoon, stung by the accusation.

"A bad nigger with a bad shotgun, that's the best motherfuckin' edge," said Walls.

The men rose from their ritual. Walls pulled on his flak jacket too. He'd nixed the night vision stuff. There were picks, shovels, grenades, and a few other gimcracks to be arranged, but essentially they were ready. Then he noticed a red bandanna on a bench, left over from some cracker handyman or other. Quickly, Walls flicked off his watch cap, snatched it up, expertly spun it into a roll, then tied it Apache-style around his forehead.

"You see, boy," he said to the horrified Witherspoon, "in the hole it's

hot as shit, and the sweat sting up your eyes. Saw a white guy once
blown away 'cause he missed a first shot 'cause he couldn't see nothing."
He smiled for the first time.

An officer yelled, "Game time, rats."

The moment had come. Walls grabbed his Mossberg, felt the heave
and slap of the automatic at his hip, the weight of the flak jacket. He
lumbered out to the chopper.

The tough-looking old white guy stood off to one side as they ran to
the slick, watching them go with numb eyes. Brass, Walls thought.
White brass. Shit, he hated white brass, stern fuckers with little squinty
eyes who looked at you like you were shit on their shoes.

But then the white old guy gave him a little thumbs-up for happy
hunting and—fuck it!—hey, *winked* at him. Walls saw the radiance of
something almost never on the pale, slack faces of the white race—
belief. That is, belief in him, in Walls.

You may not be much of anything, motherfucker, the old white guy
was saying, but damn, boy, you one hell of a tunnel rat.

You got that right, Jack, thought Walls, running the last few yards
through the breeze to the bird.

The Vietnamese woman, in black with an M-16 and a pair of gym
shoes, was already aboard, a blank look on her face. But as he moved
closer, squinting in the bright sunlight, she looked at him.

Jesus, he thought, losing himself in her opaque glare, home again.

The Huey with the two Rat Teams lifted, nose heavy, a bit ungainly,
hung for just a second, and then with an agility that even these many
helicopters into his career still surprised Puller, zoomed off, and he
watched it go.

"Good pilot on that ship," Major Skazy yelled. "He'll insert 'em just
where you want 'em."

Puller said nothing. He shifted his vision. Across the white meadow,
under the bright sun and blue sky, he now saw the NG trucks in the
distance, deuce-and-a-halfs, a convoy of them, small as toys, now
lumbering into the woods to begin the ascent to the primary assault
position.

The trucks moved poorly, tentatively bunched up; one would spurt
ahead, then slow. It was an accordion opening and closing across the
landscape.

"Aggressor Force's going to see them coming," said Skazy. "Plenty of time to get ready."

"Aggressor Force was ready anyhow," said Puller.

"It's Delta's job," said Skazy.

The older man turned to look at the younger. He remembered Skazy at Desert One, his face mottled with fury, coming at him without regard for rank or protocol or career or whatever, just coming at him, screaming, "You gutless old bastard, *we can still do it. We can do it with five choppers!*" And Puller had said, "Get your men on the planes, Major. Get them on the planes," as the harsh wind, the noise, the utter confusion had swirled around them.

Now, eight years later, Skazy was still a major. He'd been passed over, his career ruined just as completely as Puller's for his legendary flip-out. He was still Delta, though, still a true believer.

"Dick," Skazy was suddenly saying, "let me go in with the NG. Those guys need some experience. Let me take Delta up to support them from the flanks, and to urge them on, give them something to see. Dick, we can—"

"No, Frank. You'll get carried away, the way you did at Desert One. You'll lose control, you'll rush in. You'll get everybody killed and you still won't stop the men in the hole."

He delivered this brutal sentence with a little bit more pleasure than was strictly necessary, as if to indulge the bully in his soul. But it was also that Skazy, brave, hardworking, brilliant, was just a bit reckless. He was a terrible accident waiting to happen. He needed to be led and aimed. He was a perfect subordinate: he wasn't the man you wanted out there on his own.

"Whatever you say, Colonel Puller," said Skazy, his face immobile.

Suddenly, he turned.

"Just use us this time, goddammit, Dick. And you weren't right at Desert One. *I* was."

Skazy stormed back to his staff, leaving Puller alone.

Puller looked back to the mountain, feeling suddenly old and a bit scared. Maybe the rat thing was pointless, maybe those tunnels weren't there at all. And certainly those kids in the trucks would be chopped up. Maybe even Delta couldn't make it.

He checked his watch. The A-10s ought to be shooting the gap any second now.

He looked back to the mountain. It was a dramatic white hump before him, the red and white aerial like a candy cane at its top, and that peculiar dark stain where Aggressor Force had built its odd tent.

He felt himself being looked at. Up there, Aggressor-One would be looking through his binoculars. Watching. Waiting. Planning.

I hope you're not half so lucky as you are smart, he thought. It was also a prayer.

Peter had found a little room off Puller's headquarters and there, with an old Coke machine moaning over his shoulder and girl scout mottos like "Always do your best!" on the rickety walls, he looked at a copy of the single communication Aggressor-One had sent from the mountain.

I wish to say furthermore that you had better prepare yourselves for a settlement of that question that must come up for settlement sooner than you are prepared for it. The sooner you are prepared for it, the better.

There was something tantalizing in it, ironic. A strange feeling he got, that it wasn't a madman's document, but something far subtler.

It's a game, he thought.

This guy is playing a game.

But against whom? And why? Why a game? Why now, a game? As if it's not quite enough to blow the fucking world away, to turn us to ash and dust; he's got to tweak our nose somehow.

He looked at the "signature" at the end of it: "Commander, Provisional Army of the United States."

Well, your standard-issue right-wing nutcase psycho, staple of fifty bad movies and a hundred bad novels. It fits perfectly: the inflated rhetorical tone, the sense of epic proportion, the delusion of one self-styled "great man," reaching out from his wisdom to twist history in the proper direction.

Why don't I believe it, he wondered.

Because it's too pat?

Because it matches all our expectations?

Because I've a feeling Aggressor-One has seen the movies and read the books too?

He touched his temple, feeling his head begin to throb. Now, try to relate *this*, the screwball declaration of intent from Aggressor-One, up there with his MX, to this, the mountain of teletype printouts that were

being sent from the FBI, at Dick Puller's order, on the investigation into
his identity.

Quickly his eyes sped over the data. A crash team from the FBI
special antiterrorist squad, working with the assistance of personnel
officers at the Department of Defense and Defense's big mainframes,
had done a fast shakeout on military personnel with a certain pattern of
experience in conjunction with a certain range of political belief, which
itself had been extrapolated from a cluster of skills necessary to plot,
stage, and execute the silo takeover and an assumed cluster of ideological
beliefs necessary to provide the key ingredient: the will.

Among the plotting coordinates in the search for Aggressor-One were
one or more of the following:

—Special Operations experience, including Special Forces (Army),
Ranger (Army), Air Commando (Air Force), SEAL teams (Navy), and
Marine Recon (Marine Corps); Central Intelligence Agency Special
Operations Division (comprised primarily of veterans of the foregoing)
and including those with experience in Operation Phoenix in Vietnam
and counterinsurgency among the Nungs in South Central RVN; or
experience in counterinsurgency operations in the third world, as in
guerrilla hunting with the Peruvian, Bolivian, and Guatemalan rangers
and paratroops; and other odd Agency scams, including the Kurdish
incursion in 1975; and so forth and so on; OSS experience dating back
to World War II, and including Jedburgh Teams who jumped into
France immediately before D-day, and long-range operators among the
Kachin tribes in Burma against the Japanese in World War II. Cowboys,
Peter said to himself, God save us from cowboys.

—public record or private reports regarding unusually fierce political
opinions, particularly as regards the Soviet Union. Membership in
groups in the FBI Index, such as the John Birch Society, Posse Comitas,
the Aryan Order, so forth, so on. The fulminators, the sparkplugs, the
geezers and whiners, Peter thought, the Red haters and baiters.

—professional officers with solid careers going who had somehow
gotten off the track—a CO who screwed them on a fitness report, a
program they were in charge of that was axed, a command that was
riddled with drug abuse that fell scandalously apart, a stupid and un-
guarded moment with a reporter that wrecked their progress—who,
surveying the rubble of their lives, might have ingeniously plotted some
kind of revenge against Defense, using their clearances and friendships

to acquire the necessary intelligence to stage the silo raid. The losers, Peter thought.

—and finally, membership in what was called the strategic community, that weird agglomeration of inside-the-Beltway types who, unbeknownst to the world in general, went about their merry way planning its destruction. This meant familiarity with strategic thought and its particulars, particularly silo culture and technology, missile silo security, launch procedures, strategic targeting initiatives, the top secret Single Integrated Operation Plan (SIOP), the game strategy by which this country would fight a nuclear war.

This was the big category. It was all well and good to know how to skulk through the night with a knife through your teeth, but in the end you had to know what Peacekeeper was, how it worked, where it was located, or there was nothing at all to the mission, it was just dreamy nonsense. For it all turned on the ability, once having gotten into a silo, to get the bird off its pad. And, in *this* silo, on knowing that it was even there—not a thousand men in Washington knew this—and that it was uniquely vulnerable, launch capable. He had to know so much, this Aggressor-One! That was the tantalizing thing about it: whoever he was, he would almost certainly be someone Peter knew and had worked with.

He has to be one of us.

He looked at the list: Rand Corporation dropouts, disgruntled SAC colonels, embittered Pentagon jockeys with an intellectual bent, bypassed generals, flamed-out academics. All the names were familiar.

Another document clattered out of the machine, and Peter examined it. It described a former civilian analyst for the Air Force of great promise who was intimately acquainted with Peacekeeper, particularly as it was to be deployed in the South Mountain installation. He was known for his hard-line attitudes toward the Russians and toward nuclear war in general and had actually published a famous essay, "And Why Not Missile Superiority? Rethinking MAD" in *Foreign Affairs*, making him a hot item on the Washington circuit, the man who believed war could be fought and won. He appeared on *Nightline* and *This Week with David Brinkley* and *Face the Nation*. He had eventually become head of the MX Basing Modes Group at the Johns Hopkins Applied Physics Lab out in Howard County. But his personal life had disintegrated under the pressure of his career, his marriage had broken up, his wife had left him.

Now he taught at a prestigious institution and still consulted with the Pentagon.

"Sir?" It was a young communications technician.

"Yes?"

"There's some men from FBI counterintelligence here. They have a warrant for your arrest."

"Sir."

Alex blinked in the bright air and looked. He could see the vehicles lumbering toward him across the meadow.

"No helicopters," he said. "They are not using helicopters, they are using trucks."

He watched the convoy come.

"All right," he said, "stations, please. Get the men out from under the tarpaulin and to their combat stations."

A whistle sounded. He could feel men around him running to their positions, hear the clink and rattle of bolts and belts.

"Steady, boys," he cried. "We have all the time in the world."

He watched the trucks come up the mountain. I would have thought helicopters, he told himself. They could have gotten more people here faster with helicopters. But maybe the troops they have aren't air-assault qualified and would have been more frightened of the flight than the fight.

No, wait: one helicopter rose. It must be some kind of medevac chopper, for casualties.

We'll give you some business, fellow, he thought.

He climbed atop a bit of ruin, and shouted, "All right, boys. Company coming for lunch! Lock and load."

"Sir—"

The boy pointed.

He could see them, low and whizzing over through the gap in the far mountains across the valley. Eight of them, low to the ground, clearly A-10s even from this distance.

Well, he had this one figured too.

"Planes," he said. "Missile teams prepare to engage."

The first assault had begun.

Gregor Arbatov took Connecticut Avenue out to the Beltway, headed east through thin traffic, then north down Route 95 toward Baltimore through even thinner traffic. He had plenty of time. He was not due until two and he had left at 12:30. The vodka had somewhat calmed him, and his call to Molly had left him with at least some hope for the future. Molly would help him somehow. His stomach churned; he wished he had a Tums, he lived on Tums, his fat tongue always glistened with the chalky residue of a Tums. But he was out of them.

Whoa, there, Gregor, old fool. You are slipping. With a start he realized he'd almost missed his exit, and he had to make a sudden dart across the lanes of the expressway, took the ramp too fast, felt the whirl of gravity fighting him for control of the car and at last—though only in this one thing—regained control. He circled over a bridge to arrive at Route 175 for another less swift but equally sleek road, and after a few minutes of zipping through rather attractive Howard County and the suburban city of Columbia, came to a glass-topped pavilion glinting in the sun.

The exuberance of the place did not faze him. He rather liked shopping malls; America at her glorious best, all glittery and shiny, all the people slick and sassy (the women, Lord, the thin, lovely, supple American women!).

Gregor was familiar with American shopping centers—White Flint was a favorite, White Marsh out beyond Baltimore, the Inner Harbor *in* Baltimore, Owings Mills west of Baltimore, the new Marley Station south of it, Tyson's Corners in Virginia—because it was Pork Chop's vanity to be serviced in them. Pork Chop—whoever he was—boasted exemplary trade craft. Pork Chop hated solitude and privacy, finding safety instead in mass, particularly in the crowded, bustling venue of the American shopping center. This suited Gregor perfectly. If he could no longer justify his existence on the paltry gleanings from his girls, then he could by his ability to please Pork Chop, whom he had never made anxious, whose signals he never missed, and whose wants and needs supplied the pretext for his survival.

Gregor never knew when Pork Chop would demand servicing. It all depended upon the *Washington Post* personal ads, which he checked each day. Most days there was nothing, sometimes weeks would pass: and then, as yesterday, it would be there.

Darling, I love you. Meet me at D-13-3. Your little Pork Chop.

The code was simple. Gregor simply referred to the previous Sunday's

Post, Section D, page 13. On that page would be an ad for some kind of chain bookstore well represented in the area, usually a B. Dalton's or a Waldenbooks. At the bottom of the ad would be listed the various locations. The third of them—in this case the Columbia Mall, in a B. Dalton's advertisement—would be the site for the beginning of the ritual of the meet on the next day. It was clever and simple and impenetrable, unless of course one knew the key, and only Gregor knew the key, which he had received on a special Eyes Only document two years earlier.

Pork Chop had been quiet ever since a furious spurt of activity three months ago; therefore Gregor was somewhat astonished when he'd come across the message in yesterday's paper. But it had made him happy, though it was his bad luck to draw the time-consuming and frequently exhausting job the same night he had communications duty in the Wine Cellar, and exactly when Klimov was so furious at him for so many other failings.

Well, that was more of his rotten luck. He journeyed through the parking lot like a lost traveler, experiencing one of the real drawbacks of capitalism: lack of adequate parking places. It was, after all, near Christmas. The Americans would be out in force today, loading up on goods for their favorite holiday. But eventually Gregor found a spot in the far environs, and began the long trek to the building proper.

Suddenly, there was a roar; involuntarily, he ducked, stunned at the noise. He looked up. Six jets whooshed overhead. So low! Incredible! They were a kind of thing Gregor had not seen before, like backward-headed flying crucifixes, their long prows so far ahead of their stubby straight wings. And they were green, not silver. Gregor shook his head.

Should I know this airplane?

But the jets were gone then, flashing over the trees.

"They're sure in a hurry," a lady a few feet ahead of him said.

"Must have a fire to go to," Gregor joked.

"Maybe," said the woman with a laugh. "Or girlfriends to show off for."

Inside, it was like the spring, calm and pleasant, climate perfectly controlled. But Gregor immediately broke into one of his familiar shirt-drenching sweats, as if he were in the jungle. As he sailed forward, all business, something caught his eye; and then another thing and then another! Capitalism! It was a festival! He loved America! He stopped to

admire a particularly nice sweater in Woody's men's department and
they had some nice colorful ties there too. Then, it was time to eat. He
bought a chocolate chip cookie and a peach yogurt and a bag of popcorn
and a chili dog. Only eventually did he find his way to the store of the
ad, B. Dalton. He stepped into it, browsed for a while, noticing the piles
of best sellers up front. The big book was a lurid thing about a dark KGB
plot to subvert America by infiltrating a television network. Then, there
was a book about a Hollywood actress with the sexual desire of a
stevedore. There was an inspirational volume by a millionaire business-
man. There were books about ways to make money on the stock market
and to make yourself thin and happy forever, about how to be aggressive
and how to be sensitive and how to get people to like you better. That's
what I need, he thought.

Gradually, he made his way to the back of the store, to the inevitable
section marked Classics. Here, he dawdled a bit longer. He'd always
wanted to study literature and still loved it, even if he'd actually been
educated all those years back as a chemist. He examined Shakespeare's
Hamlet and Dostoevski's *Crime and Punishment* and the great Tolstoi's
War and Peace and Hemingway's *For Whom the Bell Tolls*. Now, this
was more like it! Then his fingers found the inevitable copy of Margaret
Mitchell's *Gone with the Wind*, exactly the volume that every bookstore
in America would be certain to keep on its shelves. His fingers touched
the fat thing, rubbing it softly. He began to feel excited, and sent a quick
nervous look around the store. It was full of shoppers, of course, but as
an experienced watcher himself, he could see no visible signs of
observation.

The ritual was exact: He would pick it up, turn to page 300 and there
discover a very small piece of paper with one single number on it: 2 it
might say, or perhaps 3. That was all.

To anyone else it would be meaningless. Only Gregor knew that it
indicated he must leave the store, turn to the right—always the right—
and begin to walk through the mall counting exits, and at the second or
the third, leave the building.

Except that this time there was no slip.

Gregor stared in stupefaction. He felt the bell tolling for himself in his
own head. His heart began to break. The air was suddenly hot and gassy.
Pork Chop was such a pedant! Pork Chop never made mistakes! Pork
Chop was slow, calm, steady, patient!

Gregor felt the panic come over him. Was he being set up? Was this some kind of ruse? A test? He swallowed harshly, feeling the book grow heavy in his hands. The damned thing weighed a ton.

"That's a wonderful book," a woman said to him. "I've read it six times."

"Yes, it's wonderful," said Gregor, staring absurdly at her. Was she an FBI agent? He swallowed, waiting for her to speak again. He wished he could breathe, or charge his wan and twisted smile with some spontaneity. She looked at him with searching eyes, an attractive but unremarkable American. It was as if she were about to speak.

But she merely smiled enigmatically as his heart pounded in his chest, and then walked away.

He looked down at the book; it was shaking in his trembling hands. He began to flip through the pages while looting his memory for clues. Had he made some stupid mistake? Was it another bookstore, another mall, another day? The possibilities raced by like the rushing seconds on a digital clock. He grew confused. His head ached.

Think, you idiot!

He knew he could not stand there holding the book until his beard grew and the world ended.

He rifled the pages as his mind imploded on him and . . . like the dart of a white bird, quick and furtive . . . a little piece of paper from somewhere in the five hundreds broke free from the volume and began to pirouette toward the earth. Gregor watched it flutter, dip, then land. He could read the message: it was a single integer—4.

Thank God, Pork Chop! You *didn't* let me down!

His relief was radiant with bliss. His knees shuddered in pleasure. He took a deep suck of air, felt it flood into his lungs. He put the book back on the shelf, and turned very adroitly and walked out.

Light as a dancer, Gregor turned to the right, as the absolute rule of the code demanded. He continued to walk until he found the fourth exit on the right, and stepped out into the bright sunlight, which made him blink after the interior of the mall. The bitter chill attacked him also. He struggled with his sunglasses, then began to walk up the row of cars that was immediately in front of him as he clung to the right-hand margin of the sidewalk out of the mall.

He walked on through the crisp air, examining the cars in the row to his right. At last he noticed a plaid scarf crumpled in a rear window well.

In the summer it might have been a madras jacket or a picnic tablecloth or even, as it was once, a Scotch cooler: but always it was something plaid. And always the automobile was different, presumably something rented under a pseudonym. Pork Chop was very careful with details like this.

Gregor looked at the vessel of his deliverance. It was a Ford. The bright sun burned down and the clouds of his own raw breath floated majestically before him. He could feel the sweat inside his collar begin to freeze.

Yet he did not move forward; he could not. Something rapped in his chest. He could not deny that he was still extremely upset.

But he could not just stand there either; nothing attracts attention in America more than a man standing still in a parking lot. Parking lots are a thing one goes through on the way to the other destinations; no one's destination in America is ever just a parking lot. So Gregor continued his walk until he was out of acres of cars and headed into the woods, another extremely bad idea.

He headed back.

Do it, he commanded. Time is flying.

He was shaking horribly. He forced himself to go to the car and peeked in. He could see the briefcase on the floor of the backseat on his side, its top unzipped.

Just open the door, fool, and do it.

Gregor went to the car. The rear door was unlocked, as usual. He put his hand on the handle, pressed the button, and—

But then he tried to remember back, two years ago, when his services to Pork Chop started and that moment of explanation. Specifically, he pawed through his memory to recall if it was part of his official instructions that the exit code be placed between pages 300 and 301, or if that was merely Pork Chop's own personal signature, something the spy had begun doing on his own. As a long-time agent-runner, Gregor knew that agents all had signatures, little things that worked into the ritual of communication subconsciously so they were unique, a part of the subverbal language between themselves and their cutouts.

Gregor's sense of unease grew palpable. It felt like a brass egg jammed in his windpipe. The professional part of him, the deep-cover operative in an enemy country, came bristlingly alive. But so did the coward. He wanted to weep. He felt his knees begin to knock. Pork Chop, why are you doing this to me? Have you grown sloppy, Pork Chop? Have you grown cunning, or greedy? It happened to agents all the time. Pork Chop, what is going on? He realized his vanity had betrayed him again; he'd allowed himself to love Pork Chop as the only steady constellation in his whirling cosmos. He was a hopeless neurotic, always falling for lovers who were fated to betray him! It was a pattern, and now Pork Chop was repeating it. Suddenly, he hated Pork Chop! Pork Chop was slime, offal, defecation! Pork Chop was . . .

In a blast of desperation, almost more to escape his problems than to master them, Gregor walked to the other side of the car, where the doors were locked. He looked around. There was no one coming, though far off he could see people walking to and from parked cars. He reached in his pocket, took out a Swiss army knife, and with a swift plunge jammed it through the rubber seal of window and leaned against it with all his strength. Nothing happened. He looked around, almost catatonic with fear. But though he could see others moving in the lot and cars patrolling for empty spaces, no one was near him and no car came his way. Once more he leaned heavily upon the handle of the knife, calling up all the strength that he had, pulling the strength from the well of his fear. Suddenly, he felt something give. He had managed somehow to jam the window down an inch. With a mighty shove he got it down another and another and . . . he realized now he could get his hand in.

He looked around again, nervously, stunned at what he had done. No, no one had yet seen him. Breathing hard—good Lord, he was going to have a heart attack!—he pushed his fat hand through the slot of the window, reached for the lock button, and with an—oof! almost, no, almost, *yes!*—got it open. Disengaging, he quickly opened the door. The smell of the new car rose to his nostrils, a rich American smell. He reached across the front seat and tugged at the briefcase and—it would not come! There seemed to be a bit of an impediment, as if he were pulling from the wrong angle, and Gregor gave a little tug and—

Gregor had a brief impression of an insect buzzing swiftly by his face, or perhaps it was more like the sudden swoop of a small, darting bird, an angry swallow or hummingbird flashing by, harmless but nevertheless confusing, disorienting, completely stunning, and then in the next second, even as these impressions accumulated, he heard the sound of a

dense thunk, metallic and vivid with texture, and then the low hum of
something shivering rapidly. Gregor stood back, stupefied, trying to
make sense of it all. His heart began to thunder again. Quickly, he
checked himself; he seemed all right and—

Then he saw, sunk into the car roof just a few inches beyond his eyes,
something particularly bright and evil. It was the blade of a vicious
fighting knife, smooth with oil and glinting in the light. Its top edge was
savagely serrated, all the better for sawing through flesh, and, driven
with enormous force, it had sunk nearly half its length into the car roof.
What blade remained visible was a long, graceful shank of steel. At its
base were two prongs; it appeared to have no grip at all.

Gregor recognized it immediately; it was the blade of a Spetsnaz
ballistic knife, a weapon carried by the GRU's Special Raiding Forces,
his country's equivalent of the American Green Berets or the British
Special Air Service regiment. The blade was locked onto its hilt atop a
powerful coiled spring; it could be used as a conventional fighting knife,
but when a button of the crossguard was triggered, the spring sprang,
and the blade was driven forward with enormous velocity, literally fired.
It could kill silently at twenty-five meters and was a special assassination
weapon not only of Spetsnaz but of KGB and all the Eastern bloc secret
services, a favorite device of the masters of the *mokrie dela*, the wet job,
at the KGB procedures school at Karlovy Vary, on the Black Sea. Gregor
bent to the case and saw the gleaming metal of the hilt inside and a wire
rigged from the trigger button in the crossguard through the case to the
floor. It was designed so that when he picked the case up, it fired
through the open mouth of the case.

He sat back. He realized that if he'd come through the unlocked door,
the proper door, and had been leaning across the case as he tried to lift
it, the blade would have speared him through the center chest; he would
have been dead in seconds, choking on his own blood in the backseat of
this little car.

Someone had planned his murder.

He vomited.

Then, very quickly, he began to walk away.

Poo Hummel said, "Mommy. Mommy. Airplanes!" She ran to the
window, drawn by the roar of the low-flying craft. Herman, her guardian, watched her go, took a quick look at his watch.

So late, he thought.

I would have thought it would have been earlier. They are doing such a bad job of it.

"Poo, you be careful," Beth Hummel screamed from her bedroom.

But Poo had her nose pressed against the glass, drawn by the noise, the spectacle of the big, slow ships zooming overhead toward the mountain.

Herman was next to her, with a hand on her shoulder.

"Herman, what are they doing?" Poo asked.

"Oh, I don't know," said Herman. "They probably came to show off for all the children of the town, to make them happy and excited with their noise and to make the snow melt faster."

"They look like scarecrows," said Poo.

Herman wasn't listening. Suddenly grave, he said, "Let's go into the basement, all right, Poo? We'll take your mommy and your sister into the basement and we'll have a little party."

But Poo had made the kind of connection of phenomena, intuitive but brilliant, with which children often astonish adults.

"Herman," she asked, squinching up her eyes, "did the airplanes come for you?"

"No," said Herman. But he knew men would, soon enough. And he knew what he was expected to do then.

"Herman, I like you," said Poo as he lifted her up. She gave him a squeeze and a kiss.

"I like you too, Poo."

You feel like you're the king of creation in an A-10. You're up front and the plane itself—wings, engines, rudders—is way back. You sit at the end of the long snout in a fishbowl wide and bright to the world and the only thing in your head-up display is a little rubbery smudge of nose. It's really just you, slung out there. That's why pilots like Leo Pell loved the ship; you really *fly* her, you're really airborne, on the wind. It's World War II stuff, Jugs and Bostons lowlevel over the hedgerows of occupied Europe.

"Delta Six, this is Papa Tango One, do you copy?" asked Major Pell in *The Green Pig*, leading Tango flight toward South Mountain, which rose like a glob of ice cream before him.

"Uh, roger, I copy, Papa Tango One," came the response in his earphones from his forward air controller, on the ground with Delta.

"You want us to rough up this old mountain, Delta Six?" asked Pell.

"That's a big rog," said the FAC. "Twenty mike-mike only."

"Uh, I got that, Delta, and we're only packing twenty mike-mike. Papa Tango to Tango Flight, let's arm guns, boys."

Pell's finger snaked off his stick to his armament control panel on the left lower quadrant of his instrument board; he hit a switch and the red gun ready light went on up at the top of the panel. His hand back on the stick, his thumb grazed the little nipple, red and lively, beneath it.

His plane felt giddy, alive, teenaged. *Pig* was lighter than a dream today because she didn't have the usual wingload of external stores for air support jobs and wouldn't even be firing her heavy 30-mm gun that ran through the center of the fuselage. Instead, she wore the two gun pods under her wings that Leo and his boys had labored so furiously to mount up.

"Papa Tango, Delta Six, do you copy?"

"I copy."

"Leo, you all clear on targeting?"

"Hey, Delta, I read you loud and clear."

"Leo, they tell me there's some kind of tarpaulin or something on top of the mountain and some breastworks or trenches or something right at its edges. You want to put your ordnance into the trenches, you got that?"

"Map coordinates bravo zero niner, Delta, I read you, and I've got the map on my knee and I have visually acquired the target."

"You may commence your run anytime, then, Papa Tango."

"I read you, Delta. Tango Flight, time to party. On my mark, Tango Flight, five-second bursts at max altitude 3200, do you read?"

"With you, flight leader," came a stereo of replies.

Then the smart-ass Tarnower. "Wahoo, Leo, let's do this sucker up good."

"Watch the chatter on the air, Tango Two," said Leo, a sticker for combat protocol. But he himself felt the exultation. The mountain, white as a sugarloaf, was quite near now, and below it all the patchwork of Maryland spread out like a pale geometry problem of infinite detail, cross-hatched cornfields, clumps of black-broccoli trees, silvery roads.

He took a deep breath and slid from formation like a gull, feeling— even through the network of strapping, the constriction of the flight suit, the heaviness of the helmet—the swooshing, stomach-feathering sense of gravity releasing its hold. Down the plane slid, down, down, on a line like a baseball fired toward home. He flew straight and level, taking no evasive action, confident that his bus could not be budged from the air and that his butt could not be peppered by small arms, because he sat, actually, inside a titanium bathtub configured into the cockpit. Leo's sensations speeded up immensely. He had fired many times before and in 'Nam he'd fired live at gooks in his T-28 with six 50s. But twenty mike-mike against real bogies fifteen minutes out of home without even having to go to war with Russia to bring it off! Goddamn, and wahoo yourself, Tango Two.

In his head-up display, a sheet of Plexiglas on which the complex deflective computations for nailing a scudding T-72 were projected, the targeting angle solved neat as a bow tie, Leo saw just mountain against the floating neon circles of his gunsight. He had no trouble bringing the two circles together and holding the mountain in them. He could see the brown patch of canvas or whatever, looking like an OD handkerchief on the mountaintop, and there appeared to be some movement in the trench at its edge. His blood sang in his ears. The mountain grew before him. He checked his angle of attack indicator and discovered himself sailing in at thirty degrees, just right, just the way the books said to do it.

Leo touched the gun nipple.

He loved this part best. The twenty mike-mikes shuddered under him, their seven barrels whirling in their pods under the fuselage like threshing machines. He saw the tracers float out before him, fall away, disappear into the mountain. Where they fell, they destroyed. It was awesome, godlike. The snow rose in a cyclone of disturbance as the burst leapt across the tarp and at the trench.

Leo fired for five seconds until the mountain was real as a nightmare before him. He pulled up, hearing in his headphones a litany of destruction as the other elements in the flight placed their bursts in the target zone.

But then:

"Goddamn, Tango Leader, I have a goddamn missile lock-on."

It was Tango Four, Leo could tell, his voice broken with fear.

"Go to ECM, Tango Four, dispense your chaff and evade, evade—"

Leo heard the explosion.

"Ah, fuck, he, fuck, he got me, goddamn, filling with, goddamn, smoke, ah, shit—"

"Flame out your bad engine, son," Leo said, "and ride it down, Tango Four, you're okay."

Leo turned his head back as he climbed and turned, and saw his flight spread out behind him as the mountain shrank to a lump. Tango Four pulled from the parade of ships, pulling out, its left-side General Electric bleaching the day of color with white fire. It began to slide downward.

"Ride it down, Tango Four, you can pull an abort in a farmyard, plenty of parking places down there—" Leo argued, a sane voice in a crazy world.

"She's going to blow," said Tango Four, "and I'm ejecting."

"Negative, Four, you haven't the alti—"

But it was too late. Tango Four panicked and ejected at an altitude of four hundred feet. His chute was only half open when he hit the ground. The big plane hit just ahead of him, detonating in a huge smear of fire.

"All right, Tango Flight, let's get it together," Leo said to dead silence on the horn. "Goddammit, Delta Six, where'd that fucking SAM come from? Who the fuck are these guys?"

"Tango, we had no idea they had SAM capability. Shit, it looked like a Stinger."

The Stinger was very bad news. Designated the FIM-92A, it could reach speeds of Mach 2.2 and used proportional navigation and passive infrared homing to engage high speed, extremely maneuverable targets from just about any angle, out to a range of 3.5 miles. It was also highly resistant to electrocountermeasure jamming. It was a bitch. Nobody wanted to go into Stinger country.

"Goddamn," said a Tango flyer, "Goddamn, Leo, I got a bad hydraulic light on, I'm pulling out."

"That's a big negative," said Leo, "we got some business to finish. Delta Six, you want us to hit it again?"

A new voice came on the net.

"Uh, Tango, Colonel Puller here, that's an affirmative to the max, you got that? We've got some kids about to jump off against the position, and they need all the help they can get."

"Leo, this goddamn hydraulic is—"

"Off the air, Tango Seven, do you copy. Off the goddamned air!"

Leo led the flight around in a twelve-mile left-hand circle for a second run. The mountain grew before him.

"All right, Tango Flight," he ordered, "we're going in in two elements,

I'll take the first element, the two and three ships. We'll come in north to south, say at 2200, evasive action, electrocountermeasures. I'll dump some flares if they send the Stingers up. Captain Tarnower, you take the second element, the six, seven, and eight ships, from east to west. Okay, on my mark divide. Let's mark it, guys, and *now*."

Leo pulled from the formation, dipped to the earth, seeing in his rear mirror that three of his six remaining ships stayed with him, while Tarnower, in the Tango Five ship, banked right, taking two birds in behind him.

Who the fuck are these guys? Leo was thinking. Where the hell did they get Stingers?

"Let's shake it, Tango Flight," he ordered.

"Flight leader sounds solid," said Puller to the FAC. They could see the dark ships splitting into two formations, rolling apart from each other and getting down to an assault altitude.

"Leo's the best," said the FAC. "Humps tourists for Continental. But damn, he likes that *Green Pig*."

Around them, the Delta commandos stood watching the show. The drifting tendril of smoke from Tango Four's crash inscribed a crazy line against the bright blue sky.

Puller blinked. His head ached, all the noise from the jets. He looked at his watch—1442. He could see the National Guard trucks pulled off about halfway up the hill, where Aggressor Force had blown the road and had made out some activity through his binoculars as the officers got the men out and into some kind of attack formation.

"They're going in again, sir," said Skazy.

"Lookin' good, lookin' real good, Tango Flight," the FAC said into his microphone.

The planes hit the mountain from two directions, one flight then the other. When they fired, Puller could see the empty cannon shells cascade from their pods in a fur of smoke. The tracers plunged from under the fuselage like darts. Where they fell against the mountain they ripped it.

But something was wrong.

"They're firing much longer," said Puller. "Goddammit, they're firing much longer."

The FAC said, "Uh, I think some of the guys are really pouring it on."

"Bullshit," said Puller, "they're just hosepiping their ammo away so they don't have to go back."

He grabbed the mike away from the FAC.

"Tango Flight, Delta Six here, goddammit, you men, slow your fire down, you're wasting rounds on nothing."

"Tango Flight, this is Tango Leader, you guys conserve your ammo, you hear. Goddammit."

"Leo, I'm dry," a voice came.

"Six, you pumped most of your shit into Washington County, goddammit, I saw—"

"Missiles," said Skazy on the ground. "They've fired more missiles."

"Heatseekers," said the FAC.

The missiles, leaking thin streaks of white gas, went like fast dogs for the planes, which themselves began to fantail and scud, breaking this way and that as the missiles hunted them. They broke from their formation like the petals of an immense rose unfolding over the white mountain. Most of the missiles failed to lock on, whirling off until they burned through their few seconds of fuel, at which point their contrails disappeared and they fell to earth. But—

"Missile lock-on, goddamn, missile lock-on!" came the scream over the radio. A missile hit an A-10 engine with a thud heard on the ground, and dissolved it in a burst of light; the plane wobbled; a second missile, seeking the larger heat signature of the burning power plant, plunged into it, and the plane fell from the sky dead.

"Goddamn, I've got no controls, nothing's respon—"

The sentence ended in a cornfield.

"Leo, I'm down to zero lead," came the call.

"Leo, my hydraulics are shot. They put some shit into my wings."

"Leo, my controls are all mushy."

"Tango Flight, you stay on station," said Leo Pell.

"What's your ammo?" Puller demanded over the radio.

"Sir, I'm all dry," came the response.

"Delta Six, this is Tango Leader. I've got about seven seconds left. I'll go in again. Tango Flight, form up on Captain Tarnower and head for home."

"Leo," said the FAC, "you can't go in there alone."

"Hey, I've got seven seconds of rock and roll left, you think I'm going to park this pig with it?"

"Jesus," said the FAC to Puller. "If he's got the only signature in the sky, their heatseekers will nail his butt sure. Those were Stingers, too, the best. Where the hell they get Stingers?"

Puller didn't answer.

"What's his name again?"

"Leo Pell."

"Major Pell, this is Colonel Puller, do you copy?"

"I copy, Delta Six."

"I am advised you have a low to zero survival probability."

"I came to dance, Colonel, not to sit."

"Good luck, then, Tango Leader."

Okay now, it was just Leo Pell and the mountain. He wasn't worried about the small-arms stuff, though a spider web jinked his bubble where a LMG round had popped through at about ten o'clock, because he was sitting in his titanium bathtub, carrying self-sealing tanks, and had plenty of redundancy in his control systems. And he wasn't worried about delivering his packages. Going in wasn't the problem, even if you could see the tracers floating up to swat you. You were okay going in because your exhaust was behind you and their heatseekers wouldn't see it to read it and chase it. You were okay until you showed them your hot ass.

When you passed the crest, you were wide open. You were like a bitch in heat and the missiles, like stud hounds, came up after you with one thing on their mind. They wanted you up the ass, that's all there was for them.

So Leo, who wanted to live almost as much as he wanted the sheer gut-thumping joy of pumping twenty mike-mike into the mountain, resolved to juke in like a rock 'n' roll melody, up and down and down and up, straighten out for his seven seconds of deliverance, then cut hard to the left, dive for the deck, keep his engines astern from the mountain as much a possible, and just maybe Aggressor Force might not punch him out.

The mountain was fat as a tit in a centerfold. Leo began to evade. He pumped his rudder pedals, he diddled his decelerons, and he rode his stick. His ship, *Green Pig*, dipped and skidded through the air in a flight pattern that was more like a controlled catastrophe than a conscious design. And in his harness Leo felt the plane's moves to the pit of his stomach and to his heart, which seemed to have gone on vacation for this last long ride.

Meanwhile, blobs of color floated up to smash him. He felt as if he were going down the drain of a brightly lit bubble bath. Strange radiances, odd visions, nightmares, fantasies, dope hallucinations, fever dreams, all floated by. There was a queer underwater quality to it, aquamarine and pastel, everything wonderfully graceful and stately. His plane bumped when hit; they were hitting the *Pig* pretty regularly now, all the guns on the mountain having their way with her.

He felt air suddenly as a stitchwork of holes sparked through the bubble just over his head; something like a firecracker went off in the cockpit. His left arm went numb. His mirror blew off. Smoke, acrid and rancid, began to fill the cockpit. Didn't they know the No Smoking sign was lit?

"Tango Leader, watch yourself, lookin' good, lookin' real good," FAC was saying.

Okay now, Leo thought, get in real close, blow those motherfuckers away, hurt 'em, hurt 'em bad now.

Leo saw the mountaintop lined up in the floating circles of his head-up display. The trees were alive with fire and light and commotion. He checked his airspeed, 220, his altitude, 1,450, his angle of attack, 37, the onrushing hump, corrected his deflection just a touch, and it was gun time.

He hit the nipple.

The guns spent themselves in seven long seconds. The twenty mike-mike bursts flicked out like flung pebbles and splashed into the huge sheet of canvas. He had no idea if he was doing any damage at all; he just watched the tracers sink into it.

The crest flashed by and the last few shells flew out into Maryland. Leo cut his throttle, hit his left rudder pedal, banged his decelerons, dipped his nose, and began to dive for the deck and bank at the same moment as his right ailerons cranked up. Something white and mad flashed by as one missile missed, followed in a second by another. No lock-ons yet. A third burned past him from underneath.

He felt cold air again, more of it. The bubble around him seemed to liquify into smaller bubbles, until finally it was a cascade of glittering diamonds. Smoke rose from beneath him, everywhere. The controls were a mess. The stick had turned into a delinquent child, a horrible

son with a mind of his own and no respect for poor old Dad. Leo could
see no sky, but only Maryland, the Free State, big and white, reaching
up to absorb him.

The plane hit in a wild blur of thrown snow and earth, and for an
instant there was no fire and then there was nothing but fire, fire
everywhere, fire forever. The fire rose like a ritual offering. Smoke
peeled away from it, fanning in the breeze.

"Shit," said the FAC stupidly. "Goddammit. What I want to know is,
who are those guys? Where'd they get Stingers? What are they, the U.S.
Army?"

"We don't know who they are. Kids?" asked Puller.

"What?"

"Kids, did he have kids?"

"Ah, he had a lot of kids. Five, six, I don't know. Six of 'em, I think.
Goddamn, Leo Pell *dead*, I can't believe it!"

"The good ones always have kids, for some reason," Puller said. "I
don't know why, I've never figured it out, but the real good ones always
leave a mess of kids."

He turned to Skazy, murder in his eyes.

"Beep the Guard," he said. "Get 'em moving."

1500

"**T**his is absurd, isn't it?" said Peter Thiokol, extravagantly offended. "I mean, the reason you're trying to find out who breaches security at the South Mountain installation is so that we can figure out who's *in* there and then from that maybe I can figure out a way to get by the elevator shaft door, but now you're interrogating *me*."

The two agents had little appreciation of the absurd. They weren't collectors of ironies, either, and in some future time they wouldn't hoist a glass in salute to the ludicrousness of this moment.

"Dr. Thiokol, there were thirteen senior people in the MX Basing Modes Group at the Hopkins Applied Physics Lab that the Department of the Air Force Strategic Warfare Committee employed to design South Mountain. There are arrest warrants on all of them. It's a technicality, designed to speed things up, just in case. Now, we have some questions, I'm afraid."

Peter wondered if he had the energy to explain anything. He felt himself tumbling toward incoherence, as he had before his students that morning. And he knew also where the questioning would go, where it would *have* to go: toward Megan. He could not stand to go over it, to work out the theories. He had just put it into his bottom drawer and thrown away the key. It was in the deep under-mountain silo of his subconscious.

But the two agents were grimly bland men of indeterminate age and strong will who simply plunged ahead. They were probably not all that different from the Delta officers: hardworking types who drew their power and identities from the potent organizations they had chosen to join and to whose dictates they would not be disloyal.

"For the record, you're the son of Dr. and Mrs. Nels Thiokol of Edinah, Minnesota."

"Dr. and *Dr*. Thiokol. My mother was a damned good ob-gyn. My father was a surgeon. Do we have to go through my whole life?"

They did. This went on for a little while and he answered all the stupid who/when questions curtly, pretending to a charmless boredom in his eyes. But as usual, he felt himself tightening when it came to his twisted adolescence, his wretched relationship with his father, whom he could never please until it occurred to him he wasn't *supposed* to please him, and what this led to, all the schools, the expulsions, the business with the sleeping pills, the time he thought of now as only a long dark tunnel as he crawled through slime toward the light.

"Yet you got excellent grades through all this. And your test scores—"

"I'm smart, yes. I finally got my act together my sophomore year at Harvard."

"What did you discover there?"

Yes, it was the crucial question of his career. He remembered it well, November of '66, that funky, dreary room in Brattle Hall, which he shared with Mike De Masto, who was now a shrink in Oakwood, just outside of the glamorous burg of Dayton, O. Mike had long hair to his shoulder blades that year and was about Peace. Mike smoked dope and read his sacred texts and organized, orchestrated, and led the burgeoning Harvard antiwar movement. Which of course meant he was getting laid, sometimes two, three, and four times a day. Meanwhile Peter, the soggy little grind with a history of instability, spent the months in the exile of the library, depressed near unto suicide, working like a demon to figure out a way to keep himself alive. And one day he found it.

He found the bomb.

"I became interested in strategic thought at Harvard," he told the FBI agents. "The bomb, you know. The big bomb. For reasons that were doubtlessly pathological. I drew some queer comfort from an instrument that could wipe us all out in a blinding flash. It gave point to the pointlessness."

Peter still remembered the image of the nuclear mushroom climbing from its fiery birthing, clawing ever skyward, opening, devouring its way through the heart of civilization.

The bomb became a kind of focal point for his existence: he lost himself in its culture, its byways, its traditions, its intricacies. He learned how to build one, how to hide one, how to plant one, how to use one, how to deliver one. He pored over the interesting work in strategic thought being done at Rand and later at Herman Kahn's Hudson Institute. The strategic thinkers, men like Bernard Brodie, Albert Wohlstetter, Henry Rowan, and Andy Marshall, were his heroes, outlined against the blue-gray November sky of his imagination. His senior thesis reflected their thought but was his own in the way a promising apprentice can take the line of the masters and push it way out until it's something altogether new: *Strategic Reality: Crisis Thinking for a Nuclear Age,* which was later published by Random House.

In fact, everything that Peter ever became, that he ever got, he owed to the bomb. Sometimes, he thought back on that crimped, desperate, achingly lonely little shit he'd been in prep school.

You beat them, he'd tell himself, swelling with radiance at the power of his becoming what he wanted to become, which was important. Everything you have is because of the bomb.

And most of all, he had Megan because of the bomb.

He'd met her in England when he was on his Rhodes studying the impact of weapons systems on policy decisions in immediate pre-Great War Europe in a political science seminar at Balliol. She was on a Rhodes, too, studying art at Keeble, after four years at Bennington. They met at the Bodleian, far from the radical unrest of America and the Vietnam War. She was dark and Jewish and he'd known she was American because she was blowing a bubble.

I beg your pardon, he said, is that *real* Double-Bubble? *Fleer's* Double-Bubble?

She just looked at him. No smile, her frank eyes devouring him, her beautiful jaw ripping away at the gum. She blew another bubble. Then she reached into her purse and pushed a single piece of genuine Fleer's Double-Bubble across the three-hundred-year-old oak table at him.

Who are you?

He told only the truth.

I'm the smartest guy you ever met in your life, he had said.

"Did you meet any Communists at Oxford?" one of the agents said.

Peter just looked at him. What could one do with such idiots?

"No. Look, I don't see any of those people anymore. I haven't seen them in years."

The agents exchanged looks. He could tell they thought he was being "difficult." They tried a different approach.

"Of the eleven senior members of the MX Basing Modes Group, were any of them politically suspect?" asked one of the agents.

"You've seen the files. *I* haven't."

The two agents looked at each other, then sighed. One of them wrote something down.

"I'm running very low on time here, guys," Peter said, smiling with what he thought was a great deal of Ivy League charm. They appeared not to hear.

"Well, then, psychologically suspect? It seems to be a pattern among senior defense analysts, and defense engineers and researchers, particularly the farther reaches of—" The agent struggled for a word.

"The farther reaches of blowing the world up, right?"

"Yes, Dr. Thiokol. Anyway, our investigations have shown that a significant number of these men and women burn out. That is, lose heart, have radical changes in religion, sexual orientation, political ideology."

"It's a very intense life. You're gaming out the end of the world nearly every day, trying to figure new wrinkles, new ways to do it. Nobody gets old."

"What about this Dr. Michael Greene?"

"Mike? Mike found out he was queer. Anyway, he bailed out before we'd really gotten to the interesting stuff."

"He's disappeared, that's what makes him so interesting. And he's got AIDS, did you know that, Dr. Thiokol?"

"No, I didn't. My God, that's awful."

"Isn't it possible that a man who's dying—well, he'd be vulnerable emotionally to pressures or, rather, too fragile to withstand them. And someone—"

He didn't know what to say. He knew the weakness of each member of the MX Basing Modes Group. Mike Greene's was for thin-hipped Gentile athletes, Maggie Berlin's for greasy mechanics. Niles Fallow had an alcoholic wife; Jerry Theobald suffered from almost incredible drabness; Mary Frances Harmon was a virgin who talked dirty; Sam Bellows was perpetually horny, yet so hangdog he never got laid; Jeff Thaxter was a workoholic who abused his kids; Jim Diedrickson had a son with cystic fibrosis; Maury Reeves's wife Jill walked out on him for a Marine colonel. And on and on . . . each of them held in a matrix of weakness and duty. They used to have a joke about what they were doing. They

called it the Revenge of the Nerds: little techies, sealed away in anony-
mous offices in the beast of a building complex called the Johns Hopkins
Applied Physics Lab out in picturesque Howard County, figuring out
whether the world would end in fire or ice, and if fire, how hot, what
color, spreading at what rate, and influenced by what wind patterns?

At last they moved to him.

"Any approaches in the last few months? Any sense of being watched?
Any peculiarities in your mail, say, being intercepted, your house being
broken into, your papers messed up."

"Absolutely not," he said, swallowing hard.

They missed it.

"What about your wife? You hear from her?"

"Leave her out of it, please. She's—she's off somewhere, that's all."

"The marriage. When did it break up?"

"Nine months ago. I don't talk about it with anybody, do you
understand?"

"Megan Wilder, she never gave up her maiden name?"

Peter didn't like this at all.

"I said I'd prefer not to discuss my private life. She's with another man
now, all right? That's all there is to say. I upset her, she went with
somebody else. How much longer is this going to take?"

"When did you last see her?"

"She came up to Baltimore two weeks ago. It was a kind of a stab at
reconciliation. It was kind of okay at the beginning, but the next
morning it turned into catastrophe again."

"This was before or after your breakdo—"

"It was months afterward. That was in July, when I left the committee. But it was no big deal. It was a very mild nervous breakdown, yes,
created by a great deal of work stress and the end of my marriage. I just
felt used up and incapable of being with other human beings. I spent
four weeks at a very discreet loony bin in Ellicott City, where I reread
the collected works of Agatha Christie and talked to an insufferable fool
about my God complex. In the end I allowed him to convince me that I
wasn't that august gentleman. I was too smart for the job description."

The agents didn't crack a smile at this deflection. Nevertheless, tacti-
cally the gambit worked; both agents missed his discomfort, and the
interrogation headed into less interesting areas.

"Now, let's go back to this Mike Greene . . ."

The agents asked their little loaded questions, trying to probe or trick him. But it wasn't much of a contest. Peter began to feel a little like Raskolnikov—superior, implacable, a "new kind of man." He could see them set up their ambushes, and popped counterambushes on them, reducing them to hostile silence. They couldn't touch him, and in time they understood this themselves. When they got close they didn't know it; they couldn't read him. In time, perhaps, they could break him down and get at . . . at *it*, but they didn't have time. Also, he saw, they were a little bit afraid of him by now, and a little bit unhinged by the theater of reality swirling around them.

The surrender was prosaic, without ritual.

One of them finally said, "We're going to leave you with a card. If you should think of something, you call us."

So Peter had his perverse little victory. Mess with Peter Thiokol and see what it gets you!

Peter looked out the window. He could see the mountain itself. He felt a little of that radiant selfhood again. It thrilled and pleased him.

I'm the smartest boy in the class! I can do anything!

Then why couldn't you hang on to the one person you ever loved, he asked himself.

"Don't go yet," he said suddenly.

He rose, went to the window. Outside, on the plain, he could see the jagged streaks of smoke from the wrecked jets rising funereally against the bright blue air. From up on the mountain, the sounds of small-arms fire reached him; the National Guard Infantry, like the Brits of World War I, having taken their wages these long years, now were dying.

He could see Dick Puller hunched over the radio gear, talking frantically to his Guardsman on the mountain; meanwhile, the Delta officers stood by. They looked restless, even hungry, and desperate with frustration. Skazy, their gloomy leader, was clenching and unclenching his hands in anger.

You think *you* got problems, Peter thought.

He turned to the two agents.

Time to face it, Peter, he told himself. Time to face it at last. Time to stop denying the thing that's been eating at your stomach lining all these months and that put you in the bin.

"I think my wife betrayed South Mountain," he said.

*   *   *

Phuong clutched the M-16. They whirled over the mountain, and as they shot up, she felt the strangeness in her stomach; it was as if a window had been opened and the cool air could blow in. The deck beneath her began to rattle and shiver.

"Small arms," one of the crewmen screamed over the roar of the engine.

She looked; across from her the black Americans, all dressed up like frogmen, clung together. Their eyes were eggs. Her partner, the blond man called Teagarden, another frogman, stared into space, his eyes locked in a faraway glare. His lips moved.

Then they were over the mountain, sliding down its side at an angle, the craft around them feeling warped and broken.

She had seen helicopters die before. You always wondered what it was like when they blazed in flame, then plunged to earth and hit with a detonation like a bomb. Later you went to see them. They looked like the shedded skins of insects, broken metal husks on the floor of the earth. Inside you could see the men, burned meat; the faces were so terrible. Then more helicopters would come and it was time to go back into the tunnels.

"Hang on, everybody," the crew chief shouted. "Touch down."

The chopper hit hard. Dust and smoke flew; the air was heavy with vibration. Suddenly men in camouflage, their faces green, their manner urgent, were among them.

"Out, out. Come on, into the trench," they were shouting.

They scrambled from the helicopter to a fresh ditch nearby, jumping in to find other men there.

"Fire in the hole," somebody yelled; a huge explosion that sounded like a charge from a terror bomber high up in the clouds where it could not be heard clubbed her in the diaphragm. Trees flew through the air; smoke poured around her. She coughed, taking in the acrid odor of gunpowder.

Mother, it's all so familiar, said her daughter.

"Okay, Rats," said the leader-officer. "That was thirty pounds of C-4 and primacord planted into what our maps tell us was once upon a time the entrance to the main shaft of the old McCreedy and Scott Number Four mine. Let's take a look-see and find out if we punched a hole into it for you."

They stood and moved toward the smoke. All around, trees had been blasted flat; the snow was black and the smoke still gushed from the crater. Above, the mountain, dense with more trees, rose at a steep angle. They were at its base, completely isolated in the forest. The sounds of gunfire came from far away, and a few other soldiers crouched around, keeping watch.

"I think we poked through," said one of the soldiers. "That was a shaped charge; it ought to have cut real deep."

"Okay," said the small black man, "let me just check this sucker out."

With a surprising agility he lowered himself into the gap in the earth. In seconds he was back.

"Hoo boy. Got us a *tunnel*," he said. "One long, mean mothafucking *tunnel*. Party time coming, Jack." He smiled; his teeth were very white and he radiated an electric confidence.

The man Teagarden had explained. This black soldier knew tunnels also; he'd been in them in her country, spent a long time in them. He was a great tunnel fighter.

He now winked at her.

"Me and this lady," he said to the others, "we the whole show now. This old-time stuff for us, right, pretty lady?"

Yes, it was true. Black men had come into the tunnels too. She had killed black men. They were as brave as any of them.

She smiled, but it wasn't much of a smile.

"Okay," said an officer, opening a case, "what we got here is the original 1932 map of Number Four. Shit, this was some operation; you look back through the trees, you see that gap? That's where the railroad went. Some of the old track is still there. And the foundations from some of the buildings are still here. Anyway, as we figure it, this shaft'll take you in maybe five hundred feet. Then you get to what they call the lateral tunnel, the connector that held all the actual mining shafts together. There were five deep mining shafts they called Annie, Betty, Connie, Dolly, and Elizabeth. Betty, Connie, and Dollie were the bitches: they caved in. But Annie and Elizabeth ought to still be there. And they should be in pretty good shape, although nobody can say for sure, because sometimes there's shaft erosion based on moisture, earth shifts, anything. So you head on back through them maybe one thousand feet. Anywhere beyond that point you may run into intersections with the water flues from over the years. We called around to a batch of mining engineers. They think the flues ought to be passable, though it's going to be real tough going. Uphill all the way. Anyway, if you get close enough to the installation, you'll hear 'em; the ground is a great conductor. Your target would be the exhaust shafts of corrugated metal that run out of the silo. If you reach those shafts, you let us know. We'll get a Delta unit here in two minutes, and you can take 'em in the back door."

"What we do if we run into any little strange men in there?" said the small black soldier.

"Just like in 'Nam, you waste 'em. But there won't be anybody in there except ghosts. Ghosts don't bite. You all set?"

"Yes, sir," said Teagarden.

"Okay, I want a radio check the first two hundred feet. Call signs: You're Alpha, Witherspoon; Teagarden, you're Baker. I'm Rat Six, okay? Any questions. Miss Phuong, any questions?"

Phuong offered a tight little smile but shook her head no.

"Okay, and God bless you," said the officer. "We're all praying for you."

"Let's go to tunnelsville, you peoples," said the small black man with another of his smiles.

And they began to enter the smoky shaft.

Darkness swallowed them.

Puller could hear the unsureness in the National Guard captain's voice. It was close to panic.

"Th-there's a lot of smoke from up ahead, Delta Six," the man was saying from up on the mountain. "We can't see too good."

"Bravo, this is Delta Six," Puller said, staring in frustration at the white hump a mile before him. "Are you taking fire?"

"No, sir. At least they're not shooting at us yet. I think they're waiting to see if the planes are coming back. There was a lot of gunfire on that mountain, Colonel."

"Bravo, you've got to move now. The longer you wait, the harder it's going to be. You've got to get your people into the assault line and get them up the hill."

"Colonel," said Skazy, "let me get up there. I can—"

"Shut up, Major. Bravo, do you read?"

"Some of the men don't want to leave the trucks."

"Christ, he hasn't even got 'em out of the trucks yet," Puller said to no one in particular.

"Bravo, this is Delta Six."

"I copy, Delta."

"Look, son, let me talk you through this, okay? I've been on a few hill jobs in my time." Dick's voice was reassuring, authoritative. He'd take this guy in and make him his and make him perform.

"Yes, sir," came the voice, all thought of Commo protocol having vanished. "We've been on exercises for years. It's just so—so different."

"In combat, confusion is normal, son. Okay, you want to cross your line of departure, if possible, with platoons abreast and squads abreast within the platoons. You want the squads in column rather than file, so that you can respond instantly with a broad front of heavy fire if you make contact. Got that?"

"Yes, sir."

"Your sergeants ought to be able to handle the men," said Puller, knowing that sergeants may be ornery, bassackwards assholes, but they were the gears that made an army—any army—operate.

"Get your sergeants involved directly. Brief them *with* the officers and speak to them directly. You want to minimize levels of interpretation, and your officers are probably too distant from the men. The men are going to want the reassurance of the familiar."

"Yes, sir."

There was silence from the mountain. The seconds ticked by. Dick lit another cigarette. Its harshness somehow soothed him. Around, several of the Delta officers stood with binoculars.

"He should have picked out his LD and hit it from the trucks running," said one.

"Yeah, and he should have been tied in with Air," said the other, "and gone on the dime."

Sure, they were right. But they were wrong too, Puller thought. Unblooded troops need to be coaxed and nudged; nurtured. You need a mother for your first fight, and a daddy for the next hundred. Then you need a body bag or a shrink.

The National Guard officer's name was Thomas Barnard and he knew he was in way over his head. The volume of gunfire during the aerial attack had upset him greatly. He was, furthermore, not exactly sure who awaited them; the order from the Governor had simply obligated them to emergency duty at the disposal of the United States Army under a phase four ("nuclear emergency") alert at the specified locale. The unit had been very close to the end of its two weeks of active duty, and the men were not happy to clamber aboard trucks for the hour drive from Fort Richie to this godforsaken spot.

And they were furthermore baffled to detruck and discover themselves in the middle of some movie. These were mainly young blue-collar workers from the Baltimore area who had signed up because the weekend a month and the two weeks a year of low intensity army games added a nice little chunk of bucks to a parched family budget. Now they had stumbled into a little war. It was particularly intimidating to be issued large amounts of live ammunition and grenades. It had put a chill through the men, the grenades especially; in training, live grenades are treated with the awkward care of nuclear weapons because they are so dangerous. Now they were handed out like candy bars by grinning, loosey-goosey commandos. It scared his guys. None of them had a particular desire to be Rambo.

"Okay," Barnard told his NCOs and his officers with a transparent heartiness, "let's get 'em spread out, platoons abreast, through the trees."

The guys just looked at him.

"Tom, the fucking professionals are sitting on their asses down there. Why are we the ones up here? I heard machine guns. Those guys on that mountain have missiles."

"Phase four nuclear emergency. We're working for them now, not the Governor. If they say we go, we go. Ours not to etc., etc. Look, the head guy told me those planes laid so much hurt on our friends up the hill, our big problem was going to be matching up body parts. So let's get humping, huh, guys?"

"Lock and load?"

"Lock and load 'em up, righto," sang Barnard. "Full ammo, get the clips into the weapons, get the weapons unslung, have the guys open their clip pouches so they can reload on the double if there's any kind of a fight and please, puh-lease, tell the boys to be careful. Semiauto. I don't want any hotshot shooting his foot off."

Grumblingly, his people started out.

Barnard went back to the radio, a little more confident because his officers and NCOs had obeyed. Around him he could hear them yelling, the men beefing, but, yes, everybody was filing off into the woods.

"Delta Six, this is Bravo, we are deployed and ready to jump."

"Good work, Captain. Now, you've got 60s, right?"

"Yes, sir."

"I want your 60s in play earliest. We found out in 'Nam it helps the men if their own fire support is emplaced before they move."

"Yes, sir."

"Get the medics circulating behind the assault line. Don't let 'em cluster together, get 'em into the open. The men like to see the medics. It'll help them."

"Yes, sir."

"Major, finally, this is important. Don't wait to take fire. Get your fire support going just as you cross that LD, do you read? I want to hear some noise. If any of these gooks are left alive, I want your boys to blow 'em away as they're coming up the hill. Plenty of ammo. Okay. You copy?"

"I copy, Delta Six."

"Okay, son," Dick cooed. "One last thing. Keep the assault line up and moving forward. Don't let the men hit the dirt and get pinned down. Keep up a heavy, steady volume of effective fire. And keep that fire low—ricochets kill just as dead as Charlie incoming."

"Yes, sir," said Barnard.

He turned to his RTO man.

"Wally, you stay near me, okay?"

"Yes, sir. No sweat."

"That's our unit motto," said Barnard. "No sweat."

He picked up his own M-16, drew a thirty-round magazine from his pouch, and clicked it into the magazine housing. Up ahead, he could see the trees and he could see his own men spread out through them. It was a bright, white day, the sun on the trees so brilliant it hurt his eyes. The sky was blue as a dream.

Jesus, he thought, I'm thirty-seven years old and I'm a tax accountant. I ought to be sitting at my desk.

"Okay," he said to his executive officer, "Let's move 'em out." The line sounded too John Wayne to be real.

The flame was a silver needle, a blade almost. What it touched, it destroyed. Even through the thick black lenses and amid the showering sparks he could see that its power was absolute. It turned the world to a puddle.

Jack Hummel held the plasma-arc torch against the metal and watched the flame devour the titanium. Down here in the hole the world was serene and logical. He had a job to do, one he knew and almost loved, one he had done many, many times before. It was, after all, only cutting. He had, by this time, opened a deep wound in the smooth block of metal.

But at the same time, and despite the mesmerizing, messianic quality of the flame a few inches beyond his eyes, it was hard to concentrate. It was all so strange, and Jack had the terrible knowledge that he was doing something wrong. He should have fought harder. He should have made them beat him.

But he kept thinking, it wasn't my fault. It happened so fast. It was . . . it was hard, you know. You're in a no-win situation.

And he kept thinking how the world required heroes, but instead, it had gotten only him, Jack Hummel, podunk welder and former high school glory boy who had the guts of a rat. He began to hate himself.

You fucking scum, he said to himself.

But he knew they'd kill him and kill his kids. What difference did it make if the world got blown up then?

Barnard was amazed, really, at how well it seemed to be going. The guys were handling it like a wild game of cowboys and Indians, racing through the tree stumps, pawing up the slope in their platoon-abreast formation, keeping good contact with each other, John Wayneing it with the best of them. Even the machine-gun crews, with their twenty-three-pound M-60s and their forty to fifty pounds of ammo belts were keeping up, whereas in the exercises the gunners had tended to fall way back while the younger men gamboled ahead, fleet as deer.

Barnard had picked a tree about fifty yards ahead as his last line of departure; he'd fire there. He could see the crest now, the white-and-red striping of the radio mast against the blue sky, and some kind of low, dark tent just barely visible, but everything else was quiet. The trees had been chopped up by the A-10s; it was like hustling through an exploded toothpick factory over rough ground where the twenty-millimeter shells had plowed the earth. The smell of gunpowder hung in the air.

"Bravo, this is Delta Six."

"Delta, I have no contact yet. It's all quiet. Maybe they left or something."

"Get your assault support fire going, Bravo."

"I thought I'd wait just—"

"Get it going, Bravo, that's a command."

"Affirmative, Delta," said Barnard, handing the phone mike back to his RTO.

"Open fire!" he screamed.

Along the lumbering line, the Guardsmen began to hip-shoot their M-16s, jinking out rounds in semiautomatic. Up ahead, Barnard saw, the snow was beginning to fly where the torrent of 5.56-millimeter bullets popped into the earth.

"Go," he screamed again, "come on, goddammit, hurry."

His sergeants took up the cry and the volume of fire increased as the men syncopated their shots to their own rushing footsteps. So full of the blood-thinning joy and terror of the moment as they were, they began also to scream. The noise rose, unwilled, from their lungs. It was a moment of glory: the rush of the screaming infantry against the white hill under the blue sky, the punctuation of the rifles, and now the higher, faster whipping of the M-60s anchoring either end of the line, really pouring out the fire, raking what was visible of the hilltop less than a hundred yards ahead now as they—

Alex shot the officer in the throat from about two hundred meters with a scoped G-3; he'd been aiming for the head but the captain, bumbling along beside his RTO man just off the assault line, must have stepped on a log or something and so he rose in the scope just as Alex's patient finger carefully stroked the trigger.

But it was still the shot he'd been waiting for.

You want to take down the senior commander at the first opportunity, Alex knew; nothing quite so devastates an attacking force than to see the man they've bonded to over the long years slide backward with his head blown away. And Alex had picked him out almost immediately as the attackers broke from the cover of the trees.

The unit began to fire. He could see them going down.

Because the wound that Alex delivered was not quite what Alex had intended, the bullet missed the brain and tore through the muscles and cartilage to the left of the larynx, and, since it was a full metal jacket in 7.62-millimeter NATO, didn't mushroom and didn't deliver a killing blast of hydrostatic shock, but rather exited neatly. The captain felt as if he'd been whacked in the throat with a baseball bat; the world went instantly to pieces as he fell backward into the snow. In seconds, however, his head had cleared, and his first thought was not for himself but for his men. He could see many of them were down and that the tracers floated out toward them like confetti thrown at a parade of triumph. The air seemed alive with buzzing, cracking things.

"Oh, Jesus, Jesus, Jesus, sir, Christ, Captain, oh, fuck, *Captain*," came some terrible moaning next to him. His RTO man had been shot in the stomach.

"Medic!" screamed Barnard.

A burst of fire, kicking up snow and bits of wood, lashed by him. He scrunched into the earth. His left side felt numb; his head hurt terribly. He rolled over, fighting for breath.

"Captain, Captain, what do we do?" somebody yelled.

Alex only had two heavy automatic weapons, the M-60 from the van and the H&K-21, but he knew he had to break the assault's spine in the very first second or fall victim to a messy perimeter fight that would sap the energy of his men.

He'd therefore placed the two guns together in the center of his line, thereby, of course, violating all infantry doctrine, because a single grenade or even a well-placed burst of fire could destroy them both. He'd also directed that several two-hundred-round belts be ripped from their canisters and linked, so that they could fire continually without reloading for one full minute. This meant the barrels overheated dangerously; thus, stationed next to each barrel there crouched a trooper with—an astonishing improvisation, come to think of it—a fire extinguisher from the ruins of the installation. As the guns fired, these men squirted cold carbon dioxide onto the barrels and works.

The guns fired for one minute, one solid minute of full automatic. It didn't really matter, Alex believed, how accurate they were; what was important was the volume of fire and the impression of endless ammunition hurtling at the attackers. Still, they were very accurate.

*　　*　　*

"Bravo, this is Delta Six. This is Delta Six, do you copy? Bravo, what is your situation? We can hear heavy fire. What is your situation? Bravo, don't let your men bunch up, keep them moving. Act aggressively, Bravo, you've got to act aggressively." Puller gripped the phone. He was aware he was violating his own most precious principle, which was not to interfere with ground forces during maneuver, knowing from bitter experience at Desert One that a staff commander on the radio merely screwed things up. But the sound of the fire from the mountain was heavy and terrifying.

"I think you're talking to a dead man, Colonel," said Skazy.

Down at the girl scout camp they could hear the gunfire rising from the mountain for a long minute. Then it stopped, and there was silence. Then, now and then, the pop and crack of a single rifle, or a burst of automatic fire.

"Return their fire, goddammit," Barnard yelled back, coming out of his shock. Anger, confusion, finally bitterness, began to gnaw at him. He groped around for his M-16, found it, and rolled over. Other shots were beginning to rise from his troops. At least we're answering them, goddammit, he thought.

So where was the great Delta? Back on its ass down the mountain! All this shit about Delta in the magazines, and Delta sits on its ass while Bravo Company of the 123d Light Infantry, Maryland National Guard, the butcher, the baker, the candlestick maker, gets ripped to ribbons.

Barnard got his black plastic rifle up against his shoulder. Squinting over the sights, he could see the gun flashes from Aggressor Force, yet he felt in no particular danger. Languidly, he began to fire, jerking off rounds one, two, three at a time. The rifle had very little kick. He fired a magazine, reloaded, fired another one. After a while it seemed a little stupid.

"Captain!"

Someone slid into the snow next to him. It was a Lieutenant Dill from the second platoon, a phys ed teacher at a Baltimore high school.

"Captain Barnard, I have a lot of hurt men, a lot of dying men. Jesus, let's get the fuck out of here."

The captain just looked at him.

"God, sir, are you—you're all covered with blood! *Medic*, get over here."

"No, no," said the captain. "I'm not hurt that bad. Look, if we just pull back they'll chop us up. I'm going to slide over to where the machine gun should be and see if I can't set up some covering fire, okay. You wait a minute or two; when I get the fire going, you get the men out of here. Don't leave anybody behind, Lieutenant!"

"Yes, sir."

"Get the men firing. If they're not firing, they're not helping."

Barnard began to crawl through the snow. Now and then a bullet would come whipping in his direction. But he made it down the line and found his company's machine gun, lying on its side half sunk in the snow, a loose belt nearby and a batch of dead shells lying around. He recognized his gunner, a steelworker; half his face was gone where a heavy-caliber bullet had punched through.

The captain wiggled forward through the snow, breathing hard. God, it was cold now. He seemed to have stopped bleeding, but he was so wet with the snow that he'd begun to go numb. Pulling the gun to him, he managed with his stiff, fat fingers to get the latch off the breech and get a belt unrolled, and set the lead cartridge into the guides. He slammed the latch shut and drew back the bolt.

"Movement?" Alex asked his gunners.

A bullet hit the logs before them, kicked up a cloud of smoke.

"On the left; there's a group on the left."

The gunner swung the H&K-21. Indeed, a wretched huddle of men appeared to be crawling forward. Or perhaps not crawling forward, but merely crawling anywhere, forward being the direction they'd settled on.

"Yes, there"—Alex pointed—"take them down, please."

The gun fired a long burst and Alex watched as the tracers flicked out and seemed to sink toward the men. Where they struck they kicked up snow and the men disappeared in its swirl.

"Some in the center," somebody said. "However, I think they're retreating."

"You have to fire anyway," said Alex. "It will give the next assault team something to think about."

The H&K-21 fired briefly; more tracers streamed down the mountain, found their targets.

"Rather horrible," said one of the loaders.

"Not a good attack," said Alex. "I don't think these are elite troops I'd anticipated. I think they were amateurs. Casualties?"

"Sir, two men dead in the covering fire and three wounded."

"Well," said Alex. "They did do *some* damage then. And ammunition. We used a lot of ammunition in a very short time. That, too, I suppose, hurts us. But it cost them so much. I didn't think it was their style, to die like that."

The captain drew the gun to him. He couldn't see much now, just barbed wire, some smoke, the aerial, the damned tent, and lots of high blue sky above.

He wished he weren't so tired. On the slope before Aggressor Force's position, he saw bodies. What, thirty-five, maybe forty? Jesus, they caught us in the open. They just let us get close and they blew us away.

He squinted over the gun barrel. Nope, nothing. Couldn't hit a goddamn thing with a machine gun, even.

It occurred to him that he might see a little better if he stood up. He thought about it; yes, it made sense. He'd just—oof!— stand up, yes, and then he'd be able to see much better to shoot.

He stood. It worked! He could see them now, or their heads moving, clustered at the center of their line behind the barbed wire. He thought, boy, sure am glad I thought to stand. It seemed entirely logical. He'd worked it out. With his covering fire, most of his guys could get out of the kill zone. That's why they made me a captain, he thought. 'Cause I'm so smart.

With that thought, he fired.

The gun bucked through twenty-round bursts. He fired at the center of the line. He could see the far-off puffs where the bursts struck. The gun was surprisingly easy to control, though a bit muzzle-heavy, with the bipod out there pulling it down. Trick was to keep the bursts short, then correct for muzzle drift. Firing it was actually quite a bit of fun. He could move the thing slightly and watch as the bullets stitched small disturbances into the earth. He felt the hot brass pouring out of the breech like the winnings at a slot machine. The gun began to steam; its barrel was melting snow packed in the cooling vents. He had no idea if he was hitting anything. He fired a belt that way in about thirty seconds.

Then laboriously he began to change belts.

*   *   *

"The right, the right, goddamn, the right," screamed Alex. Who had fired at them? In less than thirty seconds he lost seven men and one of the rounds clipped the breech of his H&K-21, putting it out of action. The bullets swept in on him. Alex felt their sting and spray. One of his gunners lay on the mud floor of the trench, his right eye smashed.

"The right!" Alex screamed again, sliding to the earth as the bullets began to rip up his position again. He heard the firing rise. All up and down the line his men were answering.

Quickly, he crawled back, turned his binoculars. He could see the gunner, about two hundred meters off on the right. The bullets searched for him, cutting into the snow around him. Yet still he fired, just standing there. *Standing there.* Like some kind of hero. The bullets finally found him.

"Cease fire," Alex yelled.

"Sir, a bunch of them slipped away while the fire was hitting the gun."

"You saw them?"

"Yes, twenty or thirty, just got up and ran down the hill."

"Well, whoever that man was, he was a soldier. I'll say that."

"My marriage," said Peter Thiokol not so much to the agents but somehow to the air itself, "if it had a script, it was written by Woody Allen and Herman Kahn."

"I don't understand the reference to Herman Kahn," one of the FBI agents said.

"In the sense that it followed the classic pattern that Herman identified. The slow, gradual buildup of hostilities, the real arms race, the breakdown in communication, until finally open conflict seems the lesser of two evils. And that's when you get your classic spasm war. You know, multiple launches by both sides, multiple hits, the global catastrophe, nuclear winter. The end of civilization. That was the drama of our marriage. We blew each other away in the end."

There was silence from them.

"It was a very intense union," Peter told them, "but not at first. I just told her I was there at Oxford studying poly sci, which is true. I didn't tell her about my thing for the bomb or that I had a good line on an Air Force job and that I was heading for D.C. That came out later. I—I couldn't really figure out how to break it to her. She wasn't much interested in what I did, at first. She was rather self-involved. Beautiful, the most beautiful woman I ever saw."

"So when did she figure out how you were going to make a living?" said the sharper of the two.

"Oh, finally, I told her. 'Seventy-four. We'd been in Washington a year. I'd just moved from the Strategic Study Group to the Targeting Committee. It was a big leap for me and it meant about ten extra grand a year. Not that we needed the money. Her folks had plenty, but it was nice to be doing well suddenly, and she said she'd finally figured out what strategic meant."

What does it mean? he'd asked.

It means bombs, isn't that right?

Yes.

You think about bombs. You think about war all day. I thought it was more abstract, somehow. Thinking about strategies and that sort of thing, chess and so forth. Or about history, like your project at Oxford. But it's very specific, isn't it?

Yes, very, he said. He'd spent the day contemplating the effects of a nine-megaton fused airburst from a W53/Mk-6 reentry vehicle delivered by a Titan II at four thousand feet versus the same hardware and throw-weight in a fused airburst at two thousand feet in terms of fireball circumference vis-à-vis damage radius to a soft target like an industrialized urban base the size of, say, downtown Vladivostok.

I look on it as thinking about *peace*, he said. Ways to keep the peace.

By building more and better bombs?

He sighed, not at the stupidity of it, but because he knew that from that moment on, there was no turning back, no recall.

"How did your wife take the news?"

"Not too well."

"No kids?"

"The bomb was our baby, she used to say. But Megan was too beautiful for pregnancy. She didn't want to lose her waistline. She'd never admit that, but that's it. And the bomb. It wasn't that it would blow the world up, it's that it would blow *her* up. She took it personally. She took everything personally."

Peter, she once said to him, do you realize you are the only man in the Western world who has nightmares about nuclear bombs *not* exploding?

"She's famous, your wife?"

"In a very small world. She makes sculptures that are highly thought of. She gets great reviews, and sells the stuff for a ton of money. I liked it. It was very impressive. And I think the reason she never left me was that she drew off of me and what I did. Her art would have suffered. She made these anguished things, these masses of mashed tin and plaster and painted surfaces. It was our old pal, Mr. Bomb."

"Was she untrue?"

It took Peter a long second to make sense of the word. It was so quaint and comical.

"I don't know. She went to New York once a month or every six weeks. She said she had to get out of Washington. At first I went with her, but I didn't really go for those people. Assholes, all of them. It was still the sixties for them. It always will be."

"Politics. Was she in a ban-the-bomb group or anything?"

"No. She was too vain to join groups. She wouldn't join any group she couldn't be the leader of. Then I published *my* essay, and I became the celebrity and started going on the tube and that really hurt her."

" 'And Why Not Missile Superiority? Rethinking MAD'?"

"Yes."

He remembered: the argument was simple. MAD—mutual assured destruction, the crux of strategic thought—was a fallacy. We could deploy our MXs before the Soviets improved their 18s and got their 24s on line and it would be possible, under certain rigidly controlled circumstances, to make aggressive moves against the Soviet Union without fear of retaliation. Eastern Europe, for example. In other words, it was theoretically possible, if we could get our MXs out and Star Wars going, to win without the big launch. Reagan loved it. It made Peter the superstar of the sunbelt right.

"That's what got me the head of the MX Basing Modes Group. I was making eighty thousand a year, I was suddenly very high-profile, I'm on TV, journalists are coming courting. And she hated it. I think that's what finally drove her to him." He paused. "She started up with him right after that. I think she's with him now."

"Who is he?"

"I met him once. His name was Ari Gottlieb. He was an Israeli painter, briefly big in Manhattan. Very handsome man, taught a course at the Corcoran. She met him at some Washington art thing. It was a very difficult time. We were in the middle of this squabble over MX basing modes."

"She was different after meeting him?"

"Yes. It was about two years ago. Congress had settled on an initial deployment of one hundred missiles to go into Minuteman II silos and we *knew* that was tragically wrong because it completely invalidated the premise and that it was dangerous and we had to put at least one in an independent-launch-capable super-hard silo, to beat the new inertial guidance system of the SS-18, to say nothing of the next-generation missiles. So we were working crazily on South Mountain to be our first deployed independent-launch-capable Peacekeeper unit, but trying to keep it within the congressional guidelines. We were cheating, in other words. And she hated it, because the thing just was eating up my time and my mind. And I was fighting for this fifteen-million-dollar gimmick called the key vault, which *nobody* wanted, and let me tell you, it was maximum-effort time. She hated that the most, I guess. That it absorbed me so completely. And maybe that finally pushed her over."

"How was she different?"

"I'd finally screamed at her"—he remembered the night, a livid memory, like a scar, still tender to the touch—"that maybe she hated what I was doing, but I was doing something. *Something.* That I believed. That she sat around making wisecracks and playing at despair but never *doing* anything, never *believing* in anything. That she was too *precious* to do anything. For some reason that really cut into her. After that she was different. And then I began getting these reports that she was seeing this guy for lunches in various obscure spots around town. That was all."

"And that was it?"

"In January, I think. I smelled his aftershave on the pillow. She hadn't even bother to change the pillowcases. She had to let me know. She had to hurt me."

He thought about it: the last provocation. After all the years, the final, the ultimate provocation. It was as if she'd finally launched, and now he had to counterstrike on warning or lose his hardware in the silos.

"Cheap aftershave," he said. "English Leather, can you believe that?"

"What happened?"

Peter couldn't reach it, couldn't touch it.

The pause lengthened.

"And?"

"Look, it was a very intense relationship. I was capable of . . ."

"Capable of what, Dr. Thiokol?"

"I guess finally I hit her." He remembered the evening, June it was, leafy June, the air full of light, the trees green, the breeze sweet and lovely. He'd never hit anything before. He remembered the way her head jolted on the impact and the way her eyes went blank and then her face broke up with fear. She fell back, leaking blood, her nose mashed. Spasm war: the end. She cried. He felt so shitty, he tried to help her, but he was afraid he'd think about Ari Gottlieb again and hit her some more. He told her he was feeling pretty fucked up in the head, she ought to get out of there. He might kill her. And he told her he was going to get a gun and kill Ari Gottlieb. That was June.

"It was something else too."

Peter turned so that he didn't have to look at the two of them. After all the denying, it was time to reach in and go where he was most terrified to go. He finally faced it.

"I'd also—well, I did a lot of work at home, and I found stuff— rearranged. Out of order. Slightly scrambled. It really scared the hell out of me. I guess I couldn't deal with it."

"It was her?"

"It had to be."

"Why didn't you *say* something?"

"I just put it into the deep part of my head and covered it up with everything I had. Have you ever heard of denial? You *refuse* to deal with reality. That's when I flipped, I really flipped. I crashed in July."

There was another long silence.

"It sounds like a classic," said one of the agents. "They probably had the two of you under surveillance for a long time, knew exactly how vulnerable she was. They built her a dream man, tailored exactly to your weaknesses. He seduced her. And recruited her. That's how they did it."

"Who? Gottlieb was an Israeli, for Christ's sake. They're on our side, for God's sake."

"Well, in some things. In others, maybe not. Maybe—well, who knows? She'll have to tell us."

This struck through Peter's defenses. Ashamed, he still reacted instinctively. "Go easy on her. The truth is, no matter what, I still love her. I never loved anyone before and I'll never love anyone else. It was *my* fault. It wasn't hers—"

Finally, he'd run out of words.

He sat for a while after they rushed off with their little treasure, feeling awfully rocky inside. Had he just betrayed her? He wasn't sure anymore where the higher loyalties lay. He hated the idea of disappointing her again, after everything else. He also felt close to her. He realized it had pleased him to talk of her. He wanted to reach out for her. It was dark in the room. He thought of Megan, Megan's laugh, which he had not heard for ages.

He remembered the last time he'd seen her. Two weeks ago, after such a long time. They'd talked for a while, and for a while everything seemed fine and there seemed to be some chance for them. He was out of the bin and teaching at the Hopkins and everything was fine. The key vault thing was finally going through, they'd just sent him the final design configuration and the Northrop design team had really done a good—

But in the morning she'd been angry with him. She said he was happy only because the project was going well. He was still a part of it, wasn't he? He still drew power and pleasure from its evil.

He'd gotten angry. Shouts, screams, accusations, the same old business, the air hot with neurotic fury. He'd watched her go off.

Still, she'd looked so damn beauti—

Certain things clicked in the machine of a brain he had and Peter recognized from the pattern that a wondrous possibility had just been opened.

But he also had a moment of real loneliness. Jesus, Megan, what the fuck have you done now? What the fuck have *I* done?

And then he thought, Where is Puller? Where is Puller?

They reached the lateral tunnel without much trouble, and Rat Team Alpha headed one way, toward the shaft called Alice. That left Team Baker to veer toward Elizabeth.

"We goin' to *fuck* this Elizabeth," said Walls. "We goin' crawl up this white bitch's pussy, and *fuck* her to death. Give her some lovin' like she never thought of. Once they go black, they never go back."

"Shut up," said Witherspoon, an edge on his voice.

"Man, you talk like you *married* to a white bitch."

"I am. Shut up."

"Man, no wonder you so mellow. Man, I was cashing in on white pussy every night, I tell you—"

"Shut up. Nobody talks about my wife like that. She's a terrific gal who just happens to be white, goddammit."

Walls snickered, a deep contemptuous sound. So rich. This jive-ass white boy nigger is full of himself, Mr. Delta Mean Motherfucker, see how he do if Charlie's up ahead. He shit up his pants real good.

He liked the darkness, the cool air of the tomb. The tunnel was narrowing, too, closing down. The initial shaft had been cleanly cut into the mountain, almost like a stairwell, its walls flat and more or less smooth. A little railroad track had run through it where the miners pushed their little trains. It had a comfy feel to it.

But now, after the separation of the teams, the walls were closing in. It was coolish and clammy in there; he could smell the coal dust in the air, and something else, too, a tang or something. Witherspoon's powerful beam cut like a sword all around, jiggering nervously this way and that, its white circle roaming all over the place like a man's hands on a woman's body. Meanwhile, Walls kept his beam straight ahead.

"Man, you must be nervous or something."

Witherspoon didn't say a thing. The night vision goggles pressed against his head tightly, pinching it, and it was less than pleasant. And he was a little jumpy, it was true. In Grenada he had been amazed by how un-nervous he was, but it had happened so fast, there wasn't *time* to be nervous. The stick had landed, they shucked their 'chutes and were hauling ass up this little ravine toward the airfield HQ, when literally, all hell had broken loose. Some lucky Cubie had been gazing skyward when the black-painted Charlie-130 Herc had flown in for the insertion, and had seen the black-clad commandos floating to earth.

And Jesus, after that, *forget* the mission, the job had just been to stay alive. It was like crawling through the Fourth of July, all the fireworks in the world floating out at you, trying to knock you off.

But this was different. Witherspoon hadn't thought a lot about the underground. He was Special Forces, Ranger, and Delta, the best of the best of the best. Courage was his profession. But, uh, like, a *tunnel*? In a *mountain*? He cleared his throat. Soon he'd have to face the horror of dumping the beam and going to infrared. Ceiling getting real low.

"Hey, man?" Walls's voice, soft now, its mocking edge gone. "Man, you scared? You ain't said much."

"I'm okay," Witherspoon said.

"Man, this ain't nothing. In the 'Nam, the tunnels so low you got to crawl through them, you know. And man, them people they shit in those tunnels, they got no other place to shit. And over the years, man, the shit mount. Man, finally, you crawling *through* shit. You think this is bad, you try crawling on your belly through shit waiting for some gook girl like that pretty number in the other tunnel waiting to stick a razor blade in your throat."

But this was plenty bad enough for Witherspoon.

He was really having trouble with his . . . breathing now. The blackness, the closeness of it, the sense of the tomb. And men had died here, hadn't they? Fifty years back, in this same hole, over a hundred of them.

"Rat Team Baker, do you copy? Baker, this is Rat Six, you guys copy?" The voice was loud in his ears.

"Roger and copy, Six," said Witherspoon into his Prick-88's hands-free mike.

"Jesus, you guys were supposed to log in fifteen minutes ago. What the hell is going on in there?" Something in Rat Six's white voice really irked Witherspoon.

"No sweat, Six, we're just bumbling along. Hey, hold your water, okay, Six?"

"Let's stick to radio SOP, Sergeant. You want to tell us what's up?"

"Affirmative, Six, we're through the main shaft and we've gotten into the lateral and we're looking for this Elizabeth. The farther out we get, the lower the ceiling is. This tunnel's drying up to nothing."

"How's your pal?"

"He's doing fine," said Witherspoon, sensing his partner next to him.

"Roger that, Baker, you guys stick to the schedule now, okay. You let us know anything turns up."

"So what's going on there?"

"National Guard guys got their butts shot off, that's what. These are mucho tough hombres, these guys, Baker, you watch your ass."

"Affirmative, Six, and out."

And then Walls said, "Shit, man, I think that's it."

His beam flicked out and nailed a gap in the wall, no bigger than a crawl space, low and ominous in the white shine of the bulb.

It was the tunnel called Elizabeth.

"Oh, baby," said Walls, "have I got a dick for you."

"Smoke," said Poo. "Smoke. It's burning. It's a fire."

They could see the column of smoke rising, drifting, on the wind. Several of the neighbors were out on their snowy lawns, staring.

"Herman, why is it burning?"

"It's an airplane," Herman said. "An airplane has crashed in the fields and now it is burning. It must be some kind of terrible accident."

They were in the basement, peering out of the small cellar window. The smoke smeared across the bright blue sky through the laceworks of the trees.

"Can we go look at it?"

"No," said Herman. "I think we'd better stay here. It will be very hot. The firemen will take care of it."

"Is the man all right?"

"The man?"

"The man that drives the airplane. Is he all right?"

"I'm sure he's all right. Poo, I'll tell you, they push a button and the tops fly off and they pop out. Just like toast from a toaster. And they float down to the ground under a big umbrella and they're all right."

"Do they get another airplane? If they break their airplane, do they get another airplane?"

"Oh, yes. They get another airplane."

Just then, the Burkittsville fire engine went crashing by the house, and headed out the road toward the field.

Beth Hummel looked at Herman now. She'd made the connection between the whirling jets and the crashed airplane and her vanished husband and Herman.

"Who are you? What do you want? Why are you here?"

"Please, lady," he said. "We mean you no harm. Please, okay, you just do what we want, no harm comes to nobody, okay? We're just guests, for a little while longer, okay. Then everybody's okay, just fine, super good. Okay?"

"Oh, Lord. Why? *Why is this happening?*"

"It has to happen," Herman said. "It has to happen. It's for everybody's own good."

Just then there was a knock at the door. They could hear it from downstairs. It grew louder.

*   *   *

Dick Puller put down the microphone, lit a cigarette. A loud roar rose and beat at them as four medevac choppers rushed overhead to the base of the mountain to pick up the wounded.

"How bad?" asked Skazy.

"He wasn't making a lot of sense," said Puller. "I gather it was pretty bad. Of the hundred and forty men in the company, he had confirms on forty fatals sure. Maybe fifty. He said he had a lot of men shot up. The walking wounded got a lot of them off the hill. Not too many guys left untouched. Unit morale shattered. Nonexistent. I told him he had to go back."

Puller smiled a crooked, sardonic smile.

"And?"

"And he told me to get fucked. His manners aren't any better than yours, Major."

"The CO?"

"Didn't make it back. He was last seen on the M-60, giving covering fire. I don't even know his name."

"I think it was Barnard."

"I think you're right," said Puller. He could see the choppers on the ground, far off, their rotors glistening in the bright sunlight, the dust and snow stirring and whirling. Tiny figures rushed around them. Above them, the mountain rose in a rainbow arc, implacable and immutable. The little red and white aerial seemed to wink at them over the black stain of the tarpaulin. They hadn't even found out what was under the tarp.

"You've got to send Delta in now, Colonel Puller. You can't let them have time to regroup or those men will have died for nothing."

"They were never ungrouped, Major Skazy. Don't you understand that yet? Delta goes when I say and not a second before. I'd advise you to back the fuck off, young Major," said Puller.

He fixed his eyes on Skazy, who met his gaze fiercely.

"When are we going?" the major said, his face impassive, his eyes unlit.

"After dark. We've got to let those rats see if they've got a chance at opening a back door. We've got to get Thiokol time to get us beyond the door of the elevator shaft. I'll get you your goddamned chance, Major. You have my word."

He turned and found a seat on a folding lawn chair some thoughtful trooper had pulled out for him. He checked his watch. There was going to be a long night ahead.

"Colonel Puller! Colonel Puller!"

It was Peter Thiokol, his demeanor adolescent and abandoned in excitement, jumping crazily as he ran toward them.

"Who would that be?" Herman demanded.

"I—I don't know," Beth Hummel stammered.

"Is it the airplane driver?" Poo asked.

"Mommy, I bet it's my teacher," said Bean. "They want to know why I'm not in school."

Herman pulled Beth close to him.

"Who?" he demanded.

"Herman, you're hurting Mommy," said Poo. "You'll make her cry. You'll make Mommy cry. Herman, don't hurt my mommy."

Poo began to cry.

"If it's a neighbor, they'll know I'm in here," said Beth.

Herman thought in a frenzy.

"All right," he said finally, "you go answer. Say nothing. Remember, I'll be behind the door. I'll hear it all. Don't do anything stupid. Please, these other men will be here with the children, don't do anything stupid, don't force us to do anything we don't want to do."

He released her.

"Don't do anything stupid. Please." He pressed the muzzle of the silenced Uzi against her ribs, just once, lightly, so she could feel it.

Beth climbed the steps. She could see the shape in the window of the door and went to it.

"Yes?"

God, it was Kathy Reed, from next door.

"Beth, what is going on, have you heard? Three planes have crashed. Someone says there's terrible shooting going on at South Mountain and that the state police have closed all the roads. There was an explosion on the road up to the mountain in the morning. They say there are helicopters in the valley and soldiers and—"

"I don't know. There's nothing on the news."

"God, do you suppose they have gas or something up there, and there's some kind of leak. What kind of telephone station could it be?"

"I—I don't know," said Beth. "If there were any danger, I'm sure the government would tell us."

"I'm so scared, Beth. Bruce is away. Beth, he's got the car. If there's an evacuation, will you take us? God, Beth, I've got the twins and—"

"Oh, Kathy, don't worry. I'll take you if it comes to that. I swear it. You go inside now and relax. If I hear anything, I'll tell you. I promise."

"You won't forget?"

"No, I swear. I swear it."

"Thank you, Beth. It means so much."

She went back to her own house. Beth closed the door.

"Mommy, why was Mrs. Reed crying? Was she scared of Herman?"

"No, honey. No, she was just upset. Was that all right?"

"That was fine," said Herman. "That was okay, lady, you did real good."

"Who are you?" said Poo. "You're not from around here at all, are you? You're from far away."

"Very far away," he answered.

"Yes, what is it, Dr. Thiokol?" Dick Puller asked, pulling himself away from Skazy.

"Something's just occurred to me. I—I should have thought of it earlier." He was momentarily put off by the sense of distance between the two officers; he had the sudden, awkward sense of being an outsider at some kind of intense family dispute. But he plunged on.

"It may be of some help. You ought to hear this, too, Major Skazy."

"Go on."

Peter said, "Well, we think we know who compromised South Mountain. I've told the FBI. All right?"

"Yes?"

"Now, we think this person was photographing documents and plans in my own home. I was very sloppy, it was—"

"Just go on," said Puller.

"Well, this person left my house before the planning was quite complete. Do you understand?"

Neither of them did, apparently. They stared at Peter as if he were stupid. Military men, he told himself, be patient. Explain it slowly. Connect all the dots for them.

"She left *before* the key vault was designed. So whoever planned whatever's going on up there never knew about the key vault. Until—"

"Until when?"

"She came back two weeks ago. She came back to tell me she'd thought it over and she just wanted to see me—well, I'll spare you the pitiful details. But she was in the house. I slept with her a last time. The vault had been improved, it was designed, they were implementing it, and they sent me the dope. She could have seen it."

"Dr. Thiokol, in all due respect, I don't know what the hell you're driving at here," said Puller, glowering furiously at him, almost rigid with impatience. "We already know there's been an intelligence leak of—"

Asshole! Peter thought. Stupid asshole!

"If they know about the key vault, they found out very late. *Two weeks ago!* Probably, maybe, possibly too late to figure it into their original operational plans. If that's the case, they probably didn't bring a welder along. So they would have had to pick one up *here.* Don't you see? They would have had to hire one or kidnap one or something like that. Now, if they did that, they wouldn't try and hold him for two weeks. They'd do it right before they jumped and they'd do it close by. I'm saying, maybe we can trace it."

"All right."

Their eyes remained abstracted, unfocused, lacking that primal spark of inspiration. They still didn't quite see it.

"Look, if you were going to force a man to perform a job for you, how would you get him to do it? Think of a bank president robbers take in order to get him to open the safe. How do they do it? Well, they find hostages. They leave somebody at his house with his wife and kids, right? Now, maybe that's what they've done here, maybe there's a wife and some kids and some very bad baby-sitters not too far from where we stand. And suppose—"

"*Prisoners!*" said Skazy, getting to it first. "Yes, prisoners. We get prisoners, we find out what and who we're up against."

But Dick Puller was already on the move. He hurried into the command post and quickly located his young assistant from the FBI, James Uckley, who for the past several hours had been ripping teletype info and filing reports himself to the Bureau on the operation and feeling sorry for himself for incurring Puller's wrath.

It didn't take Puller long to explain what he wanted, and from then it didn't take Uckley long to find what they were looking for. He began with the Yellow Pages and started calling welding services. At the fifth entry—Jackson Hummel, 19 Main Street, Burkittsville, 555–2219—there was no answer. He then called the Burkittsville police station, talked to a sergeant and had a request; the sergeant returned the call almost immediately. No, it did not appear that Jack Hummel had opened his service for business that day. The cop had asked on both sides and found that Jack was expected in Boonsboro that day at the Chalmers plant. Uckley called Chalmers, to discover that no, goddammit, the welder had not showed up, nobody knew where he'd gone, maybe he was sick. He called the cop back and asked if Jack could be sick. The cop didn't know but said he could stop by Jack's house which was just up the road. It would be real easy, the cop said.

No, said Uckley. They'd handle it themselves, but please stand by in case further help was needed. His next phone call was to the elementary school, where it only took him a few minutes to learn from the principal that Jack Hummel did have two daughters, Elizabeth called Bean and Phyllis called Poo, and that indeed both of them were unexpectedly absent today.

Uckley thanked her and got off the phone.

"I think we've got a Condition Red," he told Dick Puller. "It looks like they've got this guy Hummel in the mountain—*he's* their cutter—and his wife and kids in his house."

Puller nodded.

"All right," he said. "Major Skazy, I want four of your best operators."

"Yes, sir, I can—"

"Just go get them, Major. Get them now."

"Yes, sir," said Skazy, clearly irked at how summarily he was being dismissed.

Puller pulled Uckley aside, out of the hearing range of the others.

"I think you'll have to handle this one. He'll get you those Delta specialists and you ought to have police backup, but don't let the police get too close. They might mess things up. You never know how well these little country-town cops are going to handle heavy business. Besides, you'll do better with fewer rather than more people. But we need to take that house down and we need to talk to those people."

He looked at his watch.

"And we need to do it fast."

"Yes, sir," said Uckley, swallowing.

He looked hard at Uckley. The young man returned the stare, but seemed scattered, his thoughts not quite together.

"You've had SWAT training, I assume?"

"Yes," Uckley said, barely remembering the frenzied week four years earlier at Quantico.

"All right, good. You're clear? I mean, absolutely clear? There's a mother and two little girls in that house. I'm sure they are lovely people. But you must understand what's important, you and the men you take into that house."

Uckley looked away, through the window. The mountain gleamed.

"The men in that house are important. The mother, the two girls—" Dick hesitated a second, then plunged ahead in full adult awareness of the ruthless thing he was about to do. Did he have to *say* it, actually put it in words? Uckley shot a squirrely look back at him. Dick could tell from the hurt and confusion lurking in his eyes that yes, he *did* have to say it.

"Look, I have two daughters myself. There's nothing more precious to me in the world than the two of them, and certainly that's true for this Hummel too. But you've got to think hard here, Uckley. You have to see through to what's important. You have to weigh the potential immediate loss against the other, far greater, far more devastating loss. That's what we're paid to do."

Like an idiot, the young federal agent simply looked at him.

"The mother and the two girls aren't important. You may have to lose them. If it comes to it, you'll *have* to lose them rather than risk losing the prisoners. The Delta people are very good; they've been trained to take down a building and set free the hostages. But they'll shoot for the head, and you've got to stop them. You've got to take prisoners, Jim. Do you understand that?"

Uckley said he did.

The answer to all problems is vodka, Gregor Arbatov had decided. It was Russia's main contribution to the culture of the world, more important than Tolstoi, more passionate than Dostoevski, more lasting than world communism.

He now sat with a glass of it in a dark bar called Jake's on Route 1 in the seedy little Maryland town of Laurel, not far from Columbia. He was exceedingly happy. A beautiful American lady of perhaps sixty with perhaps half her own teeth and none of her own hair and a tattoo had just brought him a refill, with a golden smile and a hearty laugh. He loved her. She was a saint. Saint Teresa of the Order of the Vodka. She reminded him of his wife, whom he hadn't seen in years.

But what he loved most was what the vodka did to him. It blurred his terrors, it mellowed his brain. It seemed to leak straight through his skull and penetrate to the very center of the organ itself, mollifying, subjectifying, calming, soothing, as it went.

"Ah, Miss. Another, please."

"Sure, hon. You surely do sop it up."

He smiled. His teeth were not terribly impressive either. Her eyes were merry.

"You kinda cute," she said, handing the glass down to him. "Bartender's a close personal friend of mine. He said this one's on the house."

Gregor smiled. Somewhere under the bulge of his gut that hung down over his lap his dick stirred.

But then he thought of young Klimov. Trying to kill him. And his dick withered.

Clouds came across his wide face; fear flashed in his little eyes. The waitress was gone. The only thing that was there was the whisper of the blade as it darted by him, and the thrum of its vibration as it plunged into the car roof.

Gregor blinked, came out of it, and dived into the vodka.

Yes, so much better.

Gregor sat back. He had figured it out.

It was Klimov. Really, he could almost sympathize with the younger man. He wished to move his least productive agent out. He could not simply fire him, the time had passed for that, he had fired too many others, if he fires him then it reflects poorly on Klimov. Therefore, with a little ingenuity, perhaps aided by the intercession of his powerful uncle Arkady Pashin of GRU, he penetrates the Pork Chop security arrangements, sets up a phony meet, and then arranges for his rotten apple to die.

The results are interesting and beneficial to everyone except poor Gregor, who in theory is now dead, six inches of Spetsnaz blade cleaving his fat chest. But Klimov has eliminated his bad apple in a dramatic way, with a minimum of personal embarrassment. He can be protected in this maneuver by the importunings of Pashin, watching over his little nephew, wielding his great power and influence like a sword. At the same time, Pork Chop has been discredited. To what purpose? Perhaps whoever controls Pork Chop has accumulated too much power in the higher ranks and must therefore be destroyed by a rival. Surely the rival in question would be, again, Pashin.

Good God, realized poor Gregor, he had been targeted for execution by a senior general in the GRU, one of the most powerful men in the Soviet Union.

There was only one answer: vodka.

"Miss. Another one."

Gregor swallowed the liquid. It dashed down his throat. He felt his face burning red. He looked at the empty glass in his fat hand.

Lumbering with agility that might have surprised his many enemies in this world, Gregor made it to the men's room, pulled out a pocketful of change, and with studied labor and enormous effort called the one person in the world he felt he could trust, Magda Goshgarian.

The phone rang time and time again. Finally, her groggy voice came on.

"Magda!"

"Tata! I am stunned. What on—"

"Magda, listen please. I need a favor. I will be continually in your service if you can help me. Please, I cannot begin to tell you how—"

"Stop sniveling, Tata. Are you drunk? You sound pathetic."

"Magda, something is going on."

"Yes, it is. Young Klimov wants to bite your head off."

"No, something else. Magda, I am—indisposed."

"Is it a woman, Tata? Some American bitch with a baby in her belly that came from your tiny dick?"

"No, no. It has nothing to do with women. It has to do with the fact that I must stay clear of the embassy for a few days now while I sort some matters out."

"You're going over. Tata, don't you implicate me, they are watching *me* too. I swear, Tata, if you go, you'll leave such a mess—"

"No, I swear. I swear on my father's grave and the great Marx's image that I'll remain true. It's just that for technical reasons, I am indisposed tonight. Alas, I have cipher clerk duty in the Wine Cellar tonight. I—"

"Tata, I—"

"I know you did it last night. But since you have therefore rested today, you are therefore automatically my replacement. I call merely to ask you to take the duty for me. You can tell Klimov I called you from my afternoon pickup and that it was going very slowly for me and that I was afraid therefore I would not be back in time and that I therefore asked you to take the watch. And that you have not heard from me since. I think you'll find him surprisingly agreeable."

"Tata, I—"

"Please, darling. I'll buy you a dinner. I'll buy you the most extraordinary dinner in some ridiculously expensive Georgetown restaurant. I have a little squirrel fund hidden away, that's all, and I can afford it, I promise."

"Tata—"

"Magda, you know you cannot deny me one single thing. It is not your nature to deny me."

"You are such a sniveling, craven fool."

"Magda, you have no idea how desperately I need the help. You'll help?"

At last she surrendered.

"All right."

"I love you, darling."

"It means I'll have to do double duty tomorrow. My system will be upset for weeks."

"Pick your restaurant, Magda, and you shall have whatever you want."

Gregor hung up. Now, if he could call the other woman in his life, Molly Shroyer, and if she had found anything for him, then maybe, maybe he could make himself seem so important to Klimov that the young killer would desist.

Gregor dialed the second number. Molly answered curtly and he unlimbered the Sears code, then hung up and waited. And waited. And waited. He hung around the bathroom so long he thought he might be arrested for perversions, or beaten up by truck drivers or some such—

It rang.

Gregor picked it up.

"Gregor, I've got only a second," she said.

"Darling, I—"

"Gregor, shut up! Something big is happening out in Maryland, so big they won't tell even us. All the senators on the committee and the senior staff have been to the White House and there's some kind of news blackout, but nobody's talking. The only thing is that it's very, very serious."

"Out in Maryland?" Gregor said. Then he remembered the airplanes roaring over the Columbia Mall.

"But what could—"

"Gregor, as soon as I know, I'll let you know. I have to run now, love. Really, it's serious."

"Yes, I—"

The phone clicked dead.

Damn! he thought. I need vodka.

Phuong loved the darkness, the stillness, the sense of being totally alone. She felt whole in darkness.

The narrow walls of the mining shaft seemed to be leaning in, and she could feel the man beside her breathing hard. She could sense his fear.

Yet for Phuong the tunnels meant one thing. They meant safety. Up above, her child had been turned to ashes and shards by napalm. Up above, her father had died, her mother had died, her brother had been maimed. Her sunny village was blasted into nothingness by terror bombers. Hard men in helicopters came to kill them, and to poison the jungle. So she faced the darkness with something close to peace. She knew no fear. Her feet found the way. She sensed the walls and the low ceiling and the rough transit of the floor. The darkness was everywhere.

Teagarden, the American, fought against it. His beam was a desperate protest against it, a plea for mercy almost. His beam flashed nervously. In the tunnels in her homeland, one never used light. Light was an American invention; it was the invention of men who feared the dark. But Phuong and the men and women who fought with her over the long years never used light; they learned, instead, to feel their way with their hands. They learned to sense, from variations in the atmosphere and gradations in odor, the approach of strangers.

Mother, can you smell him, her daughter asked from her heart. He's terrified. His body stinks with fear.

I smell him, too, she replied.

Ahead, the tunnel narrowed even further.

"Sister Phuong, one moment please," the American said in Vietnamese. "I have to report."

He knelt, turned his beam off. The darkness was complete. She heard him fumbling.

"Rat Six, this is Team Alpha, we're about seven hundred yards in, no sign of this tunnel Alice yet. Do you copy, Six?"

"Alpha, that's an affirmative, good and clear."

"Uh, Six, we'll keep on picking our way along."

"Go to it, Alpha. We're counting on you. How's your partner?"

"She's real stable, Six, wish I could say the same for myself. Out, now, Six."

"Roger that and out, Alpha."

He flicked his beam back on.

"Are you ready, Sis?" he said in Vietnamese.

"Yes."

"Then let's go on."

"Brother Dee-gard-ahn, why do you come? Why not just stay here? I'll go on. You're very scared, Brother, I can tell. I know my way. I won't get lost."

"I have to work the radio, Sis."

"Brother, tunnels are no place for terror. Fear, yes. Fear, always. Fear, importantly. But terror, no, because terror leads to panic. Not many people can fight in a tunnel. Not being one of them is no disgrace. We learned it because it was the only way we had against your flying demons and terror bombers."

"I'm not one of them, you're saying."

"I can tell, Brother. I can sense it."

"No, it's all right. It's just walking, I can handle it. There's no fighting, it's just walking." He smiled with a great deal of effort.

"Then let's go, Brother American," she said.

Alex, in the lull after the failed attack, scampered over his position checking on his men, telling them how well they had done.

"Is that all they'll send, do you think?" he was asked.

"No, they'll come again. And again. And again. I think the troops they send against us next will be better. Finally, they'll send the very best. It'll be a night fight, great fun."

Morale was high. The boys seemed to be holding together very well. Down in the missile silo, the general reported good progress on the cutting. It would be sooner than everybody thought. He'd lost only ten dead and had eleven wounded, this from the terrifying air assault and the infantry assault. He had ample supplies of ammunition left. He was in an excellent situation, all things considered. Only two things really bothered him. First, the loss of one of his two light machine guns in the infantry assault, and second, that he had used so many of the Stinger missiles in defending against the air attack. He had only seven left.

"Sir, great shooting on that last bird," someone called. "You can still see her burning down on the plain." And you could: the smoke rose still from the wreck, drifted up through the bright sky, where it shredded and dissipated in the wind.

"No, nothing," said Alex. "It was just luck." Of course it hadn't been. When the last plane came in by itself, it had been Alex with the M-60 who alone had refused to dive, even when the cannon shells were cutting away at him. He'd tracked the pilot all the way, and when the plane had ruddered hard to the left, he'd jumped up from the gun position like a duck hunter and held the weapon in his arms, pumping his rounds into the craft. He'd seen the tracers flick into the bubble cockpit, seen the bright glass haze as they tore through and the plane began to wobble, then never gathered enough altitude to make it out of the dive, and sank to the ground.

Alex had never shot down an airplane before. He felt queerly pleased.

"Now, back to the digging," he said. "Enough congratulations. Time to get back to work. Whose turn is it? Whose shift? Red Platoon?"

"Blue Platoon," the call came. "Red Platoon's already dug down to hell."

There was some laughter.

"All right," Alex said, loving them, "Blue Platoon, in the trenches under the canvas. Red Platoon's turn to sunbathe on the perimeter."

"But Blue Platoon shot down the helicopter. Don't we get a reward?"

"Lucky shot," yelled one of the boys of Red Platoon. "Now you'll dig till you've blisters the size of coins, just like—"

But Alex interrupted the horseplay.

"You said the helicopter went down? I didn't see it crash."

There was a moment of silence.

"Sir, we shot down a helicopter. It went over the hill and crashed."

Alex listened carefully. He remembered the medevac chopper taking off at the beginning of the assault, but it should have hovered downslope. It clearly wasn't a gunship, because it hadn't brought any fire to bear on his position. But why would a medevac chopper have ventured over the firefight, particularly when it was so easy to avoid it? The more he thought about it, the more it bothered him. Then he said, "Everybody who fired on the helicopter, fall in on me, please."

In the end about twenty men from Blue Platoon came over and gathered around Alex.

"Tell me about this helicopter," Alex said. "One of you. Slowly. Not all at once. The man who spoke first."

"Sir," the boy eventually said in slow country rhythms. "Sir, during the last run of the aerial attack, a helicopter flew low over the trees. We saw it only very late in its approach, because everyone was undercover from the airplanes. Naturally—" he clapped his rifle, a Fabrique Nationale FAL, "I fired on it."

"What kind of helicopter?"

"UH-1B. The Huey, so famous from Vietnam."

"You hit it?"

"I—I *think* so, sir."

"How many rounds?"

"Sir?"

"How many rounds did you put into it? What kind of sight picture did you have? Were you leading it? Were you in the full or semiautomatic mode? Where were you firing?"

The boy was silent, baffled.

"Please be honest with me," said Alex. "I mean you no disrespect. You are a brave and dedicated man. But I have to know the answers to these questions as completely as you can tell me."

"Sir, then the truth is, I fired hurriedly. I had no time to really aim competently. I was firing semiautomatic and perhaps I got off seven or eight rounds."

"Did you see any damage? I mean, ruptures in the steel, smoke, flames, blown rotors, that sort of thing?"

"Not really, sir. It was so fast."

"How about any of you others. Who else thinks they scored hits?"

A few hands rose.

"Full-auto or semi?"

The answers were all semi; the stories were all the same: jerked shots fired desperately at a flashing target, no real sight pictures, less than a magazine apiece fired at the machine.

"Yet it crashed?"

"Yessir. It crossed the crest, whirled down the mountain, out of control. We lost sight of it from here. But there was an explosion at the base of the mountain."

"Did you see it hit?"

"No, sir. It hit behind some trees. Down there you can see how thick the trees are. It hit right there. A few seconds later there was an explosion."

"Was the explosion exactly at the point of impact?"

"Sir, it's hard to say. It seemed to be more or less at the point of impact. Perhaps the machine bounced when it hit, then exploded. It's—"

But Alex was already gone.

"Sergeant," he shouted, "I want you to put together a team of ten of your very best men. I think something's up, something I don't like. I don't know what. I want you to go down the hill and check out that helicopter wreck."

1600

"I don't know," said Delta Three. "I hate to go in blind. It's against everything they teach us." He was looking through binoculars from well back in the room of a house on Main Street, in Burkittsville, at the front of Jack Hummel's place some two hundred yards down the road.

"We don't have time for a recon," said Jim Uckley. "Listen, it's even possible there's *no one* in there except the mother and her two sick little girls."

"Then what happens," said Delta Three, "if I get a peripheral cue, turn and fire and blow away a child? It's no good, Mr. Uckley. I'm not going to risk civilians like that. I couldn't live with myself if—"

Some Delta! thought Uckley.

"Look, man," he said, "we don't have a lot of time. We got to help those guys on the mountain. We've got to improvise something."

"I'm not going in without a floorplan, sure information on how many guys there are and a good idea of where they are in the house and where these children might be. And I'm not going in without multiple simultaneous entries. You're too fat a target. I don't mind taking chances. I was hit twice in Vietnam, in fact. But goddammit, I'm not going in and risk kids' lives."

Delta Three was a sanctimonious southerner in his late thirties with the righteous jaw set of a zealot. He was rawboned and tough, a master sergeant. Uckley hated him. The other three Deltas—he didn't have time to learn their names so he'd simply christened them Deltas One through Four—seemed like decent kids. But goddamn this adult!

"Officer," Uckley called to the Burkittsville cop who was with them in the house. "Any chance you could, uh, get us a floorplan or something. So we knew—"

"No," said the cop. "That house is one hundred years old and they didn't make floorplans in those days, they just built 'em and built 'em a damn sight better 'n they do now."

Great. Another zealot who loved to express his opinions. The cop was about fifty-five and plainly pissed off that all this government beef had come gunslinging into his town. But in a phase four emergency, federal officers called the shots, and he'd buy the idea that young Uckley was calling these.

"Neighbors," said Delta Four. "They'd have been in the house, right? Maybe you could round one up and get some kind of a drawing or diagram. Then we'd at least have some idea."

The cop chewed this one over. Finally, he allowed that Kathy Reed lived next door.

"Call her," said Uckley. "Tell her it's an emergency, ask her to walk down the street to us."

"That's good," said Delta Four. "Maybe we can rock and roll after all."

In a few minutes, Kathy Reed, her twin boys, Mick and Sam, and a scroungy mutt that turned out to be named Theo showed up. Kathy was in her housedress still and looked as though a few days had passed since she'd last washed her hair.

"Bruce is away," she began to explain, "I'm sorry about the way I look, but it's so hard to—"

"Mrs. Reed?" Uckley asked. "I'm James Uckley, Special Agent, Federal Bureau of Investigation. These men here with me are a special assault team from the Army's Delta Group."

He watched her mouth lengthen, then form the perfect rictus of an O. She was a woman who at one time or other might have been attractive but had been ground to a nub by the trenchwork of motherhood. She swallowed, her eyes going big, then said, "Is this about the mountain. There's something going on on the mountain, right?"

"Yes, this does have to do with the mountain. Now, what I wanted to ask you about was your neighbor, Mrs. Hummel."

"Beth? Is Beth in trouble?"

"Well, that's what I want you to tell me. Did you talk to her today?"

"Yes, sir. About an hour ago."

"And how did she seem?"

"Uh, the same."

"The same?"

"It was just Beth, that's all. *I* was the scared one. Because I thought there was gas or an atom bomb on the mountain. She said she'd drive us out of here if there was an evacuation. Bruce has the car. He travels a lot."

"Did she invite you in?"

"Uh, no."

"Was that unusual?"

"Well, we have coffee nearly every morning. Beth's my best friend. She's *everybody's* best friend. I guess it was."

"Was she nervous? Unsettled?"

"Come to think of it, yes, I suppose she was."

"What about her kids?"

"What about them?"

"Did she say anything about them being sick?"

"Sick! What have they got? Sam was with Poo all yesterday. That means Sam will be coming down with it. Did she tell you they were sick?"

"They're not in school. She called in."

"That's peculiar. I *know* she would have said something about it. But she didn't mention it."

"Mrs. Reed, I'd like you to talk to the sergeant here. I want you to draw us a diagram of Mrs. Hummel's house. Meanwhile, I think I'll go down there and knock on the door and see what I can see."

"Be careful," said Delta Three.

"Oh, I will," said Uckley.

The knock on the door surprised them. Herman looked at his men, then at the lady and her children. Goddamn! Who could this be?

"All right," he said. "As before. Remember, no fancy stuff, lady. These men here are with your children. You don't want anything happening, do you understand?"

Beth Hummel nodded gravely.

"Don't hurt my children."

"Nobody gets hurt," said Herman.

He knelt at the foot of the cellar steps, crouching in the darkness. His silenced Uzi covered the entrance. He watched the lady walk to the door, peek out, then open it.

"Mrs. Hummel?"

"Yes."

Herman could see a bland young man in a sports coat and tie under a bland black raincoat. He looked to be about thirty.

"Hi, my name's Jim Uckley, I'm with Ridgley Refrigeration, we're putting in the plant out in Keedysville. Listen, I had an appointment with your husband today at two and he wasn't there. I was just wondering if—"

"Oh, I'm terribly sorry, Mr. Uckley. Jack's in Middletown. There was a breakdown in the high school heating system. The main duct split and he had to go weld it up. I'm real sorry if he missed his appointment, but sometimes these emergencies come up and—"

"Oh, listen, that's all right. I understand. Would it be all right if I came in and—"

Herman put his hand on the Uzi trigger and drew the weapon to his shoulder. Let this man come in and he'd squeeze off a three-round burst.

"Mr. Uckley, have you had the flu this year? It's horrible stuff. Would you believe that *both* my girls are down with it. Why, Bean's been vomiting for *two* days. It's a horrible thing. And the house is a disaster. You can imagine, with two sick children, how terrible it is."

"Well, ma'am, I sure don't want to add to your difficulties. Maybe you could tell your husband I'll call him in the morning. It's a pretty big job we have in mind, and we'd like to talk to him soon as we can."

"Yes, sir, Mr. Uckley. I'll see that he gets the message."

She closed the door.

Herman slithered to the window, peeked over the edge, and watched the young man mosey down the walk and climb into a little blue car and drive away. He raced to the back of the house and followed the car after it had turned up the block and headed on down to Route 17 and out of town. All right, maybe it's just a man about a job, he thought as he lost track of the car.

"Yep, they're there, you bet, I could almost smell 'em," said Uckley.

"How many?" asked Delta Three.

"I couldn't exactly *ask*," said Uckley, who was feeling somewhat heroic in regard to his exploit. "So what have you got?"

"Three-bedroom house, living room, dining room, kitchen, pantry downstairs. Stairs up front from the living room and out back from the dining room. Tough to crack with five guys."

"Hmmm," said Uckley. He was basically an accountant. He had an M.B.A. from Northwestern and had heard that five years in the Federal Bureau of Investigation Embezzlement Division looked great on a résumé, especially if you wanted to go into tax accountancy, where the bucks were. He was engaged to a girl named Sally and had been born and raised in Rockford, Illinois. He had begun the day going over the books of Mid-Maryland Federal Savings, where the vice-president had fled with over $48,000 in bank funds, looted from a variety of accounts over the past several weeks. The man had left with his twenty-three-year-old secretary, leaving behind a forty-two-year-old wife and three children.

"Tough to crack especially when we don't know how many there are or where they are."

"Is it best to infiltrate slowly or hit 'em with a rush?" Uckley asked.

"The Israelis like to go in fast, low, and hard. GSG-9 will wait until the cows come home, inserting their operators a lick at a time."

"That's a tough place to rush," said Uckley. "You could stage from Mrs. Reed's place next door, but nothing on the other side." He looked at his watch. Time was really flying. It would be dark soon.

"So, who's got an idea?"

They just looked at each other.

What am I doing here, Uckley thought. He wished he could concentrate a little bit better.

"Look, what about this?" said Delta Three. "We set off a smoke grenade in Mrs. Reed's house, call the fire department. Say, you and me ride in on the truck, rush up the lawn. Except we hit the Hummel place instead. We're in raincoats. Meanwhile Rick and Gil move in on the place from behind; they go through that back door, into the kitchen. We go in, yelling 'Fire, fire, you have to evacuate.' We've got our pieces under our raincoats. Then we take 'em out."

It was better than anything Uckley could come up with.

Megan Wilder took the tin can and put it in a vise. She spun the handle, watched the tin crumple. The can imploded and ruptured, achieving various interesting configurations of destruction as she drew the jaws of the vise closer and closer. It finally became a fully formed blossom of catastrophe, the light glinting in fascinating patterns off its tortured sides.

Quickly she spun the handle the other way, plucked the crippled thing from the vise's grip, and took it over to a table. There she had several dozen other crumpled cans.

She stared at them. Some had collapsed neatly; there was something bland and banal in their demise. Others, like this one, had a curious inner vitality and force; they fought the jaws with every last shred of resilience. And when they died reluctantly, they died most spectacularly, forming orchids of broken metal. Of the dozens there were perhaps less than five that really touched her, that *spoke* to her, including the last one. She took them all to another part of the room.

Megan Wilder specialized in what she called "constructions" or, sometimes, "destructions," depending on her mood and her honesty. Their form attempted to push out the boundaries of art; they would not fit into conventional categories. They were not quite sculptures, because although they occupied space and had plastic form, they had at the same time not escaped entirely from the tyranny of the frame and the organizing impulse of two dimensions. They were meant, in short, to be viewed only from one angle, and although certain influential critics had denounced this as cowardice to the tyranny of convention, she could not force herself to abandon it.

But neither, of course, were they paintings, although they depended for their impact on color as it defines form. For she implanted the twisted tin buds with other shapes that took her fancy—beer bottles, for example, the insides of burnt-out calculators, filaments from light bulbs, this, that, and the other thing, the detritus of American society—and stapled them inside rough frames and shelves that she had constructed herself, against a plasterboard backing. When by accident she found harmony, she destroyed it. She was interested in disharmony, the radical lack of symmetry and structure that somehow especially pleased her since Ari had left. Anyway, when she got these items arranged just so, she painted them. Not flat black like Nevelson's bleak little masterpieces, but comic-book colors, hot pink, Popsicle orange, sunburst yellow, mashed-banana yellow, a rainbow, a riot of flat, harsh, hot colors. There were critics who also despised this. Color is dead, they had decreed, and it irked them that she hadn't read their position papers. They could really be nasty, too, particularly one faggot on *Art News*.

It didn't matter. Megan was really beyond other people now. After all the years and all the pain, she'd finally fought her way to her own private place. She'd finally found her own voice. It felt authentic and passionate. It satisfied her.

The work was going so well now, it was a shame it had to end. In fact, the imminence of its end gave it all a certain perishability and poignance that made her almost cry, something no man had ever been able to do, short of punching her, and both Peter and Ari had punched her. You could forgive Peter, he was an asshole genius with an IQ of about 900 and an emotional age of about eleven, but Ari had been different; she had expected so much more.

Thus when the knock came and she became aware of the shapes of men in suits moving around the studio, up on its roof, out back in the frozen garden, it did not surprise her, but merely filled her with regret. It had to happen sooner or later and it was happening sooner. What seemed to her tragic was that she'd never see the series of constructions played out unimpinged upon, untainted by the inevitable scandal.

"It's open," she called.

There were three of them, Gentiles, strong-looking older men without irony or outrage in their eyes. They identified themselves as something or other from the FBI; she immediately forgot their names and ranks. Their blankness surprised her. She didn't see the need for it. People could be so cruel. They said she ought to call a lawyer. She didn't feel like it. She just wanted to go on working, she was so close to being finished.

"Do you have a lawyer, Ms. Wilder?"

"I have an agent," she said.

"It's not the same thing."

"I suppose I have a lawyer. My father would be able to call him, I suppose."

"I hope you'll cooperate with us, Ms. Wilder. Time is very important, and your cooperation would help you enormously later."

"I'll make you a deal," she said.

"Ms. Wilder, we don't have a lot of time. Time is of the essence."

Original line, she thought. Where do they get these guys? You'd think they'd at least go to the trouble to find someone that she could relate to. But then she understood that in the whole apparatus there was nobody she could relate to; by the very act of joining the apparatus, such a man would forever lose purchase on the possibility of relating to her.

"Here's the deal. You let me work for a little while longer. Turn on your little tape machines or whatever. You let me work, and as I work I'll answer any question you want. Is that fair?"

"I take it you understand you're in grave trouble."

"I guess I always have been," she said.

She was a beautiful woman, with a high, aristocratic face, a strong nose, and piercingly intelligent eyes. She had a supple body under jeans and a paint-spattered smock. She wore black high-topped Reeboks and round, owlish glasses. Her hair, black and lustrous, was drawn back tightly into a surprisingly girlish ponytail.

"We have information that suggests—"

"Let me just start where you want to end up. Won't that save some time?"

"Yes," the older man said.

She took a deep breath.

"Well, I did it. Yes. Whatever he says I did, I did it."

"You gave foreign agents certain materials which—"

She laughed, involuntarily. "Foreign agents" sounded so forties.

"Materials?" she said. "I gave them *everything.*"

They just looked at her.

"I had a little camera. Called a Minox, very cute. Later, sometimes, I'd just haul the stuff to the library and make Xerox copies of it. He made it so easy. He was so sloppy. The stuff was everywhere, he just left it lying around. He must have been in love with me or something."

Then she looked at them hard.

"But the joke's on him. And you. I gave it to a guy who's on our side. He's just another Jew. He's an Israeli. The Israelis are our side. So you can do to me what you did to Jonathan Pollard, and it doesn't matter. Throw me in prison and send the key to the dead-letter bin. What do you think of that?"

"Maybe you'd better start at the beginning," said the oldest of the men.

"Do you have ten hours and a bottle of very cold white wine?"

"We have ten minutes and a thermos of very hot coffee."

"Then I guess I'd better hurry," she said, and began to explain.

*　　*　　*

The shattered unit collapsed in the snow reminded Dick Puller of his own A-detachment after the fight at Anh Tran in July of '65. When the 82d had finally fought its way through, the survivors of the thirty-eight-day siege by the NVA in division strength just watched them come, numb and flat. He knew the feeling: the sense that your bones have melted, the way your brain fills with white fog and your joints are stiff and slow; and another thing, too, like persistent background music that will not go away—the terrible guilt you feel at the whimsy of the battle and all the good people who've died in spaces you've just moved out of or are about to move into. He shook his head. At the end, they'd depressed the 105s point-blank and fired canisters of fleschette into the NVA waves that had come at them as the perimeter shrank so small you couldn't even call in Tac Air. Dick shivered. Fuck if that hadn't been a fight. That was the fight to end all fights, a month of taking frontals and watching them burn away your best people until you were left with a shell of your team and less than a third of your brave, tough little Nungs. In the end we won. But won what, and why? He could still taste the bitterness.

Bravo, having straggled down the mountain, had made a stab at reforming just at its base, where the forest met the meadow and where the road began its switchbacks up to the summit. Dick rode in with the first medevac chopper and with several of the Delta officers to debrief the survivors.

Now he walked among them. The boys sat singly in the snow, having found one another and then collapsed in a loose circle, their olive drab uniforms dark blots against the blinding whiteness that surrounded them. Many were wounded though many were not. Some had weapons, some did not. Some cried. Some laughed hysterically; some merely stared at Dick with furious, dark hostility. Some chattered helplessly with the cold, their lips blue, their faces drawn and slack. They looked exhausted or sick. Their young faces had the shock of nihilism. Their gear was all fouled up, their pouches open, their straps tangled, their boots unbloused. Not many had helmets.

He knelt by a boy, one of the few who still had his weapon. He didn't have his helmet, but he had his weapon.

"Pretty tough up there, Specialist?"

The boy's eyes swung to him at an idiot's cadence. The boy just looked at him like a jerk. What, twenty-two? In 'Nam they were younger, even, in their teens. Dick, then a captain, had even had a seventeen-year-old; the gooks had caught him coming in off an ambush patrol and he'd died screaming in his own guts out beyond the wire.

"Son, I'm talking to you," Dick said in a stronger voice.

"Huh? Oh, sorry, uh, sir."

"They hit you pretty bad?"

"They had us cold. Just cut us up."

"Did you do much damage?"

"Sir?"

"I said, did you hurt them?"

The question had no meaning.

Dick seized the M-16 from the boy's limp hands, brought it to his nose, pulled the charging handle under the sight assembly. The ejector port snapped open; Dick sniffed the breech. It smelled of clean oil but not powder. He could see an immaculate cartridge sitting in the chamber.

"You didn't see any targets?"

The boy looked at him, ashamed.

"I—I was too scared to think about that," he said.

"I see," said Dick. "Well, you've got a few hours to pull yourself together. Then tonight you go back. Tonight we all go back."

The boy looked at him.

"I don't want to go back," he said baldly.

"Neither do I," said Dick, "but I don't see anyone else here, do you?"

"No, sir."

Dick stood, winked at the kid, earning a little smile.

"I'll try to do better tonight, sir," the kid said.

"You don't have to do better, you just have to be there."

He could see the other Delta officers moving through the collection of dazed men while the Delta medics worked to patch the walking wounded.

Finally, Skazy came over to him.

"It's not good," he said.

"Anybody get close enough to get a peep under the canvas?"

"Nobody got within a hundred yards of their position."

"So who are we fighting, Major? What's your reading?"

"Whoever he is, he's very good. He read the terrain, so he knew exactly the point of attack. He put his automatics in the center of the line and he must have linked belts. The volume of fire was terrific. The kids seem to agree there were two heavy guns hosing them down, plus lots of small arms. Lots of fire, so ammo must not be a problem. But that guy up there, he's been in a fight or two in his time. He knows his business. I'll bet we find he's Forces. I mean, this is straight 'Nam, your basic A-team scenario, defending a tight hilltop perimeter against superior numbers way, way out in Indian country. That's Forces work."

"I was in a few fights like that," Dick said.

"I was too," said Skazy. "As long as his ammo holds out, he's going to be a motherfucker to kill."

"Did Bravo do any damage?"

"Evidently someone covered the withdrawal with some fire from one of the M-60s and some of the men think he may have hit people."

Dick shook his head sadly.

"Where's the CO?"

"Over there. Young guy, first lieutenant. Named Dill. The real CO, that Captain Barnard, he didn't make it off the hill."

Dick found Dill sitting by himself smoking a cigarette, staring out into the distance in the bright sun.

"Lieutenant?"

Dill looked up slowly at him.

"Yes, sir?"

"Lieutenant, when you're talking to me, you'll be on your goddamned feet, if you please. Stand up."

Dill rose to the unpleasantness in Puller's voice with the look of a martyr.

"Excuse me, but, sir, we've just been through—"

"Lieutenant, you let me do the talking, all right? You just nod your head when I say so." The young National Guard officer blinked. "This is pathetic. This is disgraceful. Get these people together. Get them out of the open. Do you have security teams out?"

"No, sir, I thought—"

"What happens if the people on the hill send an assault squad down here? They could set up an LMG about four hundred meters up the slope and dust every man here. Or maybe there's another enemy unit in the vicinity, and they're going to come out of the trees firing full automatic."

Dill, a thick-set, athletic-looking man who nevertheless had something of the surly melancholic about him, simply responded by falling into a deeper glumness.

Finally, he said, "We got killed up there while you guys sat down here and did crosswords. That's not fair. That's just not fair. I want to know who's up there and why we have to die to get them and what is—"

"There's a madman with an ICBM and a launching pad. Lieutenant, if we don't get up there, all this, everything you see, everything you've ever dreamed or hoped for and loved or cherished, it's all gone in a few seconds. Do you understand?"

"Who?" was all the stunned officer could say.

"We'll know when we kill him."

"He's one of you, isn't he?" the officer said. "He's some kind of Delta guy or Green Beret. He's one of your little club, isn't he?"

Dick had no answer to this charge.

"Get your men organized, and get them under shelter. Form them up into their squads and platoons, and take roll. Get them fed. You've got to make them a unit again, Lieutenant, because we go back tonight. If you can't do it, I'll find somebody that can."

The lieutenant looked at him, sighed, and went to look for his sergeants.

It had to be Delta Three, goddammit, thought Uckley. He knew he had to say something and that time was slipping away. But Delta Three wouldn't sit still. He was exceedingly agitated and kept repeating himself to the firemen, who milled in jittery excitement around the big red truck in the Burkittsville Volunteer Fire Department.

"You guys go to the house on the right. Only to the right. The one with the smoke coming out of it. Don't worry about the smoke; it's just a chemical device in a pail or a pot or something up on the second floor. Get in there, and take cover; we think there's going to be some shooting next door. No matter what you hear, you keep your heads down, is that understood?"

The firemen nodded and giggled excitedly among themselves. They were amateurs, too, volunteers, townspeople, and this was shaping up like a great adventure to them.

Finally, Delta Three came back, breathing hard. Uckley was aware that he ought to have been more assertive, but Delta Three had one of those flinty, righteous personalities that assumed its own perfection as a basic operating principle.

"You set, sir?" he asked.

Uckley thought he was set. He had on a black fireman's slicker and helmet, remembering that when he was a kid he wanted to grow up and be a fireman; he had an ax; he also had his own Smith & Wesson 686 .357 Magnum, which he had bought used from a retiring agent and hadn't fired in eleven months. Delta Three meanwhile took the moment to do a fast check on his own weapons for the upcoming close encounter, an accurized Colt .45 automatic for backup and a H&K MP-5 with the thirty-round mag and the collapsing skeleton stock, which had been jammed shut, hanging on a sling under his slick and shiny coat. Both men had Kevlar bulletproof vests on also.

"Delta Three?"

The soldier didn't look at him. He was still checking gear. It was getting so close to Go time. He had two smoke grenades on his belt and two stun grenades and two teargas grenades. He had a gas mask in a case. He had a fighting knife.

"The boots," he said to Uckley. "You think we ought to change our boots?"

The man looked down to point out that he had on Corcoran jump boots.

How could he be thinking about shoes at a time like this?

"I don't think there's time," said Uckley, who was wearing black Florsheim wingtips.

"Yeah, I suppose you're right. Things are going to happen damned fast."

"Delta Three?"

The man finally looked at him.

"I just want to make one thing clear to you. They made it very clear to me, it has to be clear to you."

Delta Three's eyes were guileless and blue. They were somehow Baptist eyes, Uckley thought. They wouldn't know sophistication or irony or cynicism; they'd know only duty, honor, country. They'd know mission.

"This is a prisoner mission. Not a hostage-freeing mission, a prisoner-taking mission. We've got to stick by our priorities. D-do you understand that?"

Delta Three just looked at him.

"You have to understand what's important here," said Uckley, not quite believing it himself.

"She's smoking!" came the call from one of the firemen at the binoculars. "Boy, she's really smoking."

The men climbed aboard the fire engine.

"Whoo-*eeeeeee!*" some idiot yelled.

Teagarden thought: I am in a jam.

"Sister Phuong?"

"Yes," came the voice back to him in the dark.

"I think I'd like to rest."

"Yes."

He sat down, considering.

He could tell from his dancing beam that the tunnel grew smaller still ahead and began to curl and meander. It looked like an intestine. Teagarden was having trouble breathing. He was having trouble keeping his eyes open and his legs working. He was aware that exceedingly weird things were going on inside his head. He'd never really thought of the dark before, not of this kind of dark anyhow.

It wasn't night. Teagarden had fought in the night. The night was not a problem. Because in the night there was space. You could put your hand out and feel the air. You could look up and see the sky, however indistinctly. The night had textures to it, striations in the darkness. One could befriend and ultimately seduce the night, turn it for you.

But not this. It was absolute. It had no gradations, no subtleties, no nuances. It seemed as leached of meaning as of color. It was too stark. He didn't really think he could go on.

Yet he couldn't really go back. Teagarden was Delta, top of the pyramid. Delta culture, surprisingly informal in a lot of ways, was also unforgiving in others. It had its own Bushido. The guys got to wear shaggy hair and blue jeans and sweatshirts as long as they kept their rounds in the 9-zone on the range, could crack an occupied 747 in less than thirty seconds, could fieldstrip an AK-47 blindfolded. But there were lots of guys—Berets, Rangers, FBI SWAT, SEALS, Air Commandos—who had those skills. So what Delta had was this other thing, this, uh, spirit: if you were Delta, you never said no. You just went. It really came down to that one thing: if you were Delta, you never said no. That was an absolute as binding as the dark. When it came time to go, you put aside the bullshit, threw your life into the hot frying pan of fate, and you went.

I cannot go, thought Teagarden.

I am thirty-seven years old, a Green Beret, a 'Nam veteran, the holder of several medals, by all credentials one of the bravest professional soldiers in the world. I cannot go.

He began to cry. He hated himself. He wanted to die. He bit his lip, hoping for blood. Searing pain flashed from the wound. He hated himself. He was weak and worthless. There seemed to be no escape at all.

Teagarden pulled his .45 from the holster. There was a shell in the chamber and the piece was cocked and locked. He thumbed the safety down; it unlocked with a little *snik!* that sounded like a door slamming in the dark. He put the muzzle in his mouth. It had an oily taste, and was big, enshrouded as it was in its slide housing. With his thumb he found the trigger.

"Brother Teagarden."

He didn't say anything.

"Brother Teagarden, don't do it," she said in Vietnamese. "Go back to the big tunnel. Wait there. I'll go as far as I can, and if I find something, I'll come back. Then we'll call them. We won't tell them. Nobody will ever have to know."

"You're so brave, Sister," he said. "I'm not brave. Not down here."

"Brother, nobody will know."

"*I* will know."

"Learn to forgive yourself. That is the lesson of the tunnels. Forgive yourself."

He couldn't see her at all. He could almost sense her, though, her heat, her nearness, her living flesh. Next to it he felt a little stupid. The pistol grew heavy. He put it down. He locked it and put it into his holster.

"I'll just go back a little ways, okay? I just can't go any farther, Sister Phuong."

"It's all right, Brother Teagarden," said Phuong.

Turning, she went deeper into the tunnel.

"Mommy," said Poo Hummel, "Mrs. Reed's house is on fire!"

Herman turned, went to the window. Yes, black smoke poured from the upper floors of the old house next door. He watched it gush and float up to the sky. Then he heard sirens.

Herman licked his lips. He didn't like this at all. First a man in a sports coat, now this.

"Herman, is Mrs. Reed going to die?" asked Poo.

"No, I don't think so, little girl."

"Will the firemen come and save Mrs. Reed?"

"I'm sure the firemen will come," said Beth Hummel.

They were all gathered in the living room of the Hummel house. Herman looked out the window again. He could see just smoke, and otherwise nothing.

"Does the lady smoke?" Herman wanted to know.

Beth looked away. Then she said, "No, she quit last year."

Herman nodded. His two men looked at him.

"Get your weapons out," he said. "I think we're going to be hit. You go to the kitchen—"

"Oh, God—" said Beth, "Oh, God, the girls, don't hurt the girls, I tell you, please—"

Bean began to cry. She was older than her sister and may have just understood it all that much better. She didn't like the guns, because they made people dead on television.

"Herman, I'm scared," said Poo. "I don't want to be dead."

"Please let us go," said Beth Hummel. "We didn't do anything to you. We never did anything to anybody."

Herman looked at the woman and her two terrified children. He tried to think what to do. He hadn't come all this way to make war on children and women. Little Poo came across the room to him and put her arms out, and Herman swept her up.

"Don't go away, Herman. Please don't go away. Don't let the firemen make you dead."

"Nothing's going to happen to Herman," he said. "You and your sister, you go upstairs, you stay in your rooms no matter what. *No matter what!*" he finished savagely. "Now, run. Run, Poo. Take care of your sister."

Poo scrambled up the stairs, pulling Bean along. The younger one was the stronger one.

"You, lady, you're grown-up. You gotta take your risks with the rest of us."

"Who *are* you? What is this?"

"Here they are," said the man at the window. He had an FAL, not a house-to-house weapon, with an utterly worthless Trilux night sight. "Should I fire?"

"No, no," said Herman. "Maybe they are just firemen. Get up on the stair landing, get ready to jump in either direction, depending on which way they come. You"—he pointed to the other—"you get to the rear, in the kitchen. If they come—"

The man cocked his weapon, a Sterling sub-machine gun, in answer.

"Get to the door, lady," Herman ordered, his voice taut and ugly. He pressed the silenced Uzi against her back. Then he slid the bolt back, locking it. As he held it tightly he felt the safety in the grip yield to the pressure in his palm.

Peering through the window, he saw the firemen racing to unlimber hoses, and others heading into the Reed house with axes and oxygen masks on.

Two firemen in heavy slickers broke from the truck and headed toward the Hummel house.

He could hear them yelling, "Anybody in there? You've got to get out!" They were knocking on the door.

Uckley's heart was pumping like crazy; his knees felt like jelly, loose and slippery. He didn't see how they'd support him on the run to the house. It bounded in his vision as he and Delta Three careened toward it, though, of course, he was the one doing the actual bounding. Delta Three had a slight lead as they clambered up the porch steps and made it to the door. He saw Delta Three's slicker open and billow like a cape as the muzzle of the sub-machine gun came out.

"Anybody in there? Goddammit, you've got to get out, the flames may spread!" Delta Three screamed, pounding on the door.

Nothing happened for just a second. Delta Three leaned into the door, dropped his ax, his eyes shooting toward Uckley. Uckley now had the Smith in his hand, though he was surprised to find it there, not having remembered reaching for it.

"Mark your target," muttered Delta Three under his breath, then paused for just a second to hit the speaker button on his belt and talk into the radio mike he had pinned to his collar. "Delta units, this is Delta Three, green light, green light, green light!" the words increasing with energy and urgency.

Delta Three kicked in the door.

*   *   *

Herman heard a burst of gunfire from the kitchen, things breaking, men screaming, everything mixing together in a welter of confusion. "Attack, attack," yelled the man in the kitchen, firing again. Herman pulled Mrs. Hummel to him and back as the door before him burst open and the two firemen who were police agents plunged through the door. Though the gunfire rose from the kitchen, he stared for just a second at the bulging eyes and distended faces of the men opposite them. Then he fired, the gun pumping with that terrible noiseless stutter of the silencer, its shells cascading out. He put a burst into them, knocking them back, pushed the woman forward at them, spun, and ran for the steps. A bullet came after him, hit him high in the arm and pushed him down, bloodying his lip. He screamed, spun to see the wretched woman in the crossfire, crawling, her face wild with terror. He fired again, watching the bullets rip up the room. The man upstairs came to the landing to give covering fire, his big FAL jacking out heavy .308s that exploded chairs and set curtains aflame. But Herman could see nothing to fire at, had no idea where the shot had come from that had hit him. He pushed his way up the stairs, slipped once, felt the blood on his arm, and then the pain erupted, freed from its sheath of shock. He'd been hit before, but not like this, in the bone; the pain was awesome, huge, enveloping. He tried to switch the Uzi to his good hand as the blast of covering fire gave him the time, but now he saw shapes in the window. They were firing fast, and the man above him pitched forward and slammed down the steps. Herman turned, dropping his Uzi, and clambered up, clawing for his pistol.

"My babies, my babies," the woman was screaming, "Oh, God, don't hurt my babies."

"Go after him," wheezed Delta Three. "I don't think I can move anymore."

Uckley was all right. He'd been hit three times in the first burst, but the Kevlar, combined with the subsonic velocities of the silenced 9-millimeter ammunition of the Uzi, had saved him. He felt as though he'd had the shit beat out of him, which, in effect, he had, for the vests, which will stop a pistol bullet, won't absorb its impact entirely, and the strikes had been like well-delivered punches to the midriff. Delta Three, on the other hand, was much unluckier. One of the bullets had hit him

high in the leg. He was bleeding badly, even though he'd been able to
fire a magazine, hitting the big one once as he ran up the steps and
completely taking out the small one at the landing where he'd stood
firing randomly into the room.

"You okay?" asked Uckley. He wasn't sure he wanted to go after the
vanished big guy.

"Go after him, goddammit," said Delta Three, busy trying to get a
tourniquet around his leg. "Go, go *now*, man. I'll be okay."

Uckley knelt, thumbed the cylinder free on the now empty Smith,
and ejected the shells. Then he dropped a speedloader into the cylinder,
the six slugs held in a metal disk. He spun the release knob on the
device, depositing the six 125-grain Federal Magnums in their chambers. He snapped the cylinder shut, shucked off the rain slicker.

"Here," wheezed the Delta operative. "Take this too." He held out
what appeared to be some kind of customized .45 automatic, with a
fancy wraparound rubber grip. Uckley took the new gun, wedging it into
his belt in the small of his back. It was cocked and locked.

Breathing hard, he said, "Okay, I'll go get him."

He lurched by, but Delta Three grabbed him.

"Be careful, Uckley. There's kids in there."

Beth Hummel saw one of them with a big pistol like a cowboy dip
gingerly through the door and peer around, his eyes wide with excitement. She could hear his ragged breathing. He seemed to pause, gather
himself up. Nimbly he dashed past her, stooped to the man on the floor,
satisfied himself that he was dead, kicked his rifle away, then ducked
back.

"Are you hit?" he whispered hoarsely.

"My children! God, please, my chil—"

"*Are you hit?*"

"No. I—I don't think so. My children are upstairs. Please don't let
them get hurt."

"Listen, you crawl to the door and out. There's medical personnel
outside."

"My children. Please—"

"Your kids will be all right. I'm FBI, Special Agent. I can handle
this." But she didn't think he could. He seemed very young and frightened. She watched him go to the foot of the stairs.

"Uckley!" The call came from outside.

The man paused. "Yes?"

"The guy's dead in the kitchen, but so's Delta Two; Delta One is hit. You're on your own."

"Check," said Uckley. "Get the goddamn state cops here."

She had the terrible sense of a man not wanting to do what he had to do but doing it anyway. With gun as a kind of magic device, as if he could draw his strength and power from it, he threw himself up the first flight of steps to the landing, whirled up the second flight, pointing with his big silver gun.

Oh, Jesus, she thought, oh, Jesus, let my babies be all right.

Uckley reached the top of the stairway and looked very quickly down the hall. Using the two-handed grip, he thrust the Smith in front of him, searching for a target. He just saw doorways, some opened, some closed, all more or less dark.

They told you never, absolutely *never*, go down a hall or room to room against an armed man. Wait for backup. Always wait for backup, the guy has such an advantage over you, he can hear you coming, he can drop you anytime. Action *always* beats reaction.

But Uckley didn't have much choice, he figured. The whole thing had teetered out of control in that first crazy second of gunfire, and now the only thing was to stay alive and not to kill anybody wrong. He didn't really think he had the grit for this. This was supposed to be a Delta thing, all these special operators, and where were they? Out on the porch.

"Hey!" he called. "This is Special Agent James Uckley of the Federal Bureau of Investigation. The house is surrounded. Give yourself up."

He heard his voice bang around the empty walls of the old house.

He thumbed back the hammer on the Smith.

Herman was hardly conscious. He kept slipping in and out, as if the gears weren't holding in his mind. He cowered in the lee of the doorway in Jack and Beth Hummel's bedroom. He was trying to keep a tight grip on the pistol, a Czech CZ-75, with his weak left hand. His right was useless; the bullet had smashed into the shoulder. He was sitting in a pool of blood. His head ached; he was very sad but not especially frightened.

"Give yourself up," the call came again.

Now, that was a laugh. He knew what he had to do. It was very simple what you did in enemy territory to save yourself the horror of interrogation and the danger of compromising yourself. You always knew.

But Herman thought, why not one more? After so many, why not one more, why not this blundering policeman who shot my men. He edged his way up until he was on his feet. He cocked the CZ. All right, he thought, all right, Mr. Policeman.

He slid to the doorway. He thought he could make out the man at the end of the hall, low. How many others would there be? There'd be hundreds, hundreds and hundreds. So many. But just one more for now. Then he heard cars pull up in front of the house, sirens blaring. Red and blue light pulsed through the windows.

He lifted the pistol with the weak hand at what might have been the man but might also, in his blurry eyesight, have been a shadow. He fired.

Uckley panicked as the bullet came plowing his way. It smashed against the wall behind him, showering him with dust. Two more shots came and he drew back. Then he plunged forward, firing wildly, insanely, six fast blasts with the Smith until he'd reached a doorway across the hall. He got out a speed loader, popped open his cylinder, ejected six shells, set the nose of the new rounds in their chamber, twisted it to free them, then snapped the cylinder shut. He got out the .45 from his belt and thumbed off what he took to be the oversize safety. It was a new gun to him; he wasn't especially sure how it worked, and so it scared him. He peeked down the hall, saw only darkness.

"Mommy," somebody called. "Mommy, help me."

Oh, shit, Uckley thought. Then in his peripheral vision something flashed and he flinched, ducked back, aware from the buck and the blast that he'd fired the .45, one reflex shot (it had been so easy).

It was the mother. She'd come up the steps. He hadn't heard her, it wasn't his fault! He'd told her to get out. He looked at her. She'd sat down against the wall, her legs weirdly akimbo. Her head hung forward in a way no living person's would hang. There was a lot of blood on her.

Oh, no, goddammit, goddammit, oh, shit, I shot the woman!

He stared at her, ashamed and disgusted. The gunsmoke reached his nose, acrid and dense.

I told you not to come up, he felt himself screaming. I didn't hear you! *I didn't hear you!*

Footsteps clambered at him.

Uckley spun, dropped to a knee, found the target picture and—

It was a child on churning legs, just a small shape in the darkness, screaming "Mommy" and coming at him.

"Get back," he shouted, because behind the child now he saw another shape from another dark doorway, leaning out with a pistol.

Uckley dived.

He hit the little girl.

"Get down, get down, get down," he screamed, louder than she did. He hit his head on the wall, a stunning blow. His weapons dropped away. He felt the girl squirming under him. He heard footsteps.

The man stood over him.

The little girl was screaming, "Mommy, Mommy, my mommy is dead!"

Uckley held her tight to him.

He looked up.

The man, bleeding badly, stood over him. He was a heavy blond guy with a crew cut and a thick face.

"Let the kid go, for Christ's sake, let the kid go," Uckley begged.

The man turned and walked away. Uckley said to the girl, "Run downstairs. *Run,* now!"

He picked up the pieces, and with a gun in both hands he started down the hall.

Then he heard the shot.

"If you've spoken to Peter," said Megan Wilder, "then you know our relationship became spectacularly deranged at the end. I'm not sure even yet if he did it to me or I did it to him or, out of some kind of crab nebulae of neurotic energy, we did it to each other." She laughed ironically at the lunacy of it.

The three agents watched her without cracking so much as a snicker. She thought of them as the Three Dumb Men. They just sat there, their faces slack and dull, listening. They hadn't even taken their coats off, and it was tropical inside the studio.

Megan bent forward, trying to find a new angle into her construction. She saw now that she had committed a fundamental design error at the very beginning. She had found the circuit board to a personal computer and loved it: it was so intricate, so cunning, so full of texture and meaning; and she had put it exactly in the center of the piece. Then she had painted it hot pink with a spray can. It was an inescapable fact. It was the absolute, the total, the implacable. But that was all wrong, she saw now. Then you could not *discover* the image, and meet it on your terms. Rather, it hit you in the face: it was like an ugly truth that would not go away, so obvious and pitiful that it dared you to recognize it, and made you aware of your cowardice for the fact that you could not.

"This," she said to the Three Dumb Men, pointing to it, "this has to go. It's too *clever.*"

She pried the board off the backing, ripping her finger on a staple in the process. She began to bleed. She chucked the thing away, and it hit with a clatter in the far reaches of the room. Only the pink-edged silhouette was left where the board had been pulled out, and small specks of furry pink light, where the spray paint had penetrated. She liked it; it was much better that way, suggestive and elliptical rather than pontificating.

Almost at once she began to feel better about the piece. Maybe she had solved it after all; maybe there was an end to the equation in sight.

"You see, he lied. I lied too. In the end I lied more than he did. In the end all I did was lie. But Peter lied first and he lied worst. Worse, he was a coward. He didn't tell me because he *couldn't* tell me. He knew I would hold it against him, what he did. And he was right, I would have, and maybe I would have left him. But I didn't really and truly know until I was in love with him and we were married and the *gestalt* had just gotten too complicated and there were no easy answers."

She paused. "He didn't tell me, you see, because in his heart of hearts, way, way, down, Peter is *ashamed.* That's the key to him."

The Three Dumb Men just looked at her, with their long, glum, midwestern faces, like Grant Wood's gothic Americans.

"So here I am, married to this bombthinker with an IQ of several thousand, whom I love so desperately I think I may die from it. But he always had his mistress. That bitch. He'd never give her up, he was so selfish. To have him, I had to have *her.* Oh, these brilliant men, I tell you, they can be real motherfuckers. So I—"

"You mean this Maggie Berlin?" one of them interrupted.

She laughed. The idiot!

"No, no, Maggie was just another screwed-up defense genius. No, it was the other bitch. I always thought of her as a woman, you see, and I still think there was sex under it all. He laughed at me, and maybe Freud is both wrong and dead, but I think there was sex under it always, all the time, ever since the start, ever since Harvard, when he couldn't get laid and his roommate was the big stud for peace. No, *her*. The bomb. He could never leave her alone. He couldn't stop thinking about her. She was his Circe, his Alice Through the Looking Glass, his Ginger Lynn. He really did love her, in his way. And so she hurt me and so I chose to hurt him *through* her. That's the pathology of it. Surely it's transparent. I mean, you must see stuff like this all the time?"

The Three Dumb Men were silent.

"Well, that's context, at any rate. It enables you to understand why I was vulnerable to Ari Gottlieb."

She bent to the piece again. She began to regret having so summarily dismissed the computer circuit board. It occurred to her that she ought to retrieve it. But she knew to do so would be to stamp herself as an idiot forever in these men's minds. She looked at her watch. Time was flying, wasn't it? Getting close to five. We're all getting older until one day, poof, Peter's Ginger Lynn goes down on her knees, opens her mouth, and sucks off the world—the ultimate blowjob. She laughed, a little more crazily than she had intended. She felt a little like crying.

"So, anyway, Peter is the flavor of the month in Washington circles because his let's-nuke-the-Russians number is just the tune Reagan and his chums want to hear. It's got a good beat and they can dance to it. They give it an eighty. And suddenly he's Mr. Bomb, he has this terrible committee job, and it's eating up his time and he's *loving it*. I admit it. I couldn't handle it. And who should show up then but Ari Gottlieb. I guess if I had to design the PJM, I'd design Ari. That's Perfect Jewish Male. I mean, he was like Alan Bates in *An Unmarried Woman*, just too good to be true. He was incredibly good-looking but not in a pretty or an offputting way. In a kind way, somehow. He never raised his voice. When he laughed—oh, listen to me, I sound like I'm in a musical—when he laughed, he really made you feel like it was you and he alone in the most brilliant private joke ever told. I liked the way his skin crinkled right by his eyes, into two little deltas, like flint arrowheads. It had a nice texture to it. He was very gentle, very confident. He wasn't afraid. Peter was rigid with fear and guilt, but Ari was without fear. When he saw you, Jesus, how he lit up! His gift was for *focus*. He made you feel like you were the only person in the world, there was nobody else. I met him at an opening two years back."

"Date please."

"Who remembers *dates*?"

"Could it have been January?"

"No. The weather was warm. It was very warm, I remember, because Ari and I had a Coke from one of those hot dog wagons on the street outside the Corcoran and—no, no, yes, it *was* January. It was a surprisingly warm January day. Peter was locked up. It had really gotten crazy with the group, Congress had just done something about putting the MXs in old silos or something and—"

"January eleven?"

"Maybe."

She hated them. She just looked at them.

"Anyway, it was my idea. It wasn't Ari's idea. It was *my* idea. He was an Israeli citizen. He'd been in their Airborne troops or something, which I heard was a big thing over there. He knew people in the embassy. I just wanted to—to hurt Peter."

"Was he interested?"

"No. Not at first. He thought it was foolish. Israel doesn't have big missiles, Israel doesn't *care* about big missiles, that's what he said. But I said the information was valuable. Israel could *use* it somehow, they were clever. Jews are always clever."

"And so he relented?"

"Finally. You see, for me it gave me a chance to do something. And it wasn't like giving it to the Communists. It was to people on *our* side. To other Jews."

"Yes."

"And he went to them, and they said yes, they'd look at it, and finally he said this man wanted to meet me and talk to me, but it wouldn't do to be seen at the embassy, could I go up to New York and meet him at the consulate. The Israeli consulate."

"Yes."

"Yes, and so I did. I met an Israeli intelligence officer at the Israeli consulate and it was very nice. He was a brilliant, commanding man, very considerate, very charming. He said he didn't want me to get into trouble, did I know what I was doing, was I sure, blah blah blah. He pointed out that Jonathan Pollard had been arrested and that our government was making ugly noise about prosecuting him to the max, and that if I got caught, maybe there wasn't much they'd be able to do about it."

"And—"

"And I didn't care. I was sure. And so I started doing it. It was easy." She felt so smug when she said it. She'd had a great deal of curiosity about this moment. Would she turn her confession into what Peter used to call one of her "productions"? Well, yes, she had.

She felt the eyes of the Three Dumb Men upon her.

"After all," she said, "it was only the *Israelis*. I mean, they *are* our friends, the last time I looked at the *Washington Post*."

"Mrs. Thiokol—do you mind if I call you that?"

"No, that's fine."

"Mrs. Thiokol, could you tell me a little about Ari Gottlieb? I mean, I don't suppose you have any pictures."

"Yes, I have three of his pictures. Abstract impressionism. He was not very good, that's the fun—oh, you mean, his *photograph*. No, I'm sorry. I don't."

"Could you tell us about him?"

"He was just everything I wanted. Except he had one flaw."

"What was that."

"It wasn't his fault. He couldn't help it."

"What was it?"

"He wasn't Peter Thiokol."

She continued. "If anything, he was too perfect. Ari was beautiful and loving and never moody and very sexy. And dull."

"He left you?"

"After an odd weekend in an inn in Virginia a while ago. Very strange."

"How strange?"

"I can't say. I slept through it all. I passed out after too much champagne. He was very offended. He left the next day. He had to go back to Israel. To his wife."

"When was this?"

"Two weeks or so. I don't really remember. Who remembers *dates*?"

"And so you're alone."

"I was alone even when I was married."

"Tell me about this Israeli intelligence officer."

"Oh, you know. Very clever man, very warm. Charming. Mysterious. I could tell he was a legend, even there in the consulate. They all looked at him. He was a special man. I remember after it was over, we went out on Seventy-third Street and he helped me get a taxi. You felt safe with him. And he—"

"Excuse me, Mrs. Thiokol?" It was, she saw, the youngest of the Three Dumb Men. He was slightly more tentative than the others and he could see his interruption irritated her.

"Yes?"

"You said Seventy-third Street."

"Yes."

"I used to be in our New York bureau. You mean Eighty-fourth Street."

She was confused to sense no softness in his position.

"All right, I got the address mixed up. Who remembers addresses? And what dif— No, I'm sorry, it *was* Seventy-third Street! I'm not going to let you bully me. It was between Madison and Park. A lovely old brownstone. The Star of David on the flag, all the pictures of Ben-Gurion and Golda Meir and Menachem Begin and Shimon Peres, all the bustle, all the workers, all the—"

But she could feel him staring at her.

"I'm sorry," he finally said. "I know the building very well. It's a brownstone all right, but it's at Eighty-fourth, between Madison and Fifth, near the museum. I worked there, I used to go into that building regularly. We had a cooperating deal with Mossad for security."

"I—I mean—"

And then she could think of nothing to say.

"Are you *sure* it was Seventy-third Street?"

She nodded dumbly.

"You see," he said, "it would be pretty easy to do. Rent the house. For one morning you hang out the flag. You hang some pictures. Some people rush around, looking busy. An hour after you've gone, they've cleared out. That's all."

She felt a hole open: it was dark and huge. She was falling. No one was there to catch her.

Peter! she thought. God, Peter!

And then she said, "They fooled me. They just fooled me."

"Yes, ma'am. I'm afraid they did," said one of the Three Dumb Men.

She began, very softly, to weep.

"Oh, Peter," she wept, "oh, Jesus, what have I done?"

1700

Uckley sat in the front of the state police car by himself. He felt cold. Somebody had gotten him a blanket, which he pulled around himself. He sat in a festival of pulsing light. It seemed to be the world convention of police cars, and in the dusk, their red and blue lights bounced off the houses and the trees back at him. He had a headache and his guts hurt from the bullet impacts on the vest, but at least he was done vomiting.

Everybody was staying away from him, at least for now, and he was grateful for that small mercy. He stared ahead, seeing nothing. He was exhausted, flattened out. He preferred the numbness, however, because he knew that if he thought about it too much, he'd want to die, just to make it all go away.

The kids were with a state policewoman, but no one really was sure what to do with them, what with the father missing. He thought he'd heard something about them going to their grandmother's in Hagerstown. He couldn't look at them, the two little girls, little perfect angels, untouched by corruption or evil. He'd caught just a glimpse: they looked like little petals, perfect and rosy.

Why had she come up the stairs?

Why did I fire?

She came up because she was a mother.

I fired because I'm a policeman.

There: hubris, fate, kismet, karma, whatever. It was somehow written; it was inevitable; it had been decreed.

When he'd gotten back to her, there was nothing to do. Her daughter sat next to her, holding her hand. Soon the other little girl came out and sat on the other side and started to cry. Uckley just looked at them, and at the dead woman, and then went out and got into the car, while various medical people and cops and firemen and citizens rushed about. He yielded to anybody who seemed to know what they were doing.

"A tough break," said Delta Three suddenly.

Uckley looked up, dazed.

"You okay, Sergeant?" he asked blankly.

The man was on crutches, his thigh heavily wrapped.

"I think I'll live. Look, if there's any trouble, I'll tell 'em how it happened. Shit, Mr. Uckley, you went up there alone against a real bad customer who had two kids hostage, and you cleaned his clock. That's a good day's work."

"Yeah, but I didn't even do that right."

"We went into a house where there were three hostages. We got two of them out. That's a pretty damned good operation anyway you slice it. And that mother, she was a good mom, she'd have rather her kids made it out than herself. So, there you go."

"The point was to take prisoners," Uckley said.

"Begging your pardon, sir, but fuck taking prisoners. We put three assholes in the ground, and that's what we get paid for."

It was no help.

"Sir, you better report in. You know, at the mountain they're waiting, and I bet it's pretty tense there."

"Yeah," said Uckley.

With a grim sense of futility he took the radio mike off its arms, feeling his ribs knit up in pain with the effort, and pushed the send button.

"Base, this is Special Agent Uckley, can you give me a call sign and patch me into Delta command?"

"We read you, Bureau One. You're all set for transmission, over."

"Delta Six, do you copy? This is Bureau One, over."

There was static and scrambled noise in the furriness of the transmission, but eventually a voice came out of it at him.

"Bureau One, Delta Six affirmative, we copy. Go ahead."

"Assault complete. Two hostages freed. We lost one man killed, and two wounded but stable. Uh, we are in command of the situation now. We found three aggressors, heavily armed."

"Prisoners?" came Dick Puller's voice through the fog.

"Uh, negative, Delta Six. That's a negative. Too much firepower. We, uh, we couldn't get you any prisoners, Delta Six."

There was silence from the radio.

Uckley rushed to fill it.

"Delta Six, I accidentally shot a civilian. I'd like to request a release. You ought to get yourself another—"

"Negative, Bureau One."

"For Christ's sake, I shot a woman to death. I'm no goddamned good to—"

"Bureau One, this is Delta Six. Civilian casualties are a necessary hazard of combat operations. Get a hold on yourself."

"Colonel Puller, I shot a mother in the heart in—"

"Bureau One, stop feeling sorry for yourself and listen up."

"Sir, I—"

"Listen up, Bureau One. This is combat operation, and you follow orders, or I'll have you arrested, goddammit. Son, I don't have time to screw around here with your delicate feelings. Do you copy?"

"Copy," said Uckley through a knotted throat and blurry eyes.

"Collect their firearms, feed the serial numbers to the Bureau, and see if you can get a make on them. Then I want you to conduct an examination of the bodies. There should be a medical examiner or something there. Check out those bodies. And the clothes too. Check out the clothes. Do you copy, Bureau One?"

Uckley just looked at the microphone, a dead thing in his hand. He felt impossibly old and impossibly fatigued. It was almost night now and the streetlights had come on.

"I copy," said Uckley, and got up to do what he had to do.

"End of story," said Nathan Walls. "As in, end of *muthafuckin'* story."

And so it was: their lights came up onto sheer wall, where the livid pick marks of the mining tools of fifty years or so back still gleamed in the light of the beam.

The tunnel called Elizabeth had simply ceased to exist. She yielded to mountain.

"Son of a bitch," said Witherspoon. "You mean that's it?"

"Less you wants to start to *dig*, man. Figure you got to dig about a half a mile straight up. Then you be at where you want to be at."

"Goddamn," said Witherspoon, really pissed. All this way, all this low walking and crawling through this damn tomb, and here they were; they had come to nothing.

Walls sat down.

"Goddamn this bitch. Can't never trust no white woman. You looks at 'em and they crosses they legs. Oh, except your old lady, of course." He reached into his pocket, took out a cigarette, flicked a light from a Bic lighter, and inhaled.

"You smoke here?" asked Witherspoon.

"Hey, why not? Not nobody here but us spooks." He laughed. "Man, I thought I was gonna be a muthafuckin' hero. Man, now we just walk back, and that's that. You know, Spoon, here's what I was gonna do. I figure we run into some shit, man, smoke and lights and fireworks everywhere, man, old Walls just pull a fade. He go for a nice walk in the country. Not too bad, huh? I tell you, boy, only way old Walls going to get his ass a little quiet time to hisself." He laughed again.

"Yeah, that's real great," said Witherspoon. "You're really talking like a hero now. Your momma would be proud."

"My momma be dead," said Walls, laughing again.

Witherspoon slipped off his MP-5, his flak jacket, slid the night vision goggles off his head, and tried to arrange the angle-head flashlight upon them so that its beam fell on the end of the tunnel. Then he went to the wall and began to feel around. The light caught him and he cast a giant shadow.

But he could feel nothing. It was solid rock. His fingers, long and ebony, flew across it.

"Man, you wastin' your time. Relax. Have a smoke. Then we go back to the world."

In time Witherspoon gave up. There seemed no point. They were licked.

He fumbled with the Prick-88 strapped into the webbing of his vest, and picked up the earphones and put the hands-free mike in front of his lips.

"Rat Six, this is Rat Team Baker, do you copy?"

He listened intently. There was no answer.

"Shit," he said, "we must be inside too far. They aren't reading us."

"Maybe they asleep," said Walls. "You get an easy job like sitting on your butt while two niggers do all the shit work, man, you get a white man's job, you fall asleep. Call their asses again."

"Rat Six, Rat Six, this is Team Baker, do you copy? Do you copy?"

Silence.

"Is anybody there? Is anybody, I repeat *anybody*, there?"

"Maybe that damned bomb finally went off, all the white people dead," said Walls.

"Then all the black people are dead too," said Witherspoon.

"Man, some nigger scientist ought to figure out a bomb kill only white people. Man, I'd *pay* for something like that." He laughed, flicked out his cigarette.

"Rat Six, this is Team Baker, do you copy?"

By now Jake's had filled with workingclass men. Gregor hated them. They were truck drivers, fork-lift operators, warehousemen, painters, postal clerks, all large, most dirty, all tired, most loud. They smoked. The air of the place was blue with smoke. His headache had not gone away even though he'd been splashing vodka on it for some time now.

He was watching the clock crawl through the day until it would be time to call Molly again, and then he heard someone talking about soldiers and a training exercise in central Maryland and looked up to the television set. It was the news hour and the reporter was at a state police roadblock somewhere, where the cars were lined up like it was the end of the world or something.

Gregor leaned forward intently.

"Hey, Mister, who you pickin' in Eastern Division?"

"Redskins," Gregor said. "Shhhh, the TV."

"Redskins won't even *make* the playoffs!"

The reporter was talking about a military exercise being conducted in the mountains, rumors of plane crashes and helicopters, how traffic was backed up and how civil authorities weren't able to say when it would all return to normalcy, but that this was one of the prices you had to pay for your democracy.

The reporter, a childish boy, nodded enthusiastically as he spoke, narrowing his eyes for emphasis. Behind him, far in the distance, Gregor could see the fat hulk of a snow-covered mountain. It was white and glistening and looked lovely.

The boy now was rattling on about new troops headed out to the exercise. He'd thrust his microphone up to some soldiers sitting in trucks that were momentarily stopped. The men in the trucks were saying they didn't know anything about it, they'd just been put on alert that morning in D.C., and about eleven they'd been ordered to load up on the vehicles and here they were.

"But," the young soldier now told the young reporter, even as the truck was pulling away, "tell you this, we gonna kick ass!"

"Man, that must be some exercise they got going out there," said a man at the bar. "They say traffic's backed up all the way to goddamned Baltimore. Never heard of nothing like it."

"Where?" Gregor asked, adding, "I don't want to get stuck in traffic."

"Ah, out Alternate forty, from Middletown to Boonsboro. You ought to be okay you stick to seventy. That mountain, that's South Mountain, A-forty goes right by it. They got it closed off. Also, all them little hick burgs out there. Funniest goddamn thing, though."

"What's that?"

"Ain't no government land up there. Plenty up at Aberdeen. Plenty at Fort Meade. Plenty at Pax River, over on the Shore. Plenty out at Fort Richie. Ain't no government land at South Mountain though. Damnedest thing, you can bet."

"Ummm," nodded Gregor.

Should I go out there?

I'm closest. Maybe I could get out there and hear something from a soldier or something.

Yes, with your accent and your Soviet visa, yes: and end up in Danbury for twenty years, then home for twenty more in the Gulag. No, the answer was Molly.

He now saw that there was some kind of crisis and that Molly would find it out for him and that he would be first with the news, the whole *apparat* would be working on it, and he, the great Gregor Arbatov, he would find it! He stood, wobbling, and ambled awkwardly back through the crowded room to the men's bathroom. Inside, he deposited his coins in the slot and tried to call Molly again.

There was no answer.

Oh, Molly, he prayed. Oh, please, please, don't let me down, when I need you so bad.

The news continued to be bad at Delta Command, even after the debacle at the Hummel house. The Rangers had run into heavy weather over Indiana and had to divert south and take on fuel in Tennessee and were now ETA'd at 1900 hours earliest, and that was with a twilight night drop which Puller didn't want to risk, so make it 2100 before they were on station and ready to assault. Meanwhile Third Infantry was hung up in the traffic building up outside the roadblocks and were having a hell of a time fighting their way through it. Pentagon analysts had made no further penetrations of the queer message sent by the "Provisional Army of the United States." Peter Thiokol had come to a standstill in his attempts to understand the identities of Aggressor Force, and therefore was mum on his chances of breaking the reset door code at the shaft entrance. There was, furthermore, no word from the FBI regarding its investigations of his wife, Megan, and any help she could have given then. The two surviving little girls at the Hummel house were too distraught to provide any clues as to the identities of the three men who had held them hostage for most of the day. The Pentagon kept inquiring as to progress in breaking the seizure; Dick Puller had no progress, but he had final casualty figures of Bravo Company's assault: fifty-six dead, forty-four wounded, leaving an effective force of less than fifty men. The field hospital set up by Delta medical personnel was being strained to the maximum, and men had already begun to die who would have survived in Vietnam, where the airevac system had been set up much better.

It was six o'clock. Six hours to go.

Puller headed off to find Thiokol and monitor the latest in FBI investigation reports. But he didn't make it very far.

"Colonel Puller! Colonel Puller!"

It was a Spec 4, one of the Commo specialists.

"Yeah?"

"Sir, we were supposed to get a response every fifteen minutes from Rat Six on the other side of the mountain. They've missed two checks now."

"Have you tried to call him?"

"Yessir. No answer."

Puller took the microphone.

"Rat Six, this is Delta Six, do you copy?"

There was no answer, only silence on the radio.

Puller tried a few more times.

"Who's in that area?" he asked one of his sergeants.

"Sir, besides the Rat Six Team, nobody. Except we've got the mountain ringed with state policemen, so there should be a cop a little farther out."

He consulted a map, then went to the radio and called state police headquarters at the roadblock on Route 40 a few miles away.

"Ninety-Victor, this is Delta Six, do you read?"

"Affirmative, we have you, Delta Six, we copy."

"Ninety-Victor, you got a man on, uh, looks like Moser Road?"

"Yes, sir, had that one sealed off for quite a time."

"Can you patch me through to him, 90-Victor."

"Yes, sir. You just hang in there."

A few moments passed.

"Delta Six, this is 22-Victor, at the roadblock on Moser Road, about three miles due west of South Mountain. I've been requested to contact you."

"Yes, 22-Victor, I copy. Listen, son, you heard anything recently?"

"Just what I figured on, sir."

"And what was that, 22-Victor?"

"Well, sir, I figure the helicopter finally burned down to the ammo."

"Say again, 22-Victor."

"Well, sir, right from where that helicopter crashed and exploded, about twenty minutes ago, all the ammo cooked off. It was about ten or twenty seconds of gunfire. That was all."

Dick put the microphone down.

"Delta Six?"

Dick said nothing.

"Delta Six, this is 22-Victor. Do you require further assistance?"

But Dick said nothing.

Goddamn him.

He turned, looked at the mountain about a mile off.

Goddamn him: he'd found Rat Six. He'd wiped it out. And he'd sent men into the tunnels after the Rat Teams.

"Sir, do you want to send a party around to check out the Rat Six position?"

Puller shook his head. What was the point? Aggressor-One had topped him again. His rats were dead in their holes. And there was nothing Puller could do about it now except order up the body bags and pray for Peter Thiokol.

*   *   *

"Thiokol?"

Peter looked up from the Aggressor-One document, from his notebook, from his FBI counterintel reports. It was Skazy.

"Look, we have to talk."

"About what? I have a lot of—"

"Out in the barn."

"What is this?" said Peter, reading at once something tense and guilty on the officer's face. "What's going on?"

"In the barn, please, Dr. Thiokol."

Peter waited a few minutes, then went out and moseyed around back to where Skazy and two other Delta officers awaited. The men were smaller, leaner Skazys: lean, serious guys in cammo fatigues, bulging with belts and knives and grenades.

"So? What's the—"

"We want you to keep an eye on someone for us."

"That's not my job," said Peter. "I'm not here to keep an eye on anybody."

"On Dick Puller," said Skazy.

Peter felt his face betray some shock.

"There was a time," said Skazy, "when Dick Puller was the best man this Army had. It was an honor to serve under him, let me tell you. He was a great officer. He was a professional's professional. But he lost it."

"What are you talking about?" Peter didn't like this a bit.

"Sometimes these guys who've seen so much combat lose the edge. They can't send boys to die anymore. They don't have the balls for the big leap. They delude themselves; they don't close out the engagement, they don't get in tight, they're not willing to take casualties, they're not willing to see their own troops die to take an objective. And so you get what you've got right now: a sense that all around us things are going on, but right here, right at the point of the crisis, nothing is happening, except that we're marking time."

Peter felt himself a poor advocate for Puller.

"Look, he's trying, he can't do much until—"

Skazy bent close.

"In the Iranian desert there came a moment he'd trained his life for. It didn't come down like it was laid out, and it meant taking a big chance, it meant going for it. You know what they say in this business? Who dares, wins. That's the first principle of special operations. In the desert,

Dick Puller lost the talent to dare. That guy up there on that mountain, he's still got it."

"What are you saying?" Peter said.

"I'm saying if he panics again, I'm going to take him out. And push forward and deal with the consequences later. It's what I should have done in the desert. You just watch him. If you see signs that he's breaking down, you let me know, got it?"

Peter saw now that he was in some twisted, sick family drama. It was some humorless parody version of a sixties sitcom, *My Three Sons* as written by Edward Albee, in which the oldest boy, Crazy Skazy here, was going to knock off Dad, Fred MacMurray/Dick Puller, while the two younger boys, himself and the other son, poor dumb Uckley, sat around wondering what to do.

"You'd better reconsider what—"

"Thiokol, if he freezes, you sing out, you hear. That's your real job. Now, you'd better get back to your goddamned door."

The farther along he got, the better Teagarden felt, when he knew it should be just the opposite. No matter how you cut it, he knew, he was welshing out. He was ejecting. Color him gone.

Yet his relief as the tunnel called Alice widened, as its dog legs and juts eventually straightened themselves out, was enormous and liberating. Goddamn, it felt so *good*; he'd felt this way in 'Nam, way out in Indian country, he'd been just a kid, it was '71 or so and he was new to the Forces. It was after a long goddamn time in a little place, getting hit every night, that at last a relief column had broken through. It felt just like that. He couldn't smell the sky yet, or see the stars—if there were stars; he had no idea what time it was—but he wasn't going deeper and deeper into the goddamned darkness.

He almost wanted to whistle. But suddenly he heard something just ahead. It was like a little rustle or something, up against the rock. What, had Rat Six sent more guys in? He froze, caught. To run into an officer and have to explain what the hell he was doing broken off from his partner, here, hundreds and hundreds of feet back, almost in the lateral tunnel, that was trouble. He ransacked his own mind for an excuse, something to put between himself and his disgrace.

The radio!

The Prick-88 wasn't working, they weren't getting through, he'd come on back to reestablish contact before—

A light beam shot out, hit him in the eyes, pinning him.

"Hey! Jesus, you guys, you scared me. What the hell, you checking on us, Rat Six? I lost radio contact, came back to get a clear line. Listen, we're way the hell back there."

Another light struck him, blasting his vision, filling his brain with exploding sparks. He heard muttering, the soft jingle of equipment.

"What's going on, guys? Like, is all this really—"

A hand like a darting bat flew in front of his eye, landed at his chin, and with a strong yank pulled him back until he crashed against a strong body; the hand pulled his chin up, opening his throat to the attack. At almost precisely the same second, though Teagarden never saw it, the other hand drew the evil edge of a very sharp combat blade across his throat, cutting with icy precision through skin, cartilege, and on down to the carotid artery, which it severed.

My sons! he thought, Jesus, my sons!

But, stunned as he was, Teagarden at least had a second left for a reflex, and as he died, his finger tensed on the MP-5's trigger and the little gun barked out a four-round burst. The bullets smashed pointlessly into the ground, and immediately other men were on Teagarden, beating at him with rifle butts.

This was the hard part.

The guns were easy: A Fabrique Nationale FAL, in 7.62-mm NATO, or .308, serial number 1488803-213; a 9-mm Uzi, manufactured also by Fabrique Nationale under license from the crafty Israelis, serial number 10945873-38771 with a very professionally made but otherwise untraceable silencer that extended a good seven inches beyond the barrel; and a British L2A3, called a Sterling, in 9mm also, serial number 129848-555; plus one handgun, a Czech CZ-75, serial number ground off. This information had been forwarded to Washington, but the stuff felt as though it came from the immense pool of surplus weapons held in obscure warehouses the world over and belonging to no country but only to the fraternity of international arms dealers. It could have all been bought from *The Shotgun News*.

The clothes and personal effects were easy, too, though Uckley had felt a little ghoulish going through them. As for the personal effects, there were none. Each of the three dead aggressors had gone into battle without pictures of loved ones, without Bibles, without even wallets, with nothing tiny or human to sustain them: they were men who seemed to have never been. Their clothes were well-washed but equally vague: heavy black boots of obscure manufacture, also picked up somewhere on the military surplus market. Also, black fatigue pants with huge bellows pockets at the thighs; blue watch shirts, perhaps naval in origin; black sweaters and watch caps. They had gloves, found stored in the shot-up house, and heavy parkas, perhaps for outdoor work. All of the clothes would perhaps in time yield their secrets to the sophisticated microscopic textile testing the Bureau had back in its labs in Washington; but that would take weeks, and in hours the world would be ending. The clothes were therefore of no immediate help.

This left the bodies. This left the hard part.

The three naked men lay on a tarpaulin in the middle of the Burkittsville fire department. Sooner or later a doctor would surely get there who could do this thing more professionally than poor Uckley, the mother killer with the black and blue stomach, but he had not arrived yet and nobody else particularly wanted to do it. So there was Uckley, alone with the three bodies.

Look at them, he told himself.

The big one who'd died upstairs seemed the worst. He'd put the Czech pistol into his mouth and squeezed off a round. The bullet had blown out the back of his skull, leaving his head queerly deflated in appearance, like a melon halved by an ax. But more amazing was his right shoulder, which looked as if a buzz saw had hit it; one of Delta Three's bullets had really ripped it up. God, how could he go on, hurt like that? Yet Uckley had seen him, climbing the steps, firing, the whole works. In pain like that? This was some kind of Superman. Even the corpse grinned a little at him. What was there in that white-toothed smile? Was it superiority?

Yeah, okay, Uckley thought. So you were the better man.

The other two had taken more hits but looked better. They were just dead men with what looked like red scabs the size of quarters scattered across their bodies, three across the chest of one, eleven spread randomly across the other. Bullet holes, lovely, Uckley thought. He thought of a picture from a history book of proud townspeople standing next to some old-time desperado, hit about a dozen times and now propped up like a cigar store Indian in his coffin, his mustache drooping, his bullet holes shining like buttons in the sun.

Think, Uckley told himself.

Okay, all of them were lean, strong men. They had the flat bellies and sinewy muscles of well-trained professional military men, elite troopers. Their hair was all cut short; one of them had nicked himself shaving that day. They looked to be in their late twenties. All three had patches of scar tissue on their upper arms, and one had quite a few on his wrists and chest. Tattoos? Yes, tattoos, somebody had surgically removed their tattoos!

And goddamn, they were tan. Their faces and their arms were tan; they had the burnished deep color that fishermen get, men who spend their lives in the sun.

Uckley went back to the first one. He looked more closely at his body. Yes, there was a lacework of stitches running up his chest, intersected by another line of stitches.

You've been hit before, he thought. You've had a very adventurous life, my friend. I'll bet you could tell me some things if you were alive.

He checked the others for wounds. The one was clean, but the other had a pucker of scar tissue up high, near his collarbone on the right side. It was another bullet hole.

These were clearly tough customers, all right. Somebody else's Delta.

He wished he knew what to do next. He walked back to the leader. What am I, a forensic pathologist? I just look and see dead guys, their heads shot away. He remembered the man standing above him, the little girl squirming beneath him. Let the girl go for crissakes, he'd said, and the man had just stared at him.

You had me cold, pal.

Instead, you walked back and blew your brains out.

Uckley knelt. Something in that smile, something mysterious and bright. A commando with movie-star teeth blowing his brains out in the back room of an old house in Burkittsville, Maryland.

Almost involuntarily, Uckley put his finger out. It was the unnaturalness of the dead man's smile that disturbed him. The teeth were so white. He put his finger in the dry mouth, felt the dry lips and the dry, dead tongue, reached up, pinched, tugged and—

Yes, they were false.

The porcelain bridge came out in his hand.

He checked quickly. All three men had completely false teeth, and almost brand new bridges placed in their mouths.

Witherspoon began to chatter.

"Wow, did you hear that? Man, that sounded like gunfire. You suppose—"

But then Walls's hand stole over his mouth and pulled him down with more strength and will than the larger, younger man ever thought the smaller, older one possessed.

Then he heard the whisper in his ear.

"Okay, now, man, you just take it easy, you just keep it quiet. Okay, man? Okay?"

Witherspoon nodded and Walls let slip his mouth.

"Shit, you—"

"Shhhhhh. Old Charlie, he in the tunnel. Yep. Charlie here. Charlie come a-hunting. Yep, old Charlie, you can't hold him back. He's come a-hunting."

Witherspoon looked at him, feeling his eyes bulge and his heart begin to triphammer.

"Hey—"

"Hey, nothing. You listen to Walls. Walls knows Charlie. Walls and Charlie, man, them two go way back."

Walls seemed, queerly, to be fading on him, to be transfiguring into some other creature: he slid back, as if to allow his blackness to be absorbed by the tunnel. At the same time, Walls had unslung Mr. Twelve, and adroitly peeled off the black tape that masked the muzzle and the ejector port. With one swift metallic *klak!* the old tunnel rat pumped a big double-ought into the chamber.

"Okay, you listen," Walls said softly. "Time to gear up. Get your shit on, get your piece ready. Tunnel be hot. Charlie hunting us, man, we got to hunt Charlie. Only way to stay alive."

Witherspoon threw on his flak jacket and picked up his German machine pistol. He cocked it, drawing back the knob that ran through the housing over the barrel; it clicked locked and solid. He slid the night vision goggles down across his face, popped off the lens cap, and turned on the device from the battery pack at his belt. As he diddled with the image intensifiers and the focus, the tunnel leapt to life in a kind of aquamarine as the electro-optics picked up the infrared beam from the lamp atop the goggles; he had a sense of being underwater, everything was green, green and spooky. He turned to Walls and faced a man on fire. The convict's face burned red and yellow like some hideous movie special effect; Witherspoon almost laughed at the strangeness, the comedy of it all, but it was only that Walls, excited, had begun to pulse with blood, and from so close, all that heat, all those agitated molecules, came through the lenses like a movie monster.

"Okay," said Walls soothingly, "now, this is how it got to be. We got to move forward, and make our contact as early as we can. Okay, we hit Charlie, we fall back. We hit him again, we fall back. See, in a one-way tunnel, you got only one chance, man. You got to hit that sucker and hit him over and over. You got to hope he runs out of men before you run out of tunnel. Because if you run out of tunnel before he runs out of men, you're one trapped rat. Man, the tunnels I been in all had holes at *both* ends, this fucker only one end. These white bitches, they always let you down."

"Okay, I'm with you."

Something flashed in Witherspoon's psychedelic vision: it was Walls's teeth.

He was smiling.

"Whistle while you work, man," Walls said merrily.

Phuong, in the tunnel called Alice, also heard the gunshots.

Mother, her daughter said, Mother, the Americans are coming for us.

I know, she said. Let them come.

But her response was different, because unlike Rat Team Baker, she had not come to the end of her tunnel; she still believed there was something ahead. Thus her thought was to continue her movement.

She reached to her belt and swiftly removed one M-26 fragmentation grenade, smooth as an egg. Then she knelt, took off her tennis shoes, and quickly unlaced them and threw the shoes away, behind her. She swiftly tied a loop around the lever of the grenade with just enough tension to hold it in close enough. Then, gingerly, she pulled the pin. She felt the lever strain against the shoelace. With her knife she began to saw through the lace. At last, only a hair's width of lace remained, just the thinnest, tiniest membrane of woven cotton. Gingerly, she set the thing down in the center of the tunnel, on its base. She knew that if men came through the tunnel single file, without lights, they would kick it; when they kicked it, or bumped it, the thing would fall on its side, the shoelace would pop and—

Two hundred yards farther on she repeated the process with the other lace.

Let the Americans come, she thought. Let them come for Phuong, as before. And as before, Phuong will be ready. I will save my child from the fire.

Turning, she fled deeper into her home, the tunnel.

Peter was writing.

Provisional army of us??? code// 12 digits // suppressed integer// syllabification correspondence????vowel repetition significance??? 12 = 12 = 12 = 12//Simple integer equivalence??12 = 12 = 12 = twelve????

He set up a simple $a = 1$, $b = 2$, $c = 3$ scheme to see what the thing decrypted out to. It decrypted out to . . . nonsense.

He played with themes of 12: 4 3's, 2 6's, 3 4's, 12 1's . . . 12. Twelve, he kept thinking, *twelve!*

Suddenly bells were ringing. What the fuck? He looked up as a bunch of Commo specialists in the room jumped, shocked out of what they were doing.

"What the hell does that mean?" Peter asked.

"It means Priority One," said one of the kids. "It means they've got something for us."

"You better go get the hotshots."

But by the time Peter got to the flash teletype, Skazy had already taken up the prime position.

"Okay," he said greedily, "okay, here it comes," as the machine spat out its information.

Skazy read the document quickly and summarized.

"They've identified the original source of Aggressor-One's communication and they think from that their psychologists can extrapolate his motivation, his psychic dynamics, a profile of who he is and what he's liable to do, what he's capable of, and what we should do."

"So?" said Puller.

Skazy's fast eyes ripped through the letters as they spewed out. Every twenty or so lines he peeled the paper off the roller and passed it around the room. The machine clicked for several minutes.

"Of course," said Major Skazy. "That's why it's so familiar, yes."

Puller said nothing for the longest time, letting the younger men absorb the information.

"All right," said Puller. "Let's have it."

"It sounds familiar," said Skazy, "because it *is* familiar. It's John Brown."

There was quiet in the room.

"Yes, it's the same, don't you see?" Skazy rushed on, tumbling with the information. "It's John Brown's Raid, before the Civil War. He's taken over a key installation at the center of the military industrial complex. Right?"

"In 1859," Peter said, "in Harpers Ferry, in fact not seven miles from here, John Brown led a force of about twenty or so men and took over a federal arsenal and musket factory. This year, with a few more men, he's taken over a federal missile silo. Strategic muskets, in other words."

"And the goal is the same," Skazy said, "to start the big war, and to unleash the forces of good and to drive out the forces of evil. And, this time, as last time, there's a bunch of elite troops outside the place who've got the job of going in with bayonets fixed to try to stop him."

"What's the source?" asked Peter laconically, feeling quite beyond surprise.

"The message he sent," Skazy answered, "it's from John Brown's interrogation by federal authorities in the jailhouse at Charlestown, West Virginia, October 17, 1859, after his capture and before his execution."

Skazy read from a CIA psychologist's report: " 'Empathetic connection with historical figure suggests paranoid schizophrenia to an unusual degree. Such men tend to be extremely dangerous, because in their zeal they tend to exhibit great will and charisma. Well-known examples include Adolf Hitler, John Brown himself, Joseph Stalin, Ghengis Khan, several of the Roman emperors, Peter the Great. The standard symptoms are highly developed aggressive impulses and the tendency toward the creation of self-justifying systems of illusion. In the classical cases such men tend to be the offspring of broken families, generally with fathers either absent or remote, and strong matriarchal units replacing the patriarchal. They are usually marked by abnormally high IQs and extremely well-developed "game intelligence." Such men, typically, are extraordinary tacticians and brilliant at solving narrow technical or strategic problems. They almost always operate from the narrow basis of their own self-interest. They lack the gift of perspective; their power stems from their ability to see only the relevant, narrow slice of the "big picture." They lack associational abilities; they lack, furthermore, any tendency toward moderation. They are highly narcissistic, usually spellbinding speakers and almost always completely ruthless. Historically, their flaw arrives in "overreaching"; they tend to think they can change the world, and almost always go too far and are destroyed—usually at great cost to self and families—by their inability to compromise.' "

"Everything we need to know about him except how to kill him," said Dick Puller.

Skazy continued. "From this they expect him to be American military, extremely proficient in a narrow range, nursing obscure political grudges. They think his men are Americans, possibly a reserve Green Beret unit that has come under his spell. They think he's bankrolled by conservative money. Man"—he whistled—"they've worked up a whole scenario here. It's about what you'd expect. Screwball general, impressionable troops, maybe some paramilitary outfit, those pretend mercs who read *Soldier of Fortune* and wear camouflage fatigues to the shopping malls. Survivalists, nut cases, that sort of thing."

Dick listened, his eyes fixed on nothing.

Finally, he said, "So what's their recommendation?"

"Frontal attack. They say that his green troops will buckle when they start taking heavier casualties. They want us to throw frontals at 'em again and again."

"They better send some fresh body bags," was all Dick said.

Then he asked, "So is that what you think, Major? Frontals?"

"Yes, sir. I think we ought to hit him again. The sooner, the more often, the better. Let me saddle up Delta and we're off. Bravo in support. Leave a small reserve force here in case that radio message this morning was to another unit ready to jump us from the rear. When the Third Infantry and the Rangers arrive, you can feed them in if we haven't taken the place down yet."

Puller went around the room. Everybody said yes. Hit him. Hit him and hit him, and he'll crack. Waiting solved nothing, especially now that Rat Six had been zapped and there was nothing going on inside the mountain.

Even the morose Lieutenant Dill, the gym teacher who now led what was left of Bravo, had to agree: hit 'em, he said. Hit 'em until they crack.

Finally, Puller got to Peter.

"Since this has become a democracy and we're polling the voters, Dr. Thiokol, you might as well throw in your two cents. You tell me. Should I hit him until he cracks?"

Peter considered. He felt Skazy's hard eyes boring in upon him. But Skazy didn't scare him; he'd been glared at by furious five-stars in his time.

He said, "And what if he doesn't crack? What if his men are the best, and when they take casualties they don't break? What if he's got enough ammo up there to hold off a division? And he knows you can attack only over a narrow front, up one side of the mountain?

"What if, most important of all, the subtlest part of his plan is convincing you that yes, he's a nut case, he thinks he's John Brown, and that he'll come apart under the pressure. What then? And what if you hit him until you run out of men and the bodies pile up like cordwood just outside his perimeter. The Rangers show and the Third Infantry shows, and he guns them down too. And the men that you've got left are exhausted and broken. What then?"

"Then he wins."

"Right. We don't get in. What if they're wrong in D.C.?"

"These are experienced guys. Doctors," argued Skazy.

"Major Skazy, I know a little about psychiatrists. I'm here to tell you there aren't three of them in the world who could agree on the results of two plus two."

Skazy was quiet.

Peter said, "I don't think he's insane. I think he's very, very smart, and he's set up this whole thing, this phony John Brown thing, because he knows our prejudices, and he knows how eager we are to believe in them. He's encouraging us to believe in them at the cost of our own destruction."

He didn't express his worst, most frightening thought, the source of his curiously dislocating sense of weirdness over the past several seconds. The whole thing seemed pulled not out of history, but out of something far more personal. Out of, somehow, memory. His. His own memory. He remembered. Yes, John Brown, but who *thought* of John Brown first and used him as an analogy for a takeover in a missile silo in *Nuclear Endgames, Prospects for Armageddon?*

Peter Thiokol.

Peter thought: This son of a bitch has read my book.

But Puller was speaking.

"I just got a call from Uckley, who examined the three dead aggressors in Burkittsville. They had false teeth."

He let it sink in.

"Nothing gives a man's national identity away to forensic pathologists faster than dental work. So these guys had their teeth pulled—all of them—and bridgework from a third-party country inserted, so that in the event of death or capture, their origin couldn't be traced," Puller said. "These guys aren't psychos or fringe lunatics or right-wing extremists or a rogue unit. They're a foreign elite unit on a mission. They're here for a specific, rational purpose. We have to wait until we know who they are. Then we'll know what to do. To squander our limited resources right now is to doom ourselves to failure. We don't know enough to jump."

"When will we?" said Skazy bitterly.

"When I say so," said Dick Puller. "When we know who they are. And not before."

1800

Witherspoon should have seen them first, but Walls did, or rather sensed them, smelled them, somehow felt them, and his swift elbow into Witherspoon's ribs was all the signal needed. In Witherspoon's field of electro-optics, they emerged as phantasms, swirling patterns of dense color swooping abstractly through the green chamber at him. They were dream monsters, humped and horrible, their shapes changing, one beast leaking into another; they were straight from his hyperfervid id, white men with guns in the night.

So die, motherfuckers, thought Witherspoon.

He fired first, the MP-5 bucking in a spasm as it hurried through its little box of bullets. How good it felt! It drove the fear from him. Through the lenses he could not see the streak of the tracers, nor their strikes. But he saw something else: the red darts of sheer heat, which the infrared picked up and magnified, flew into them like glops of color from the brush of a maniac. The shapes slithered, shattered, quivered, and seemed to magically recombine and reform before him. The stench of powder rose like an elixir to his nose. The gun wrenched itself empty.

He scrambled back, laughing madly. God, he'd hit so many. He heard screams behind him. Man, we hit those motherfuckers cold, we blindsided them, man, we took their butts *out!*

"Down!" screamed Walls, who in the roar of their race back had heard something bounce off the walls, and as if to make the point clearer, he nailed Witherspoon with an open field hit, knocking him down in a tangle of ripped knees and torn palms. Then the grenade detonated.

It was very close. The noise of it was the worst, but not by much. The noise was huge; it blew out both of Witherspoon's eardrums and left traces of itself inside his skull for what might be forever. Its flash was weird and powerful, particularly through the distortion of his night vision glasses, the hue so hot and bright it had no coefficient in nature. Finally, following these first phenomena, the force of the blast arrived in an instant, and was as mighty as a wallop from God. It threw him, rag-doll-like, against the wall. He felt himself begin to bleed abruptly, though as yet there was no pain.

Witherspoon sat up, completely disoriented. For just a second he forgot both who and where he was. He blinked and peeped about like a just-born baby bird, chunks of shell and fluid stuck to his face. In the dark, bats of light flipped and swooped toward him. The air was full of dust and broken neon and cigarette smoke from forties movies. His head ached.

"Come on, boy, shoot back!" came the shout from close at hand, and he turned to see an interesting thing. He was by now only half in his night goggles, which had been blown askew by the grenade, so he saw half of Walls in the stylized abstractions of the infrared, a glowing red god, all anger and sinew and grace; but the other half of Walls was the human half: a soldier, scared to death, full of adrenaline and responsibility, standing against the tide of fire in the blackness and cranking out blasts from his Mossberg, eruptions of flash which, for however brief a fragment of time they lasted, lit the tunnel in pink-orange and almost turned the fierce Walls into a white man.

Walls pumped up dry, but by that time Witherspoon had shaken the dazzle from his brain, gotten a new clip into the German gun, and turned to spray lead down the tunnel, watching the bullets leaking light and describing a tracing of a flower petal as they hurled off into the darkness. The fire came back at him after a pause, angry and swarming. It seemed to be hitting everywhere, pricks of hot coal sent flying against his skin by the bullet strikes.

He knelt, fumbled through a mag change.

"Grenade," said the resourceful Walls, having thought one step ahead, and Witherspoon caught a glimpse of him as a classical javelin thrower posing for a statue. Then he uncoiled, and as he uncoiled fell forward. Witherspoon heard yells of panic from surprisingly close at hand, but was unfortunately and stupidly looking into the heat of the blast when the grenade detonated. His vision disappeared in a confusion of deep-brain nerve cells firing off and as he fell backward, his night shades fell even farther awry, then slipped away.

"I'm blind, man, I'm *blind!*" he screamed. Walls had him. The firing seemed to have stopped. Walls put a strong hand around the fleshy part of his arm above the elbow and pulled him backward in a crazy old-nigger scuffle. He felt like one of those clumsy black fools in an old movie.

Walls pulled him back farther and deeper. Gradually, his vision returned to normal. He could see Walls's sweating face just ahead.

"I can see now."

"Man, don't ever look at those suckers when they go off."

"How many did we get?"

"I don't know, man. Hard to say. In the dark, it sometime seem like so much more, you know?"

They fell into silence. Witherspoon breathed raggedly, looking for his energy. He felt as though he could sleep for a hundred years. He could smell Walls next to him. Yet he sensed no stress in Walls.

"You like this, don't you?" he asked, amazed.

Walls sniggered. "Shee-itt," he finally said, "a chance to kill white boys? Man, this is like a *vacation!*"

"You think they had enough?"

"No. Not these white boys. *Most* white boys, not *these* white boys. These white boys *pissed.*"

From the footsteps she guessed no more than five. She heard them rushing along, their breathing ragged under the equipment they wore and their urgency. Then the first explosion came, its flash bouncing off the walls and through the turns all the way to her, its hot, dry concussion arriving a half second later. There were screams and moans. But then—the sound traveled surprisingly well under the ground, for it had no place else to go except straight to her—she heard the scuffle of feet.

Mother, they are still coming.

I hear them.

This surprised her. In the war, the Americans almost always turned back when they took casualties. On the surface, when they started losing people, they withdrew and called in the airplanes. But in the tunnels there were no airplanes; they simply retreated. Yet these footsteps came on, if anything, more determined than before.

She turned, upset, now frightened, and began to withdraw deeper still into the tunnel.

Hurry, Mother. They must have found the second grenade and disarmed it. They are coming faster.

She raced into the tunnel. By now it had almost disappeared into a trace and the beams the miners had erected for their operations had long since vanished; instead, it was the classical Cu Chi passage, a low, cramped crawlspace, fetid and dense. She rushed through it, her fingers feeling the way. She felt as if she were crawling back into the black womb and knew she was very deep and very far.

She halted after a time, turned, and listened. She could no longer hear the men. She thought she was safe.

Am I safe?

Mother, be careful. You must wait.

She was still. Time slowed.

Mother, be patient. Haste kills.

What was it? An odor? Some disturbance in the air? An odd flash of mental energy from somewhere? Or only the return of her old dark instincts? Somehow she knew she was not alone.

Her hand slipped to her belt. She removed the knife. She willed herself to stillness. She willed her body into the walls. She lay motionless and silent in the dark and the loneliness with her daughter. She felt herself attempting to enter into the fabric of the underground, to still the whirl of her atoms and the beat of her heart. She thought she heard something once, and then another something. The time passed; she had no idea how much.

Then again something else came. The sound of men in heavy equipment crashing through the tunnel, much farther back now, much more frightened, much more reluctant to go on now that the tunnel was shrinking.

She could imagine them right where the bigger tunnel was absorbed into the smaller one, their bravado frozen by its sudden shrinkage and the difficulty of the path that lay before them. Western people did not like to go into the dark alone, where they could not maneuver or talk or see or touch one another. It would stop them if anything would: their simple terror of the close space and the darkness.

The men made brave sounds. They were arguing. One seemed louder. She could not quite understand the distorted sounds. But the yelling grew louder, and then halted entirely. She heard them walking away. Their sounds slowly disappeared.

She almost moved then. But she did not.

Wait, Mother. When you move, you die. Wait. Wait.

The dark pressed upon her like the lid of a coffin. Her hip was wedged against a jutting rock; she could feel it bruise. Her muscles stiffened and began to ache. Her scalp tingled. A cramp tightened her upper arm. Her whole body screamed for the release of movement.

She tried to think of her village before the war came. It was near a place called Ben Suc in the Thanh Dien forest. She had a sister and nine brothers; her father had been a Viet Minh and fought the French with an old carbine until it fell apart, and then he fought them with bamboo spears. But for a time it was a prosperous area, Ben Suc; there were many fruit trees, many cattle; life had not been easy, but they lived well enough by their modest endeavors. She was fifteen and still helping with the housework when her home was obliterated by bombs.

She tried to remember: she thought of it as the golden time, those few years before the bombs came. She held on to it, sometime, in the tunnels, and would tell her daughter, Some day you'll see. We'll live in the sunlight. There will be fruit and rice for all. You'll see, my little one. Then she would sing the child a lullaby, holding her warm and tight and feeling her small heart beating against her own:

Sweet good night, baby sweetness
in the morning comes calm,
Sweet good night, baby daughter
all the war will soon cease,
Sweet good night, baby sweetness
in the morning comes—

There, Mother. Her daughter spoke to her from her heart. Do you feel it? There is another.

Phuong lay very still because she felt his warmth.

He was very good, and like her, he was barefoot. He had no equipment. He moved like a snake, in slow, patient strokes, nothing forced or hastened. He had come ahead under the noise of the men who had halted, covered by the loud drama of their chatter and yelling. He'd moved quickly and soundlessly, hunting her. He was immensely brave, she understood, the very best of them. He was a man she could love, like her husband. He was a tunnel man. Now only the faintest blur, a different shade of dark, he grew larger as he drew nearer; she felt his heat. And then she felt the softness of his breath, and the sweetness of it, and his terrible, terrible intimacy.

I must abandon you, my daughter, she thought. Where I must go next and what I must do, you cannot be a part of. I love you. I will see you soon.

Her daughter was silent . . . gone. Phuong was alone with the white man in the tunnel.

They were as close as lovers in the dark, his supple body so close to hers that she felt a terrible impulse to caress him, to *have* him, she who had not had a man in a decade.

But she had him with her blade. It struck with amazing force in the dark as he crawled by. She felt it sink into the living muscle and she felt the muscles knit to fight it as she forced it deeper, and their bodies locked. Their loins embraced. In the hole sex and death were so much the same it was terrifying. She felt his arms enclose her and his breath was labored and intense as if with sexual energy. His blood felt warm and soft like a spurt of sperm. In frenzy he thrust his pelvis against hers, and the friction, bucking and taking, was not unpleasant. Somewhere in all this his blade probed desperately after her, and he cut a terrible gash into her shoulder, through the cloth, through the flesh, almost to the bone. She felt the knife sawing against her and muffled her scream in his chest.

She pulled her blade out. And jammed it home again. And again. And . . . again.

Then he was still. He had stopped breathing.

Spent, she pulled away from him and cupped her shoulder. She was covered with their mingled blood. She could not even see him anymore. Her arm throbbed, and she managed to rip a strip of cloth off her tattered shirt, which she tied into a loose tourniquet. Inserting the knife blade, she screwed the thing clockwise until the bleeding stopped and only a huge numbness remained.

She tried to crawl ahead somehow, but her exhaustion was endless. She surrendered to it, lying back, her mouth open, her eyes closed, in the dark of the dark tunnel in the very center of the mountain. It was completely silent. The roof of the tunnel was an inch from her face; she could feel it. She wanted to scream.

And then she heard it from just ahead: a drip of water striking a puddle. And then another. She reached out and felt the water, and pulled herself to it. She drank greedily from the puddle, and only when she was done did she think to reach into the pouch on her belt and find a match.

The light flared dramatically, hurting her eyes, which she clamped shut. Then she opened them. There was an opening in the roof of the tunnel. She looked and realized it was another tunnel, impossibly small.

But, more important, it led up.

He had been hit twice. It didn't seem fair. Witherspoon lay back, trying to get it all clarified in his head. How many of them could there be? How had the world turned so surrealistic on him?

"You doin' good, sonny," said Walls next to him. "Man, like we make these white boys *pay*, no shit, huh?"

Witherspoon could hardly answer, he hurt so badly. It was a dream fight. Total silence, then the sudden flashes as the bullets whipped by, tearing into the walls of the tunnel, their own quick answers, and the stumbling fallback before the detonation of the grenades. How many times now? Three, four. How many had they killed? How many of their own grenades were left?

But worse: how much tunnel was left?

The answer was depressing: not much.

"Whooo-eee," moaned Walls softly now, "we at the end of the line, boy."

Behind them the tunnel stopped. It ended here.

"Nobody's going home from this party," Walls said, loquacious at the end as he had been at the start. "But we made them white boys do some paying, right, man?"

Witherspoon was silent. He'd long since lost the MP-5. He had his automatic in his hands, though he was shaking. He could hear the quiet slide of plastic against metal as Walls slid more shells into his Mossberg.

"Shame I couldn't get this piece back to the guy," said Walls, cycling the slide with a ratchety *snik-snak!* "Real nice piece, you know? He take good care of it. No shotgun let you down like no woman."

"My wife never let me down," said Witherspoon.

"Sure, boy. You just lie quiet now."

The smell of powder was everywhere in the tunnel. Witherspoon's mouth was dry. He wished he had a drink of water or something. His whole left leg was numb; he didn't think he could move anyway, so at least it was good they had no place to run anymore. He was thinking a lot about his wife.

"Man, Walls. Yo, Walls."

"Yeah."

"My wife. Tell her I loved her, you got that?"

"Man, you think I'm going to be around to do any telling?" Walls chuckled at the absurdity of this idea. "Anyway, man, I bet she knows."

"Walls, you're a good guy, okay?"

"No, boy. I'm a very bad guy. Fact, I'm a motherfucker. I just happen to do good tunnel work. You best be quiet now. I think it's coming on to nut-cutting time."

And so it was. They heard the scuffles in the dark but had no targets. That was the terrible thing about it all: they could not fire until fired upon; it was a question of lying still and waiting for the world to end. Witherspoon raised the pistol, a Browning 9-mil. He had thirteen rounds in the mag, and then that was it. And there was no place else to go.

They could hear them getting closer now, edging along. Damn, these were brave men too. It pissed Witherspoon off to be matched against such good ones. It didn't seem fair, somehow. But these guys, no matter how many you killed, they just kept coming. They were the best.

The 1st Battalion of the Third Infantry was only three hours late, the convoy having gotten all fouled up in the amazing pile-up of traffic outside the operational area.

There was something peculiar about these men, Puller thought, watching as they climbed down from the big trucks just outside his headquarters in the falling dark. Then it struck him: they were all handsome and white and their hair was cut short around their ears in a style he hadn't seen for years, what used to be called white sidewalls; they had the odd appearance of Prussian cadets. He noticed next that instead of the ubiquitous M-16, black plastic and famous, they carried the old wooden-stocked M-14 in 7.62mm, a real infantry battle-fighting rifle. And then he noticed, good Christ, their fatigues were starched!

"Who the hell *are* these guys?" he asked Skazy.

"Ceremonial troops. They guard the Tomb of the Unknown Soldier, shit like that. They march in parades, bury people in Arlington. Pull duty at the White House. Hollywood soldiers."

"Jesus," said Puller.

He found the CO, a full bird colonel, rare for a battalion, even a reinforced one, and introduced himself.

"I'm Puller," he said. "Colonel, get your men out of the trucks and distribute ammo. You can even chow 'em down if you've got time. But keep 'em near the trucks. We're going to get the ball rolling real soon now, I hope, depending on what I hear from the Pentagon and whether this young hotshot I have working on the door problem thinks he has a shot at getting the shaft open."

The colonel just looked at him.

"Sir, maybe you'd like to tell me what this is about."

"Nobody briefed you, Colonel?"

"No, sir. I'm under the impression it's some kind of nuclear accident and we'd be pulling containment duties."

"It's a night infantry assault, Colonel, and you'll be pulling perimeter penetration duties, supported by a shot-up company of National Guardsmen who've already lost half their manpower, some state policemen, a local cop or two, and any high school ROTC units I can round up, and maybe, if the goddamned weather holds, a Ranger battalion now somewhere between here and Tennessee in a couple of C-130s. Your job is to get Delta in close so it can jump the silo. You might want to think about reforming your squad heavy weapons teams into an ad hoc machine-gun platoon."

"Yes, sir."

"Good. Brief your senior NCOs and your officers now. There'll be a final briefing at 2000 hours. You can check with Delta staff for maps. I'll expect all your officers to know the terrain backward and forward by then."

"Y-yes, sir."

"You in Vietnam, Colonel?"

"Yes, sir. I was a captain with the 101st, a company commander."

"Well, you're back there, Colonel, except that it's a little colder and a lot more important."

Walls fired. He fired again. He fired again. Beside him, Witherspoon fired with the pistol. Walls could hear it going off like the bark of a dog. Meanwhile, heavy automatic fire came at them, tracer, and as it skittered overhead it whistled on back to the end of the tunnel, and began to ricochet. Spent rounds whirled through the dark space over their heads. It was like being in a frying pan at full sizzle, bubbles of hot grease dancing everywhere, flying through the air in angry flecks. That's what Walls thought of. But of course it wasn't. It was just the tunnel.

The Charlies broke off contact.

"Okay," Walls said. "Goddamn, I think I got one that time. Man, can't be too many left. Man, we may be out of tunnel, but them boys goin' be out of *peoples* real soon now, you hear that, boy?" He laughed deeply at the idea.

"Man, like to kill me a whole muthafucking platoon of them boys before I'm done!" He laughed again, and then noticed the silence from Witherspoon. He reached to him and found that the young soldier had died sometime during the fight. He had simply and quietly bled to death.

Walls shook his head in disappointment. Now who was he going to talk to? Man, this was worse than solitary.

He heard noises up ahead, the click of guns being checked and readied. Okay, white boys coming again. He tried to think of them as Klansmen, big crackers in pickups with ax handles and flaming crosses. Or big Irish Baltimore cops with red faces, motherfuckers on *horses*, man, who'd just as soon smash you as look at you. Or fancy white-boy suits look at you like you a piece of shit a dog dumped on the street.

He laughed again, threw the slide on the Mossberg, felt a shell lifted into place.

"Hey, come on, motherfuckers!" he yelled, laughing. "Come on, white motherfuckers, Dr. P got some shit for you boys!"

It then occurred to him that there was an even larger joke he could play on them! He could blow them all up! For hadn't Witherspoon, the perfect little soldier boy, hadn't he carried C-4 explosive in a block somewhere on him? Walls had blown tunnels in the 'Nam with this stuff; he knew it well. He rolled to Witherspoon's body.

Sorry, boy, he said to the corpse. Got me some lookin' to do. He probed, scared that the white boys would hit him before he could rig his big surprise. But then he came across it in a bellows pocket of the field pants, a greasy brick about the size of a book. He got it out and began to squeeze and mold it in his strong hands, working some warmth and flexibility into its chilled stiffness.

Gonna make me a *bomb*, he thought, blow those muthafuckers up.

Okay, finally, he had a lump about the size of a deflated football, maybe a pound's worth of the stuff. He had one grenade left. He took it off his belt and carefully unscrewed the fuse assembly and tossed away the egg. He bent to Witherspoon and probed him until he came across a coil of primacord in a pocket. He unraveled a bit of the primacord—it felt like putty and was an extremely hot-firing explosive fuse substance— onto the tip of the grenade's blasting cap at the end of the fuse, and then he plunged this into a glop of the C-4, quickly kneading the C-4 around the grenade fuse, but careful to make sure that the grenade lever was free, so it could pop off when he pulled the pin. He worked hard, laughing softly to himself, knowing that time was very, very short. For sure, they'd seen the tracers striking the rear wall. They knew he was out of tunnel.

"Hey, white-boy motherfuckers, you boys want to get laid? Hah, old Walls got some fine-lookin' bitches for you, man. Got a nice high yaller, got me a couple white chicks, got me a redhead, got me some real *foxes*, man. Come on and get it, white boys."

Three automatic weapons fired simultaneously and the bullets struck around him, hitting the walls, the back of the tunnel, cutting him off, kicking up clouds of coal dust from the floor. But he got the pin from the grenade, and with a kind of lob-heave launched the thing, felt it leave his hands, traveling slowly, not far enough, and he knew then he'd die in the blast too. And he began to scramble backward, away, away, though there was really no away to go to and—

In the small space the blast was huge. It lifted and threw Walls through hot light and harsh air. And dirt, or stone. For the world had been ruptured and the old mountain heaved, and the ceiling of the tunnel gave. He felt the earth covering him. He could not move. The tunnel caved in. He was frozen. He was in his tomb. He was in total blackness.

It occurred to Peter that he should eat something. He was beginning to feel shaky and his head ached. It had been hours since he'd eaten, way back in another lifetime.

But he could not leave the door behind.

The damned door.

It was a simple idea really, you just had to write the program and that was that. That, in fact, was its brilliance—its simplicity. Peter knew that if Delta fought its way to the elevator shaft in the launch control facility, he'd confront the computer-coded door to the shaft itself. It was the mega-door, the ultra-door, the total door. To pop it, you had to know the twelve-digit code. Except that the aggressors would have changed the code—easily done from inside the launch control center at the computer terminal.

Change it to what?

There it was: the new code would be twelve letters or numbers long, or a combination thereof, or less (but not more). Peter assumed that it would be a consciously selected sequence, because—well, because, it would be part of Aggressor-One's game. That's how his mind works, and I'm beginning to get a feel for it.

The terror was in the computer program itself. The program, conceived and written by Peter Thiokol of the MX Basing Modes Group, had been designed exactly to prevent what Peter now had to do. That is, he had built into its system a limited-try capacity. If the right code were not hit in the first three attempts, the program reasoned that interlopers were knocking at the door and automatically changed the code to a random sequence of numbers, and it would take another computer at least 135 hours to run through the millions and millions of permutations, even working at macrospeed.

Three strikes and you're out, Peter thought.

But it had been so smart—so *necessary*—because the heart of South Mountain is that it's independent-launch capable. Suppose the missile base is under assault by specially trained Soviet silo-seizure teams of the sort CIA said they were working up? Suppose Qaddafi sends a suicide team in? Suppose—oh, no, this is *too* wild!—right wing elements of the American military attempt to take over the silo in order to launch a preemptive strike against Johnny Red? In all those scenarios, exactly as projected in the chapter in his book on the John Brown scenario, it fell to the door and the key vault more than any complement of air security policemen or the doppler radar to hold the intruders at bay.

The joke was, he was fighting himself.

Through the medium of his poor wife, he had provided John Brown, Aggressor-One, or whoever he was, with all his stuff: his ideas, his insights, his theoretical speculations. He knows exactly what I know, Peter thought. In a terrible way, he *is* me. I've permutated. I've cloned a perfect twin; he's absorbed my personality.

Peter turned back to the documents the Agency psychologists had put together on "John Brown." As he read the psychological evaluation, he realized they could have been talking about him. And that's what troubled him the most. It was as if John Brown had *begun* with him, or with his book, or perhaps with his famous essay. And that he'd built his plan outward from that, mastering not so much South Mountain as Peter Thiokol.

He shivered. It was getting cold. He looked at his watch. The digital numbers rushed by:

6:34.32
6:34.33
6:34.35

Less than six hours to go.

John Brown. John Brown, you and your door. Three strikes and I'm out.

He started to doodle: Peter Thiokol = John Brown = 12 = 9 = 12 = 9?

Goddamn, he thought, it would make so much more sense if John Brown had twelve letters in it—the way Peter Thiokol did.

The general was on the phone most of the time with Alex up at ground level, listening impassively. Or he was standing politely back, watching Jack Hummel dig through the block of titanium that stood between himself and the second launch key.

Jack was quite deep by this time. It was difficult finding the space to maneuver so deep in the metal. And his arms ached and the sweat ran down his face. And, Jesus, he was hungry.

"Mr. Hummel. Mr. Hummel, how would you say it's going?"

"Look, you can see for yourself. I'm in here all the way. I'm really getting deep now."

He felt the general over his shoulder, peering down the shaft he'd opened, the wound in the metal.

"You're on the right line?"

"Absolutely. I'm going right into the center, that I can tell you. If this chamber or whatever you say it is is in the center, then I'll get it."

"How much longer?"

"Well, I can't say. You said the block was two hundred forty centimeters in diameter, and I've gone maybe a third of that. So I'm close. Another two, three hours, I don't know. We'll just see."

He looked into the flame, which was consuming the titanium with a voracious appetite. Even through the density of his lenses he could sense its extraordinary power. Nothing on earth could stand before it; all melted, yielded, liquified, and slid away against the urgency of the heat.

He tried to imagine this little flame grown a million times. He tried to imagine a giant flame, devouring as it flashed across the landscape; he tried to imagine a giant torch cutting its kerf of destruction around the globe, through cities and towns, turning men and women and babies to ashes. He tried to imagine all the death there was, a planet of death. It would be a lone zone that just didn't stop.

Instead, banal movie images flooded through his head: the mushroom cloud, the wrecked cities, the piles of corpses, the mutated survivors, bands of starving rat people scurrying through the ruins, and now a word from our sponsor, liquid Ivory, for truly *smooooth* hands.

I can't see how it would really be, he thought. I just can't. And the further leap, by which he would admit that such a fate could occur as a direct consequence of his own actions, was entirely beyond him.

It's not my fault, he told himself. What was I supposed to do, let them kill my kids? Sure, tell me my kids are less important than the world in general: that's easy for anyone except a dad to say.

He did know it called for an extraordinary man.

And I'm an ordinary one, he concluded. Bomb or no bomb, war or no war, *those are my kids!*

He looked back to the flame, in its hunger licking its way toward midnight.

"I told you," Megan told the Three Dumb Men. "How many times do I have to tell you? They claimed they were Israelis. I swear to you I thought they were Israelis. Jews. Just Jews. Are any of you Jewish?"

The Three Dumb Men shook their heads.

"The FBI doesn't have Jews?" she asked, incredulous. "In this day and age the FBI doesn't have Jews?"

"You're changing the subject, Mrs. Thiokol," said the harshest of them. "We're under an enormous time constraint here. Please, could we return? You've told us of your recruitment, you've told us of your mental state, you've detailed the information you gave him, you've described Ari Gottlieb and this mysterious intelligence officer in the Israeli consulate."

"That's all I know. I've told you everything I know. Please, I'd tell you anything. But I've told you everything."

It was dark by now, and through the windows she could see lights on in the neighborhood.

"Would anybody like any coffee?" she said.

There was no answer.

"Could I fix myself some coffee?"

"Of course."

She went to a cabinet where she had a Mr. Coffee machine stored, got it out, fiddled with filters, coffee grounds, water, and finally got the thing to working. She watched the light come on as the coffee began to drip into the pot.

One of the agents went to talk on the phone, then came back.

"Mrs. Thiokol, I've directed our counterespionage division to bring our photos by. We've also got some photos from the Pentagon for you to look at. We'd like you to try to find the face of the man who recruited you and the face of the man you saw in the consulate, is that all right?"

"I'm horrible at faces," she said.

"We wish you'd try very hard," said the man. "As I said, time is very important."

"What's going on?"

"It would be difficult to explain at this time, Mrs. Thiokol."

"It's something out there, isn't it? Something because of what I told these people, that's what's going on, isn't it? It involves South Mountain, doesn't it?"

There was a pause. The Three Dumb Men looked at one another, and finally the eldest of them said, "Yes, it does."

"Has anyone been killed?"

"I'm afraid so."

Megan stared at the Mr. Coffee. You ought to be feeling something, she thought. You've got blood on your hands, so *feel* it, all right? But she felt only tired. She just felt exhausted.

"It's Peter," she said. "He's out there, isn't he? You'd want him out there, wouldn't you?"

"Uh, yes, I believe Dr. Thiokol is on-site."

"On-site? Is that your word for it? He's where the shooting is. He's an awful coward, you know. He won't be any good around guns at all. He's best in some kind of room full of books. That's what he loves, just to read and think and study and be left alone. He's so neurotic. They won't put him near the guns and the danger, will they?"

"Well, Mrs. Thiokol, we really don't know. Some other people are handling that operation. I don't know if he'll be up near the shooting or back where it's safe. If it comes to it, I suppose he might have to be where there's firing. And I'm sure, given what's involved, he won't be a coward."

"Maybe that's what I wanted. Maybe what I really wanted was to get him killed."

"You'd have to talk to your psychiatrist about that, Mrs. Thiokol. Fred, call counterintel again, those damned books ought to be here by now."

"I just called them, Leo."

"Well, call them again, or something, don't just sit there."

"All right."

"The coffee's ready," Megan said. "Are you sure you don't want any coffee?"

"Yes," one of the Dumb Men said, "I'd like some, please."

She poured it.

"Mrs. Thiokol, let's talk about this. How did you contact your friend and how were the materials picked up. Was it through Ari?"

"Only once, just a few weeks ago. He sent me specially. But more commonly we had it set up in New York so that—do you really want to hear this? I mean, it's just *details*, you know, the little silly business that seemed so ridiculous to me and—"

"Please, tell us."

She took a sip of coffee.

"Well, it was so stupid and complicated. They explained it to me very carefully. I checked the Sunday *Post*. I picked an ad with the name of a chain bookstore in it. Then I dropped a personal ad off for the *Post* classifieds. Cash, they said, always pay cash. Through a code, I identified the store. Then I rented a car. Oh, and I had to remember to get something plaid. Then I went to the store on the appointed day—it was usually in a mall someplace around the Beltway—and I wrote a number on a scrap of paper, and I put it at page 300 of *Gone with the Wind*, which I loved when I was a girl and which they always have. And then . . ."

"Who serviced the drop? Do you know?"

"Well, I was so curious I once stayed to check. A fat nervous-looking middle-aged man. He looked like a slob. He was no—"

The door opened, and several agents, laden with material, began to troop in. The photo books had arrived.

Arbatov drove aimlessly through the traffic, down Route 1 to the Beltway. He almost turned down it, but decided at the last moment not to and was glad of that decision, for when he passed over it, he saw a ribbon of light, signifying a terrible traffic backup, all the car lights frozen solid on the big road.

The Americans, he laughed drunkenly. They build more cars than anybody in the world, and take them out and dump them in terrible traffic jams. The only thing crazier than the Americans were the Russians, who never had traffic jams because they didn't have cars.

He thought he ought to try Molly again. Pulling off the road, he went into a crummy little place in College Park. He stepped into the same thing he'd left behind at Jake's—his life wasn't getting any better! —which was another crowded, seedy bar full of smoke and lonely drinkers, except that by this time a new, ludicrous note had been added, a go-go dancer, a fat one of the sort Gregor specialized in. She looked like a truck driver's woman. She undulated to dreadful rock music up on a little stand, a bland, dull look on her bovine face. She looked a little like Molly Shroyer, that was the terrible thing.

Gregor found a pay phone, and dialed. He heard the phone buzz once, twice, three times, four times, damn! Where was she? She could not possibly still be at her office! What was going on?

He saw his great coup slipping away. Suppose Molly had not been able to find anything else out? The thought made him extremely nervous, so instead he instantly conjured up his most comforting illusion, seeking solace and serenity in the scenario.

Molly found him some wonderful stuff, absolute top of the line, and tomorrow he'd walk into little monkey Klimov, throw the documents down on the desk and say, "There, there, you little piglet, look at what Gregor Arbatov has uncovered. The great Gregor Arbatov has penetrated to the very center of the capitalist war machine. He has extraordinary documents on the crisis in central Maryland, and you thought he was nothing but a sniveling fool. Well, young whelp, it's you who'll do some sniveling soon enough, you and your powerful uncle Arkady Pashin, who'll do you no good at all. You're the one who'll be recalled to the Mother Country, not the great Gregor Arbatov."

It was such a wonderful moment, he hated to relinquish it, but at that second some equally drunken American prodded him, wanting the phone, and he realized he stood in a smoky bar in College Park while a great American whore shook her milk-jug tits at him and he stood and breathed cigarette smoke and clung to a phone that was not being answered.

Walls was dead and had begun to putrefy. The smell of decay, foul and noxious, reached his nostrils through death, and involuntarily, he squinched his face to avoid it, and threw his arm over his face, even in the grave. Amazingly, the arm still moved, if only in the medium of dirt. He had a brief moment of black clarity, and then the stench penetrated again, enough to make a man insane it was so foul, and he coughed, gagging, and a shiver rolled through him, deep from the bone, and as he shivered he shook himself from the shallow coating of coal dust that covered him.

Alive!

He blinked.

God, it was awful, the smell.

He pulled himself upright. His head ached, one arm felt numb, his knees knocked and quivered, and he was terribly thirsty. The air was full of dust; his tongue and lips and teeth were coated in dust. He tried to stagger ahead, but something held him back, pulling at him. He spun to discover it was the damned shotgun, its loose sling looped around his arm. With a grunt he pulled it free, searching his belt simultaneously for his angle-head flashlight. He found it.

Whoo-eee. No going back, no way, no how, no sir. The collapse of the tunnel, in whose rubble he had been loosely buried, completely sealed him off. His beam flashed across the wreckage, revealing only a new and glistening wall of coal and dirt. He was cooked, he now saw.

Dead, he thought. Dead, dead, dead.

He turned to explore what little remained of the sarcophagus. Blank walls greeted his search in the bright circle of light. It was the same end of story they had discovered before the tunnel fight. It was like the door in his cell. *Fuck Niggers.*

Walls laughed.

You die slow, not fast, he thought. Them white boys have their way with your nigger ass anyhows.

But still, the smell. He winced. The odor of corruption he recognized instantly, having encountered it so many times in the long months underground back in the 'Nam, when the gooks could not get their dead out of the tunnels and so left them buried in the walls, where occasionally, after a fight or a detonation, they fell out, or rather pieces of them did, and with them came this same terrible odor.

Man, how could it smell so? It only your old pal death.

Yet as he pieced the situation together, his curiosity was also aroused. For the smell had to come from somewhere. It could not come from nowhere and it had not been there before the explosion.

He began to sniff through the chamber for that spot where the odor was at its most absolutely unendurable. Led by his nose, his fingers searched the crevices in the walls. It didn't take long.

Shit, all right. Yes, sir, here it was. Walls found it. A kind of crack in the wall, and from the crack, which was low off the floor, there came a kind of breeze and from the breeze the moist, dank, terrible stench.

Walls searched his belt. Yes, dammit, he still had it, a goddamned entrenching tool. He remembered now that the damned thing had banged against his legs in the long tunnel fight. Removing it, he quickly unfolded the blade, locked it into place, and with strong, hard movements began to smash at the wall, scraping and plunging. The air filled with more dust, and his eyes began to sting, but still he kept at it, thrusting and banging away, amazed at how swiftly it went. With a final crack the wall before him heaved and collapsed. He stepped back. The dust swirled in his single beam of light, but yes, yes, there it was, a tunnel.

A way out.

Or no, maybe not out. But to somewhere.

Faces. The world had become faces.

"Now, these are American military, Mrs. Thiokol. We put this file together rather hurriedly, but these are the faces of men who possess the skill necessary to plan and execute the sort of operation we're dealing with at South Mountain."

She was amazed by how much she despised soldiers. These were exactly the kind of men she was never attracted to, that made her yawn and mope. If she had seen any of these bland, uncomplicated serious faces at a party, she would have run in the opposite direction. They looked like insurance agents, with their little haircuts all so neat, their eyes all so unclouded, their square, jowly heads atop their square, strong shoulders, over neatly pressed uniform lapels, with great mosaics of decoration on their square, manly chests. They looked so boring. Their business was supposed to be death, but they looked like IBM salesmen. They looked grim and task-oriented and hideously self-important and dull.

Still, now and then there'd be one a little more interesting than the others—with, say, a little pain in his eyes or a faraway look or a peculiar haunted look. Or maybe even the suggestion of evil, as if the owner enjoyed the power of death that was his profession.

"This one."

"This one. You know this one?"

"No. No, I'm just curious. He looks as if he's had an interesting life."

One of the men breathed heavily, almost a sigh.

"He was a colonel in the Special Forces. He was in Vietnam for seven straight years and spent a long time out there in what they called Indian country."

She couldn't begin to imagine what that meant.

"But, yes, he has had an interesting life. He's now in Bangkok, Thailand, where he runs a very proficient private army that protects a heroin merchant. Could we go on, Mrs. Thiokol?"

"I'm not being very much help, am I?"

"Don't worry about pleasing us, Mrs. Thiokol. Pleasing us has no meaning. Finding the man or men behind all this, that has some meaning. Fred, would you get me another cup of coffee?"

She went on. But none of them bore the faintest resemblance to that charming, forceful man in the Israeli consulate that morning.

"I'm sorry. They're beginning to blur together. I've been looking at them for hours now. I don't think he's here." Somehow she suspected he wouldn't be.

"You've been looking at them for about half an hour. It doesn't appear to me that you've been concentrating."

This irritated her.

"I *have* been concentrating. I have a visual imagination, and that man's face is in it. I *know* that face. I can call it up even now, I can remember it. Do you want me to go through it again?"

"No."

"Maybe if you had one of those police sketch artists I could *describe* him, and then the computer could help you find him."

"We've found that's a very long shot. Statistically, it almost never works out."

"Maybe I could draw him. I mean, I'm—"

They looked at one another as though they really were Three Dumb Men. You could fly a plane through those open mouths. It seemed so elementary to her.

"An artist, goddammit!" one of them yelled. "Yes, goddammit. Why the hell didn't we think of that sooner?"

"It's my fault, I should have—"

"Don't worry about that now. Fred, get her some paper and a—is a pen all right?"

"A pen is fine."

She took the Bic, a fineline, and faced the blank sheet in front of her.

"All right," she said, taking a deep breath. She hadn't drawn in years. She felt the pen in her hands grow heavy and then, experimentally, she drew a line, which seemed to lead her to another and then another and then . . . suddenly, she was in a frenzy of drawing, she didn't want ever to stop drawing. And as she worked, she felt the details pouring back into her mind. She remembered the curious formality to the man, and yet his cheer and his sense of command. You just knew this was a man who got things done. Then she reminded herself that at the time she had thought he was a Jew, a hero of Israel. How could she have been so wrong? Still she felt herself drawing a hero of Israel, a Jew. So there was something in him that she responded to, that was genuine even under the cleverly constructed fiction and the guile that had gone into con- structing the fiction. She decided then that he really *was* a hero, of sorts, and that he was probably as brave as any Israeli hero, and she tried to draw that, too—his courage. She decided that he was a special man, and she tried to draw that. She tried to draw his charisma, which was the hardest. Is it in the eyes, some steely glint, some inner fortitude? Is it in the jut of the chin, the set of the mouth, the firmness of posture, the clarity of vision, the forthrightness in the way he turns his whole face toward you and never gives you the half- and three-quarter looks so much a part of the repertoire of the people who like to think themselves "charming"? She tried to draw that.

But a face was emerging from all this thought, and her fingers hurt where she had pressed down upon the pen. Somehow, through her illusions, her eyes and her hands had not lied.

She looked at him. Yes, that was him. Yes, forget the bullshit, that's him. Maybe his vitality obscured his age and his bright eyes obscured the tension deep inside him, but that was him. Maybe the hair wasn't right, because she tended not to notice hair. But that was him.

She felt them crowding around, watching.

"There," she finally said. "Does that look like anything?"

They were very quiet. Then, one by one, they spoke.

"No. It's real good. You really made him come alive. But no, no, that's not anybody I've looked at today," said the first Dumb Man.

"Just for a second," said the second Dumb Man, "it was shaping up like a SAC colonel who got the ax seven years back when he got involved in some crooked real estate deal. He was a leading candidate early this afternoon, until they found him in Butte, Montana, teaching junior high."

The long seconds passed, and then it became extremely obvious that the third Dumb Man, who was the youngest, the one who did the phone calling and gotten the coffee, had not yet spoken.

"Fred?"

Finally, Fred said, "I think you better get the Agency."

Then he walked over to the table, where four or five more huge volumes of photos lurked. He read the words on their binders, selected one, and as he brought it to her, she could hear their breaths come in harshly. She could not see what the book was, but he opened it quickly, found a certain page.

There, before her, were about a half dozen men, all in uniform. But it was not an American uniform, as had been the case with all the others she had looked at. It was a tunic-collared uniform, with off-colored shoulder boards and lots of decorations. The faces were flinty, pouchy, grim, official.

She put her finger out, touching one.

He was heavier here by several pounds, and he wasn't smiling. He had no charisma, only power. But it was the same, the white-blond hair, the wise cosmopolitan eyes, the sureness of self and purpose, and the wit that lurked in him. It was all there, though in latent form.

"That's him," she said.

"You're sure, Mrs. Thiokol?"

"Leo, look for yourself. That's the face she drew! That's it!"

But Leo didn't want to believe it.

"You're absolutely sure, Mrs. Thiokol?"

"Leo, look at the picture!"

"Fuck the picture," Leo said. "Mrs. Thiokol? Megan, look at me. Look at me. This is the most important thing you'll ever do in your life. Look at me, and tell me this is the man you met in what you thought was the Israeli consulate in New York City."

"She drew the picture from *memory*," Fred said. "She couldn't have known."

"Yes, it's him."

"Leo," said Fred, "I should know, I spent nine years in counterintel. He was one of our big bad bogeymen. We tracked him all over New York back when he was operational. He was a hell of a pro, I'll say that."

Leo just said, "You better call the White House. And the people at South Mountain."

"Who is he?" asked Megan, and nobody would look her in the eye until finally Leo, the oldest of the Three Dumb Men, turned to her and said, "You've just identified the lieutenant general who is the head of the First Directorate of the Soviet GRU, Mrs. Thiokol. Head of Russian Military Intelligence."

She didn't believe him.

"I—" she started, then stopped.

Finally, she said, "His name. Tell me his name, just so I know it."

"His name is Arkady Pashin."

The dust floated up through the hole in the wall, drifted in layers through the flickering beam of Walls's light. Cool air, dense and almost gaggingly sweet with corruption, raced through his nose. He fell back, vomited, retched himself empty in a series of dry, shivering spasms. At last he stood.

Man, he thought, I don't wanna go in there, no, sir.

You gotta, boy. No other place to go. You maybe find something in there. You go on forward now, boy.

Shit.

Stop your cursing. You go forward, black and proud, or you die. Same as the streets, motherfucker, same as any tunnel ever made. Man stand up, man be black and proud, man go ahead. No one gonna raise up against you, not down here.

Black and proud, he thought, black and *proud*!

Ducking, he willed himself through the space into some farther chamber. He was braced for what he saw, yet still the power of it, when the circle of light fell upon it, was shattering.

Black and proud, he said to himself, holding himself together, yes, sir, black and *proud*!

It was the face of death. He'd seen it a jillion times, of course, from cartoon pirate flags and halloween masks and scary movies and even cereal boxes, jokey and funny—but not jokey here: the leering skull's face, its splayed grin hideous and total, the face from beyond the Great Divide. Yet its power still shocked him—that, and the fact that flesh, rotted and filthy, still clung wormlike to the clean white bone of the skull. The eyes were gone—or were they merely swollen grotesquely, so they no longer looked like eyes? The hair hung in stiff hunks down across the face, and atop the head, which was at the crazy angle of uncaring, was a metal miner's helmet, its little light long since spent. The spindly creature's hands, frail and bony-looking, held a pick that had fallen across and joined the dead man's chest, sinking through its blackened corruption, joining the slithery lungs—things moved in there as the beam disturbed them. Quickly, he flashed the beam about, and everywhere the bright circle prowled it revealed the same: dead men, commingled with their still-hard equipment, now in the process of rejoining the elements, sinking into the maggoty forever. He had the horrified sense of not being alone: other small living things, grown fat on this feast, moved and shook their scaly tails at him as the light prodded them.

Walls fell back. He had an image of the world gone to death: the world, like this desperate chamber, filled up with corpses, heaped and rotting.

Black and *proud*! he told himself.

Again he vomited, not even having the strength to lean forward to avoid befouling himself. But there was nothing left to puke. His lungs and chest seemed to rupture in the effort of expulsion, but nothing remained to expel. Shakily, he stood, wondering if he could step forward blindly, did, felt something beneath him fight just a split-second, then yield to the impact of his boot.

He was in something.

He shook his boot off, staggered forward. Everywhere the maggoty, glistening bodies lay, beyond color, beyond everything except their own disintegration. He stumbled ahead, finding himself in a larger chamber, then saw the drama of it. His beam flicked backward in confirmation, and there revealed the fallen tunnel, a hopeless no-exit of collapsed coal. These men, what? fifty or so? had been trapped back here in the coffin. They'd known they hadn't the strength or the time to tunnel back out through the fallen chamber, and had thought therefore to dig laterally, from their tunnel—Cathy, wasn't it? something beginning with a C—into his tunnel, Elizabeth. But Elizabeth, that bitch, that white bitch, had betrayed them as she had betrayed him. She had been just inches away before exhaustion and airlessness had overcome the last of them, and they'd died in a frenzy of effort.

Walls wept for their effort and guts. White boys in a tunnel, digging for their lives. Tunnel men, like he was. Hey, man, dyin' underground no way to die, Walls knew, having seen enough of it himself in his time.

But why are they rotting now?

Walls worked his mind against it and then he had it. Of course. They'd been sealed off in airless, germless protection down here for their long half-century, and without air, there is no rot. They had quietly mummified, turning to leather and sinew, perhaps even refrigerated by the coolness. But then—he struggled to remember the details as they had been explained by him—the hole had been left open for years and years and finally, last summer, when they excavated for the missile shaft, it had rained even more, and the rain had poured into the open mountain and eaten its way down through the coal, and eventually reached and punctured this coffin. And when it violated the grave, it admitted grave robbers, the millions of germy little creatures that turned flesh to horror.

Git your ass going, boy!

Walls had entered the main tunnel now, where the rest of the miners were. His light flashed upon them. The ceiling was low. Walls tried not to imagine it but he could not avoid it: thinking of them trapped down here in the dank dark, feeling the air ebb in slow degrees, waiting for a rescue that wouldn't—couldn't—come.

He walked forward, bumped his head, crouched, walked forward some more. He felt the cool pressure of air, and had a bad moment as he imagined his lungs filling with microscopic maggoty things, with the wormy crawlers and creepers that scuttled through the flesh. He felt very close to panic, even he, Walls, the hardest, meanest, baddest tunnel dick of all time, and not a slouch of a street player either, thank you, ma'am. Maybe this was the worst moment for him: standing among the corpses, no place to go, it seemed, but to join them. He saw an image of himself, a ragged, mealy hunk of rot spangling a few old African bones. Years later white people would come and hold up a Walls drumstick and with great distaste say, "Good Lord, Ralph, this fellow's limbs are so darned much thicker than the others; why, he must have been a colored man!" But then Walls got hold of himself, yessir, saying it over and over, black and *proud*! black and *proud*! and the panic flapped out of his chest and found some other chest to fill somewhere in the world: old Walls was back.

No stiffs going to get the best of this nigger, no, *sir*!

This boy goin' *live*, Jack, don't you know?

Walls crawled forward, feeling. He didn't need his lamp now, he didn't need nothing. He flicked it off. He loved the darkness. He was the man of darkness. He was home in the darkness; it was his natural element. He had this tunnel *beat*. This motherfucker was his, its ass belong to *him*.

In the dark his fingers reached out. He was alone with the dead but no longer afraid.

Then he saw the light. Milky, luminous, faraway, but light nonetheless.

Okay, motherfucker, he thought.

The breeze continued to blow, and he was surprised at how strong and sweet it smelled. He crawled over bodies, feeling them crumble beneath him. They couldn't harm him, they were only the dead.

He came to it at last. Air poured down from the hole in the roof. He looked up. There was the light, far away, a long life's upward chimney crawl or squirm. But light. The light at the end of the—whatever.

Okay, Jack, he thought. Here comes Walls.

He wrapped his friend and companion Mr. Twelve tightly to him, and began his journey toward the light.

It was a chasm by now, a tunnel into the heart of the metal.

"Mr. Hummel?"

"Yes, sir?"

"How much farther?"

"Last time I measured, I'd gone one hundred twenty-five centimeters. That puts us maybe ten or fifteen away."

"Time, please."

"Oh, say three, four hours. Midnight. We get there at midnight."

"Excellent. And then we can all go home."

He'd been cutting for hours now, and the ache in his arms from the awkwardness of holding the torch deep in the guts of the titanium block was terrific. Yet he was proud, in a terrible way. Lots of guys couldn't have done what he'd done. He'd done a beautiful job, clean and elegant and precise. He'd just quit bitching and gotten it done. But he was still scared.

"The Army. It's up top, trying to break in, isn't it?"

"It is, Mr. Hummel."

"What happens to me when those guys kick the doors down and start shooting?"

"They can't get down here."

"They'll figure out a way. They're smart guys."

"Nobody is that smart."

"Who are you guys? Tell me, at least."

"Patriots."

"I know enough to know all soldiers think they're patriots."

"No, most soldiers are cynics. We are the true thing."

"But if you shoot this thing off, *everybody* will die. Because the Russians will shoot off theirs, they'll shoot off everything they've got, and *everybody* dies!"

It scared him to defy the man. But it just blubbered out.

The general smiled with kind radiance.

"Mr. Hummel, I could never permit a full-scale nuclear exchange. You're right, that would be the end of the planet. Do you think I could convince all these men to come with me on this desperate mission only to end the world?"

Jack just looked at him and had no answer.

"You see, Mr. Hummel, war doesn't make sense if everybody loses, does it? But if we can *win*? What then? Then, isn't it the moral responsibility of a professional soldier to take advantage of the situation? Isn't that where the higher duty lies? Doesn't that save the world rather than doom it? Millions die; better that, over the long run, than billions! Better a dead country than a dead world? Especially if the millions are in the enemy's country, eh?"

The man's eyes, beaming belief and conviction, radiated passion and craziness. It frightened Jack. He swallowed. "I hope you know what you're doing."

"I assure you, Mr. Hummel, I do. Now, please, the flame."

Jack put the flame in the hole. He had a feeling of terrible guilt.

"We're done," announced the engineer sergeant.

"At last," shouted Alex. "God, you men have worked so hard. Get the tarpaulin pulled back."

With grunting and heaving the men of the Red Platoon pulled back and discarded the heavy sheets of canvas that had obscured their work.

In the darkness Alex couldn't see much, but he knew what was there.

"They'll never get through that," he said. "We should know, eh? We learned the hard way?"

"Yes, sir," said the engineer sergeant.

The air was crisp and cold and above them the stars towered, spinning firewheels, clouds of distant cosmic gas. All around it was quiet, except for the press of the breeze through the trees and the occasional mumble or shiver of a man in the dark.

"And just in time too," Alex said. "They'll be coming soon, and in force."

"No signs yet?"

"No, it's all quiet down there. They brought some trucks up a few minutes back."

"Reinforcements," somebody said. "We hurt them bad, they needed more men."

"*Sir!*"

The call arose from a dozen places on the perimeter. Alex turned with his binoculars, even as he heard the roar. At first he could see nothing, but then someone screamed, "The road! The road!"

He lifted his binoculars and watched, and even at this distance could make out the spectacle. A plane came down and even though it was only a phenomenon of landing lights, glowing cockpit, and blinkers at the wingtips, it seemed heavy in the air as it floated awkwardly down, touched the straight-running line of the highway, bounced once, twice, skidded a bit as a braking chute popped, and then slowed.

"C-130," Alex said.

The plane eventually halted to let out its men; then it simple taxied off the roadway and into the fields, where it fell brokenly into a ditch to make room for another plane, which in seconds followed the same drunken path downward to the highway. Then another, and finally a fourth.

"Very neat," said Alex. "Nicely done. Good pilots, brave men, landing on a roadway."

"More visitors?" said one of the others.

"Elite troops. Rangers, I suppose. Well, well, it's going to be an interesting next few hours."

He looked at his watch. Midnight was coming. But would it come soon enough?

1900

There wasn't much to it, really; Dick Puller was a great believer in simplicity and firepower, not ornamentation and cleverness. What he'd come up with seemed like something out of World War II, say, the Pointe du Hoc assault at Normandy, a Ranger legend.

Here, as there, the Rangers would carry the primary site assault responsibility, moving over the same ground as Bravo earlier in the day. There were more of them, and they were much more proficient. Their commanding officer, an old Puller buddy, had already dispatched the men directly from the planes to the mountain. They were already moving up the hill. They would be supported on the right by Third Infantry, which with its longer-range M-14s would provide accurate covering fire, before moving in after the Rangers had reached the perimeter. On the radio the Rangers would be Halfback, Third Infantry Beanstalk.

"Lieutenant Dill?"

"Sir?"

"Dill, congrats. You and your people get to sit this one out. I want you on the left, separated from the main assault force, as high up the crest as you can get. Point being, we may need stretcher bearers if casualties are high, we may need runners if these guys can jam our radios, and we may need the extra firepower if they're pressed and try to break down the hill in your direction. I make it map coordinates Lima-niner-deuce, have you got that? You can find that point in the dark?"

"Got it," said Dill, trying to keep the elation out of his voice.

Meanwhile, Puller continued, the Delta Assault Team, the actual shaft-busters whose job it was to rappel down the elevator chute, break into the corridor, fight their way to the launch control center, and disable it, would be choppered in when the launch control facility was taken. Along with them would be Peter himself, ready to do battle (he hoped) with his nemesis, the door.

"Any luck on the door, Dr. Thiokol?"

Peter smiled wretchedly. His tweed coat was rumpled, and sweat soaked through his dense blue shirt. The white delta of his T-shirt showed in his open collar.

"I'm working on it," he said, too brightly. "Confidence is high."

The party would start at 2200 hours, Puller continued, as the various units continued to move into position until that time. Peter had told them that given the key vault's construction, the earliest the people inside could get through it was midnight.

"You're sure of that?" Puller asked for what must have been the millionth time.

Yes, he was. It was the only thing he was sure of. Peter nodded.

Puller turned to the group.

"Any questions?"

"What's the go code?" somebody asked.

"We go on 'Heaven is falling.' From an old poem. Got it? 'Heaven is falling.' "

An officer wanted to know about medical evacuation; he was told that the Delta insertion choppers would double as medevac ships, but they wouldn't be active until after the insertion.

Tac Air?

Two of the Delta choppers had been fitted with Emerson mini-tats, that is, rotary-barreled 7.62-mm General Electric miniguns on carriages that looked like a 1934 Johnson outboard motor and hung beneath the skids. In the early moments of the assault, these ships, call-signed Sixgun-One and Sixgun-two, would be available to provide suppressive fire on enemy strong points. But since there was a premium on the choppers, they wouldn't close within one thousand feet of the targets and their target-time would never be more than twenty-five seconds, because of the Stingers, a devastating SAM, as demonstrated earlier.

"We lose more than two helicopters, then we have trouble getting all our Delta people in there in time," Puller said. "It's like the Iranian rescue mission. We need X number of birds to get the job done and there's not a lot of redundancy in all this. Sorry, that's just the way it is. You'll lose some people because we can't get 'em medevacked out and you'll lose some people because our air support isn't top rate, but the alternative is to wait until more stuff can arrive. And that's no alternative. We go with everything we've got."

"Everything?" somebody wanted to know.

"Yes. In the assault reinforcements I've asked the state policemen to join. Anybody know any boy scouts?"

There was some hollow laughter.

"What about our fire restrictions?" the Ranger executive officer asked. "Can we use grenades with that computer up there?"

"Dr. Thiokol?"

Peter cleared his throat.

"I'm sorry, this has to be a gunfight. The titanium casing ought to be able to withstand any number of small-arms hits, up to 7.62 full metal jackets, but I can't sanction explosives. If you could stick with the gunfire and forgo the explosives, we might get out of this. If that computer goes, it's all over."

"Suppose they mine the computer to blow?"

"They won't," said Peter. Of this one thing he was absolutely positive. "No, not Aggressor-One. There's just a little part of him that thinks he's smarter than everybody. The limited-try code will keep us out, because that's the way his mind works."

And because that's what I designed it to do. He wants to use my stuff to beat *me*.

Peter tried to think about the man.

What have I done to deserve such an enemy? How did I become his Moby Dick? What did I do to him?

"What about in the shaft? Can we use explosives?"

"Negative again," said Peter. "I know you've got to use explosives to get down there. But once you get close to the command center, I'm sorry to tell you you can't. We just don't know quite what would happen if you blew the wiring. You might make it impossible for me to abort the launch if they've gone to terminal countdown, which is tricky enough anyway; and you might even *cause* a launch. You've got to do it with guns once you're close to the place."

"Is there any late word on what's under that canvas?" an officer wanted to know.

"Our analysts in the Pentagon think it might be the emplacement of a heavy artillery piece," said Puller. "In 'Nam, we used 105s to fire

fleshette canisters at the NVA. It's possible they brought a heavy piece
up there disassembled. Or maybe it's a Vulcan or one of those fast-firing
Czech 23-mm cannons. You'll know soon enough."

When he wasn't talking, Peter sat with a kind of rigid politeness
through all this. He knew it wouldn't do for these guys to see into what
he was thinking. But there was a joke in it all, and he thought of the
line, *all dressed up and no place to go*, for that's exactly what it might
work out to be if he couldn't get them through the door.

"And then Dr. Thiokol opens the door, and Delta goes in, and it's all
over but the cheering," said Puller. "Right, Dr. Thiokol?" Peter nodded.

Right, he thought, nodding politely, except he had no idea in hell
what the door code could be and so knew only one terrible truth:
Aggressor-One had done it.

Welcome to Armageddon.

Bells were ringing, men were hopping around.

Peter looked up from his daze. He heard them shouting, a lot of nos,
and no ways. The general discipline of the briefing was completely
disintegrating.

"What's going on?" he asked the man next to him.

"Didn't you hear, man?" said the fellow, a helicopter pilot. "They got
an ID on these guys. They say they're *Russians*."

And he heard Skazy talking about something called a Spetsnaz Silo
Seizure team, but others were saying no, no, it couldn't be, why'd they
want to blow away their own country, what the hell did it mean?

And then there was silence.

Peter saw they were all looking at him.

"Dr. Thiokol, here. You make some sense of this for us, will you
please?"

He handed Peter a yellow teletype sheet, with the words PRIORITY:
FLASH across the top. He read the contents swiftly.

FBI hq believe team leader of aggressor forces at South Mountain to
be PASHIN, ARKADY Colonel-General, GRU, First Deputy of
GRU, head of Directorate V, Operational Intelligence. Subject PASHIN
according to CIA records has primary responsibility in GRU the past
decade for penetration of U.S. strategic warfare compounds. He is a
graduate of the Intelligence Faculty of the General Staff Academy; the
Training Centre of Illegals; the Military-Diplomatic Academy; the

Military Institute of Foreign Languages, where he learned to speak brilliant English; the Special Faculty of Higher Communications; the Kiev Higher Military Command School; the Special Faculty of the Second Kharkov Higher Military Aviation and Engineering School, and the General Staff Academy. He spent a decade in United States attached to the Soviet U.N. mission. One identifying peculiarity is that he is only high-ranking Soviet command-staff figure on record to have formally rejected the use of his patronymic. In November of 1982 ARKADY SIMONOVICH PASHIN formally notified his head-quarters that he would henceforth be known simply as ARKADY PASHIN. No information is available as to the reason for such an unprecedented decision. None of our sources have any idea as to its meaning. One last item: Subject PASHIN has been twice named as possible sponsor of group known as PAMYAT (Memory), thought to be a collection of right wing thinkers agitated into action by Gorbachev's apparent willingness to meet with West, sign an INF, and to permit policy of glasnost. PAMYAT has senior analysts worried; information on it, however, is scant. More follows.

Peter put it down.

"Is it some kind of coup?" asked Dick Puller. "Would the Soviet military, or this nut-case PAMYAT outfit, be taking over the country, and they want their finger on a nuclear trigger somewhere for a certain period of time?"

"No," said Peter. He realized in a second what it was all about. He saw it. He had been pulled along the pathways of the same argument, knew its temptations, its hypnotic allure. He knew how it could seduce a man into believing in the moral good of pushing the button.

"No, it's not a coup. It's simply logic, or rather strategic logic, and the willingness to follow it to the end."

He gave a grim little smile. He knew Pashin, knew how his mind worked, because it worked the way his own did.

"You see," he said, "it's really very simple. This Pashin . . . he's done something no one else has ever done. He's figured out how to win World War Three."

He felt the power of Pashin's mind, its reach, its grasp, its subtleties and, most of all, its will.

He took a deep breath.

"Pashin believes that MX is a first strike weapon, and that when it is fully operational and we have the advantage, we will push the button and blow them away—furthermore, that by our own logic, we *have* to. That's where these missiles take us. And since the MX is so clearly superior in terms of accuracy and silo-busting capacity and since our own command, communication, and control system is so fragile and so unable to withstand a Soviet first strike, we've *got* to use it. It's use it or lose it, and he thinks we'll use it. That's his first position: it's unassailable, and I can't say—no man can say—that it's not a distinct possibility. It's not that we want to, it's that we'll be afraid not to."

There was silence.

"So from his position the choice isn't between peace and war, it's between losing and winning an already inevitable war. That's all. Once you accept that, it all follows, particularly if he's of a conservative bent, as his membership in this PAMYAT thing would indicate. There's going to be a nuclear war. It will be fought as soon as our system is operational, in six months to a year, via an American first strike with clear weapons superiority, and a complete victory for the United States, with all their cities ruined and all their birds fractured in their silos and all their command bunkers turned to barbecue pits. Or it will be fought now, tonight, in a few hours, and"—he paused, letting it sink in—"and they will win."

There was silence in the room.

"This is how it works. He fires our MX into the Soviet Union. But it's important to understand the targeting of this particular missile. Those ten warheads are zeroed on what we call third and fourth generation hard targets, as opposed to soft targets such as cities, people, that sort of thing. Our W87s are sublimely accurate; they never miss; they're sure as death and taxes. And because of their accuracy the bombs can be quite small. So the ten warheads deploy against three key long-range radar installations, the Soviet air defense command, a deep leadership bunker thirty miles outside Moscow—the point is to decapitate their leadership—and five Siberian missile silos, which, by the time they strike, will be empty. The reason, of course, is that once the Soviet radar identifies the ten incomings, the Russians go crazy and punch out with everything they've got. Our ten nukes detonate with a total megatonnage of thirty-five; they take out the installations I've named and they kill—I don't know, tops maybe thirty thousand people. Seven to nine minutes later, they hit us with four thousand megatons; they tag all our cities and missile silos; they EMP our radars and computers to craziness, they kill maybe three hundred million of us; they effectively wipe us out. That's it. Game, set, and match, Soviet Union. Essentially the point of this Pashin's exercise is to goad his own country into what amounts to a first strike, because the premium on a first strike is so high. But of course neither the Politburo nor any sane command group would push the button. So he does it himself, maybe with the help or under the inspiration of this Pamyat thing, and with this little commando unit, based on his intelligence. See? It's easy. It's more than easy, it's brilliant. And when it's over, he climbs out of the mountain, a chopper picks him up, and he's tsar of all the Russias."

"But our subs, with our subs we can—"

"No," said Peter, "sorry, but they've got our subs zeroed. They can take some of them out in the first few minutes of the spasm. Then they can hunt down and kill the Tacamo VLF aircraft that are our primary sub links and are set to deliver the retaliation message. They'll go straight for those babies, jam them, EMP them, or just blow them away. The subs will be out of contact, and will wait to fire while the Russians hunt them down in the following couple of weeks. At the worst, they'll have plenty of time to evacuate their cities. They can outlast or outsmart the subs if they have to and Pashin has forced them to. That's all; he'll make them beat our subs. They aren't going to want to fight that fight, but he's taken the element of choice out of it. And he'll make them do it. And in a terrible, deep way he probably thinks he's cleaning up the mess the rest of his leaders have made. He's the cleaning lady."

"Why didn't he take over a Russian missile compound and get his first strike that way?" somebody asked.

"Because this is the only independent-launch-capable silo in the world. It's the only one he could take where he himself could push the button. He's made the hardest choice of all, but by his lights, it's the logical one. I suppose by a certain moral system it's even the right choice. He's not a madman, really, he's just operating within the rules of the game, the game that his country and ours invented."

"Who are those men with him?" somebody asked.

"Washington's sure it's Spetsnaz," said Major Skazy. "Soviet Special Forces. In the control of the GRU, not the regular Army, and remember this Pashin is a big-time GRU heavyweight. Anyway, they've been trained in silo-seizure and blooded in Afghanistan. That explains those tans and the false teeth, meant to cover up their foreign origin. And there were sixty? That's four fifteen-man teams, which is the operational unit in the Spetsnaz organization. And it explains where the goddamned Stingers came from. We've shipped Stingers to the Muhajadeem, to take out the Soviet MI-26 gunships. These guys must have bounced a shipment, and they've turned the stuff around on us. These are very, very good guys. That's why they've been so tough."

But Puller hadn't been listening. He'd been thinking. He'd gotten close to the last wrinkle. "Dr. Thiokol," he said suddenly, "doesn't your theory fall apart on the issue of our response to their launch? As soon as our radar sees the Russian birds coming, *we* launch. And *they're* blown away. And the world dies in the rad—"

"You haven't seen it yet, Colonel Puller. Just as I said early on, something else has to happen. Something to prevent us from launching, something to totally de-coordinate our response in the crucial seven- to nine-minute envelope between the launch of this Peacekeeper and the launch of the Russian massive retaliation."

Again, the silence.

"The launch is only one half of the operation. There's another half of it, there has to be. I told you this from the very beginning, but I didn't know what it was. Now I see it. It explains the radio message that he sent out this morning immediately after the seizure. He was talking to his other half, telling it to hold off for eighteen hours because of the key vault."

"Hold off on what?" asked Skazy.

"It's called 'decapitation,' " said Peter, "or leader killing. It means cutting the heads off. And all the heads are in Washington. You better bump me through to the FBI fast, because they've got to get hopping on this. This Pashin's going to launch at South Mountain and then he's going to nuke D.C."

This was the hardest thing yet. Uckley would rather do anything than this, but now events were whizzing by and it had been explained to him in Washington that he had this last job left to do.

"I—I'm not sure I can do it," he said. "Can't you get somebody else?"

After a restrained moment or two of silence, the voice at the other end of the line at last said, "They can't get there in time. We can send the photos and documents over the wire to the state police barracks on Route 40 outside Frederick and have them to you in twenty minutes. You're the senior federal representative there, it has to be you."

Uckley swallowed. What choice did he have?

And twenty minutes later, a state police car whirled into town, its siren blaring, its flasher pulsing. Seconds after that, the messenger was delivered to Uckley.

"We got these over the computer hookup from D.C. just a few minutes ago. Hey, you okay? Man, you look like you had the worst day of your life."

"It wasn't the best."

"I hear there was a bad shooting."

"Yeah. Mine."

"Oh, Jesus, sorry, man. Hey, don't they give you time off for—"

"There's no time for that today. Thanks."

Uckley took the envelope from the man and headed up the walk. The house was full of lights. A minister had arrived and the family doctor and, a few minutes back, an older couple he took to be grandparents.

He paused at the door, wishing he were several million miles away, wishing the whole thing were over, wishing it weren't him. But it was him, and eventually he knocked.

Minutes seemed to pass before someone answered. It was a man about sixty, heavyset, with expressionless eyes.

"Yes?" he asked.

"Uh, my name is Uckley. I'm a special agent with the Federal Bureau of Investigation. I'm sorry to have to do this, but I've got to talk to the girls."

The man beheld him for the longest time.

"The girls are very tired," he finally said. "They've been through a lot today. Too much. We've just gotten them down. I was going to sedate them if they have any trouble sleeping. Their grandparents are here. Can't this wait until some other time?"

"I wish it could, Doctor. But I've got to talk to them. This is a very urgent situation and time is important."

"Young man, these girls saw their mother shot and killed today. Have you any—"

"Look, I hate to have to act like a jerk, but you've got to understand how terribly, terribly urgent this all is, Doctor. This is what's known as a phase four nuclear emergency, and technically I have all legal rights to get what I want. Please don't make me have to be an asshole about this." He felt himself swallowing uncomfortably. His breath was heavy and his knees felt watery.

The doctor simply glared at him. Then he stepped back and let him in.

Uckley stepped into a terrible silence. The two older people sat on the sofa. The woman was crying. The man looked numb. There wasn't enough light in the room. The neighbor, Kathy Reed, fussed at the dinner table. She had evidently brought some casserole over, but nobody had eaten and the food lay on the plates glazing with grease in the dim light. There were still chips of wood and plaster and shreds of tufting everywhere from the gunfire, and a gritty layer of dust lay over every-thing, but evidently the police had covered the blown-out windows with plastic. The room filled Uckley with the nausea of memory and terror.

"Kathy," said the doctor, "do you think you could go up and get the girls? This officer says it's urgent that he talk to them."

"Haven't they been through enough—" began Mrs. Reed, her voice rising with emotion.

"I'm sorry," said Uckley. "It's necessary. But maybe I only need the oldest one. Uh, Poo?"

"Bean," she said. Then she started up the stairs. But she turned.

"You were so *positive* this afternoon. You were so *excited*. And look what happened. Look what you did to this family."

Uckley didn't know what to say. He swallowed again.

"They were such a happy family. They were a *perfect* family. Why did you have to do this to them?"

Uckley just looked at his shoes. The doctor came up to him.

"Were you the man who went upstairs?"

"Yes," said Uckley, swallowing. "You've got to believe I didn't want anything like that to happen." But the doctor looked as though he didn't believe it at all.

In a few minutes Kathy Reed brought Bean down the stairs. The girl's face was wrinkled from sleep, and she had on a pink robe and a pair of rabbit slippers. She was scrunching her eyes, but when she saw Uckley waiting for her, she just grew still and grave. She had a peculiar presence to her, an almost eerie luminescence. Kathy Reed led her down the steps to Uckley.

"Hi there," he said, his tone chipper. "Hey, I'm real sorry I had to wake you."

"You don't have to talk to her like a chipmunk," said Mrs. Reed.

Uckley had no talent with kids. He somehow never saw them, and his few exchanges with them in the past had been perfunctory and stupid. But now, looking at the girl, her solemn face, her pale button nose, her huge, dark, questing eyes, her perfect little hands gathered in front of her, he had the terrible urge to kneel and clasp her to him and beg her for forgiveness. The skin of her neck was so soft.

"My name's Jim," he said. "Honey, I have to ask you to look at some pictures."

"Are you going to shoot me?" she asked.

The ache he felt splintered into a couple of thousand pieces, and each of the pieces began to hurt.

"No, honey. What happened was a terrible, terrible accident. I am so sorry. I'd do anything if it wasn't so."

"Is my mommy in heaven? Nana said you sent her to heaven because Jesus wanted her as his best friend."

"I guess so. Jesus, uh"—he didn't know what to say—"Jesus is sometimes a mysterious guy, you know. But I guess he knows what's the best thing."

She nodded gravely, considering.

"Jesus loves us very much but he loved Mommy best of all. My mommy will be very happy with him," she said.

"I'm sure she will. Now, sugar, please, do me this one little favor and I'll get out of here forever. I've got some pictures. They sent them from Washington. I want you to look at them and tell me if these are the men who took your daddy away."

He led her to the table, and she went through the pictures, one after another, in her deliberate way.

Finally, she picked one, and handed it over.

"Him. He was here this morning. He's my daddy's new boss. He took him to his new job. He was Herman's friend."

Uckley looked at the picture. It displayed the remarkably robust face of an obvious professional soldier, a man with a broken nose, a short crew cut, and a set of hard, flinty eyes. He wore some kind of camouflage tunic, and Uckley could make out the spout of an AK-47 over his shoulder, obviously carried on a sling. The picture had a fuzzy quality in its background, as if taken from hundreds of feet away through an extremely powerful lens.

He scanned the accompanying sheet.

CLASSIFIED TOP SECRET
CENTRAL INTELLIGENCE AGENCY
RESEARCH DIRECTORATE; SOVIET MILITARY DESK/ELITE UNITS
SUBDIVISION
YASOTAY, ALEKSANDR, Major. Last authenticated posting, 22 Spetsnaz Brigade, GRU, attached 15th Guards Motor Rifles, Kabul, Afghanistan. Subject YASOTAY graduated Reconnaissance Faculty of Frunze Military Academy; the Cherepovetski Higher Military Engineering School of Communications; the Spetsnaz Faculty of the Ryazan Higher Parachute School, the Serpukhovski Higher Command Engineering School. Qualified member Parashutno-Desantny Polk (Soviet Airborne), sniper and HALO-insertion trained. Thought to have seen action in Angola, Central America, the Sino-Soviet border. Subject YASOTAY first identified by Israeli Mossad when instructor at Iraqi guerrilla camp in 1972. Subsequent sightings place him at Karlovy Vary, KGB training camp on the Black Sea and as infantry adviser to 15 Commando, Cuban force operating in Angola. Presence Afghanistan authenticated by Agent HORTENSE, Kabul, 14 January, 1984. Mentioned by source FLOWERPOT, Moscow, 1986, as possible member PAMYAT (Memory), held to be right wing nativist movement of indeterminate strength, possibly extending to higher councils of government. PAMYAT remains of great interest to Western intelligence units.

"Is he a nice man?" asked Bean.

"Yes, honey, he's a very nice man."

"Will he bring my daddy back to me?"

"Yes, honey. I promise you, he will." He looked at her eyes, bold and honest. "Honey, I promise you, he'll bring your daddy back to you."

2100

The phone buzzed and buzzed.

"Hello?"

Gregor's heart leapt! The sound of her voice was lyric pleasure, so intense he thought he'd gag. He was almost too dumbfounded to say anything, and then he found himself blurting out, "Molly, oh, Molly, it's you, sweet Jesus, it's you!"

What he heard in response was equally marvelous.

"Oh, God, Gregor, darling, I was afraid I'd missed you and you weren't going to call anymore! Gregor, I've got it! You won't believe what's going on, Gregor. It's incredible, and I've got the whole story for you."

"Molly, what is it? Please, tell me now. I have to know."

"Gregor, this is more than you could have hoped for. You won't just save your career, you'll make it. It's incredible. I've got it all for you. Where are you?"

Gregor was in another bar, this one on 14th Street, one of the few remaining go-go places in the District itself.

"Uh, I'm in Georgetown," he lied.

"Gregor, how soon can you get here? I've got documents, I've got pictures, I've got reports. God, you won't believe it. It's going on right now, out in central Maryland. It involves—listen, darling, get here as fast as you can."

"I'm almost there now. Oh, Molly. Molly, I love you, do you know that? I love you, I'm so grateful."

Sniveling with joy, Gregor lurched out of the bar. The night air was fresh and clean; it smelled of triumph. He needed a drink to celebrate. He looked, saw a liquor store open down the block. But when he got there and stepped into its fluorescent brightness, he found he had only three dollars.

"Vodka. A pint, how much?" he demanded.

"Russian stuff's best," the clerk said. "Stolichnaya, four twenty-five. Absolut, five fifty. Then, there's—"

So Gregor, as he had that morning, bought something called Vodka City, an American concoction which, quickly sampled outside, had the mere strength of a small woman's slap to it and didn't quite amplify the joy he felt hugely enough.

Well, no matter. Any vodka being better than no vodka, he took several more hits on it as he ran back to his car, which had picked up a fresh parking ticket. Merrily, he crumpled the ticket into a ball and sent it sailing into the street. He climbed in, and drove to Alexandria.

It took twenty minutes and several more bolts of the drink before he pulled into her parking lot. He'd left it this morning in the dark and now he returned in the dark: full circle. From despair to triumph, his course magically assured by superior cunning and tactics. He slid the vodka into his coat pocket and raced to the foyer. There he took the elevator up and all but flew down the hall.

He knocked.

She threw the door open.

"Gregor!"

God, what a lovely woman! Molly, as usual, wore a muu-muu, but her meaty shoulders gave her the odd look of a professional football player. She'd applied two great vivid smears of blue eye shadow; her hair was waved and exquisite; and she wore, at the end of her stocky legs, two gold lamé strapped high-heeled slippers. Her toenails were painted pink.

"I wanted to look beautiful for this evening," she said.

"You do, my dear. Oh, you do, you look glorious."

She took his hand and pulled him into the room. He was so eager, his heart was beating like a metronome. He had an erection like an SS-24. He was set to blast off. The room was candlelit; he could see a bottle of wine on the table in the rear and two beautiful dinner settings.

"I thought we had something to celebrate," she said.

"We do! We do! This means I can stay forever!"

"Please sit down darling," she said. "May I pour you some champagne?"

"Champagne! Yes! God, wonderful!" The champagne would combine with the vodka to incredible sensations.

He sat in the big easy chair in the dim living room. She returned immediately with an unopened bottle and a glass.

"Now, darling. I'm all ears," he said, smiling in the face of her extraordinary radiance, sucking all the pleasure from the moment he could.

She sat opposite from him.

"Now, Gregor," she said, "there is one little thing I should tell you before I begin. One widdle ting." The baby talk brought a foolish, girlish smile to her plump face. "Pu-wheeze don't be angry with me."

"I forgive you anything," he said. "I absolve you of all your sins. You can do no wrong. You're an angel, a dear, a saint." He took her surprisingly tiny little hand and looked into her eyes. Odd he'd never really noticed before now, she didn't even have cheekbones. Her face was a white pillow with eyes.

"I am also," she said, "a special agent in the Counter-Espionage Division of the Federal Bureau of Investigation." She smiled.

He thought it was a hilarious joke.

"Oh, Molly, you're such a *character*," he said, laughing, and then he noticed that the reason the room was so dark was that there were so many other people in it, and he was so swiftly gobbled up by men in suits, it stunned him. The lights came on. An agent walked from the bedroom and snuffed the candles. Others emerged from closets, the bathroom. It was like the terrible moment at the theater when the play is over, the lights come up, and you see you've only been in a drafty old building all along.

Molly stood.

"Okay, Nick," she said. "He's all yours." She turned to him. "Sorry, honey. Life's sometimes tough. You're a pretty good guy, but Jesus, you're a shitty spy."

Molly disappeared into the bedroom, and a middle-aged man sat across from him.

"And so," he said, "we meet at last, Gregor Ivanovich Arbatov. Name's Mahoney. Nick Mahoney. I've been a close observer of you for two years now. Say, isn't that Molly a peach? One of the best. She's really terrif, huh?"

"I—I—"

"Now, Greg old guy. We got us a problem."

Gregor stared at him, stupefied.

"Can I have a drink?"

"Sorry, Greg. Need you sober. Oh, Jesus, do we ever need you sober."

Gregor looked at him.

"Greg, we got us a real, pure-D mess. A grade-A, godawful, major league mess."

He looked at his watch.

"You ever heard of a guy named Arkady Pashin?"

"I—"

"Of course you have. Well, right about now, Arkady Pashin is the most powerful man in the world. He's sitting inside an American missile installation fifty miles outside of Washington and he's about to start the Big One. Shoot off a bird that will start the last dance. He's got some Spetsnaz jokers along with him to see that he gets his way. You've heard of Spetsnaz?"

Gregor swallowed. "Raiders. Cutthroats. Heroes. The very best killers, it is said. But *why*?"

"Well, evidently he's trying to goad your people into a first strike while there's still weapons parity. He's going to fire a ten-warhead bus targeted against your command and control network, and he knows you guys will launch on warning. Presto, bingo, World War Three. He knew he could never get it by the Politburo. So he just did it, you know? Can you feature that? I mean, you kind of have to admire the guy's gumption."

Gregor said nothing. Yet it sounded like Pashin.

"Ever hear of some kind of nutsy outfit called Pamyat?"

"Memory," said Gregor. "Lunatics. The ones who hate Gorbachev and glasnost and INF and everything modern and hopeful and wish to return to the years of Stalin. Yes. They frighten all of us."

"Yeah, well, it appears your pal Pashin is a charter member. He's got a great memory, that's for sure. Well, the long and the short of it is that we have about eight hundred of our best boys up there, just about to jump off for what looks like a very busy evening, to try to stop this guy from—"

"But the world will end when you retaliate," Gregor said in horror.

"There you go," said Nick Mahoney with a phony smile. "Our strategic people think there's another wrinkle. That it's not enough for Comrade Pashin to twit your people into a first strike, but that he's also got to do a little something to give your team a big advantage in the seven-minute envelope between launch and detonation. So that when our birds fly, they fly poorly, they are uncoordinated, they are clumsily handled. Hell, brother, they may not even fly at all. You ever hear of this doctrine the intellectuals call 'decapitation'?"

Gregor looked at him.

"As in cutting the head off. And the head of this country is in the very city you're sitting outside of right now." He smiled.

"Yep, Greg. We figure your pal Pashin's gonna detonate a nuclear bomb tonight. In an hour or so. Right here in D.C. Bye-bye White House, Joint Chiefs of Staff. Pentagon War Room, CIA. NSA, National Bureau of Standards even. Bye-bye the whole shooting match. Bye-bye a couple of million sleeping dreamers."

He smiled at Gregor.

"Now, the question is, where would he get a bomb? I mean, if he doesn't have a Russian missile silo or a missile sub at his command, where does he get a bomb? Does he buy it at Eddie Bauer's?"

Gregor swallowed. His mouth was awfully dry. If there were going to be a nuclear detonation, wouldn't it be wiser to get out of there now, while there was still time? Shouldn't they be evacuating?

"Gregor, do you know where there's a bomb floating around?"

"I don't know what you're talking about," Gregor said.

"Now, that's not what I hear. In fact, we work real hard at covering your place, and we know the rumors just about as well as you do. We believe there's a one-kiloton nuclear device in the Soviet Embassy. It's there under strict GRU control, in case push ever comes to shove and the word goes out for a decapitation mission. That would cut reaction time to the seconds it took some brave boy to walk over to it and push a button."

Gregor held his breath. The rumors had always been dark, a sort of bleak Slavic joke, horrible black rumors, unbelievable. But they were persistent and had lingered for years.

"See, in the old days," Mahoney explained, "a bomb weighed a couple of tons. No way anybody was going to smuggle one in. But now we've got something called Special Atomic Demolition Munition, weighs one hundred sixty pounds. Delivery system, the big book says, is one strong soldier with a backpack. Now, we figure there's just such a sweetheart somewhere on Sixteenth Street, four blocks from the White

House. What do you think of this, old Greg? Anybody in that building dumb enough to pull the switch on himself?"

Gregor suddenly understood. Now it was clear. Now it made sense.

"Yes, I know such a man. His name is Klimov," said Gregor. "He is the Deputy *Rezident*, GRU apparatus, protégé and nephew to Pashin."

The agent nodded.

"Probably another member of Pamyat."

"It's worse," Gregor said. "The bomb would be downstairs. In the code cell, what we call the Wine Cellar. It's the most secure point in the embassy. Last night my friend Magda Goshgarian was on cipher watch. If Klimov wanted to detonate this bomb, poor Magda alone could not stop him."

"Yes. They wanted to launch early this morning. But they ran into an eighteen-hour delay. In fact, this morning Pashin sent a short burst of raw noise over the silo radio out into the great beyond to anybody who has a sophisticated radio transmission and receiving system. Like at your embassy. We figure it was some kind of signal to whoever is going to push the button, to tell him to hold off for further instructions. Tonight the show is set for around midnight. If we don't break in, Pashin will send another signal to whoever it is and—well, the button gets pushed. The bomb in Washington and the missile to Moscow must go off near simultaneously."

"Yes," said Gregor. "And now I know why they tried to kill me. They planned so far ahead that they had it set up that this afternoon Klimov tries to kill me with a Spetsnaz ballistic knife. Because with me dead, cipher duty reverts to the previous night's officer. To Magda. Again Magda is in the Wine Cellar, and Klimov will have no problem with poor Magda. Oh, Magda. Oh, poor Magda, what have I done to you?"

"She's there now?"

"Yes. I called her, asked her to take my duty. Jesus, it's the same thing, I gave him the same thing. She'll die without a whisper. And the little piglet will do it, laughing at history and his own glorious importance."

The two men were silent.

Finally, Gregor said, "This must not happen. You must stop it. Invade the embassy, no? With police, go in and stop Klimov."

"The embassy is your territory."

"But the rules, they can't mean much now."

"Gregor, old goat. You got KGB with AKs set at full auto, and kamikaze orders, shoot the hell out of anybody who comes over the wall. And when the ruckus starts, your friend Klimov goes downstairs a few minutes early, and pop goes the weasel. Listen good to your pal Nick, your long-lost best buddy. The only scenario that plays is the following. We need a guy—a good, brave guy, a guy with no nerves, and balls the size of Cadillac hubcaps, a tough, smart, shrewd guy, a James Bond guy, but Russian—to get into the basement and stop this Klimov. That's the best shot, really the only shot. We got eight hundred commandos in the mountains; here in Washington we've got room for only one. You dig?"

"Where you going to find this guy?" asked Gregor, still wondering how he could assist. He figured now they needed help with the floor plans, with the layout, the entry protocols, the Wine Cellar arrangements, maybe with the documents that would get the American agent past the KGB door guards, and . . .

And then he noticed Mahoney looking at him. God in heaven, they were all looking at him. Molly was looking at him, her big, stupid cow eyes hot and moist and radiant.

"Oh, Gweggy," she said, "how much better if we had a Green Beret, a policeman, a federal agent. But we don't, dear Gweggy."

And then Gregor grasped it.

"We have only you, Greg," said Mahoney. "Time to be a hero type. Time to join the Green Berets, Gregor old pal."

2200

Now the data was pouring in: the FBI had located the farm rented six months earlier by one "Isaac Smith" on the border of South Mountain from which the Spetsnaz operation was mounted: there the feds found piles of ammunition crating hidden in the barn, a variety of cars, trucks, and buses by which the men had assembled over the past month by a multitude of soft routes down through Canada or up from Mexico, as well as plans, schedules, a food dump, maps, and an informal barracks—all beds made. And they found a few sheets of what appeared to be chemically impregnated white canvas—four, to be exact. The Bureau guessed that these were some sort of crude Stealth technology for defeating South Mountain's Doppler radar, and reckoned that they were left behind, unused, by the four men who took down Hummel's house that morning.

The Pentagon, the CIA, and the DIA had further information on Spetsnaz history and theory. Spetsnaz people were said to be either the very best, or the very worst, as the case might be: highly motivated, extremely competent, utterly ruthless commando units that had operated most furiously in Afghanistan, where they were thought to be responsible for a number of village atrocities.

Going back through the years, it was clear that wherever the Soviets needed quick, deadly strikes, they used Spetsnaz units: the Prague airport, for example, thought to have been seized by airborne troops in the spring of 1968, when the Russians closed down the Czechoslovakian revolution under Dubcek, was actually taken by a crack Spetsnaz seizure team. And it was a Spetsnaz wet squad that aced the Afghanistan president Hafizullah Amin in his Kabul palace in December 1979. Spetsnaz personnel routinely formed the training cadres that the Russians circulated in the third world, having operated in such varied climes as the Peruvian mountains, the Iraqi mountains, the Malay peninsula, the Asian mainland, the paddies of Vietnam, and the highlands of Salvador.

"They're very good people," said Skazy, "but we can dust them."

"The worst part of the operation," Puller said, "will be the rappel. Sliding down that rope into the darkness. You know they'll be firing up at you. You'll put your grenades and maybe a good dose of C-4 down the shaft first, but then there'll come a moment when the first men of your team have to slide those ropes down into the darkness. And you know enough of the Spetsnaz tunnel defense team will recover to be firing on you as you descend. It'll be pretty bad, Frank. You figure out yet who'll be the first man on the ropes?"

Skazy laughed, showing strong white teeth. He was West Point, '68, and in those days had loved to bus to Princeton, the closest Ivy League school, on weekends, and lounge around in his ludicrous plebe uniform and white sidewall haircut, and just dare the punks to make a comment. He loved to fight. He dreamed of fighting all the time. He burned to test himself in the most fiery of all possible crucibles.

"You don't lead men from behind," he said. "I'll be Number One."

The answer did not surprise Puller, which was why he asked it.

"I want you to reconsider, Frank," he said. "A commander risks his operation if he exposes himself pointlessly and gets fataled in the early going."

"I'd never ask a man to do what I couldn't," said Skazy, meaning it and believing it.

"Frank," said Puller, "look, I'm not going to tell you how to run your assault. But don't go down that rope first out of some idiotic notion of showing me up. I know you're pissed at me because of Iran. I know you think I fucked your career. For what it's worth, I talked to Bruce Palmer and tried to get you your eagle. I told him what happened at Desert One was my fault. It wasn't yours. Okay?"

Skazy didn't look at him.

"I'm just trying to do the mission, Colonel. That's all. I just want the chance. The chance I didn't get in Iran."

Puller, who never explained anything, felt the temptation to this time. We couldn't go with five choppers out of specific mandate by the Joint Chiefs, who overcontrolled the mission beyond belief. I had no choice. I'm an army officer, I get paid to follow orders, and I get paid to take the heat afterward, when they all walk away because of their careers. I could have made a stink, but I didn't. Which is my way.

But he didn't say anything.

"Well, Frank, good luck to you, then. It's Delta's baby now."

"Just let us go, this time, Dick. Whatever you do, *let us go*."

So many turns and twists and dark ladders now, Walls felt as though he were in somebody's intestines, following the little trace of light upward. Sometimes this meant almost straight up, as if he were crawling up a chimney, supporting himself on the tension between his knees and his hunched, pressing shoulders, all of it made more difficult by the heavy weight of the remaining shotgun shells in his bellows pockets and the gun itself, wrapped awkwardly about his arm.

Dump the sucker, he thought.

But he could not. He loved the piece. It had never let him down.

And sometimes it meant almost walking rather than climbing, where the floor went to a slant, then switched back, but always, always, it went upward. So upward he fought in the darkness, seeing before him only the little bounce of illumination from the mazelike warren of tunnels. He knew only that there was this hint of light and that there was air in the tunnel, more now, cool and clean, whispering in from somewhere.

Maybe you dead, and this is hell, boy, he thought. Maybe this is forever, crawling through these damned holes, the tunnel rat's final fate: tunnels to other tunnels. Walls saw it before him: tunnels to heaven, tunnels into space, tunnels forever.

He paused. Sweat was in his eyes. Beginning to craze out a little. There, boy, he told himself. He breathed, realized how hungry he was. He'd kill for a piece of chicken about now: he focused on it for a second, thinking about the crisp outer crust and how he used to rip through it with his teeth, feeling it crunch beneath them, then get at the tender white meat inside that would fall off the bone into your hand, sweet in its own sweet grease. He smiled: his brother James was across from him. They used to joke—when white people died they came back as chickens so black people could eat them and finally do black people some good.

He laughed to himself. Hadn't thought about that shit in years. Hey man, be nice, get out of this jam, get out of this hole, go back and see James, have some of Mama's chicken.

Mama was a big Baptist woman. She worked for many years at some Jewish people's in Pikesville and they treat her good. But nobody else treat her good, not Tyrone, her husband, who disappeared, and Willis, who moved in and used to beat her. His mother was a large, sorrowful praying woman who worked very hard every day in her life and died when her eldest boy, Nathan, was in tunnels in Vietnam and only heard about it from his brother James. Then James got killed. Another boy at a basketball game had a gun, said James called him something bad, shot him.

So Nathan came home to no Mama and no brother James, and all the men he'd fought with in the tunnels were dead too. Death was everywhere, like the rats that prowled the hot alleys behind Pennsylvania Avenue, in B-more, Maryland, and he could get no job or when he got a job and his head would ache because of the time he was blown up and buried in the tunnel and couldn't work, he got fired.

TODAY IS THE FIRST DAY OF THE REST OF YOUR LIFE, the sign had said in the DEROS station on the way back from 'Nam, but it was another white lie: today was the first day of no part of your life.

The sign should have said what another sign did say: FUCK NIGGERS.

Walls shook his head. He was gripping the shotgun hard enough to break it; no one understood how full of rage Pennsylvania Avenue could turn a man. Man do *anything* to get off of Pennsylvania Avenue, and bury his mama and his brother in a nice place in the country. He missed his mama, he missed his brother. He never got off of Pennsylvania Avenue, but he became the dude of Pennsylvania there for a while, boy, the Dr. P of Pennsylvania, he could do anything for you, foxy pussy, some magic pills make you feel good, a piece to make you a man. He was the sultan of Pennsylvania Avenue until—

Walls came out of his reverie when a drop of water hit him in the cheek. Was only this motherfucking tunnel, no lie, Jack, that seemed to go on forever and ever and—

And then he saw it.

Well, a long way to climb to see this shit, but this was it all right, this was what he'd come for.

It was a metal pipe, corrugated, cutting through the tunnel up ahead. But goddamn, it was rusted, and it was from the hole in it that the light originated.

Walls scrambled ahead, not straight up exactly, but on an angle toward that pipe. Was this where white shit came out of the fort in the mountain? But no, didn't smell like no shit. He got up to it and crouched. Yes, the water came through here and had eaten the flues into the mountain from this spot. This was the main mother of all the tunnels he'd come through, this itty-bitty little thing. He reached up, touched the hole. Yes, by God, man could get through. Walls pulled himself into it. It was like being unborn: it was like crawling back into a pussy. His body had to work in an odd way to get into the rotted pipe, bending here, twisting there, wiggling his skinny hips this-way-that-way and—dammit, fucking gun *caught!* uh, c'mon, goddammit, uh—yes, yes, yes, again yes.

He was in the sucker.

Okay, motherfucker, where you go? He began to slither forward. His shoulders could barely move. The roof of the pipe was an inch above his nose. He wiggled ahead. He couldn't turn to see. He could smell the metal. The gun was under him, it hurt—goddamn, it hurt—but he was so trapped he could move forward only by inches. Panic hit him again. Oh, shit, to die like this in some pipe like a turd in the sewer. He screamed, his scream coming back in his face off the metal above him. This was the worst. There was almost no room for movement at all in here; he just had to keep pushing himself forward inch by inch. A man could die in here, stuck and starved to death and the little rats would come and eat the skin and muscles off his bone.

Walls tried not to think of the rats, and thank God there weren't any for him: only the pipe, above him, all around him, and the vague sense of light ahead and the rush now of absolute cool, dry air, and a vague hum. He squirmed on, and the seconds seemed to expand into hours. He felt like he'd been down here forever. He felt like this was his life. He couldn't remember a goddamned thing, except that this morning he'd been worried about the Aryans whacking his ass in the shower as they'd sworn to do. He figured he ought to pray, but now he was out of gods. He could think of no gods to pray to. The Baptist God of Momma was no good down here. Besides, lots of guys believed in a Baptist God and they got wasted easy, the most recent of them being poor Witherspoon some hours back in the tunnel. But this guy Allah was no treat either, and the guys that ate up his action died just like the Baptists. Larry X, head Fruit of Islam in the pen, he got his throat splayed open as a fish mouth by an Aryan, Allah did his ass no good at all. So Walls could think of no one to pray to, and he just sang a verse of "Abraham, Martin, and John," thinking, those dudes the closest thing to God I ever heard of, and squirmed ahead, and came, centuries later and awash in his own stench and sweat and terror, to the end of the tunnel.

He squirmed out. And there was God.

Tall and black and blank, God looked down on him impassively, in an air-conditioned chamber with the hum of machines. God was enormous. God was huge. God had no mercy, no meaning, no human face. God was flat and cold to the touch.

God was a rocket.

The teletype clattered for the first time in hours. The general made no move, however, to approach the machine and read the message. He simply remained crouched over Jack Hummel's shoulder, seemingly mesmerized by the flame so deep inside the block of titanium, as if he were *willing*, somehow, the flame to cut more swiftly.

"Sir," Jack heard someone say. "There's a message here."

The general finally tore himself away from the spectacle of the flame, went to the machine and ripped the message off the platen.

Then he went to the phone.

Jack heard the call.

"Major Yasotay. Tell the men they no longer need to obey language discipline. The Americans seemed to have figured out who we are."

He put down the receiver and spoke quickly in another language to one of the guards in the command capsule. The silent boy responded and raced out; Jack heard them all talking, and then he recognized the language.

Impulsively, he turned and stood.

"You guys are *Russians!*" he shrieked. "I heard you. That's Russian. You're fucking Russians!" His heart pounded in the awful loneliness of the moment. He couldn't believe he was defying the general.

The general looked at him, and for just a moment Jack saw a hint of surprise flicker across the man's smooth, handsome face.

"And so if we are, Mr. Hummel? What possible difference could that make to your family?"

"I'm not helping any Russians," Jack said with absolute finality, feeling that he'd somehow made his breakthrough and had located sufficient grounds upon which to make his stand, though he felt his heart's thudding go off like a jackhammer and his knees begin to knock.

The general spoke quickly in Russian, and instantly two of the young troopers ducked into the room, their weapons aimed at Jack.

"Let's end the farce, Mr. Hummel, without any silly fuss. If I say the word, my men fire. Then I'll have to put a message through to the men at your family's house and your wife and children die. There can't be but an inch or two of metal left in there. We'll get through it, with or without you. Your sacrifice accomplishes nothing; the sacrifice of your family accomplishes nothing."

"Oh, no? Buddy, you may know missiles, but you don't know welding. I give a yank on the tubes here"—he yanked the rubber hoses that ran from his torch to the cylinder of gas nearby—"and rip the sealers out, and you lose all your gas, then you're out of fucking luck until you get a new cylinder in. Like, say, by noon tomorrow, huh?"

Jack's knees shivered with desperate bravado. He felt the torch trembling in his hand. But he was right, of course; the whole crazy thing depended on nothing more than the seal between the hose and the tank; give it a hard yank, and this was all history.

The Russian understood immediately.

"Mr. Hummel, don't do anything foolish. I haven't lied to you, I guarantee it. Your wife and children are safe. Listen, you've been working hard. Take a break. We'll leave you alone. Think about it, then give me your answer. All right?"

He smiled, spoke to the two soldiers, and the three of them exited. Jack felt a surge of triumph. It had pleased him to see the suave general suddenly at a loss, scuttling backward absurdly. But the triumph turned quickly to confusion. Now what should he do? Pull the hose? Boy, if he did that, they came in and blew him away and blew away his family. The world lived, the Hummels died. Fuck that. As long as I hold this goddamned tube, I got some power. It occurred to him that he could hold them off. He looked and saw the big metal door to the center. If he could get that locked, then maybe—

Then he saw the yellow sheet from the teletype lying on the counter and picked it up.

Arkady Pashin, First Deputy of the Glavnoye Razvedyvatelnoye

Upravleniye, you are hereby directed to cease operations within the South Mountain Silo Complex. The following conditions are offered:

1. You and all men of Spetsnaz Brigade No. 22 will be given safe escort back to the Soviet Union. Soviet authorities have not yet been notified of your identities or to the extent of your operation or your connection to the group PAMYAT.

2. All your wounded will be tended for and returned to the Soviet Union at their earliest convenience.

3. No intelligence interrogations or debriefings will be held.

4. If the condition listed in paragraph 1 is unacceptable, the United States will also guarantee your delivery (and delivery of any men who chose to accompany you) into neutral country of your selection.

5. A tender of asylum is also hereby offered for you or any of your men who chose to so decide, and with it the offer of a new identity in comfortable surroundings in this country.

General Arkady Pashin, the mission which you have planned cannot succeed. I implore you, in the name of our common humanity and your code of ethics as a military professional, to cease and desist before the gravest possible consequences result.

It was signed by the President of the United States.

The President! The President was involved. This really impressed Jack. His spirits burgeoned. If the President was involved, that meant it was just about over. The Army would be here at any moment! If I can just get the door sealed, I can—

He looked up and the world disintegrated in red dazzle and befuddlement as a dot of gunsight laser struck his eyes, blinding him.

Yank it! he thought, and pulled on the hose, but something exploded in his leg and he fell yelping as his leg collapsed. The pain was extraordinary, but even as he fell, the torch slipped from his fingers, and as he hit the deck he rolled, scrambling, full of athletic passion, to reach it and yank that son of a bitch. But the commando who had shot him was through the opening of the capsule and on him. It was over in seconds.

"Stop the bleeding," said the general.

"You're crazy," Jack Hummel shouted. "You're fucking crazy, you'll—"

People were all over him. He lay flat on his back. Somebody shot something into his leg, and it stopped hurting and began to feel as if it were filling with whipped cream. A bandage was applied.

"He shot you very cleanly, Mr. Hummel. Right through the meat of the thigh. You'll live to be a hundred."

"You're crazy," shouted Jack again. "You're going to blow up the world. You're a fucking screwball."

"No, Mr. Hummel, I'm quite sane. I may be the sanest man in the world. Now, Mr. Hummel, you're going to have to go back to the torch, and as you cut, bear in mind that this man here will have a pistol on the back of your neck every second of the time. One slip and you're dead and your family is dead. They will go unmourned in the funeral pyre of the world."

The general leaned over. His charm ducts opened and Jack felt the scalding bliss of attention rush across him.

"But listen here, young man. When you get the key loose and we do what we must, I'll let you call them. There'll be time. I'll have my men bring them up here. Don't you see, Mr. Hummel. In here, in this mountain, it's the only safe place. Mr. Hummel, think of the world you'll inherit. It's all yours for a little bit of further effort."

It wasn't that the guy was nuts that was so unsettling to Jack Hummel; it's that he seemed sane—that he knew, absolutely and without doubt, what must be done.

"Think of your kids, Mr. Hummel."

"Why are you doing this?" Jack blurted out involuntarily. "Jesus, why? You'll kill a billion people."

The general smiled bitterly. Jack had the sense he was really seeing the man for the first time.

"The fact is, I'll kill only a few hundred million. I'll *save* billions. I'm the man who saved the world. I'm a *great* man, Mr. Hummel. You are lucky to serve me."

The general gave another little smile.

"Now, cut, Mr. Hummel. Cut."

Jack felt himself surrendering again. What could he do against such an operator, so much *better* than he was, so much stronger, smarter, who had it all figured out.

The flame ate into the metal.

Scurrying like a swift night lizard, Alex moved from position to position with a sweet word, a pat of encouragement, an invocation to patriotism and sacrifice, a reminder of the traditions. He was not an eloquent man and certainly not a glib one, but his blunt simplicity and, most of all, his belief, did what it was supposed to.

"How are we here, boys?" he said, glad to be speaking in Russian again.

"Fine, sir. Ready. Ready as we'll be."

"On our nightscope we picked up their trucks moving toward the mountain. Our infrared also picked up the heat of their helicopter engines turning over. The Americans will be here soon, boys. And this time there'll be lots more of them."

"We're ready, sir. Let them come."

"Good lads. This isn't Afghanistan now, where the issues grow hazy and you wonder why the fellow next to you has to die. This is the battle we all trained for."

He believed it. The general had explained it all to him, and he believed in the general. The general was a great man, a man who understood the whole world and what was best. You could believe in the general. Alex had come back from Afghanistan hungry for a fight to believe in: he'd seen too much meaningless death in the gulches and canyons and enfilades, too many guts spilled out on the rocks, seen too many black flies corpulent with Russian blood. Yet he came back, like the veterans of many another war, unappreciated and unloved, to nothing except a bitter peace. He came back needing a faith, a redeemer, a confessor, a messiah, and he'd found them all in the general.

"It's changing," pointed out the general. "This Gorbachev, with his damned glasnost, is turning the country your men fought and died for into a little America. We are becoming soft and bourgeoisfied. We are becoming our enemies, even as our enemies are preparing to destroy us. In America this second they are preparing to deploy a new generation of missile that dooms us, the madmen! And this fool Gorbachev has stripped us of mid-range nuclear weapons and hints of yet broader initiatives. Jews are brought back from the Gulag and allowed to become celebrities for their antisocial tendencies! American music is played on the radio. Our teenagers no longer join the Party, they are too busy dancing. And all this was going on while your men were bleeding slowly to death in Afghanistan. Only a few of us have the memory to understand this. Memory, Alex, that is the key. From memory, Pamyat, comes everything, a belief in our land, the courage to do something about the unpleasant present. Few enough have the guts to realize this, and fewer still the guts to do anything about it. Where is the leadership, the passion, the courage?"

"Sir, it's with one man. It is with you."

The general especially hated America. He called it "One big moral and intellectual concentration camp." Only men of courage could stand against the hated America and its plans to destroy Russia.

"Alex, did you know that Ghengis Khan had a special operations team, a Spetsnaz himself, under the leadership of a brilliant young officer who refused all promotion? Do you know what he said? I offer you this to think about: he said, 'Give me forty picked men, and I will change the world.'"

Alex nodded.

"I will change the world, Alex. With you and forty picked men. Or, rather, sixty."

They were a perfect team: the general the father who saw and knew all, the major a son who made his father's vision possible with his own willingness to sacrifice.

"Now, boys," he said to *his* children, the tough young heroes of 22 Spetsnaz, who would change the world from the perimeter defense of South Mountain, "think of your fathers scrambling through the wreckage of Stalingrad in the subzero weather, throwing themselves against the SS juggernaut all those long and bloody years. Then think of your grandfathers, who made a revolution and fought great battles against the West to save the world for you. Then be thankful that your test isn't half so severe as theirs: you've only a single night to fight, on a mountaintop in America."

"Let them come," said a boy. "I'll talk in bullets."

"That's what I like to hear. And remember this: you're Spetsnaz. No men on this earth have trained as hard or learned as much or given as much to become as good as you. You are the very best in the world. You carry your country's destiny because you're strong enough. Your shoulders are broad, your minds clear, your wills strong."

Alex paused in his thoughts and a twitch played across his face. He realized that it was a smile.

God, he was happy!

He couldn't wait for it to begin. It was the battle every professional soldier since the time of the Legions had dreamed about: a small-unit defense with the fate of the world hanging in the balance. But only one soldier of all the millions had gotten a chance to fight it, and that was Major Aleksandr Pavlovovich Yasotay of 22 Spetsnaz.

And one other: the unnamed American assault team commander, whom he would soon be meeting.

Skazy was alone with Delta now. He checked his watch and saw that it was 2145; the plan called for them to onload the choppers at 2150. Puller had gone back to the command headquarters to work up his nerve or whatever; and the guy Thiokol, gone too, back to his anagrams and code sequences, tensing up to crack the door.

There was one outsider here, Skazy knew, but said nothing. The young federal agent Uckley, who'd fucked up at the house, had arrived a few minutes ago in Delta cammos, presumably borrowed from one of the men he'd cracked the house with. Somewhere he'd got an MP-5 and an accurized .45. Uckley was here to tag along. All right, kid, thought Skazy. It's your party too.

"Okay, guys," Skazy said, "your attention please, just a sec."

They turned to look at him, faces now blackened, gear checked for the thousandth time, the very best guys there were, weapons cocked and locked, boots tied, all concentration and intensity.

"Guys, it's just us. Some of you were in 'Nam in the airborne or the Rangers or out in the boonies in an A-team detachment and you remember how it came apart in the end despite all the blood you and your buddies poured into it. And some of you were on the fucked-up Iranian mission with me and remember how it came apart, and how we left bodies burning in the desert. And some of you jumped into Grenada with me, and remember being pinned in that ditch during that long night. Well, the truth is, Delta's had its ass kicked each time out. Now, right now, I know there's a guy on that mountain who's a lot like us, hardcore, pro military, lots of ops under his belt. The Spetsnaz commander. Right now he's telling his guys how good they are, and how Delta will be coming and how they're going to kick more Delta ass. Okay? That doesn't make me too happy, and I don't think it should make you guys too happy. So no matter what happens, I just think we ought to have a little moment of seriousness here for a moment before we get on board the slicks. I fully expect to die tonight and that doesn't scare me a bit, because I know if I do, some Delta asskicker is going to come in the hole I opened and finish the job I started, right? So let's just shake hands, clear our minds, and concentrate on our profession tonight. In other words, guys, let's just get it done. Tonight, Delta gets it done. Tonight, Delta kicks ass. Fair enough?"

The roar was an explosion.

Skazy smiled. God, he was happy!

Peter stared at the face. It was a shrewd, wary face, cosmopolitan, comfortable, sure. It was also handsome, radiant with confidence. You could almost feel the charisma leaking from it. The eyes were bright and hard.

Arkady Pashin, he thought. I never even heard of you. But you certainly heard of me.

His eyes scanned the biographical data. Military and engineering all the way, another smartest boy in the class.

He tried to see a pattern, a meaning, in the Agency information. But he found nothing—it read like your run-of-the-mill defense pro, like any of a hundred generals he had known, only Russian style, with one of those famous cold, hard, serious defense minds, with the inevitable right wing twist, the Pamyat thing.

But there was this one peculiarity: "In November of 1982 Arkady Simonovich Pashin formally notified his headquarters that he would henceforth be known simply as Arkady Pashin. No information is available as to the reason for such an unprecedented decision. None of our sources have any idea as to its meaning."

Why on earth would he have done this?

A weirdness passed through Peter, some twisted nerves firing, and the strange sensation that the name alteration had to do with him too. It was connected to him. He shivered.

Peter tried to think about the Russian thinking about him and realized how important he was to the guy. He sends a guy to fuck my wife and then he himself comes over to this country and he charms her. He has her in that room in that fake Israeli embassy, and he looks at the woman I'm in love with. He's probably seen movies of her fucking Ari Gottlieb.

Peter shivered again; it was so *intimate* somehow; he felt hideously violated. His most closely held vulnerability—Megan—had been taken from him, turned, and used against him, used as a weapon. He had an image of this guy going through telescopic photos of him, going through the detritus of his life, trying to figure it all out, trying somehow to enter Peter—to, in some perverse and pathological way, to *become* him.

He reached back, pulled out his wallet, and got out his wife's picture. She still looked good to him. He set the photo down next to Pashin's and looked at the two of them together. Megan's shot was a head-on, without angle, casual. It caught her grace and the brains behind her ears and maybe just a little bit of her neuroticism. Looking at her, he suddenly acquired a terrible melancholy.

God, baby, I set you up for them, didn't I?

I made it so easy for them.

He looked at Pashin, the man in the mountain.

Your whole thing is that you think you're smarter than me. You and your little tribe of cronies, what's it called, this screwball outfit, Pamyat, Memory. He felt a little twist of shame. He knew himself he had no memory, no sense of the historical past.

It doesn't mean anything to me, he thought. Only one thing means anything to me.

Megan.

And you took her from me.

He looked again at the picture. No, Comrade Pashin. I'm smarter than you. I'm the smartest guy in the class. I'm the smartest guy you ever met.

He began to doodle with the name, Arkady Pashin and the name Peter Thio—

He stood up suddenly. A terrible excitement came over him, and a terrible pain. He had some trouble breathing, and yet at the same time he filled with energy.

I think I have you, he thought. The only thing I have to do is look where you think I don't have the guts to look. But I'm a realist. And this is how I beat you.

I can look at anything. Even if it kills me.

He left his desk, strode through the operations room, not seeing Dick Puller or the others, and pushed his way to the Commo room.

He picked up a phone.

"Is this a clear line?"

"Yes, sir," said a young soldier.

Swiftly, he dialed a number, heard it ring, ring again.

A man's voice answered with a name.

"This is Dr. Peter Thiokol," he said, "calling from the South Mountain operational zone. I want to speak to my wife."

Now was the lonely time. Dick Puller felt he ought to be doing something better, smarter, harder, more brilliant. Instead, he just sat there, puffing on a Marlboro, wondering why he ever decided to become a soldier, while inside it felt as though cold little spiders were crawling through his intestines. He felt so tight he could hardly breathe.

You became a soldier because you were good at it.

Because you always dreamed of leading desperate men in a desperate battle.

Because it seemed important.

Because it was in your genes.

Because you were scared to do anything you weren't sure you'd be good at.

Dick puffed harshly on the cigarette. He was an old man, he knew, fifty-eight his last birthday, with lovely daughters and a wife he'd die for, the perfect soldier's wife, who did much and asked little.

Your life has been one long self-indulgence, he thought, hating himself, wishing he could call her or the girls. He couldn't. Jennie was married to a good airborne major in Germany and Trish was in law school at Yale. And Phyllis—well, Phyllis wouldn't know what to do if he called. He'd never called before, only sending her his dry little letters from various hot locales, lying cheerfully about the food (which was always bad) and the danger (which was always high) and the women (who were always numerous). If he called now, he'd scare her to death, and what good would that do?

"Sir, Sixguns One and Two airborne, checking in."

His air force. The two gunships that would double as troop carriers and fly into the sure death of Stinger country.

"Acknowledge," said Puller, listening as the battle began to orchestrate itself, outside his hands now that all the planning was done, all the speech-giving over, and it came down only to the boys and their rifles.

"Sir, Halfback and Beanstalk are in position at the IP."

This was the Rangers, backed by Third Infantry.

"Acknowledge."

"Sir, Cobra-One reports onloading the slicks accomplished. Any messages?"

"No. Just acknowledge. You hear from Bravo yet?"

"That's a negative, sir."

"Figures," Puller said, seeing in his head the slow and clumsy progress of the reluctant remnants of the National Guard unit in the dark toward their reserve position to the left of the assault line, straggling awkwardly through the snow and the trees, out of contact, scared and exhausted and very, very cold. Bravo would be slow tonight.

"Sir, it's almost time. Will you be on the mike?"

"Yes, just a sec," said Dick, lighting another butt.

Inside, he felt himself tightening even further. Somehow it hurt to breathe. His lungs ached, his joints pinched. So many things could go wrong. So many things *had* gone wrong. In any operation, count on a sixty percent fuck-up rate. The way you win a war has nothing to do with brilliance; it has to do simply with showing up and fucking up less than the other guy. Some Napoleon! And now there was nothing to do but wait just a few more minutes.

At this point at Midway, Raymond Spruance went to bed, figuring he'd done his best.

U. S. Grant got drunk.

Georgie Patton gave a lecture on patriotism.

Ike Eisenhower prayed.

Dick Puller went back to work.

Thinking, yes, still, now, with just minutes to go he might have missed something, he began to page again through the various Spetsnaz documents and photographs that had poured in the past hour or so. There was too much to be gotten through; he was simply scanning the material, hunting for associational leaps, for blind luck, for—well, for whatever.

The dope included more reports on known Spetsnaz operations, defector debriefings (significantly all third party; no known man had defected from a Spetsnaz unit proper); satellite photos, newspaper accounts, everything the CIA had vacuumed up in thirty years of Russia watching, which had been shipped him high speed via phone computer line.

Lazily, more to drive the anxiety from his brain than for any real reason, he skimmed through it.

What if the Rangers bog down and the pretty kids of Third Infantry turn out not to be worth a shit off a parade ground?

What if the Soviets have more men and ammo than we ever suspected?

What if there's not as much titanium between Pashin and that key as we thought?

What if Thiokol can't get through the shaft door?

What if the Delta assault team can't fight its way to the LCC.

What if—

And then his eyes hit something.

"Stop the attack!" he screamed. "Tell all units to hold!"

"Sir, I—"

"*Tell all units to hold!*"

There was a pause and some fumbling at the other end as the FBI agents debated among themselves what to do. He thought they might be trying to cross-check the authenticity of his call over another line while he waited, and as he stood there, he felt his chest seem to fill with gravel and his breath wheezed between the loose stones.

Funny, he thought. The world may end tonight and yet that doesn't mean a thing to me. But here I am waiting to talk to my wife and I'm shaking like a leaf.

He wondered if he had the strength for the next few minutes.

And then he heard her voice.

"Peter?"

Her voice had a sadness in it, as if weighted with regret. Megan never apologized, not formally, not for anything; but she had little signals by way of indicating her small responsibility for whatever might have happened, and it was in this softened tone he heard her say his name. It did exactly what he had willed it not to: it earned his instant and total forgiveness and his total surrender. Shorn of his moral certitude, he knew he was lost.

"Hi," he said softly and raggedly. "How are you?"

"God, Peter, it's so awful. These awful men. They've been here for hours."

"It's unpleasant, yes," Peter said, irked instantly at the way he immediately agreed with her. "But look, you've got to give them everything
you can. Later, if you can demonstrate how hard you worked for them,
it'll help. I guarantee it."

"I suppose," she said. "It's just all so awful. They're going to send me
to prison, aren't they?"

"A good lawyer will get you off. Your father will know some hotshot;
he'll get you out of it. I guarantee it, Megan." He took a deep breath
and plunged ahead. "Look, I don't know what they've told you—"

"Not much. It's something terrible though, isn't it?"

"It's a mess."

"It's all my fault, isn't it?"

"No. It's all *my* fault. I see that now. How I played into their hands
and made it easy for them. Now I need your help. Your absolute, total,
trusting help."

"Yes. Tell me what I can do."

He paused.

"This Soviet officer you identified. The older man, Pashin."

There was silence. He waited as long as he could, until he could wait
no longer.

"Somehow," he said to her finally, "it was personal with him. That is,
between him and me. It was intimate and personal. That's why you were
so important to him. Megan, I have to go where I'm scared to go, and
look at what I don't want to see. You've got to take me there, and be
strong, and make me see the truth. It the most important thing you'll
ever do, do you see?"

Too much emotion tainted his voice, and he struggled to hold the
words in proper register. But the words were treacherous; they broke and
splattered on him and odd high notes, strange sounds of anxiety, splashed
through them. He felt as if he were weeping, but he could feel no tears.

Megan was still silent.

Then she said, "Peter, there are men here. All around me. Don't
make me talk in front of them. Can't we do it later, in private? I'll tell
you everything in private."

"There isn't time. There's a question I have to ask you. Only one."

He waited, but she wouldn't help him.

In the silence, he thought, the sex with Ari. He was good at it? He
was really good at it? He was better than me?

Stop it, he told himself.

He'd played the whole thing to get here, and now that he was here, he had a moment's terror.

You can look at anything, he told himself. *You're a realist. That's your strength. That's how you'll beat him.*

"Tell me if I'm not right. I've figured out how his mind works. I can read him now. I get him now."

"Ari?"

"Ari! Ari's nothing, Megan. Ari's a tool, a big stud for hire. No, it's this other guy. He's the one that's pulling the strings. Megan, there was a night, wasn't there, where you passed out? Where you had too much to drink or you were tired or something? Some night where you can't quite account for four or five hours? In fact, you probably haven't really acknowledged it in your own mind, because at some subconscious level you're not quite ready to face it. But wasn't there a night when . . . when you can't really remember what happened?"

Her silence grew, and as it grew it confirmed his suspicion.

Finally, she said, "He said it was the champagne. That I had too much and that I passed out. We had gone to an inn in Middleburg, Virginia, for a 'romantic weekend' at a very lovely inn. But I passed out Saturday night. When I awakened I could tell . . . that it had been romantic."

Peter nodded.

"When was this?"

"Two weeks ago."

"After—?"

"Yes. After I had been with you. I went straight from you to Ari. I'm sorry."

"And that was the last time you saw him?"

"Yes. I took some pictures of some documents you had. I just gave him the camera. We didn't use the usual routine. And then we went to this inn. And the next morning he left me. Said he was returning to his wife in Israel. He just walked away from me. I cried, I begged. He hit me. Peter, he hit me, and then he just left me in that place, as if I didn't matter to him."

You didn't.

"Okay," he said. "You've been a great help."

"Peter, is that all? You called—"

"Megan, you should be all right. That lawyer, he'll get you a walk. Those FBI guys, throw a little charm at them. They'll melt. They're men, after all. And when this is over—"

"Peter, God, it's dangerous out there, isn't it? But you're safe, aren't you? You're back, far away from the guns, aren't you? You're not going to do anything stup—"

He was lost now. He felt it slipping away. He saw her in the room, in the dark, drugged, helpless, and unresistant. He wondered what they used and how compliant she'd been. He knew she'd been utterly, totally compliant. He felt her shame and debasement. The image of it brought the tears at last from him, and he felt himself begin to sob like an idiot child.

"Baby, when it's over," he heard himself saying, "we can go to New York. We can have another life, I swear it. We can move to New York so you can be with the people you like and I can teach, maybe, or—"

He could hear her crying too.

"I miss you so," she was saying. "Peter, I'm so sorry this all happened, I'm so, so sorry and be careful, please, stay away from the—"

"Dr. Thiokol!"

It was the hard voice of Dick Puller punching at him through his grief.

"Megan, I have to go."

"Thiokol! I need you ASAP!"

"I have to go," he repeated. And then he said, "Thanks, I think I can take the guy now," and hung up. The sport coat seemed to constrict him strangely and he pulled it off and threw it in the corner. He felt much better.

He turned, tried not to see the men staring at him in amazement, and discovered Puller bearing down on him like a juggernaut, waving a photograph.

"Peter, look at this," said Puller. "Tell me if it's what I think it is."

Peter blinked to clear his eyes, felt like a fool, an idiot, but noted that Puller was far too intense to notice. As his focus sharpened he saw what he was supposed to see. It appeared to be an extremely high aerial view of South Mountain; he could see the launch control facility roof, the barracks roof, the wire perimeter, and the silo hatch, and the access road leading up. Yet there was something subtly wrong with the photo, in the relationship, say, between the buildings, the angles of the siting, in a hundred little areas. He concentrated, but couldn't quite—

"It just came over from CIA. They got it with a Blackbird three months ago over Novomoskovsk near Dnepropetrovsk where Spetsnaz has its big training camp. Damn, if they'd have only read it *then*. If they were sharp in that damned agency, instead of—"

But Peter just stared at the picture.

"It's where they prepped the mission. It's their rehearsal site."

Peter stared hard.

Something's wrong with it, he thought. He saw what looked like diagonal slashes in the earth, or sergeant's chevrons, or a giant tire track rolling across the mountaintop.

"What are these marks? I see these marks in the snow, what are they?"

Puller looked at them.

"Yes, that's it, isn't it? They're trenches. That's what's under that goddamn tarpaulin."

Peter didn't get it.

"What you're looking at, Dr. Thiokol, is his plan. Yasotay's defense plan. You see how the trenches take the configuration of a V and fall back toward the elevator shaft?"

"Yes."

"He'll fall back, trench by trench, toward that last redoubt. When we assault we're always in a crossfire kill zone from the two arms of the V. You can't flank it because it's too wide. You can bet the trenches are linked by tunnels, which they'll blow as they fall back. It's the way the Muhajadeem fight in Afghanistan. He must have lost a thousand men trying to take hills like this. He's the hill expert of all time. Each one of these trenches will cost us an hour and a hundred casualties. In effect, we have to take the same trench, over and over. The attack will never make it. It'll get hung up in the trenches."

But Peter wasn't really paying any attention. He was staring, fascinated, at the photograph. There was something weird about it. He could not tear his eyes away. It was something he knew, yet something he didn't know. His mind struggled to interpret the competing phenomena; he searched for a theory to unify his perceptions of distress.

"Look!" Peter suddenly shouted. "Look! Look at this!" He *knew* there was something about the picture that bugged him; he'd been over and over the top of South Mountain before and during the construction. He knew it as well as he knew Megan's body. No man knew it better.

"See, here. They haven't bothered to plant the trees to the left and the right of the assault site. They've just left the area bare, but you can see the way they've sculpted the land form to match the shape of the earth. But their original satellite pictures must have been taken early and they didn't bother to check the later ones carefully; see, we actually moved the site of the barrack about fifteen feet to the left, and we didn't build this additional wing to the launch control facility, although it was in the plans they got from Megan. But most important, the creek's missing. They don't have the creek because there *wasn't* a creek."

Puller looked at him strangely.

"What the hell are you talking about?"

"You told me the problem with the assault site was that it had such a narrow front that all the attacks had to come across this meadow here. Right? And those are the men that go into the guns, right?"

Puller looked at him.

"But that's not right. There's a creek bed, here, on the left." His finger probed at a place on the denuded photograph that showed sheer cliff.

"It's supposed to be impassable, too steep to climb, but I'm telling you, the creek cut into it. You could get people up it and hit them from this other side, I know you could. You don't have to attack on that narrow front only. You could get soldiers up there and hit them from the left and bypass the fall-back trenches. I swear to you, there's a creek bed. You don't see it in the winter because it's dry and under snow and you don't see it during the summer because of the trees, but it's there and it's another way to the top."

Puller looked at it hard.

"Come with me."

They ran to the command center to look at the national geodesic survey map.

"Dr. Thiokol, there's no creek marked here."

"That's a 1977 map. The creek, we opened the creek when we excavated for the shaft, last year. That's why. I'm telling you, you can get soldiers up that side of the mountain and the Soviets don't know." His finger shot out to a marker on the map. "Those men are the men you send. They're the ones who'll get you into the perimeter and to the elevator shaft. Your Rangers and regular infantry won't make it."

Puller leaned forward.

"Those guys," Peter yelled, pointing at the mark on the map that stood for a group of men. "Who are those guys?"

"That's Bravo," said Puller. "Or what's left of it."

Walls was in the cathedral of the missile.

It towered above him in the gray half-light. He felt so small.

He reached out and put his hand to the skin of the thing, which was not cold and clammy and metallic as he imagined. Indeed, it had no sense of *machine* to it. Even as his fingers lingered in stupidity upon it, it did not warm to the touch. It drew no energy from his hand. It was . . . most peculiar . . . it was nothing.

He could not know it. He could not feel it. It had no meaning. It wasn't exactly that he was dwarfed into nothingness, that his smallness was made manifest by his proximity to the seven-story bigness of it, it was just that it was so blank. It was an abstraction. There was no feeling of its having any sense. He could not begin to figure out how to connect to it. It was just an immense black apex, smooth and blank, huge beyond knowing, disappearing as it rose above him, throwing in the half-light the tiniest smudge of his own reflection back at him, but more shadow than anything, a sense of movement and shape, that was all. It had no human face. He sensed that it didn't . . . again, this was very peculiar . . . it didn't care about him.

It befuddled him. He felt his reactions slow way down, as if he'd been drugged. It had a weird radiance, a kind of halo. It almost felt as though it came from some dead religion or something; he'd once come across something just as strange in the 'Nam, a giant stone head with thick lips and staring eyes amid the bougainvillea and the frangipani, and you could look at it for a century or two and not learn one thing from it.

Tentatively, he walked its circumference, though there wasn't much room between the skin of the thing and the concave of the cement wall that encircled it. His head was back, his mouth was open. It never changed. From any angle it was the same.

His head ached. He became aware of small noises, tickings, pingings, obscure vibrations. At the same time he smelled the odors of wiring and cement and wax. It smelled like electricity in there.

He looked at it again, in wonder. It wasn't at all like the rocketship he'd imagined, to the degree that he'd imagined rocketships at all. It had no fins, for one thing. How could they steer it without fins? It had no numbers either, and he had the vague supposition that it should have black and white checks on it somewhere, as well as big fat USAF initials, like the Tac ships in 'Nam. He also had this idea that there'd be a huge superstructure like a battleship's control tower up next to it, and lots of guys scurrying around: nope, nothing. It was so huge it didn't look like it could fly at all. The big tube just sat on a tiny framework of girders, nothing elaborate, and its exhaust cupolas extended beneath that, into a pit. As he looked up it, it disappeared, yielding some seventy feet up to nothingness. Then, another hundred or so feet up was the circular image of the sealed silo hatch, which appeared from down here to resemble a manhole cover.

He wondered what to do. Should he blow it up? He wasn't sure. He tried to remember. Goddamn, if that Witherspoon were here, he'd know what to do. But Walls wasn't at all sure if he should blow it up. He might get in big trouble. And even if he was supposed to blow it up, there was the problem of *how* to blow it up. He had no grenades left. He had no C-4 left. He could see no cables to cut or hoses to rip. He didn't think firing a few Mr. 12s into a thing this big would do any damage. And anyway, wasn't there an A-bomb in there? He wondered where it would be. He didn't think it would be a terribly good idea to shoot the rocket and make the bomb blow up, because wasn't that what they were trying to stop?

Shit, he thought, baffled by it.

At last he stumbled on a ladder. It was really a series of rungs in the concrete and, craning, he saw that the rungs led a perilous way up the yawning side of the concrete tube to a very small door, halfway up to the silo hatch.

Walls tried to figure out what to do. A certain part of him said, just wait here until they come get you, you're okay now. But another part said, they wanted to get into this place real bad, only way to get into this place is up that ladder.

Maybe you're the only dude get into this place. The *onliest*.

He laughed at that. All those white motherfuckers running around with their helicopters and shit, and here little nigger Nathan Walls, Dr. P of Pennsylvania Avenue, son of Thelma and brother to James, both dead, but Nathan, Nathan, he the onliest peoples to make it *in*. And what then?

Then you kill more white boys, he thought.

He had at that second just the briefest animal sensation of warmth and motion, and then he was hit hard by a flying bunch of muscle, yanked down, as if under the pounce of a cat, and pinned against the cement. And he felt the blade come up hard and tight against his throat, and he knew he was going to die.

In the first slick, Skazy was on the radio.

"Delta Six, this is Cobra One, I'd like an amplification of that last order, please."

"Cobra One, hold tight in your ships, that is all."

Skazy sat, breathing hard, feeling it all come apart in his mind. He remembered Desert One, the confusion of rushing men, out-of-control machines, and unsure command. He remembered Dick Puller off on his own like some kind of moody Achilles, out of reach.

Colonel Puller, there's rumors all over the—

It's an abort, Frank. Get Delta on the—

An abort! We can still take these motherfuckers! Goddamn, we don't need six chops! We can do it with five, we can get in there and blow these motherfuckers away and—

Back to the ship, Major!

That's when Skazy had hit him. Yes, he'd hit a superior officer in the face, and remembered the shock, the totality of it, when Puller fell back, his face leaking blood, the unexpected look of hurt on it.

Someone grabbed him.

Frank, get out of here. Dick's decided. Get back to your people.

You cowardly motherfucker, you don't have the guts for this kind of work, he remembered screaming, the wounded, enraged son who'd just learned his father was merely a man.

"Delta Six, Cobra One, what the hell is going—"

"Off the net, Cobra One, you're in a holding position until release, out."

Goddamn, said Skazy to himself.

"I'm going back to command," he told McKenzie, and disengaged himself from the chopper, dipped under its roaring rotor, and headed back to Puller.

There were fifty-five of them and they were lost and had been lost and they were way behind schedule, and it was cold as shit and even if the world was hanging in the balance, they didn't care, they just wanted to be warm. Sure, okay, you can make so many speeches, but the guys had been shot at today and most of them were still in bad shock from the first fight. These guys had been playing at war and they'd never seen anyone die and suddenly they'd seen a whole batch of people die, mostly their friends.

"Lieutenant, I think we're lost," said the sergeant.

"We can't be lost," said Dill. "It's just over here."

"I'm afraid some of the guys may have wandered away."

"Goddammit," said Dill, "they were supposed to stay in close. You get lost on this mountain, you could be in real danger."

He looked back. Bravo was spread out through the trees; he could see the blurry shapes against the white of the snow, each trailing a bright plume of breath, each groaning laboriously, each cursing under the discomfort, strung out, uncoordinated. Jesus, what a parade to save the world, Dill thought. You poor guys. You couldn't lick a stamp to save your life. He almost laughed.

"Tell the sergeants to get the guys together. I mean, we're just supposed to *wait* is all, in case they need us."

Jesus, he thought, poor Bravo can't even *wait* right.

"Yes, sir. But we're already way behind. Like, it's quarter after and those guys should have started shooting and I don't hear a damn thing."

"Yeah, well," said Dill, not sure what to do, "I'm sure they have their reasons."

It had seemed so easy in the briefing. Bravo was to move up behind the Rangers and Third Infantry, then peel off to the left to get out of the way of the support groups, the medics, the ammo carriers, that sort of thing. And just wait in good order in case they were needed. So they were essentially out of it. The ones that were here, they'd made it. They were alive! Whatever, they had made it. It was time for the pros to take over.

But he was anxious that he hadn't heard anything on the radio for a while.

"MacGuire?"

"Sir?"

"You sure that thing is working?"

He heard fumbles, mumbles. MacGuire was new to the PRC-25. Huston, his regular, was dead.

"It's not working."

"Oh, shit," said Dill. "Can you fix it?"

"Uh, sir, it's the batteries. They're dead. We've been out of contact now for about ten minutes."

"You got any extras?"

"Yes, sir, in my pack."

"Great. Maybe they've surrendered and we don't know it yet."

He crouched as the boy struggled first with his pack, then with the radio. Dill thought he ought to say something to the kid about checking stuff like that before they started out. But Dill was gentle; he was good with kids, and they responded to him, which is why he coached basketball for a living at a high school outside Baltimore.

In a few seconds there was a gravelly growl as the boy got the walkie-talkie back in working order, and then handed it over to Dill, who hit the receive button to hear himself being vigorously paged by the old bastard colonel who was running things.

"—vo, goddammit, Bravo, this is Delta Six, where are you, Bravo? Goddammit, where—"

"Delta Six, affirmative, Bravo here, do you copy?"

"Dill, where the fuck have you been?"

"Ah, sorry, Delta Six, we had a temporary malfunction and lost contact there for a second or so, over."

"You were out of contact for nearly ten minutes, soldier. Are you in position?"

Dill grimaced.

"Well, not exactly, sir. Tough going up here. We're more or less where we're supposed to be, about halfway up. I can't see the Rangers or Third Infantry. But it gets real steep ahead, I can see that, and I—"

"Dill, there's a change in plan."

Dill waited. The colonel said nothing.

"Delta Six, I don't read you, ah, over."

"Dill, I'm advised that ahead of you there's a creek bed."

"Sir, I don't recall any creek bed on my map. I really looked hard at it, too, sir."

"I am advised that it's there, nevertheless, Dill, and that you ought to be able to get a raiding party up that—"

Raiding party?

"—up that groove in the rocks and onto the perimeter flank pretty easily."

"In support of the main attack, Delta Six?" asked Dill, computing the problem.

"Negative, Bravo. You are the main attack."

Dill looked at the little box in his hand. Goddamn that kid, why hadn't he discovered his dead batteries ten minutes from now rather than where he was.

"Sir, I don't think my men are—"

"Bravo, this isn't a request, this is an order. Look, Dill, sorry, but it's how things have to go. The Rangers will never make it in the face of the heavy fire without help from the side. The front is too narrow and we believe there's a network of trenches in their position. We have to take this fucking place in one stroke. You guys are it. Get humping, Lieutenant. It's time to go to war."

Tagged again, Dill thought.

He wished they'd leave him alone so he could get at the vodka in his pocket. At least with vodka he'd have a chance or something. But no, the Americans just kept drilling him, going over and over it again, where the bomb was, its fusing mechanism, the disarming steps, just in case, a crash course in nuclear technology, all a blur to him.

I want *vodka*.

But now the van had stopped. They were out of time.

"Okay, Greg," said the FBI agent called Nick, "we're on I Street, two blocks down from the embassy, right in front of the MPAA. You know the neighborhood. Just a few feet down to Sixteenth, then your left and there you are. We've halted traffic, we've got the place sealed off, and we've got enough SWAT people around to crack Nicaragua. But we've been feeding cars along so they won't catch on. Okay, the street is clean, it's sanitary, no mugger's going to knife you on the way in."

Gregor thought the man was hyperventilating. He looked as if he were going to have an attack of some sort. He looked as if he needed a bottle of vodka himself.

"Greg, you paying attention here, fella?"

"Yes, of course," said Gregor.

"You sort of looked like you were dreaming about what was between Molly Shroyer's legs there for a sec, old guy."

"Actually, I am fine."

"Good man, Greg. Anybody going to give you a hard time getting in? You code-cleared, all that?"

"I'm known. No difficulties. Well—"

"Well what?"

"I have been out of contact for twelve hours. It is not possible to know how they're going to react. There might be a few questions, maybe an unpleasantry or two. But nothing I cannot handle."

"Great. In other words, these guys may roust you just going through the door?"

"No. No, I am a trusted man. Nothing will happen."

The American looked at him with great doubt on his plump, tough face. Then he said, "You want a piece, Greg, in case it should get hairy down in the Wine Cellar with this Klimov? I've got a nice HK I could lay on you."

"There's a metal detector. If KGB security finds I am armed, it will be the end. There will be no way to get downstairs."

"Sure?"

"Certain."

"Now, don't rush it, guy. That's how these things fall apart. You get anxious, you try and force it, bingo, it's history. There's plenty of time. Hell, it's not even eleven. You're just old Gregor, in from the cold, looking to relieve your pal Magda downstairs. Okay?"

"Okay," said Gregor.

"Time to go, guy."

"Okay," said Gregor again. Somebody slid the van door open and out he stepped into amber light. It was moist and chilly; the streets glowed; the air was filled with sparkly mist. When Gregor breathed it felt like ice sliding down into his lungs, a great feeling. It made him feel alive. He shivered, drawing the cheap little overcoat around him, but took comfort from the weight of the vodka in the pocket. Once he got inside, he promised himself a nice hit, a drenching, gushing gulp of it, to send all his demons away.

He walked on down to 16th Street, turned left. He could see the building up ahead on the right, just past the Public Television Office, which looked far more totalitarian than the Russian building. The embassy was a big old place, Georgian, once upon a time a capitalist millionaire's playpen. Up top, the complicated mesh of aerials, microwave dishes, and satellite communication transmitters looked like some weird spiked crown.

Gregor crossed the street. Two American cops—the executive protection service—at the embassy gate watched him come, but they didn't matter. They were nothing. He knew once he was inside the gate, KGB would be on him.

Who? Who was captain of the guard that night? If it was Frinovsky, he'd be all right. Frinovsky was an old man, a cynic like himself, another secret drinker, a homosexual, a man of appetites and forgiveness. On the other hand, in KGB as in GRU, these kids were taking over. Ballbusters, showoffs, zealots, Gorbachev's awful children, all with their pretend birthmarks. Gorshenin, perhaps. Gorshenin was the worst, a little prick who kept names and Wanted to Rise. He hated those like Gregor, who only Wanted to Stay. He was young Klimov's pal too.

Gregor arrived. He flashed his embassy ID to the two cops, who stood aside, and then he stepped through the gate and headed up the walk toward the door, toward the bronze plaque, CCCP.

He was back in Russia, and scared shitless. The door opened, a blade of orange light spilled across the pavement.

It was Gorshenin.

"Arrest that man," the awful Gorshenin shouted.

So very deep now. He couldn't have much gas left in the cylinder at all. The angle was torture. It was like surgery, he was so far inside. The light from the torch was far, far away, a blur of bright flame through his black lenses. He could see only more metal. He withdrew.

"What is wrong?" the general said.

"My leg, Christ, it's killing me."

"Get on with it, goddamn you."

"My leg's bleeding again, Jesus, can't you—"

"Get on with it."

"Maybe we missed it or some—"

"No!" screamed the general. "No, you did not miss. The center, you went into the center. I saw, I measured myself, I know exactly where the cut should go and how it should proceed. I monitored. You have not failed. Cut, Mr. Hummel, goddamn you, cut, or I'll have you shot and your children's bones ground to fertilizer."

Jack looked at him. Crazy fucker, he now saw, crazy underneath, crazy as a goddamned loon.

The general pulled out a pistol.

"Cut!" he said.

Jack turned, and again thrust the torch into the deep gash in the titanium. The bright flame licked at the far metal, licked and devoured, drop by drop and the metal fell away.

Then—pinprick, BB, cavity, Cheerio, nailhead—a minuscule black hole began gradually to appear in the metal at the end of the tunnel. He saw it expand as the titanium liquified and fell clear. Jack's heart thumped and, goddamn him, he couldn't help the excitement.

"I'm there. *I'm there*," he shouted, giddy with joy. The long journey was almost over.

Dick Puller hunched over the microphone, sucking on a Marlboro. He drew the smoke deep into his lungs, held it there, absorbed its heat, and hissed it out in a flare from his nostrils. His face was bleak and set and ash gray. Before him stood the map on the wall, with its brave little pin reading BRAVO, the radio transmitters, ashtrays, cigarette packs. Around him nervous staff guys, Commo clerks, state cops holding cups of coffee, talking quietly, just staring out into space. The air was heavy with tobacco smoke and pointless, dry chatter and despair.

And there was Peter Thiokol, who'd changed totally. He wore commando gear now, black field pants and a black sweater, the black knit watch cap down over his ears so that they were too hot. His glasses looked fogged.

Peter stood with his arms crossed, trying to get his thoughts assembled. Hard, under the circumstances. It was like a waiting room outside the maternity ward in an old *Saturday Evening Post* cartoon. There was no real sound in the room, no meaningful sound. He could hear the creak of boots as the men swayed their weight from foot to foot, or scuffed their heels against the floor, or exhaled loudly or sighed tragically. Occasionally, the crackle of static leaked from the speaker of the radio.

"What's taking them so long?" Peter finally asked, but nobody answered.

He spoke again, because no one else seemed to have the will to.

"Colonel, maybe you ought to contact them again."

Puller just looked up at him, his face gone shockingly aged, broken. He looked as if someone had been hammering on his head with pipe wrenches and snow shovels. Peter had never seen this Puller, dazed and old, caught in the crunch of the stress, the energy bled out of him.

This is what Skazy saw at Desert One, he thought in horror. An old man without an edge; an old man squashed by the pressure; an old man who'd sent too many boys to die too many times.

"They're either going to make it or they're not," said one of the other officers. "Talking to 'em during maneuver just screws things up. This, uh—"

"Dill," said Puller.

"Dill, this Dill, he either gets 'em there or he doesn't. Funny, you train all your life for a spot like this and there's maybe twenty thousand professional officers who'd give an elbow and a jawbone to be there, and it comes down to a gym teacher."

After that there wasn't much to say.

"Delta Six, this is Halfback, do you read?"

"I copy, Halfback," said Puller.

"Sir, we still holding?"

"That's affirmative, Halfback."

"Sir, if it comes to it, we'll go in. I mean, we're Rangers. We go in. You just say the word, and we'll jump off."

"That's a negative, Halfback."

"Delta Six, Sixgun-One." It was the lead gunship, still holding on the strip. "We're ready on the assault too. Give the word, and we'll rock and roll."

"I said, holding. Holding. Back to radio discipline, all units."

The crackles sputtered out.

Peter looked at his watch. It was 10:35.

"Sir, if I was you," someone whispered to him, "I'd turn that watch upside down on your wrist. You get up there, you'd be surprised in the dark, those gooks will zero on the radium in your watchface if it shows."

Peter looked at him, mumbled an insincere, "Uh, thanks," and made the adjustment.

"Sir, how long will you hold them?" someone asked Puller.

"Until Bravo checks in," was all that Puller could say.

"Colonel Puller."

Skazy stood in the door. He looked like some kind of guardian of hell's gate, his face blackened like Caliban's, his eyes leaking white rage, his grim lips pink and hot. He was draped with an immense green rope and wore several ammunition belts around him. He carried two pistols, several M-26 and smoke grenades, an angle-headed flashlight, and a CAR-15.

"Colonel Puller, I'm going to have to ask you to retire, sir. I'm officially taking command."

Puller stood. He was another large man. Somehow the men between them melted away.

"Back to your station, Major Skazy," said Puller.

"Colonel Puller, I'm prepared to put you under arrest if you don't move away from the radio."

Puller spoke quietly.

"Major Skazy, back to your station."

Four Delta commandos, heavily armed, slipped by Skazy and slid into the room. Though their weapons weren't brandished, everyone knew they were cocked and unlocked and at Skazy's disposal.

"Sir, I request once more that you move away from the radio. It's time to go."

Puller reached into his holster, removed his .45, and threw the slide with a harsh clack that echoed in the still, smoky room. The hammer locked back.

"Son," he said, "if you don't move out of that doorway and return to your ship, I'll shoot you in the head. It's that simple."

He leveled the pistol at Skazy.

Instantly, four CAR-15s zeroed on him. Craziness flashed through the air.

"We'll both die, Colonel," said Skazy.

"Be that as it may," said Puller, "if you don't move away from that doorway and return to your post, I'll shoot you."

"Colonel," said Skazy, "I have to ask you one more time to move away from the radio and relinquish command."

He started to walk into the room—

"*Stop it!!*" screamed Peter, himself almost out of control as he lurched between them. "*Stop it!!* This is infantile!"

"Step aside, Thiokol," said Puller, looking through him.

Skazy had removed an automatic from his belt.

"Thiokol, sit down. This doesn't concern you."

"This is insane," Peter shouted. He was breathing near to hyperventilation, murderous with rage at the folly and so terribly scared he could hardly stand still. His blood surged with adrenaline. "You assholes, you Delta prima donnas and your goddamned games, do your goddamned jobs like everybody else! Don't hold yourself so goddamned precious!"

There was a click.

Skazy had cocked his Smith & Wesson.

"Peter, sit down," he said. "Colonel, I have to give you one last chance to step aside or—"

"Delta Six, this is Bravo, we're *up*, we're at the top of the hill, goddammit, we're *there!*"

Peter saw Puller snap the safety on his pistol as he slid it into the holster, lean forward, just an old man with a shit-scared look to his face, nothing dramatic, no big line to deliver, and say, "All units, this is Delta Six, do you copy, Delta Six. Heaven is falling, I repeat, Heaven is falling. I repeat, Heaven is falling."

Everybody began to run. Someone cheered. Peter took a deep breath and then was running for his chopper through a commotion of other rising birds, the whip of snow and dust in the darkness, and the sound, far off and blurry, of men with guns.

"They're off," yelled the man on the night scope, "five, six, seven, eight, eight of them. Hueys."

Troop carriers, Yasotay thought. An airborne job, helicopter assault at night. Let them come, he thought. He'd been on a few and knew how they got messed up.

"Rockets," yelled Yasotay to his missile people. "Spotters ready. Men on the first line, eyes front. Get ready, boys. The Americans are coming."

But before the Delta-laden Hueys could arrive, the first of the two gunships rose over the treeline, then the other. They hung obscenely, two black shapes against the white snow of the valley. Their rotors filled the air with the wicked whup-whup-whup of the jet engines, loud enough to mask the final movement of troops through the trees to the point of attack. Worse, at an altitude of some five hundred to a thousand feet up, the gunship guns had angle on the ground troops; they'd be firing down on the compound.

"Mark your targets, rockets," Yasotay shouted in the second before the mini-guns began to fire. The stable world seemed to dissolve. The mini-guns fired so much faster than conventional machine guns that their problem wasn't accuracy but ammunition conservation. From each of the hanging birds the tracers leapt out at the mountaintop like a dragon's flame, a stream of light almost, and where the hot streaks touched, the world yielded. But of course in the dark they had no good targets, just as earlier the A-10s, roaring overhead, had no good targets; shooting at men is not like shooting at tanks or trucks. And so the bullets, as had the earlier bullets, bounced across the compound, roiling snow and dirt but little flesh; but their impact was devastating psychologically because there seemed no force on earth that could stand against them.

Down in the treeline Yasotay saw movement; infantry, coming hard through the trees, almost into the open.

"Rockets," he yelled again, knowing he had only seven Stingers left after the profligacy of the air attack in the afternoon, but knowing that if he did not push the gunships back the infantry—good infantry, he presumed, better than the boobs who'd come at him earlier—would get close. It was a question of timing now; he'd put up a hard fight, then fall back to the first of the five V trenches; they'd come ahead and he'd have them in two fires. He'd kill them all. They'd never make it. They'd never get out of the mess of ditches and counterditches with the fire pouring in on them from both sides; and every time they made it to a new trench they'd find it empty, except for booby traps, while more fire smashed at them from the flanks. He'd seen the Pathans wipe out an infantry brigade that way, kill four hundred men in ten minutes, and then retire laughing to their rice pots higher up the mountain.

A Stinger fired, streaking out into the dark at one of the birds—it missed, lost its power and sank into the trees.

A second, hastily aimed—the gunner hadn't properly acquired his target—missed worse, but the pilot in one of the gunships blinked and evaded, and his mini-gun fire swung wildly out of control, missing the mountaintop and spraying out behind them into Maryland.

A third Stinger missed.

Four left, I have four le—

The fourth hit the gunship dead on with a disappointingly small detonation and just the smallest trace of smoke; but the bird's purchase on the air was altered and it began to slide sideways, until its back rotor pulled free and it simply became weight and fell because it could not glide. It fell into the trees but did not burn.

The second gunship zeroed on the flash of the missiles coming its way, though Yasotay gauged the pilot as merely good and not special like some of the Mi-24 aces in Afghanistan. But the pilot now had a target and he brought the mini-gun to bear and Yasotay slid down into the trench as the bullets rushed at him, a torrent of light. They struck up and down the perimeter trench and dust showered down, and screams and yelps rose as men cowered under the torrent. One of the missile gunners took a full burst of the mini-gun across the chest and the bullets pulverized him.

The gunship roared in; Yasotay could hear it overhead, circling, swooping as the pilot overshot the mark, swung back; a spotlight raced out from the craft, hunting targets. And then the guns caught it. The chopper pilot, too low, too eager, had crossed Yasotay's silent first trench in hunt for the missile men; but he'd forgotten Yasotay's own gunners, who opened up instinctively, catching the craft easily in ten or twelve steams of fire and the Huey wobbled, vibrated, and then was gone in a horrid smear of orange flame spreading bright as day across the night sky.

Yasotay was up even before the flames had drained from the air, and he saw the field ahead of them filled with rushing infantry and thought it was too late. But his NCOs, blooded the many years in Asian mountains, did not panic, and he could hear their stern voices calling out in reassuring Russian, "To the front. To the front. Targets to the front."

Yasotay fired a flare, and then another.

It was sheer, delirious spectacle.

The infantry came like a tide of insects, scuttling, lurching ahead in dashes, yet still brave and steady, forcing the gap between itself and Yasotay's front line, rushing ahead in packs of four or five. Yasotay fancied he could even see their eyes, wide with fright and adrenaline. Their backup guns had started, suppressive automatic fire from the flanks, lancing out over the troops but too high to do any damage.

Then his own fire rose, rose again; the men were on full automatic. The assault force troopers began to go down, but still they came, brave, good men and the battlefield broke apart, atomized, into a hundred desperate little dramas, as small fire-and-movement teams tried to work closer. But Yasotay could see that he'd broken the spine of the attack. He picked up his scoped G-3 and began to engage targets.

Puller could hear them dying.

"This is Sixgun-One, he's got missiles coming up, ah, no sweat, they're missing, that's one past us, oops, two gone, and that's the big— Hit, hit, I'm losing it, we're—"

"Charlie, I have you, you're looking swell."

"Major, he's not burn—"

"Christ, he hit hard."

"Delta Six, this is Sixgun-Two, I have missile launchers ahead, and I've got them engaged—oooooooo, look at them boys dance—"

"Sir, belt's out."

"Get it changed, I'm going in."

"Goddammit, Sixgun-Two, this is Delta Six, you are advised to hold your position, I can't risk another lost ship."

"Sir, I got 'em running, I can see 'em running, I just want to get closer."

"New belt, skip."

"Let's kick ass."

"Sixgun-Two, hold your fucking position!" Puller roared.

"Colonel, I got those missile guys zeroed, oh, this is great, this is—"

"Shit, sir, there's fire coming up from—"

"Oh, oh, shit, goddammit, hit, I'm—"

"The fire, the fire, the fi—"

"Jesus," somebody at the window said, "his tanks went. He's all over the sky. It looks like the Fourth of July."

"Delta Six, this is Halfback, I'm taking heavy fire from the front."

"Halfback, get your second assault team up to the initial point."

"Ready to go, sir. Shit, the gunships are both down, that one guy, he's still burning. The fire is heavy."

"Are your people still advancing?"

"We've got a lot of fire going out, sir."

"But your team, is it still advancing or is it hung up?"

"I don't see much movement out there, but there's a lot of fire. There's smoke, dust, snow, whatever, I can't see through it. Should I send my backup yet?"

"Not unless you're convinced your first wave has completely lost it."

"Well, there's fire. Where's that stuff on the left? Where's Bravo? Where the hell is Bravo? Jesus, Bravo, if you don't help us, we're going to get butchered and nobody's getting any closer to that hole than they are now."

The blade touched his throat; he felt it begin to cut—then halt.

He felt the sinewy muscles so tight against him ease just a notch; then, swift and silent as his stalker had pounced on him, he was gone. The weight left Walls's back; rolling over, his fingers flying involuntarily to the break in his skin where the blade had begun to slice open his throat, he found himself staring into the mad eyes of his own death, which this time had by luck decided not to occur.

"Jesus, lady, you scared the shit out of me."

The Vietnamese woman looked at him sullenly. God, how could such a scrawny creature be so strong? Baby, you had my ass cold. Fifteen years ago you get me like that and my ticket be punched forever and ever.

He rubbed his neck, which was wet with a trickle of blood.

"I figure you come up the tunnels same as me. Then you run into one of them pipes for the rocket blast, right? You follow it, and you end up in here with me, is that right, girl? Sure it is. No other way it could be. Then, when you hear me coming, you crawl up inside there—" He pointed to the big cupola of the rocket exhaust port. He shivered, thinking of her curled up in there, like a cat actually inside the thing. "Shit, you look like you been through worse hell than me."

She was smeared with mud and blood; her face was filthy. She had a crazed look in her dark eyes and her hand kept tightening and loosening on the haft of the big knife. One of her trouser legs was ripped out. A terrible gash had left a cascade of dried blood down one arm; the cut itself had turned black and glistening. Whoever said their faces were blank? He was wrong, whoever he was, because Walls now looked hard at the thing he had all those years ago taught himself was flat and dull and yellow and saw the same play of emotions he'd seen on any face: fear, anger, pride, a big charge of guts, maybe more than a little grief.

"They jump you? Where your partner be at? You know, Stretch. That tall white dude. Where he be at?"

She shook her head.

He laughed. "He didn't make it? My boy Witherspoon didn't make it neither. Well, sugar, just you and me, we's all there is, us old-time rats. Nobody else coming." He stood, picking up his shotgun.

"Okay, lady," he said. "Now, I figure on climbing up this ladder to that little door. You see it? Way up there? Then, maybe somehow we get through the door. 'Cause the one thing I know, we don't want to be sitting next to this big cocksucker"—he looked at the missile—"in case it gets lit off. Burn us to shit. You coming or you staying? Best if you come."

She looked at him, her dark eyes crazily boring into his.

Shit, she don't even understand what this is. This is just another tunnel to her, except that now it's some shit with a rocketship.

"Come on," he crooned. "Take it from me, you don't want to be down here if this sucker go. Fire come out of the hole, burn you all up like napalm."

He began to climb up the rungs. He climbed, looking up, watching the manhole cover of the silo hatch. He wouldn't look down because it was too far, and Walls, the tunnel champion, was afraid of heights. He climbed and climbed until he was woozy. Seven fucking stories. It was high!

He finally reached the door. It was blank and solid. Hanging groggily on the rungs, he touched it, and it had no spring or give. It was another door, the door of his life.

FUCK NIGGERS wasn't scratched into it, but it could have been, for that was its message. Like any door he'd ever faced, it only said, You ain't going nowhere. You ain't invited.

His hand made a fist and he smashed it, stupidly. His hand crunched in pain.

So this was it, huh? This was the cocksucker. Another door.

Walls thought he might laugh. All this way, and he just run up against FUC—

He heard a noise, looked down to see the little Vietnamese woman beneath him a few rungs.

"That's good, mama-san," he said. "Good you came along, but there's no place to go."

She reached up and tapped his foot, then pointed.

Well, well, hello yourself. Yes, it was another small door or hatch or something, maybe two feet by two feet, covered with metal gridwork. The thing was about five feet farther around the curve of the silo wall. It looked like the entrance to a duct or a vent or the air-conditioning. But it didn't matter.

"It's too far," he yelled. "I can't reach that far."

But with her gestures she made him see that she wanted to come up.

The bitch going to try. Don't she know? Can't get in. Nothing to it now. All she wrote, end of story, the man he had them beat.

But up she came, like a cat, Jesus, she was so strong. He slid over on the rungs, and up she scrambled, until they shared the same precarious upper rung. She pointed and made interesting facial explanations and ultimately it occurred to him that *she* was proposing to go over to the little door.

He saw now what she meant. He was strong, she was light. If he could just hold her, somehow, maybe she ought to be able to bridge the gap.

Dumb bitch, don't know when the man got you beat.

"Sure, hon. You just go on. Nathan hold you."

He tried to turn sideways on the rung beneath, planting one foot real solid; with his arm he embraced the top rung.

Backward, she mounted him, feeling back with one strong supple foot, planting it on his thigh, then with her arm hoisting herself, and planting her other foot while he embraced her around the waist with his arm.

She was light, just bones and strings and skin and short black hair, but she wasn't that light either, and there was a terrible instant when he couldn't get set just right as her weight threw him off, and he thought he was losing her. He could feel her tighten, shriek a little, and scream or curse in her language, but in just a second he had her back under control.

"Okay, okay, we be okay, just cool on down, just chill it on down, sugar baby, now," he moaned through his own pounding breath. He knew whatever he did he couldn't look down: it was delicate, their position, the two of them supported on the slippery purchase of his one boot on the rung, his other out to balance them, her whole body leaning on his thighbone and the slipperiness of his muscle there.

It wasn't going to work, goddammit!

But out she strained, out, so far, Jesus, she had guts, and he clung desperately to her waist, feeling it slide against his grip as she leaned ever out for the grid on the little door.

He could hardly see what was going on, just her back ahead of him, inching away from him, and he could feel the great pressure against his forearm, holding her in, and also the great pressure in his other arm, keeping them moored to the top rung. He could feel the sweat pop out of his hairline and begin to trace little patterns down his face. He thought his muscles would cramp; his heart was thudding; he couldn't get breath and his limbs began to shiver and tremble against the strength that threatened to desert them totally. He heard what sounded like pinging or chipping and realized that she'd gotten her knife out and into the frame of the little door and was trying somehow to jimmy the goddamned thing open and—

Uh—

Suddenly, she took flight and squirmed out of Walls's grip and he lurched for her. His foot slipped off the rung and he himself fell, in his panic forgetting her as the gravity claimed his body and he knew he was going to die—but then his left arm wrenched him with a whack into the wall and was so panicked it would not let him fly loose and he planted his boot back onto a rung and with his now tragically free hand, grabbed back to the top rung again, and then and only then did he see that the woman had not fallen at all, but like some kind of simian creature now actually rode the grate on the little door which on its delicate hinges swung ever so gently back and forth.

"Jesus, watch yourself," he shouted.

The little door swung the full 180 degrees, banged into the wall with its desperate cargo; then with a toe she pushed off, clinging like a cat on a screen to the gridwork. Her foot came out, searched for the duct and found it, and she pulled herself closer, shifting in her ride, until, swinging just a bit, she was able somehow to heave herself at the duct—a sickening thud as she hit too low against the base of her spine, but pivoted in spite of the pain, and with one arm reached out and caught something inside, then with the other pulled herself in.

Jesus, he thought. She made it.

She rested for what seemed to him to be an inhumanly short time and then peeped out, pointing at his loins urgently.

Lady, what the fuck you want?

Then, of course, he caught on: his rope tied in a tight figure-eight on his web belt. He took it off the D-ring, kneaded it free, and tossed it in an unraveling lob toward her; she caught it neatly—she did *every* motherfucking thing neatly—and in seconds it was secure on something inside.

Walls tied his end into about a trillion or so knots on the rung. She gestured him on.

Oh, shit, he thought. Hope this sucker holds.

It was only six or so feet, but it seemed a lot farther. The only way he could manage it was upside down like a sloth, his boots locked over the rope, eyes closed as he pulled himself along. Jesus, he felt the give and stretch of the rope bouncing as it fought against his weight, and the dead steel of the twelve-gauge pumpgun hanging off his shoulder and all the little pouches on his belt swinging and the pockets full of loose twelve-gauge shells jingling.

As he edged along the rope, Walls prayed feverishly. His desperate entreaties must have surely paid off, for suddenly he felt her hands pulling at him, and in a squirming frenzy of panic—this was the worst yet, of it all this was the absolute worst—he managed somehow to get himself into the duct opening.

He sat there, breathing hard. In time the various aches of his body started to fire up; he saw that his palms were bleeding from the tightness with which he had clung to the rope, and that he had whacked himself in the shoulder, the arm, the hip, and the shin getting over the threshold of the duct. He didn't want to think about it though. He just wanted to suck in some air. He wished he had a cigarette.

She was saying something, and after he'd caught up on oxygen he got enough concentration back to say, "Hey, no speakee, sugar. Sorry, can't understand you, honey."

But he could read her gestures: she was pointing.

At last it occurred to him to see what they had achieved and the disappointment was crushing: they had achieved nothing; about six feet back the duct ended abruptly in cinderblock.

So what's the point of the duct, he thought bitterly, knowing it to be another government fuck-up.

But then he saw the point of the duct: a metal box up near the corner of the wall, with metal tubes running out and into it from various points in the wall.

He crawled closer.

A padlock kept the box from human touch, but the box itself looked flimsy enough to beat open.

He squinted at the words on the box:

DOOR ACCESS FUSE PANEL, USAF LCA-8566033 it said.

He recognized only one. It was familiar from his years in prison: DOOR. DOOR. DOOR.

That's how we get into the sucker, he thought, and began to beat at the metal box.

Dill could hear the firing up ahead, rising, rising still more, rising till it sounded incredible.

"Jesus," he said to his sergeant.

Then the second gunship went up like a supernova a few hundred feet ahead, its glare spilling across the sky and filling the woods with light.

Dill winced, fell back, his night vision stunned. He blinked, chasing flashbulbs from his brain. You never look into a detonation, he told himself.

He looked back. Most of them—maybe a half of them—were still strung out in the creek bed, coming up over the ice, pulling themselves up rough stairways of stone, up gulches, scrambling up little gulches and whatever. It would take an hour for all of Bravo to make it up.

But now he had twenty-five guns, M-16s, full auto, and he could hear the firing beckoning him onward, and it was time to go.

"Almost there," he said.

"Bob, a lot of us are going to get killed," said one of the men.

"Yeah, Bob, it doesn't look like we'll have much of a chance against all that."

"Yeah, well," said Dill, "I get the impression the Russians don't know we're here. And, like, those other guys are counting on us. I think there's a pretty good fight going on, and we ought to be there helping."

Dill knew he wasn't an eloquent man and even by his standards his little speech had been pretty lame, but at least he hadn't whined and sounded utterly preposterous, and so he simply walked ahead through the snow, slipping between the trees, trying to figure out if he was going in the right direction or not. He thought they were with him, but he didn't want to turn around to look, because it might scare them away.

He came to a meadow shortly. Up ahead there appeared to be a kind of fireworks display going on; he couldn't make it out.

It was all wrong somehow, nothing at all like what he expected. He had no idea if he was in the right place. The feeling was all wrong too; there was a crazy sense of festival to it, none of the noise was distinct, but simply a blur of imprecise sound. He couldn't see anything well, just sensing confusion, as if too much were going on, really, to decipher.

"Bob, is this where we're supposed to be?"

"I don't know," said Dill. "I'm not sure. I hope we're on the right hill."

"We have to be on the right hill. There's only one hill."

"Uh—"

Dill now saw someone emerge before him. He smiled, as if to make contact, and realized in a second he was staring at a Soviet Special Forces soldier with camouflage tunic, black beret, and an AK-47 at the high port. The man was the most terrifying thing Dill had ever seen. Dill shot him in the face.

"Jesus, Bob, you killed that guy."

"Bet your ass I did," said Dill. "Now, *come on*, goddammit!"

All up and down the line, without orders or thought or guidance behind them, the troopers began to fire.

They dropped to one knee and began to squeeze bursts off into the Soviet position, stunned at how quickly and totally the scurrying figures fell before them, and how long it took the Russians to respond and how easy it all had been.

Yasotay stared in stupefaction. In that second he knew the position was lost.

Delta moved in from the right, firing as its men deployed. The helicopters were a ruse, the infantry was a ruse, the brilliant American commander had somehow gotten the Delta unit up the hard cliffs to the right in the dark—impossible, impossible! thought Yasotay bitterly—and sent them in.

Now it was only a matter of seconds.

He saw the defenses were disintegrating, that he could not fight an enemy on two fronts, he was flanked, his complex scheme of drawing the frontal into the trenches had come undone. Now the job was simply to get the tunnel defense team down, and devil take the rest.

Yasotay fired a burst at the rushing figures from the right, but like the brilliant troops they were, they came low and hard, with disciplined fire and movement. He could see them now at the far end of the trench, firing their M-16s from the hip, long, raking bursts into his troops, while others broke off and hit his trenches from the side. More and more of them were coming, and as they came, they killed without mercy.

It sickened Yasotay that men so good should die so fast.

Yasotay pulled his whistle out and bleated two brief blasts, waited a second, and then bleated two more.

He watched as his soldiers rose in a scurry from their positions, first the Red Platoon, then the Blue Platoon, each putting out a covering fire as the troopers from Delta closed in from the right and the infantry poured over the main trench at the front. He saw the choppers landing and still more men pouring out and scrambling toward him; then it was time to run himself.

Turning, he slithered through the fire back to the ruined structure that housed the elevator shaft access. Time was short; flares hung in the

sky, hissing and popping; everywhere tracers arced through the atmosphere, and where they struck they kicked up blossoms of dust. It all had
a terrible slow-motion sensation to it, the desperate run to the elevator
shaft, the insistent bullets taking his men down.

He made it.

"Tunnel team inside."

Fifteen men, the maximum, wedged their way into the car; with the
fifteen below, that would give him thirty.

"The gun?" his sergeant major yelled.

The gun? Here it was. Yasotay had to face it, the hardest choice. He
had one heavy automatic left. He thought of the mad, fat American
standing out in the snowy meadow firing the M-60 from the shoulder as
their own fire splashed around him. Before he died, goddamn him, his
bullets had shattered the breach of Yasotay's H&K-21. Now he had one
belt-fed weapon, the M-60; if he took it, he doomed the boys up top.
They wouldn't have the fire to hold the Americans off. Yet if the
Americans got into the tunnel, he'd need the damned thing.

"Major Yasotay," the sergeant major shouted again. "The gun?"

Yasotay hated himself.

"In the elevator," he said. "It has to go down."

"Gun forward," yelled the sergeant major, and the weapon was passed
through the crowd until it reached the elevator.

"You boys, God bless you," Yasotay called. "You hold them. You
hold them till hell freezes. It's for the motherland and your children will
love you for it."

"We'll hold the bastards till Gorbachev comes to accept their surrender," said a voice in the darkness, sheer bravado, for now it was very
late, Yasotay could tell.

He bent quickly to the computer terminal still mounted in the seared
metal side of the elevator shaft.

He typed ACCESS.

The prompt came:

ENTER PERMISSIVE ACTION LINK

He typed in the twelve numbers the general had made him memo-
rize, pressed the command key, and the thing winked at him.

OK

He stepped inside the elevator, and the door closed with a pneumatic
whoosh, sealing him in for the journey down and sealing out the vision
of night combat left behind.

2300

"**A**nd where have you been, dear Comrade Arbatov?" asked the KGB man Gorshenin. "The alert for a possible defection went out at seven P.M. when you failed to arrive for your communications duty."

"I was detained, comrade," said Arbatov, blinking, wondering why Magda hadn't alibied for him. Like some idiotic spy melodrama, the lamp in the KGB security office on the third floor had been turned so that it broadcast a steady, irritating beam in his eyes. So stupid! "On a mission. As I explained to Magda Goshgarian, who agreed to stand in for me."

"The notification of your defection comes from your own unit commander, Comrade Klimov."

"Comrade Klimov is mistaken."

"Hmmm. Comrade Klimov is not the sort to be mistaken."

"Yes, well, this once, he's mistaken. Look, would I have come back to finish up my night duty if I were trying to flee the coop? Wouldn't I be at some FBI estate eating steak and squeezing the bottoms of tarts?"

Gorshenin, a humorless youngster of thirty-two with a brightly lit bald head and two dim little technocrat's eyes behind his glasses, looked at him without emotion. These young ones never showed emotion: they were machines.

"Explain please your whereabouts today."

"Ah, comrade, you know that GRU operations are off limits to KGB, no? I can't inform you, it's the rules. Both units operate here by strictly enforced rules. Or would you prefer the Washington station be entirely staffed by GRU and all you KGB lads could go on to some interesting city like Djakarta or Kabul?"

"Attempts at levity are not appreciated, comrade. This is serious business."

"But, comrade, that's just it, it *isn't* serious." Gregor was using all his charm, making sly eye movements at the young prick, smiling with sophisticated wisdom and slavish eyelash flutters. "Frankly, this young

Klimov and I don't get along. I'm old school, orthodox, hardworking, play by the rules. Klimov is all this modern business, he wants corners cut, this sort of thing. So we are locked in struggle, you know. This is just a little business to *embarrass* me."

Gorshenin eyed him coolly. He touched his finger to his lips.

"Hmmm," he said. "Yes, yes, I know how such things can happen in a unit."

"So it's merely *personal*, you see. Not *professional*. That's all. A misunderstanding between the generations."

Gorshenin licked at the bait. Went away. Came back, licked some more. Then bit.

"So, there seems to be a morale problem in GRU?" he said.

"Oh, it's nothing. We'll work it out amongst ourselves. Most of our chaps are good fellows, but sometimes one bad apple can—well, you know the saying. Why, only yesterday Magda was saying to me—"

But Gorshenin was no longer listening. His eyes were locked in an abstract of calculus. He whirled through his calculations.

"Ah, say, old fox, do you know what would be the wonderful solution to your problems?"

"Eh? Why, the only solution is that I'll just wait it out."

"Now, Gregor Ivanovich, don't be hasty. You know how excitable young Klimov is. Suppose he were to really fly off the handle? It could be the Gulag for you, no?"

Arbatov shivered.

"Now, Gregor Ivanovich, consider. A transfer to KGB!"

"What! Why, that's pre—"

"Now, wait. Stop and consider. I could get you in, at the same posting. A man of your experience and contacts. Why, you'd be invaluable."

Gregor made as if to study the proposition.

"It could be a very profitable move for you. Very comfortable too. None of this backbiting, this snipping and nipping like two hungry pups in a crate."

Gregor nodded, the temptation showing like a fever on his fattish face.

"Yes, it sounds interesting."

"Now, of course, I'd have to have something to take to Moscow. You know, I couldn't just say, we want this man, we must have this man. I'd have to *have* something, do you know?"

You are such an idiot, young Gorshenin. A real agent-runner is smoother; he's got that easy, cajoling charm, that endless persistence and sympathy as he guides you on your way to hell. Arbatov should know: he'd guided a few toward hell.

"A present?" he said as if he were a moron.

"Yes. Oh, you know. Something small, but just to show you were enthusiastic, do you know? Something minor but flashy."

"Hmmm," said Arbatov, considering gravely. "You mean something from the Americans?"

"Yes! Something from the Americans would do nicely."

"Well, actually, it's a fallow time. You know how it is in this business, young Comrade Gorshenin. You plant a thousand seeds and then you must wait to harvest your one or two potatoes."

Gorshenin appeared disappointed.

"A shame. You know I'd hate to have to turn you back to Klimov with a bad report on our interrogation. He'd not see the humor in it."

"Hmmm," said Arbatov, gravely considering again. "KGB has the GRU code book, of course."

The idiot Gorshenin swallowed and the greed beamed from his eyes like a television signal. The code book was the big secret; it was the treasure; if KGB could get its hand on just one code book for just one hour, it would be able to read GRU's cable traffic for years to come. And the man who brought it in . . . !

"I'm sure we do," said Gorshenin, poorly affecting nonchalance. "I mean the things are left around in installations all over the world."

Such a terrible lie, so thin and unconvincing. The books were, of course, guarded like the computer codes that launched the SS-18s.

"Yes, well, a shame. You see, though the book is locked except when the communications officer uses it to decode or to encode high priority messages, he's an old friend of mine, and one night he called up and realized he'd left delicate medicines there. Barbiturates, did you know the poor man was addicted? Anyway, in his despair he gave me the combination. I was able to retrieve his drugs for him. I actually committed the combination to memory."

"Surely it has been changed," said Gorshenin too quickly.

"Perhaps, but not the last time I had communications duty."

The two men looked at each other.

A small object was pushed across the table at Arbatov. It was a Katrinka camera.

"Aren't you late for your duty in the Wine Cellar, comrade?" Arbatov glanced at his watch.

"Very late," he said. "It's nearly midnight."

The hole glistened open, dilating as the metal around it liquified. Jack thought of a birth: a new world would come out of this orifice. The black hole would spread and spread and spread, consuming all. A terrible sadness filled him.

"There, go on. Go on," insisted the general. "You're almost there, go on, go on!"

The flame ate the metal, evaporating it.

Suddenly there came the sound of the opening of the elevator door and the rush of boots. Men raced down the outside corridor. Shouts and alarms rose. For just a second Jack thought the American Army had arrived, but it was only the Russian. The language rose and yelped through the halls. Orders were hurled at men by NCOs. Jack heard ammunition crates being ripped open, the clank and click of bolts being thrown, magazines being loaded, automatic weapons being emplaced. He heard furniture being shoved into the corridor as barricades were hastily erected. The atmosphere seethed with military drama; Jack was in the middle of a movie.

The general was talking earnestly in Russian with the tough-looking officer who'd come to Jack's house that morning. They nodded their heads together, the younger man explaining, the general listening. Then the two of them departed from the capsule to check the preparations.

Jack stood. He was alone with the guard who'd shot him. His leg had stiffened and the pain was immense. He had a throbbing headache.

"You speak English, don't you?" he said to the boy who stared at him with opaque eyes, blue as cornflowers. He had a rough adolescent complexion and teeth that could have used braces. But he was basically a good-looking, decent kid, a jock, maybe a rangy linebacker or a strong-rebounding forward.

"Do you know what they're going to do?" Jack said. "What have they told you? What do you guys think is going on? You guys must not know what's going on."

The guard looked at him.

"Back to work."

"These guys are going to fire the rocket. That's what's in here, the key to shoot the missile off. Man, they're going to blow the world away, they're going to kill mil—"

The boy hit him savagely with the butt of his AK-47. Jack saw it coming and with his good athlete's reflexes managed to tuck his face just a notch and take the blow at the hinge of the jaw rather than in the mouth and cheek, and though he knew in the instant the pain and concussion erupted in his head his jaw was broken, he had a perverse pleasure in the fact that his teeth hadn't been blasted out. He sank with a mewling scream to the floor, and the boy began to kick him in the ribs.

"No, God, please, no!" Jack begged.

"American pig shit motherfucker, kill all our babies with your god-damned rocket!" the boy howled in pain as genuine as Jack's.

Jack thought he'd blacked out, but the kicks stopped—the boy was dismissed to the tunnel defense team by the tough major or whatever—and the major pulled Jack to his feet.

"Watch what you say, Mr. Hummel," he said. "These kids know their pals are upstairs getting killed. They're in no mood for charity."

"Fuck you," Jack screamed through his tears. "The Army's coming in here and they're going to kill your asses before you get this goddamned key, and—"

"No, Mr. Hummel," said the general. "No, they're still hours away. And you're minutes away."

The major raised his pistol and placed it against Jack's skull. His eyes were drained of emotion.

"Do you wish to say 'fuck you' now, Mr. Hummel?" he asked.

Jack wished he had the guts to say it. But he knew he didn't. It was one thing to be brave in the abstract, it was another thing with a goddamned gun up against your head, especially when everything about the Russian suggested that without blinking an eye he'd pull the trigger. Hell, they could cut the last inch or so of metal away with a Bic lighter, that's how little was left.

The general leaned over, picked up the torch, and placed the sputter-ing thing in Jack's hand.

"We've won, Mr. Hummel. We've done it, don't you see?"

He turned and crossed the small room to a radio set between the teletype machines. He turned a few buttons and knobs, then looked back.

"It's all history, Mr. Hummel. We've won."

Dick Puller had left the command post and was airborne in a com-mand chopper with his radio, hovering out of range, watching, giving orders over the radio.

"Cobra Three, you people have to bring more of your automatics into play. I can see a slacking off there, do you copy?"

"Delta Six, goddammit, I have four men dead and nine wounded on this side!"

"Do the best you can, Cobra Three. Bravo, this is Delta Six, any movement there?"

"Delta One, their fire isn't dropping a goddamn bit. I've still got people coming in."

"Get 'em in and get 'em shooting, Bravo. It's the guns that'll win this thing."

It was a question of which the men hated more, the Soviets dug in at the ruins of the launch control facility who would not stop firing, or the dry voice over the radio, clinical, impatient. The bird floated tantalizingly beyond them all, its lights running insolently in the night.

The Soviets were firing flares, which hung in the air under parachutes leaking flecks of light down across the scene, giving it a horrible weirdness. It looked like some musty nineteenth-century battle painting: the flickering lights, the heaps of bodies, the gun flashes cutting through the drifting smoke, the streaks of tracer darting about, tearing up the earth wherever they struck. All of it was blue with a smear of moonlight, white with a smear of gun smoke, dark where the mud and blood commingled on the earth.

And there was extraordinary moments of valor. A Soviet trooper crawled out of the perimeter, stood, and rushed into the American lines. He had nine grenades in his belt, and when he leapt among the Americans—he'd been hit three times but he kept coming—he detonated himself, killing eleven Rangers and quelling the fire on the front for three long minutes. Then there were the three Spetsnaz gunners on the right, isolated from the larger body of troops and unable to resupply themselves with ammunition. Down to a single magazine apiece, they mounted their bayonets, climbed out of their trench in a banzailike charge, and, screaming as they came, ran at the Americans, shooting from the hip. One was hit immediately, center chest, by a burst of MP-5 fire from a Delta; but the other two leapt like fawns as the tracers searched them out. As they came they fired, but as they came they were hit, and eventually the bullets dragged them down, but the last one got into a Delta hole and killed a man with his bayonet before his partner fired the full mag of 5.56mm into him.

Another hero turned out to be Dill, the gym teacher. He took his leadership responsibilities overzealously. He led three assaults from the left side, from which his unit had come. He killed nine Russians and was hit twice. His men kept up the fire and by this time the stragglers had joined them.

The wounded crawled among the besiegers, handing out ammunition. James Uckley, with no place else to go, had separated himself from the Delta troopers with whom he'd flown in and taken up a position on the right. He had a CAR-15, and with little regard for his own life he lay in a shallow trench close to the Soviet position and fired magazine after magazine into it. He couldn't see anything except the answering gun flashes and had no idea whether or not he was helping. He just had the sense of the weapon shaking itself empty. Still, he kept firing, feeling his skin turn to black leather as the powder rose and sank into it. Overhead, the bullets whistled close and at least three times he'd felt zeroed as the bullets struck close, kicking up a spray of snow and dust. But everything had missed so far. On his left were two state policemen and two Hagerstown policemen, each with shotguns; they fired too.

Now the inevitable progression of the battle was in the American favor, no matter the ferocity of the Soviets. The Americans had more weapons and with each passing minute more were brought into play. The reserve companies of the Third Infantry got in close and with their heavier M-14s began to raise the volume of fire. Additional elements of Bravo staggered in through the woods. State and local policemen, a few FBI men, some of Bravo's walking wounded, most of the Delta intelligence staff, all arrived, found some kind of weapon, and struggled up in the dark to the firing line, found a scrap or bit of cover, and commenced fire.

Only one man in all this did not fire. This was Peter Thiokol, who lay on his face about two hundred meters off the site of the battle, feeling useless. He was terrified, yet his mind did not associate what was going on with any notion of war, which he had seen only represented on television or in the movies, where everything is clear, the relationship of friend to foe, the layout of the terrain. Now everything was strange. He could make no sense of it. An odd idea leapt into his head: he felt present at some ancient religious ceremony, where priests were sacrificing young men up there at the vivid altar with crude, cruel bronze blades. The young men went willingly to their doom, as if in doing so they guaranteed themselves a place in heaven. It had a late Aztec feel to it, or a sense of the Druid's return—the devil was here, Peter knew, looking over the shoulders of the priests up there with their bright blades, laughing, urging them on, congratulating himself on having a nice day with an idiot's drooling, half-moon smile. Tracers filled the air; he could hear them cracking. Occasionally, they'd hit close, driving him back. But he kept peering over the lip of his trench, fascinated.

"Better stay down, doc," someone said. "You get killed peeking and all this ain't worth shit."

Peter shivered, acknowledging the wisdom in the advice, and hunkered down, wishing he could make the noise go away.

Finally, the Russian response seemed to falter. Skazy, noticing the decrease, led a Delta party of six men and breached the final Soviet trench on the right side. It was a terrifying run up the hill, and all around him the fire flicked out, yet he jumped into the trench, and discovered only corpses. With an M-60 he began to pour fire into the Soviet position from up so close that the Russians had almost no chance. With his gun working from almost zero range, it ceased to be a battle and became a butchery.

There was a pause in the firing.

Smoke licked the battlefield's horrible stillness.

A Delta interpreter asked through a loudspeaker if the Spetsnaz people wished to accept an honorable surrender and medical attention. The few Russians responded with gunfire.

"Delta Six, this is Cobra, there's no answer."

"Do you have targets?"

"Most of them are down."

"Ask 'em again."

Skazy nodded to his interpreter. The man spoke again in Russian. A burst of gunfire responded, hitting him in the chest and throat, knocking him down.

"Christ," said Skazy into his hands-free mike, "they just hit our interpreter."

"All right, Major," said Dick, "body-bag 'em."

Skazy finished the job.

Walls beat the tin door off the junction box with the stock of the Mossberg, badly chewing the wood in the process. No time to worry about that now.

The box, ripped open, yielded a terrifyingly complex mesh of wires crowding in on the junctions. It made no sense to him. It was like so much of the world: all wired up, all fixed, all fancy and complicated, beyond him. It could have been the same old sign.

FUCK NIGGERS it could have said.

He looked at it, feeling the rage grow and seethe. He'd felt this way on the streets sometimes. Hey, he was a hero, goddammit, he went into tunnels for his motherfuckin' Uncle and did what Uncle said and killed yellow people and did shit no man should have to do and was hit three times and almost killed a hundred more times and then it was, thanks Jack, and good-bye to you and good luck to you.

NO BLACK BOYS NEED APPLY it could have said.

NO BLACK TUNNEL RATS NEED APPLY.

NO SILVER STAR WINNERS NEED APPLY.

NO THREE-TIME PURPLE HEARTS NEED APPLY.

FUCK NIGGERS.

That was some sign.

The Vietnamese woman said something and it pissed him off. It was that singsongy shit they all had, you couldn't make no sense out of it. She thought he knew what the fuck to do. Like he was some kind of white guy, he had all the goddamn motherfucking answers.

Hon, it don't mean shit to me. It's just some wires from white boys, that only white boys can figure out.

He felt like crying. He felt trapped in the tiny little space. Come all this way for nothing. Grief beat at him. But then he figured, fuck it, got to do something. He pulled out his knife. Hey, he was going to use it to stick in some guy instead of sticking it into some wires.

He was just going to stick it in, fuck the wires up, see what happen. But then he remembered the word DOOR from the front of the tin box. He stared at the wires coming into the box. They came out of the walls, most of them, through little tubes. Let's see, door be *that* way, let's see if we can't find some goddamned wire come from *that* way. He looked. Sure enough, most of the wires came from some other way, but one trace of wires plunged outside toward the box from his left, from the direction of the duct entrance. Walls hacked at the tubing covering the batch of wires, chipping away little nuggets of rubber that fell like raisins to the floor, until he had some bare wire revealed. He was acting just like he knew what the fuck he was doing.

The woman was so close in the little chamber. She looked at him like he knew what he was doing too. He laughed again. She didn't know shit either. He thought it was pretty funny, the two of them in a little space off a rocket that was going to end the world, hacking on some wires like they knew what they were doing, a nigger boy and a gook girl, the two lowliest forms of scum on the earth which was going to be blown to shit if *they* didn't stop it. She laughed too. She must have been in on the joke, because she thought it was funny too.

They both had a good laugh as Walls chopped his way through the wires. Then, just for the fuck of it, he cut through some more wires. With the blade of his knife as a kind of stick, he lifted one tuft of wires over across the gap and shoved it against the other wires and—

Walls shook the spangles from his eyes and found himself against the wall. Felt like his old daddy had whacked him upside the head one. His nose filled with an acrid odor. His head hurt. When he blinked he saw blue balls and flashbulbs. His teeth hurt. Someone was playing music inside his head. His knife lay on the floor, smoking. What the fuck had—

But the woman was at the mouth of the duct, screaming.

Walls crawled over. Man, he felt smoked himself. Could hardly remember who he was, Jack.

But he remembered when he saw the door into whatever the fuck else was down here: it was open.

Jesus fuck, he'd done it. He'd gotten into whitey's secret place.

He grabbed for his shotgun, seeing that it would be easy to reach the open door, swing over to the ladder, then get inside.

He pulled the Taurus 9-mm automatic out of his holster and handed it over to her.

"You know how one of these things work, hon?"

He pointed to the safety lever locked up.

"Push that down, babe," he gestured with his finger, "and bang-bang! You got that? Down and bang-bang!"

The woman nodded once, smiled. The gun was big in her tiny hands, but she looked as though she'd been born with it there.

He reached, and the shotgun came up into his hands. It felt smooth and ready and he still had a pocket full of twelves.

The woman looked at him.

"Ass-kickin' time," he said.

*   *   *

The shooting had stopped. Peter looked up. There seemed to be some kind of delay, some sort of hassle up at the launch control facility, and then he heard a roar and looked up as the command chopper, beating up a screen of snow and dust, lowered itself awkwardly from the sky and he saw Dick Puller leap out. The chopper zoomed skyward.

He heard his name called then.

"Dr. Thiokol. Where are you? Where the hell is he? Anybody seen that bomb guy? Dr. Thiokol?"

Shivering, Peter rose.

"Here," he called, but his voice caught in some phlegm and it didn't come out quite right, and so he said it again, *"Here!"* and it came out too loud, too shrill for a battlefield full of the dead, where he was the only man without a gun.

"This way, please, Dr. Thiokol," yelled Dick Puller.

Peter began the short climb up the hill to the launch control facility, or what remained of it. All around him men moaned and shivered. If only it didn't feel so unreal, if only the smell of blood and gunpowder weren't so dense, if only the lights from the flares and the hovering choppers weren't flickering dramatically, the flares hissing and leaking sparks, the chopper lights wobbling drunkenly. Up ahead, men were consumed in the drama of their equipment, clicking bolts, loading clips, smearing their faces.

Someone was shouting. "Okay, now, goddammit, everybody out of here but the Delta Tunnel Assault Team. You guys in the second element, you form up over there on Captain McKenzie. The rest of you guys, Rangers especially, please back off and give us some fucking room to operate."

He could see the men rigging themselves with complicated harnesses and thought for just a minute they were parachutes. Parachutes? No, then he realized that it was rappeling gear by which the Delta commandos would slide on ropes down the shaft. Coils of green rope lay about on the ground.

"Thiokol, hurry up, come on," said Puller, up at the door.

Peter scrambled up the rest of the way.

"It's not damaged, sir," said a young soldier. "We tried to hold our fire away from it."

Peter saw the elevator door set in its frame of solid titanium, the only hard, gleaming thing among the blown-out walls and the shattered floorboarding. Hard to believe this had once been inside a building and that the building itself had stood quite normally until just a few hours ago. And on the hard cool face of the titanium was the computer terminal, which looked for all the world like a bank money machine.

"There's still current," said Puller.

"Oh, there's current," said Peter. "There's a solar cell up top, and every day the sun shines, it recharges the batteries. The shaft access unit is independent of outside power. It can go for six days without sun and the computers inside it keep running." He was aware he was ranting like a pedant. "The question is the shield."

Peter bent to it. A solid Plexiglas sheet covered the keyboard and the screen. Now, if they were smart and had the time, they'd have jimmied the mechanism on the screen access itself, so that before he had to solve the door, he'd have to hack or bash or cut his way through the protective screen. With a screwdriver they could have won. But he thought no, no, not this Russian. This Russian thinks he's smarter than me. He's going to beat me at my own game.

Peter touched the red plastic button just under the terminal.

With a quiet grind the Plexiglas shield unlimbered from the keyboard and lifted like a praying mantis rising from the grass. It folded itself back and out of the way.

Two words stood on the blank screen.

ENTER PROMPT they said, two gleaming little green words in the bottom left of the screen.

So far, for two words.

Peter swiftly typed ACCESS and pressed the enter button.

The machine responded ENTER PERMISSIVE ACTION LiNK CODE.

Eleven hyphens blinked beneath the mandate and the prompt stood in front of the leftmost.

So here it is.

You punch in twelve numbers. No more, no less. To make it interesting, there's no limit on the integers between the hyphens. Thus the code may be twelve numbers long, or it may be twelve million; it just has to have eleven hyphens in it. And then you push Enter.

If you are wrong, the machine will shout STRIKE ONE.

If you are wrong again, the machine will shout STRIKE TWO.

If you are wrong a third time, the machine will figure out that somebody who doesn't know is trying to guess his way in, and it will shout ACCESS DENIED and arbitrarily assign twelve new numbers that only it knows and that only another computer can figure out in about 135 work hours.

"Can you do it?" asked Skazy. "Peter, I came a long way for this party. I brought a lot of people with me. Can you do it?"

He thinks all this is about *him*, Peter thought.

"Shhh," said Puller. "Peter, we could move away if it would help."

"No," said Peter. He bent to the keys, took a deep breath. Focus. Where's my focus? Just shine my focus on it and work it through. He knew it would help him to talk.

"Here's the trick. Pashin thinks he's *me*. He had to become *me* to beat me, that's his game. It's obvious, really. He dropped his patronymic in November of 'eighty-two because that was the month I published my famous piece in *Foreign Affairs* about how a well-based MX could give us more than parity. That's when he starts: he's working through my life, processing my information, trying to become me to destroy me. He's obsessing on me, looking for my code. He wants to crack *my* code. So he starts with something stupid. He gets rid of his middle name. Why? Because numbers are important to me, so they're important to him. And that left him with twelve letters in his name. Just like mine. ARKADY PASHIN becomes PETER THIOKOL."

He looked at them. Their faces were dumb.

"And twelve letters just happens to be the length of a Category F PAL code. That's the kind of perverse correspondence that would appeal to him. So if you give each of the letters in my name a simple arithmetic value, with A as one and Z as twenty-six, you get a twelve-unit entry code that stands for *me*." He gave a little chuckle, and his fingers tapped the numbers in.

He pushed Enter.

The opening was gigantic, or so it seemed. It was big enough for a man to get his hand into.

"Yes," croaked the general. "Yes, now, move aside."

Jack Hummel felt himself being shoved aside.

"Now, yes," said the general, "now we are there."

Jack saw him bend and plunge his arm into the deep gash in the metal he had opened.

"Yes," he said, his face enflamed with the effort of it. "Yes, I'm in the gap, I can feel the damned thing, Yasotay, *I can feel it*, ah, oh, I can't quite get a grasp on—Yasotay, is there a man here with small hands, extremely small, a woman's-size hands?"

Yasotay spoke quickly in Russian to an NCO, and there was a brief conference and a name was called out and—

Sirens started howling. Lights began flashing.

Jack Hummel jumped, turned in panic; he felt the men around him panic.

"Now, now, Mr. Hummel," came the reassuring voice of the general. "It's nothing to worry about."

Suddenly, the room was filled with the laconic yet lovely voice of a woman.

"Warning," she said in her slow, unhurried prerecorded voice, "there has been an unsuccessful attempt at access."

"He's up there," the general said to Alex. "My old friend Peter Thiokol, he's up there, trying to get inside. Peter, you'll never make it, my friend," the general said.

STRIKE ONE, the computer said.

"It didn't work," said Skazy.

"No, it didn't," said Peter.

"You're sure you did it right?" asked Puller, his voice suddenly older and weaker. "You didn't—"

"No, no, the code isn't right. We try again."

He crouched, and his fingers flew back to the keys.

"So maybe he's an arrogant son of a bitch and he's not quite willing to give up totally on his own identity. Not quite. So he's got the twelve numbers, but they're the numbers that correspond to *his* name, the egotistical bastard."

He computed swiftly, and typed it in.

Then he pressed Enter.

She was called Betty. She was the voice of the computer. She spoke from perfect preordained wisdom. She knew everything except fear and passion.

"Warning," she repeated. "There has been a second attempt at access."

"He thought of everything, didn't he, Alex?" said the general. "You see, it warns them when interlopers are coming. It gives silo personnel plenty of time to call SAC, and if they are in danger of being overrun, they can either fire the missile or dispose of their keys. He is so very, very smart, Peter. So very smart. A genius."

STRIKE TWO, the computer told him.

Peter let his breath slide out in a hiss of compressed disappointment. He sought to replace it but couldn't get anything in because his chest was so tight.

WARNING, the computer told him, ONE MORE STRIKE AND YOU'RE OUT.

"It didn't work either," said Skazy with something like a whimper.

Puller had sat down by himself. He said nothing. Around them soldiers stood stupidly.

"We could still try to hit the bird as it goes out the silo," said Skazy. "We could rig our 60s and hit it in a crossfire and—"

"Major," said Peter, "it's titanium. No bullet, no explosive is going to bring it down."

"Shit," said Skazy. "Well, get the C-4. Get all the C-4 we've got, we'll try to blow the door open. Then, if we've still got some time, we'll call in some real heavy air strikes and maybe—"

"No," said Peter. "No, forget it."

He stared at the keys. He'd always been the smartest boy in the class. Everywhere. Every time. All his life.

"Pashin really wants to become me," he said again, almost in astonishment. Then he gave a little laugh, rich with contempt. He thought about his wife and threw his worst secret out for them.

"He thinks that's his strength, his pathological edge. But it's not. It's his weakness. It's how he's overreached. You know, he wanted to become me so bad that he fucked my wife. Yeah, the man in the silo, the man one hundred feet below us now, this very second, this Comrade General Pashin, *having* her fucked wasn't enough for him."

"Peter," said Puller, something twisted in his voice, as if he were confronting a man on the cusp of breakdown.

But Peter rushed on, now unable to stop.

"That was the last thing," he told the horrified men, and the broken timber of his voice held them. "He had her drugged and he fucked her two weeks ago in Virginia. He *became* me through Megan. He had her, the motherfucker. So let's do this. If you mathematically split the difference between the value of the two names encrypted into numbers,

then you define the actual merge: you define exactly where he becomes
me and where he fucked my wife and where he wants to fuck us all." He
gave another little laugh, as if he were genuinely amused.

Okay, Russian, he thought. Let's party. Heaven is falling.

Peter knelt, quickly typed in twelve numbers.

He turned to Skazy.

"Piece of cake," he said.

He pressed Enter.

Betty spoke again in her seductive voice. She sounded like a lover,
rich and throaty—full of confidence on a hot summer's afternoon in
sweaty sheets, her words cutting through the siren and the pulsing red
light.

"Warning," she cooed, "access has been achieved."

Yasotay looked at the general and the general looked back at Yasotay
and there was just a moment of panic.

Then a man raced in.

"They've opened the elevator shaft!" he cried.

"He's through the doors," said the general. "Goddamn him, Peter
Thiokol, goddamn him."

It was ten till midnight.

Gregor asked the KGB security man at the front desk if Comrade
Klimov was about.

"He just went downstairs," said the man. "Just a second, comrade. I
can call down to the Wine Cellar and—"

"No, no," said Gregor. "No, that's all right. I'll go on down after
him." He smiled weakly and the KGB man looked at him suspiciously,
then consulted his list.

"You're late."

"I was in conference," said Gregor. He stepped past the man, into the
stairwell which was dark and curved away, out of sight toward the cellar.
It was very quiet. He licked his lips. Pausing, he reached into his pocket,
took out the vodka, and for courage took a deep swallow, feeling its
nuclear fire as it went down. For courage, he said. Oh, please, for
courage. He screwed it shut, put it away. Gingerly, he headed down,
twisting ever so gently as the stairs wound around on themselves.

He reached the bottom, paused again. It was very dark here; someone

had turned out the lights. He looked down the hall. Only the light in
the coding cell was open, some fifty paces ahead. He stepped into the
darkened corridor, heart hammering.

The device, he thought. The device is in the Wine Cellar, that maze
of chambers behind the vault door where all the installation's little
treasures were kept. If there's a device, and if Klimov means to set it off,
then that's where he'll be.

He thought of Magda. Klimov would come in to her; she'd recognize
a superior, and violate procedure, yes. She'd open the barred door and
Klimov would smile at her and kill her swiftly, with a silenced pistol, a
ballistic knife, his bare hands. Then he'd have to find the vault combination in the drawer, open the heavy door, and go on in to the labyrinth
in there.

Gregor hoped he was wrong. Please let me be wrong, he prayed. Let
me find fat Magda reading some absurd American romance novel or
cinema magazine or writing a letter to one of her many lovers or her
husband or petitioning for a higher living allowance or deciding whether
or not to change the color of her nails from Nude Coral to Baby Hush
or . . .

"Magda," he called softly as he walked down the hall, his head
pulsing with pain. "Magda, Magda, are you—"

The cage door to the Wine Cellar door was wide open.

Magda lay on her back, her thighs open, her garters showing, her
dress and slip up around her hips. Her face was in shadow.

"Oh, God," sobbed Gregor. The vision of her death robbed him of all
strength and will. His Magda was gone. He wanted to sit down and cry
and wail with rage. She would never call him Tata, her very own Prince
Tatashkin, noble hero who fought the Witch of Night Forever again. A
tear formed in the corner of his eye.

Then he saw that beyond Magda, the vault door lay open. Inside it
was dark; he could see the corridor leading away, like a maze, and all
the low, black openings off it. Once it had housed the liquid treasures of
exalted inebriation, inebriation in a hundred exotic hues and tones, each
more rarefied than the one before; now it was a super-hardened puzzle,
a collection of possibilities, all of them bad.

Move, Gregor. Time is short. You fat, putrid old man, move. Move!
Move!

He had an inspiration, and ran to Magda's desk and pulled open the
third drawer.

There, an old Tula-Tokarev automatic pistol should have been awaiting him.

It was gone, and so was its spare magazine.

Gregor looked into the open strong room, where the device was and
where Klimov was with the gun.

He looked at his watch.

It was very near midnight.

Walls hand-over-handed down the rope the six feet back to the ladder,
there awkwardly transferred his weight to the top rung, and pivoted,
unfolding, from the fetal to a hanging position, planting his boots on a
rung five feet below. Damn, it was easy! He scrambled up the ladder and
through the open door. The woman was right behind him. He found
that he had climbed into some sort of deserted corridor which led down
the way to another door. He thumbed the safety off the shotgun; opening
its little blazing dot to the world, saying, Ready, Jack. Then he edged
along, gun at the ready. Very tricky here. He tried to think it out: his job
had been to see how close he could get, then go back and get other guys
to plant a bomb or something. But that was all shot now. Now, he was
in the goddamn place and it was hours since he'd been in contact: he
had no idea who was here. Maybe all those soldiers had gotten into the
hole already and he and the girl could just sit down and have a nice
Coke and make their report and go home. But he didn't think so. Those
guys who came after him in the tunnel, man, they were too fucking good.
They were tough motherfuckers. You don't get guys like them out easy.

So he figured he'd managed now to get into the place where they
could fire the rocket. But nobody had told him what it was like. What
should he look for? He remembered as a kid when in school they made
them watch rockets shoot little balls or white guys into space from
Florida. It was some kind of big room with white guys in white shirts
sitting at panels. Somehow he knew that wasn't right. He figured it'd be
a little place, a little room somehow. And as they drew nearer to the far
door, Walls became aware of a peculiar sound; it was tantalizingly
familiar, coming at him from somewhere in his memory. A siren. The
police after him. He stopped. He felt her hand on his arm. He turned,
looked at her.

"Some kind of siren," he said. "You know, like the police are here or
something."

He could see she didn't comprehend.

"That's okay," he said. "We just goin' to nose ahead and see what's up. We do real slow. We not goin to do nothing stupid, okay, lady? No heroes. We ain't going to be no heroes. Being hero, that's the way you get fucked up, and Walls done being fucked up. We just ease our way on up and see what's to see."

Phuong looked at the black man. She had no idea what exactly was going on, where exactly they were. But she understood that they were very near the men who would drop the bombs and turn the world's children to flames. Her heart filled with hate and anguish. She had an image of her daughter in that one instant before the napalm flooded in searing brightness across her: The child ran, screaming, Mother, Mother, as the big jet rushed lazily overhead, and two black, spinning eggs fell from it, drifting in their stately course to earth.

Mother, Mother, the girl cried, and the wall of flames fell over her and the heat beat at Phuong, pushing her back and down and she felt her heart melt and her brain die and she wanted to run into the fire, but hands held her back.

She knew then why she was here, why she had come this long way back into her past.

Mother, her daughter called her, Mother.

I am here, she sang in her heart, joyous at last, for it was time to run into the fire.

Skazy yanked the pull-ring on an eight-second delay detonator jammed into a five-pound block of C-4, looked around, yelled, "Fire in the hole," and tossed the thing down the shaft. He had a sense of extreme maliciousness: to throw enough explosive to flatten a building down into a hole in the ground, then scamper back until it went boom. He felt giddy and dizzy as the thing fell weightlessly from his fingers and was absorbed by the blackness. He stepped back a few feet, though he knew the blast couldn't hurt him. He looked about: the dark troopers of the first squadron of the Delta Tunnel Assault Team stood around awkwardly, linked into their harnesses. All were in black; faces, hands, watch caps, armored vests, guns, ropes, knives—all black. In the second before the explosion Skazy had a delirious moment of clarity: it was all behind him now, the stuff with Puller, the so many times Delta had mounted up and gone nowhere, the stand-downs, his own career stalled out by the rumor that he had once smashed a superior in the face. All gone: now there was only Delta, and the moment rushed toward him so beautifully he could hardly stand it.

The explosion was muted from this distance, but still you could feel its force. The ground shook. It was a hard, sharp clap under the earth. Hot gas pummeled up from the shaft and gushed out into the night air.

Skazy tugged once, just for luck, on the metal bit at his belly button through which his ropes ran; he knew they were perfect because he'd done this drill a million times. He went to the shaft and heaved his long rope down it. It disappeared, uncoiling, shivering, and clicking off the walls as it fell. Other ropes fell with it down through the long distance. He looked around, and there stood Dick Puller with the earphones and Peter Thiokol looking at him.

"Delta Six, this is Cobra-One," he said into the hands-free, voice-activated mike suspended on its plastic arm inches from his lips, "we are commencing operations. Heaven is falling." He gave them the thumbs-up.

He saw Dick speak into the microphone, and simultaneously heard the words, "It's all yours, Frank," in his ears.

There was something he had to say. "Dick, I'm sorry."

"Forget it, Frank. Good hunting and God bless you."

Skazy turned to his sergeant, and said, "Let's go kill people."

Then he jumped off into the black space, hurtling down the rope, feeling the rope burn through his harness and between his legs and rip against the leather of his gloves, and he swung into the walls, bounded off the balls of his feet, and continued to whistle down the rope toward the tunnel, his CAR-15 rattling against his back. He was first, but he knew in seconds that around him, like spiders descending from their webs, would come the others of the tunnel assault team, falling through the dark.

The force of the explosion threw Yasotay against the wall of the corridor. One of his eardrums blew out and he twisted his shoulder badly on the wall. Someone shook him alert. All around he saw his men shaking their heads, touching themselves to make certain they were whole, clapping each other to touch other living flesh.

The general yelled from the entrance of the launch control center, "Only a few more seconds. Just hold them a few more seconds."

Yasotay blinked, found his whistle, blew it twice, hard and sharp. Its strident tones cut through the air of shock that hung like vapor in the air. Yasotay knew the battle would turn in the next second or two.

"On your guns, Spetsnaz, on your guns, boys!"

With that he himself did a stupid, incredibly brave thing. He stood and ran the sixty feet to the shattered elevator door, where the smoke was thicker.

"Sir, no, you'll—"

But Yasotay ran on, uncaring. He reached the elevator just as the first of the American fighters, who looked like a cossack from black hell, arrived at the end of his long rope. The man separated himself from his harness with an extraordinary economy of motion, and was unlimbering his automatic weapon, when Yasotay brought him down with short Uzi burst, the dust flying off the man as the bullets punched into him. Yasotay figured he wore body armor, so when he fell back, Yasotay fired again into his head.

"Cobra One, this is Delta Six, do you read? What's the situation, Cobra One, we hear heavy firing."

Puller got no answer.

"Skazy's down, dead probably," he said to Peter. "They were right on top of them as they came down."

"Sir," someone yelled from the shaft. "Somebody's in the shaft, firing up."

"Grenades," yelled Puller. "Grenades, now, lots of them. And then get your asses down there."

Yasotay killed the first four men the same way, gunning them as they slid off their ropes. It was terribly easy. But then the men stopped coming. Smoke floated everywhere, the smell of burned powder curled up his nostrils, and he was struggling to change clips in anticipation of more Americans, when he heard something bounce hard on the floor of the car, and then another and another and—

He'd just gotten away from the shaft when the first grenade went off, then another and another and another. He felt his arm go numb as it took several pieces of shrapnel. Leaking blood, he staggered down the corridor to his first strong point, where he had his M-60 and a batch of men with automatics.

He just got behind the barrier when the next group of Delta commandos hit the floor of the elevator shaft.

"Sir, we have targets."

"Take them, take them," yelled Yasotay, breathing hard. The M-60 fired, its tracers racing out, filling the shaft door. The others were firing, too, the bullets hitting the door, tearing it apart, ripping into the masonry and the metal. But then, incredibly, out of the door there came with a sickening thud a large chunk of doughy-looking C-4 with something stuck in it. Yasotay saw it come, land halfway between the elevator opening and his own position, and started to scream at his people to get down, when it detonated.

The explosion seemed even bigger than the last one. Again, like a rag doll, he was twisted backward by the blast, separated from his gun and from his senses. He had the sensation of going down a drain, of being swirled through a spiral of hot gasses and wild sensory impressions while large black Americans beat on him with baseball bats and American women poured hot coffee on him. His arm was on fire and he at least had the sense to beat it out against his leg. He blinked, tried to will himself to clarity and command. There now was smoke everywhere and a bell had begun to sound. A Spetsnaz trooper, shocked and disoriented by the blast, stood next to him with a stunned look on his face, and as Yasotay watched, a small red dot appeared on his center chest, and then a burst exploded it, blowing out his heart, pushing him back. The trooper fell with the terrible gravity of a building whose underpinnings had been cut out, with total animal death, oblivious and absolute, and his arms splayed out on the impact of his crash to the floor.

Yasotay gathered his Uzi and looked down the hall. He saw the Delta people had laser-sighting devices and were very good shots. They fired not out of fear or excitement but out of calm professional purposefulness, behind what cover was available, with extraordinary accuracy. The red streaks from their weapons cut through the smoke, and when they touched flesh, bullets followed. Their first premium was the gunner. He was hit twice in the head. Next to him, the loader was dying with a hurt look on his face, his blood pumping in spurts from a large gap in his throat. The blast had knocked half the barricade away and two or three men lay sprawled beyond it. The gun itself lay on its side, its bipod up like the feet of a dead animal on the road, its belt a tangle. It was useless.

Yasotay fired his clip—he was the only man in the position firing—then dropped back to the floor and slithered across it like a wily old lizard.

"Come on, boys, you've got to fire back. Come on, get the guns going, boys," he yelled as cheerily as he could. "Your mothers will curse you if you don't get some fire going, fellows." His team began to return the fire, but they were clearly shaken by the laser sights.

Yasotay smacked another clip into his Uzi. Then, with calm deliberation, he stood, aimed at a Delta commando coming at him in the dark, and killed the man with a single burst to the brain. He found another target in a second and fired into the ribs. He found a third and hit him in mid-body. By this time, like angry birds, the red streaks sought him through the smoke and the darkness. And as they climbed to find him, one of his men found the courage to race out of the shelter of the barricade to retrieve the M-60.

"That's it!" Yasotay shouted. He waited one more second, then dropped out of gun range. Overhead the world seemed to explode as the tracers tore through the air. But he heard another sound: his own M-60. God, he was glad he'd brought it, because the damned thing had so much authority that it drove anything that faced it into retreat.

"Sir, they're falling back."

Indeed, the Delta commandos, faced with the heavy gun, straggled backward. They were hung up in the elevator shaft entrance and its environs.

Then Yasotay's M-60 jammed.

It was the second big blast that panicked Jack. It was so close! He blinked, terrified, and felt his pants fill with liquid. He realized he'd urinated. Then it sounded as if hundreds of kids were beating on the walls with two-by-fours, the sounds wooden and unconvincing. What? He couldn't figure it out, until at last it occurred to him he was hearing small-arms fire.

They'd be coming, he knew. They'd come through that door there, these army guys, and they'd kill everybody, and that was it.

He turned to the mad general and said, "I don't think—"

"Burn it! Burn it, you fool. My hand must get into it! Burn it through, goddamn you, Hummel."

The pistol came close to his skull and rested there.

Jack's will collapsed. He wasn't strong enough. He was going to die, he knew. He'd never see his kids again or his wife: he was a fool and a loser and a vain and worthless man, and this was the one test that counted and he was fucking it up and this guy would kill him or the Army would kick its way in and kill him.

But he tried.

"I can't," he said. "I won't."

The general placed his pistol next to Jack's head. Jack felt the circle of the muzzle boring against the frail bone of his temple. There was a click.

"Do it," commanded the general.

Jack plunged the torch back into the long slash in the metal and watched as the hot bright needle of flame melted the last rim of titanium around the black hole. He could tell: it was done. You could get your hand in now. It was over.

He looked up.

"It's finished," he said.

The general's arm rose and came down and Jack accepted the blow across the face. It went off like a thunderclap, the sound of the pistol barrel striking bone and shaking brain and the world wobbled out of sight with the surge of pain, and then became blurry.

Jack felt himself sliding away and knew the warm wetness on his face was blood. But through his daze he saw the general reach in, struggle once, and then emerge with the key.

"Yasotay. Yasotay, I have it!"

The first blast knocked Walls to his knees and he almost fired the shotgun involuntarily. The second blast, even louder, really scared him. The gunfire rose like the sound of the ocean, beating and crashing against the walls.

He turned to the woman.

"Okay, mama-san," he said. "You just cover my ass, okay?"

Something that passed for acceptance radiated from her dark eyes for just a second and she turned and muttered something to herself and Walls, then realized she was praying. She was giving herself up to God for what would happen in the next two seconds or so. So he himself said a quick one. Dear God, he said, if you're a white man or a brown man or a yellow man I don't know, but please don't let these guys blow up the world before I move my momma and my brother James to the country. And if you do, then fuck you, cause you be dead too.

With a punch of his foot Walls kicked in the door to discover a young man in the blue beret of the Soviet airborne running with an RPG to reinforce the second strongpoint, and he blew him away with Mr. 12, felt the hard kick of gun against his shoulder, cycled the slide in half a second, popping a red from the breech, blew away another as he turned, dipped running across the corridor, blew away a young man with an AK-47 who turned to look at him, and saw himself in the kill zone of still a fourth who, before he could fire, fell back as his head exploded because the Vietnamese woman had shot him there with her Taurus.

Walls winked and gave her the thumbs-up—bitch can *shoot*, no fuckin' lie!—and dropped to one knee to thread more 12s into the shell port of the gun just in front of the trigger guard, got seven in, flipped it back upright, and threw the pump with a *klak-klak!* just in time to blow up a rather large man with a large automatic rifle. He began to slither ahead, the girl off on his right ten paces back, covering his black ass.

He was thinking, Come on, you motherfuckers, come to me, come to old Walls, Walls got the glory and the truth for you here with Mr. 12 by his side, and indeed he came upon two wounded men busily inserting ammunition into clips, and he did the necessary without a twitch of guilt, pumping the slide as the hot shells flipped from the breech and then he heard a cry and was hit by a spray of gunfire in the wrist, rib, and neck, and went down.

Mother, Mother, her daughter cried from the flames, Help me! Help me!

Phuong ran to her, past the black man who had been shot, but in her way was a white man with a rifle, and so she shot him; then another came and she shot him; there were two more and she shot them. Suddenly, they were everywhere around her and she felt herself hit, but she turned and fired twice more and was so close she could not miss, though she was hit again and again.

Mother, do not let me burn! her daughter screamed.

Phuong rose through her pain, turned to find her daughter, and two more white men fired at her and hit her, but she fired back, hitting them too.

I am coming, she screamed in her heart, and then she saw her daughter and went to her and grabbed her and the burning finally stopped.

Jesus, he hurt, but then he looked and saw that he still had the damn vest on and the bad one in the rib had just flattened itself out while kicking him like a mule. His wrist had been hit with a ricochet, his neck didn't bleed bad. He pulled himself over to the woman.

She lay quiet. Seven men lay around her. The automatic was on the floor, its slide locked back. He knelt, quickly felt for pulse. Nothing. Her eyes were closed and tranquil.

Jesus, mama-san, he thought, you're some kind of fine lady.

One of the bad guys was trying to crawl away, leaking blood. Walls put the muzzle of the shotgun against his head and fired. Then he raced on.

Yasotay gave the M-60 a good kick and when that didn't work, bent, pulled out his boot knife, and popped the feed cover. He could see that a bad shell had become stovepiped into the bolt head. With his knife blade he got some purchase, gave a mighty heave, and popped the thing out. Then, throwing the knife away, he reseated the belt, slammed the feed cover, and pulled the bolt back. He turned to the gunner, who was so overcome at Yasotay's charisma that he made no move to take over the gun. So Yasotay stood as red flashes zeroed toward him, and he saw the Delta commandos flooding toward him, visibly taken with his extraordinary courage. He pressed the trigger. The gun made him a god. The tracers flicked out, and where they hit they pushed the shadowy figures of Delta down. The gun fired swiftly: it rattled itself free of the first belt and the hot brass shells rattled from its breech, hundreds of them, spilling out and bouncing across the floor. And then it started to rain.

The water pelted Yasotay in the face, and he fell back, stunned. It fell in dense sheets, filling the air, accumulating in lurid, fluorescent-jazzy puddles on the floor, driving the sweat from Yasotay's hot body. It felt like a miracle. Greedily, he threw his head back and drank. The water poured in, sweet and glorious as vodka. Momentarily, the shooting stopped.

"Drink, boys, damn you, 22 Spetsnaz, drink! It's a message from God. He sends us water deep under the ground to quench our thirst.

Come on, drink, you lovely bastards!" Yasotay was laughing madly, aware that a stray round must have touched off the fire control sprinkler system. But he looked and saw Delta stunned at the sudden gush, and then crazily began to fall back. Where bullets had failed, water had succeeded.

Then he heard the general.

"Yasotay, damn you. I have it! I have it!"

"Delta Six, this is Cobra, do you copy?"

"Go ahead, Cobra."

"Sir, this is Captain McKenzie. Skazy's dead and so are most of my people down here. We've got maybe sixty or seventy percent casualties, dammit, and now it's raining."

"Raining?"

"The goddamn fire system went off, and it's pouring cats and dogs, Delta Six."

Peter said, "Tell him to push it anyway, it's only water."

"Cobra, you've got to push ahead. Where are you?"

"Sir, I'm into the corridor and past the first strong point, but they've set up a real motherfucker down there, they've got a goddamned M-60 and it's kicking our asses. They've got some kind of Russian Rambo down here who stands up and laughs at us. He must have killed forty of our guys already. Jesus, he is one tough son of a bitch."

"Waste his ass," said Puller. "Blow his guts out."

"Our lasers aren't working in the rain, goddammit. Sir, I've got a lot of dead and wounded."

"Delta, you've got to get into that launch control center."

"Sir, every man I throw down there gets wasted. They've got this goddamn place zeroed. I need more C-4, more men, and more time. And more lasers."

"Cobra, you've got to get it done, that's all. Now, press the attack, son, or your wives and children will curse you from here to eternity."

"Jesus," said the young captain.

The general watched Yasotay run through the rain. He moved with surprising grace, given his condition. Most of his hair was burned away, as were his eyebrows. His face was bright red from excitement, although peppered with shrapnel and bleeding from several places. One arm had

had its sleeve burned away, and the bare limb underneath was blackened and crusty with scabbing. His other arm was sodden with blood. Yet the man moved with such relish it was difficult to fathom. He was pure war.

"I have it. I have it!" the general yelled, holding the key aloft. "Come, Alex, we're there, we've won."

In his hands the general held two red titanium keys, each weighing about an ounce, each about two inches long, and jagged and fluted as any key would be.

"Here, take it. Now, on my mark."

He pressed a key into Yasotay's hand and had an odd sense that in Yasotay's mad eyes something weird and sad danced.

But the general raced to station two.

There were two stations. At each, not much: a telephone, a wallful of buttons, a computer, and all of it, really, irrelevant, except for the keyholes under the rubric LAUNCH ENABLE.

"Put your key in, Alex," the general commanded, inserting his own.

Yasotay put his key in.

Immediately, a red light began to flash in the command capsule.

The prerecorded voice stated, "We have launch condition Red, please authenticate, we have launch condition Red, please authenticate."

"The computer, Alex. Do what I do. The numbers are there."

Before Yasotay were a set of twelve numbers; they were the proper, preset Permissive Action Link for that day that he had obtained by blowing open the safe in the security shed eighteen hours earlier.

Yasotay punched in the twelve numbers, as the general had done.

"We have an authenticated command to launch, gentlemen," came the voice of the beautiful woman out of the speakers. "We have an authenticated command to launch. Turn your keys, gentlemen."

There was something tender in her sweet voice.

"Alex," said the general, "on my command."

Alex's eyes came up to meet the general's, then went back to the key.

"Alex, three, two, one."

The general turned his key.

It did not move.

The sound of gunfire rose and rose. Shouts, screams, explosions.

"Alex?"

Yasotay looked up. The general saw something odd on his face, impenetrably sad and remote. He had not turned his key.

"Is this right, Arkady Simonovich Pashin? Can you say, irredeemably, in God's eyes, in Marx's eyes, in Lenin's eyes, in the eyes of our children, that this is right?"

"I swear to you, my friend. It's too late to go back. The bomb in Washington goes off soon. If we don't fire now, this second, the Americans respond with *all* their Peacekeepers and death will be forever and ever. Come, my friend. It's time. We must do that hard, terrible thing, our duty. We must be men."

Imperceptibly, Yasotay nodded, then looked back to the key. His fingers touched it.

"On my command," said Pashin. "Three, two—"

Pashin had the impression of conflagration, of flames unending and unceasing, spreading through the world, eating its cities, its towns, its villages, its fields, of the long and total death of fire, in its immense but necessary and cleansing pain. He thought of babies in their cribs and mothers in their beds, but then he saw that it was not the world but his own hand and arm that were in flames, and then the pain hit. He turned into the mad eyes of the American Hummel and his torch, which now climbed from the blazing arm and sought him where he was softest, burned through his tissues, through throat to larynx, through cheeks to tongue, through eyes to brain, and the pain was—

Yasotay watched the general burn. In a queer sense he was relieved, and then he saw that he had merely acquired another responsibility. The general's pain was extraordinary, yet it did not move Alex. He watched as the American drove the torch deep into the face and the face melted. Alex, in his years of war, had seen many terrible things but nothing quite as terrible as this, and after a time, numb as he was, he decided enough was enough and he shot the American in the chest with his P9. The man slid to the floor and the torch went out at last.

Then Alex stood; the machinery to launch the missile was still intact. He could not turn two keys at once, however. He had to find someone, anyone, that was all. He turned and rose to get a man, and at last saw his own death, in the form of a black American commando with a red bandanna and a shotgun and frenzied eyes, and Alex, still numb, lifted the P9 in a nominal attempt at self-defense, but then the American blew him away.

*   *   *

Gregor looked at his watch.

Midnight was very close.

He looked into the welter of rooms that lay behind the vault door. He wondered if the great Tolstoi had ever conjured such a moment: fat Gregor, scared so badly the shit was almost about to run down his pulpy legs, going into a maze to stop a man with a bomb who would merely destroy the world. It was too absurd, not Tolstoi at all but more the ancient Russian folktale. He was Tatashkin, going off to fight the Witch of Night Forever. The world chooses such terrible champions to defend her! he thought bitterly.

Liquid courage. He pulled the bottle from his pocket, sloshed it to find it only half full, unscrewed the cap, and threw down a long, hot swallow. The world blurred perceptibly, turned mellow and marvelous. Now he felt ready. He put aside his servility and his avuncularity and his sniveling obsequiousness, his need to please all his masters; and he put aside his fear: he decided that he could kill and after that he decided that he would kill.

Gregor walked into the dark corridor.

Klimov had switched the lights off.

Gregor slipped out of his shoes. He began to pad down the hall. His nervousness had left him. His heart was beating hard, but not out of fear, rather out of excitement. Now he had him: little Klimov, the piglet, who had killed his friend Magda and would just as soon kill the world. With the vodka he was able to imagine pressing the life out of the piglet's throat, watching his eyes go blank and dull as death overcame them.

Gregor glanced through the first doorway; inside there was a filing cabinet, three obsolete portable coding machines, nothing else.

He walked on. He breathed in small wheezes, evenly, quietly, only through his nose. He felt his eyes narrow. In a curious way he felt himself concentrate as he had never concentrated before, or as he had not concentrated in years. He flexed his hands, tried to limber up his muscles.

He tried to remember the lessons from so many years ago.

Any part of your body is a killing weapon: the heel of the palm driven upward against the nose or into the throat; the edge of the hand against the neck; the knee, planted with thunderous force into the testicles; the bunched fist, one knuckle extended in the form called the dragon's head, into the temple; the elbow, like a knife point, driven into the face; the thumbs into the eyes. You are all weapons; you are a weapon.

Gregor slid around the second doorway: more filing cabinets, old trunks, hanging uniforms.

He proceeded. The next little room bore outmoded communications and coding equipment, too bulky to be shipped back, too sensitive to be abandoned, too imperishable to be destroyed. The following room contained weapons, a row of old PPsH-41s locked in their rack, some RPGs chained to a circular stand. Also some stores of explosives and detonating devices, left over, all of it, from the maniac Stalin's reign, when it seemed that war would break out at any moment and every second commercial attaché might be turned into a saboteur or a partisan.

And on to another room, which had nothing in it but furniture from some purged functionary's office, cast off as if it, too, had been contaminated by political unorthodoxy, and it, too, had been consigned to a Gulag.

In the last room he found the ratfuck Klimov.

And he found the bomb.

Gregor recognized it, of course, from the drawings he'd seen: it was a variation on the American W54, the famous suitcase bomb called a Special Atomic Demolition Munition. It was in the one-kiloton range, from here easily powerful enough to vaporize all primary governmental structures and, by virtue of blast, heat, and electromagnetic pulse, completely destroy the Pentagon across the river in Virginia, while doing massive damage to CIA up the river in McLean and, in its farther reaches, rupturing the communications at the National Security Agency in Maryland. The thing looked like a big green metal suitcase sitting there on the table. It was open, its padlocks sprung. The top was off, and the firing mechanism appeared to be quite simple, a crude timing device, digitalized for the modern age. The numbers fled by in blood red like a third-rate American spy movie.

2356:30
2356:31
2356:32

So the fucker was set. Klimov sat before it in immobile fascination as the digits flicked up toward the ultimate moment. He brought an old roller chair in from the storage room. He'd just sit there and be atomized in the detonation.

Gregor walked to him, waiting for the piglet to turn and rise with the pistol. Gregor knew he was close enough. He felt the murderous rage building within him. He'd kill him with his hands and it would feel good. He'd kill him for Magda already gone and the sleeping millions who'd join her.

Inch by inch he stepped closer.

Klimov just sat there.

2357:45

2357:46

2357:47

He touched the boy on the shoulder, making ready to strike.

Young Klimov slipped forward an inch, then toppled to the cement, hitting it with a sickening thud, and the crack of teeth.

Young Klimov had been shot in the heart with a ballistic knife blade that projected from the center of his chest in a sodden mass of blood. Blood also flowed from his mouth and nostrils. His eyes were open in absurd blankness.

"He didn't believe it when I shot him," said Magda Goshgarian, standing behind him in the doorway. "I wish you could have been there, dear Tata, when the blade went in and the life went out of his eyes."

"Magda, I—"

He gestured to her but she raised a pistol.

"He knew something was up. He was very smart, the little prick. He's been nosing around me for weeks now. He came down and I killed him, Tata."

Then her eyes moved to Gregor's, and he saw that she was mad, quite mad.

"And I heard you coming, yelling my name with your voice trembling in fear. So I played dead, and off you went. I will shoot you, too, Tata, though I love you. I love you almost as much as I love our country, which has lost its way. And as much as I love my lover, Arkady Pashin, for whom I would die. For whom I will die. He is a great man, Tata, a man of Pamyat, and you are merely a man. Now, stand back. It will be over in seconds, my love. You won't feel a thing—just nothingness, as your atoms are scattered in the blast."

Peter stood by the mouth of the elevator shaft, listening to the gunfire below. It sounded horrible, roaring up the dark space of the shaft, no individual sounds to the shots at all, just a mass of noise. He was at the same time fussing with something around his waist.

"Excuse me," he said to a Delta soldier close by, "is this right?"

The young man looked at it.

"No, sir, you've got to rotate the snaplink a half turn so that the gate is up and opens away from the body. And I don't think you're in the rope-seat just right. And you've got to take up some slack between the snaplink and the anchor point and—"

Peter fumbled with it. He'd never get it right.

"Look, could you fix it for me?" he said.

The soldier made a face, but bent and began to twist and adjust Peter's rig.

"Dr. Thiokol?"

It was Dick Puller.

"How's it going down there?" Peter asked.

"Not good. Lots of fire. Very heavy casualties."

Peter nodded.

Puller checked his watch, then looked at the other Delta boys queueing up for the long slide down to the battle.

"Delta, second squadron, ready for the descent," an NCO called. "You locked and loaded?"

"Locked and loaded," came the cry.

"Check your buddies. Remember your quick-fire techniques and to go to the opposite shoulder at these damn corners. No fire on the way down, the show starts about halfway down the corridor. In twos, then, Delta, on rappel, go, go, go."

As he tapped them off, the Delta men began their slide down.

"More men, maybe that'll do it," said Dick.

"That's it," said the soldier, rising. "Now you're rigged right. You just thread the rope through the bit, under your leg. You break with your right hand—you're righthanded, right?—by closing it and pressing the rope into your body."

"Thiokol, what are you doing?" said Puller abruptly.

"I have to get down there."

Dick Puller's mouth came open, the only time Peter had ever seen surprise on the leathery, unsurprisable face.

"Why?" the old man finally asked. "Look, they're either going to shoot their way in and stop Pashin or they're not. It's that simple."

Peter fixed Puller with a harsh look. "It's not simple. There's a scenario where it may come down to somebody who knows those consoles and certain launch-abort sequences." He marveled at the dry irony of it, how it had to turn out so that he, Peter Thiokol, *Dr.* Peter Thiokol, strategic thinker, had to slide down a rope to the worst game of all, war. "There's more to it than men. Your Delta people may kill all the Russians and the rocket will fly anyway. I have to go. I started this fucking thing, now I'm the one who has to stop it."

Puller watched him go. He interrupted the Delta assault descent, and the sergeant looked over at Puller and Puller gave a nod, and Peter somehow managed to get the ropes properly seated in the complex rappeling gear strapped to his waist. He was standing right there at the mouth of the tunnel. He poised on the edge for just a second, then caught Dick Puller's eyes and gave a meek little thumbs-up, more like a child than a commando, and then he was gone.

Walls knew where he was now. He was *in*, actually *inside* the white man's brain. It was a well-lit little room, covered with electronic gear, telephones, screens, dead guys. He jacked another shell into the Mossberg, stepped inside, pulled the goddamned door closed, gave a huge circular mechanism a twist and a clank, locking it. Beyond the white boy with the piece he'd just blown away there was another white guy, burned up like a pig in a North Carolina pit. Whoever he was he sure smelled bad. He went over and poked at him. The guy was barbecued. He'd been burned down to black bone. You could eat him, that's how bad he's been burned.

And then still another guy. Walls walked over and poked at him. His face was all smashed; he'd been beaten pretty bad. His leg had been shot. Blood bubbled on his chest. His eyes fluttered open.

"My kids?" he asked.

"Man, I don't know nothing 'bout no kids," said Walls.

"You Army?"

Walls wasn't sure how to answer this.

"Yo, man," he said.

"They made me do it," the guy said. "It wasn't my fault. But I stopped the general. With the torch."

"You done more than stop that general, man. You *roasted* his ass, but good."

The man's hand flew up to Walls's wrist and gripped it.

"Tell my kids I loved them. I never told them, goddammit, but I love them so much."

"Okay, man, you just rest. If you ain't dead yet, you probably ain't going to be dead at all. I don't see that you're bleeding. He plugged you over the heart, but I think he missed it. Just sleep or something while I figure out what to do, you got that, man?"

The guy nodded and lay back weakly.

Walls rose. This was the place to be, he thought, right in the middle of the white race's brain. He had the door locked and a little farther up the tunnel there was a real serious battle going on, and he didn't see what going up there and getting killed was going to do.

He looked around. These people, shit. Who could build a room like this, what kind of motherfucking asshole? Little white room way down under the ground where you could end the world by pushing some buttons. He looked and saw a key, just like the key in a car, stuck in an ignition switch. At another little place in the room he saw this other key. Like these white guys were going to drive away. There were lights, labels, signs, speakers, radios, typewriters, a wall safe, a big clock on the wall. Damn, it was late! It was nearly midnight.

He laughed.

White people.

And suddenly a white lady was there. It stunned him because he heard her voice in the bright room. He looked around, it sounded like she was just there, but no, no white lady. She was coming over the radio or something.

He tried to understand what she was saying. He couldn't figure it out, man, it was just jive. These jiving white bitches, they always gave you a hard time, something about some kind of lunch being served or some other shit like that, man, what *does* this bitch want?

"Automatic launch sequence initiation commencing," she was saying. "Automatic launch sequence initiation commencing. Gentleman, you have five minutes to locate abort procedures if necessary. We are in terminal countdown."

But then he understood. The bitch was going to fire the rocket.

2357:56
2357:57
2357:58

"Now, Magda," Gregor began, "now, darling, let's not do anything hasty here. This man Pashin? He may be a handsome charmer, but at the same time, he's clearly something of a lunatic. Now, darling, believe me, I know what a bastard I've been to you and how vulnerable you might be to someone flashy like this, but can't you see, he's merely *using* you? Once you're gone, you're gone. Poof! It's not as if he'll be waiting somewhere for you, darling. I mean, in just a bloody minute or two we're all ashes."

The gun was pointed at his heart. He had seen Magda shoot. Magda was an excellent shot. She wasn't trembling at all. The flickering colors of the fleeing digits in the timer mechanism illuminated her face, giving it an odd animation. The lights made real her insanity, her tenuous grip on reality, which had opened her to Pashin and made her capable of doing this tragic thing. Pashin had probably purchased her loyalty forever by something as elementary and unremarkable in this world as an orgasm. A quick tongue in the right place and the world was his.

"Please, darling," he said, "I—"

"Hush, my love," crooned Magda, her voice deep and throatily sexual. "Now it's just a matter of waiting as the seconds flow by and we join the great All, Tata."

He wished now he had made love to Magda. It would have been so easy. Magda had always been available for him. All he'd had to do was ask! And if he'd had her, she'd be his now. It was that simple. But he never had. He'd always taken her for granted. Magda! Silly, goosey woman, a pal, a chum, always willing to listen, to sympathize. She must have loved him secretly for years and been chewed up by the way he took her for granted. And so she turned to Pashin and his mad grandeur.

"Magda, let me tell you, it doesn't have to end like this, in a flash of flame. Magda, you and I, we can be together. I can take you away from all this. I have friends among the Americans. The two of us, Magda, we can get away from Washington, from the embassy, from all this. We can have a happy life in some American city, Mr. and Mrs. We could adopt a little girl, Magda, a whole family. The Americans will help us. We can have a wonderful life, Magda, I'll make you so hap—"

Magda's laugh, sharp and percussive, cut him off.

"What, Gregor Ivanovich. Do you imagine I'm in love with you? That I'd sell my country out for one of your caresses? Men, God, how you all value yourselves! No, Tata, my heart belongs to Arkady Pashin and to his vision of the future, which is a vision of the great Russian past, the past of Pamyat, of Memory, Gregor dear. A pretend Russian like you cannot see this, but I give up my life willingly to my motherland, and to my lover."

And to his damned quick tongue. Gregor saw how mad Pashin was: to put a tongue to plump Magda! Gregor also saw now that he was doomed. Magda's loyalty was impenetrable. Pashin had made her his forever with his lunatic's babble of Memory and Mother Russia. Magda, desperate for something to worship, had bought it all. The crazy bitch! The cunt, the dumb Russian cunt! Women! He hated them, the bitches.

She had him. To rush for the bomb would be to catch a bullet in the heart, like poor Klimov here; he'd be dead before he made it, and even if he wasn't, he didn't know how to stop it. Or if he came at her, she'd shoot him. Yes, she would. Right in the heart, hating it all, but doing it just the same, because she saw it as her duty to the damned genius charlatan, Arkady Pashin, and the motherland for which she thought he stood.

"Do you know, darling"—he tried a new approach—"the Americans know. Even now they're attacking the mountain. Even now Pashin has failed. He's probably already dead, Magda. His dream is over. At the very least the Americans are in communication with Moscow. This damned bomb will go off, and the thousands, the millions, will die, yourself and myself included, but there'll be no war for us to win, no Russian future based on a great Russian past. Just one ruined city, and the bones of babies turning black in the night."

He had begun to weep.

He could see the numbers fleeing by. They rushed on remorselessly.

2358:21

2358:22

2358:23

She simply looked at him. There was only pity on her face.

"You poor fool, Tata. You believe in nothing except the religion of the ass, your own, for which you would do anything. You snivel and beg and whine. Goddamn you, Tata, why don't you have the guts to die on your feet! Come at me, you silly, gutless bastard!"

But Gregor fell to his knees.

"Please," he slobbered, broken. "You're right. I don't care about them. I don't care about any of them. But, Magda. Magda, please. Please, I don't want to die. Stop it. Stop the bomb! Please don't kill me! *Please!*"

She made a terrible face, her lips snickering in utter contempt, her eyes rolling, and in that second the barrel of the gun wavered, and in that second Gregor Arbatov leapt.

Peter slid through the dark, slid until he thought he'd lost control and was falling, and pulled in on the rope skidding before his eyes to brake himself. Big mistake. He hit the wall hard, feeling the blow ring in his head and his body go spastic in the concussion. Lights popped in his skull; his breath came hard and hot. He could feel the blood on his face, and his will flying out the window. He blinked for control. Below he heard the firing, roaring, incessant. But he just hung there, suspended between worlds. Other men, dark shapes falling, sped past him. His nose rubbed against the shaft; the straps cut into his groin; he had an image from a World War II movie of a paratrooper hanging in a tree. He tugged, twisted, struggled—ah! oops! and there he went again, sliding down, this time with a bit more control. He felt the burn of the rope through his leather gloves and as he swung in toward the wall, this time he caught himself on the balls of his feet and propelled himself outward again, and so eventually tumbled to the bottom.

He alighted on the top of the blown-out elevator car, amid the swirls of its cable. The smell of the explosion, so recent, still hung heavy in the air. He found himself in a crowd in a small space, as other Delta people were busy shedding themselves of coils and snaplinks and D-rings and dropping through the rupture in the roof to get to the fighting. Peter did likewise, though with less agility. Even as he struggled, trying to remember what the boy up top had said, still other Delta raiders landed at the end of their long ropes, unlimbered themselves in the confusion, and dashed off. But it was taking so long!

Finally, he was free, and climbed gingerly down through the hole to discover poor Skazy on his back, staring up in a puddle of blood through lightless eyes at nothing and forever. Peter gagged, first at the sight of Skazy's hideous face and evacuated skull, and then from the smell, now that blood and bowels had been added to the stench of powder. He turned, found more bodies, stepped over them, and hurried out of the car and down the corridor.

It was his installation all right, now, however, tarnished horribly by the battle and made strange, stranger than he could imagine. The water was an inch deep, and moisture filled the air like a mist. The sprinklers had obviously popped. Bodies lay in the water, dark with their own vital fluids where they seemed to rock back and forth, like floating Marines in the Tarawa surf. He saw some horrible things, but didn't concentrate on them. Sirens were going, and half the lights were off. Sparks leaked out of wiring ruptures into the water. And he heard the voice, the sweet voice of the angel of megadeath.

". . . Launch is imminent. We have an authenticated launch command and launch is imminent. We have an . . ."

It was Betty, the prerecorded voice of the computer. He thought she sounded a little like Megan.

He tuned out the bad news and sloshed ahead through the mist to the firing, coming at last to a jog in the corridor and peeping around it to discover the epicenter of the battle. The Delta people were still a good fifty meters from the Soviet strongpoint, which was a jerrybuilt assemblage of sandbags, furniture from above, crates, whatever. It mounted at least a dozen guns, all of them firing. The air was busy with lead and noise. Where bullets struck, dust leapt off the wet wall. Meanwhile the Delta people, their guns flicking the red rays of the laser-sighting devices, plugged away, but they had stalled. They were down to the last few yards, but they had stalled. To run into the guns was to die, that was all. Peter could see that they needed explosives or something larger than what they had. It was all fucked up, a mess. It had no order at all, it was just gangs of men shooting each other up in a very small space.

Jesus, he thought, ducking back, feeling for the first time the quiver of real fear. His bowels loosened. He now saw it. They weren't going to make it.

"You the doc?" a crouching, blackened figure with a CAR-15 and a hands-free mike asked, another Delta Caliban.

"Yes," he said to the man, evidently the head commando. "Listen, you've got to get into that room down there. That's it. That's the launch control center."

"Yeah, sure. After you. Is there a back way into it?"

"No. Just straight ahead. Look, you've got to get into it. There's no other way and there's not much time."

"Sorry, but I've got to wait until I get some more firepower."

"They're all fouled up getting down the shaft," Peter said. "There isn't time. Do you hear that, do you know what that voice means?"

"Yeah, I hear it. No, I don't know what it means."

"It's the computer. She's going to launch the bird in about four minutes."

The officer looked at him peculiarly.

"You see, we found out in our tests that while all hundred percent of the men in the silos would insert their launch keys, only about sixty percent would actually turn them. So we fail-safed it. If they stick both keys in, it initiates a timing device; three minutes later an automatic launch sequence begins. They don't have to turn the key, they just have to stick it in, and the terminal countdown begins. Now, if it's a mistake or some terrible fuck-up, there is a way to stand down the launch sequence from the command center. But they can get it only over the radio, it involves a secret meaning for several of the switches pressed in a certain sequence. Only SAC HQ has the sequence. And me. Look, if you get me into that thing, I can stop the bird."

"Man, I can't get into the fucking place, you dig? It's rock and roll out there."

"You're going to let a handful of Soviet soldiers stop you? Just rush the place. Please, Jesus, please."

"Yeah, rush the place, great. Man, I can't get good suppressive fire on the motherfucks. They've got anybody who comes at them zeroed dead. I don't have enough firepower. Hey, we'll die to get it done, but there's no point in just dying to die, man."

"We can't be this close and fail."

"Doc, I'm sorry. I can't do the impossible. That's all there is to it."

"Call Puller."

"Puller's not down here. I am. If I wait a few minutes, then maybe I get enough firepower up and move a team down to get some C-4 into them and push off. But my guys are getting torn up. These Russian kids are very tough guys."

"*Please!*" Peter shouted, surprised at the violence in his voice. "God-damn, don't you see, if you don't get into that room in the next three minutes or so, all these men have died for absolutely nothing. They're suckers, jerks, fools. Please, Jesus, if not for me or your kids, for those dead guys who—"

"*I can't!*" the officer screamed back, just as loud. "It's not a question of wanting. I just can't get you in there. No one can, goddamn you."

Peter thought he might weep. The sense of helpless rage filled him. So this was it, then. Another two or so minutes, and Pashin had won. Pashin was smarter. Though Peter wondered why he didn't just *turn* the keys now and get it over with, if he had 'em both in. And he had to have them both, or he couldn't have initiated the robot launch sequence.

Then he realized: Pashin must be dead.

"Look," he said suddenly. "Our guys are in there. They have to be. Some Delta guys are *in* there, goddammit. We wouldn't be where we are if this Russian had gotten the keys out and put them in the slot, because he'd have turned them. But somebody stopped him, and that's why we're here, don't you see? Somebody blew his ass away at the last moment, but the keys were already in. We've got guys *in* there, goddammit."

The officer looked at him.

"We have an authenticated launch command," said Betty on the loudspeaker. "We are commencing terminal countdown phase. Launch is three minutes and counting."

"So call him," said the officer.

"Huh?"

"*Call* him. On the phone. Look, in the wall there. Isn't that a phone?"

Peter looked. The simplicity of it was stupendous. Yes! Call him!

He picked the phone up and dialed L-5454.

Walls stared at the board, bright with lights. The room seemed full of white ghosts. The motherfuckers were dead and they were going to kill the world anyway. White people! Assholes.

He gripped his shotgun, threw the slide, felt a shell click into the chamber. He'd blow a hole in the controls, that'd stop it! But he didn't know where to shoot.

He stood staring at the board furiously, hating himself for being so stupid. The room made him feel like nothing. He didn't know what to do.

"Terminal countdown is commencing," the white lady was saying on the radio or whatever.

Damn the bitch!

Suddenly, there was a shrill beeping.

Made his ass jump!

"Terminal countdown is commencing," the white bitch said again.
He picked up the phone.

"Yes," said Peter, shrieking almost with the excitement. "Yes, Jesus, who is this?"

"Walls," the voice said.

Some Delta people had gathered around Peter. He cupped the receiver.

"He's in there!" he shrieked. "God, a guy is *in* there. Walls. Anybody know a Walls?"

"There's no Walls in Delta," said the officer.

"Son, listen," said Peter on the phone, "are you Delta?"

There was no answer. Oh, Christ, had he—

"Uh—I come through the tunnel, man. You know, from underground."

"Jesus," Peter said, "he's one of the rats. He got in from underneath. Listen, son, what's the situation there?"

"Man, I think this rocket fixing to go off. Lights blinkin', shit like that. Man, I blow the controls away with—"

"No, God, *no!*" shrieked Peter. "Don't shoot anything. Throw the gun away."

"Yo, okay."

Peter heard the crash as the gun was tossed.

"Is the door locked?"

"Yes, suh. Them guys, whoever the fuck, don't want them gettin' in—"

"Listen, Walls. Listen to me carefully now, please, son. You can stop it."

Peter's heart was pounding. He was gripping the phone so hard he thought he'd choke it. "Yes, listen. You've got five labeled keys to hit in the proper sequence. All you have to do is listen, and read the labels, it's very simple, very easy. All set. Are you all set?"

There was a long silence, heavy and still.

Peter could hear the firing. He could hear the tick of seconds, too, running off, on the way to forever.

"Son?" he asked again, and thought he heard a sob or something.

"Son? Are you there? Are you there?"

Finally the voice came.

"Then we fucked," it said. " 'Cause I can't read."

*   *   *

She shot Arbatov twice. The first bullet hit him over the heart, blowing through the subcutaneous tissue, the muscle, ripping up a lung and nicking his shoulder blade before exiting with a terrible vengeance through the back. The second hit farther down, between two ribs, and plunged through the organs of his belly, terrible, terrible damage. Then he was on her, crushed her to the ground, and spitting blood, began to punch her in the face and head. Somehow he got the gun out of her hand, got it into his fist, and beat her savagely with it. When her eyes went blank he stopped beating her, and rolled off against the wall. He wasn't sure if she was dead and he didn't care. It wasn't important. He was surprised how much blood was in him. It poured out. Shock, numbing and narcotic, rippled through him. He had an image in his head of golden wheat weaving in the sun and had a terrible impulse to lay his head down and rest for a time. But instead, the numbness in the stomach wound began to wear off and the pain was extraordinary. He couldn't make much sense out of what was happening.

Bomb, something about a bomb. An atom bomb, that was. Slightly moot now, however, since he seemed to be dying.

He forced his head to turn, and yes, from the lurid play of light on the ceiling he could see that the numbers of the timing device were rushing onward toward 0000. Gregor thought he should get over there. Thus he ordered his reluctant body to topple forward. Like a tree it went. It hit the floor with a thud, and his ears rang, though there wasn't much pain. He began—somehow—to crawl through his own blood toward the thing, having no idea what he'd do if he actually got there.

Damn you, Pashin, you took from me the one woman I loved. And also my life. Goddamn you, Pashin.

Hate was helpful because hate was energy. He began to crawl, but the damned thing was still far off.

Words. Goddamn motherfuckin' white-boy words.

Their shapes were like snakes or bugs, maybe. They swirled and coiled and twisted about him. Everywhere he looked he could see words on little black plastic plates that stared at him. They were meaningless. They had no mercy, they never had, the motherfuckers.

"Walls? Walls, are you there?" the voice came over the phone. It was twisted with urgency. It connected with so much. All the times white people had looked at him, their features quizzically perturbed. Son, can't you read? Son, the world is a threatening place to a young man who cannot read. Boy, you'd better learn your ABC's, or you'll stay black and dumb and be one of the little streetcorner fucks forever and ever.

"Son?"

"Yes, suh," Walls said, hot and bent with shame and furious hatred— some for himself, and some for this Mister White Man with his concerned voice, and some for whoever had put him in this white man's room with the seconds running out and some bad motherfuckin' shit about to go down.

"Uh, son, tell me," the voice asked, trying to stay calm, odd currents firing through it. Walls had heard this voice a million times. It was a white guy who'd just realized he was dealing with Mr. Dumbjiveass-niggerboy, but also knew if he pissed Mr. D. off, Mr. D. he take top of the motherfucker's head off, and so going real poh-lite, you know, like real sloooow, so as not to rile him.

"Uh, son, do you know the letters? Do you know your alphabet? Not words, now, but do you recognize the letters?"

Walls burned with shame. He shut his eyes. He could feel the tears running down his face, hot and bright. He squished the phone so hard he thought it'd snap in two, or maybe melt.

"Terminal countdown has commenced," said the white bitch, snooty and far off and so much better than him. He wanted to kill the white bitch.

"Yes, suh," he said. "I know my letters pretty good." He was speaking slow, like a goddamn houseboy.

"Ah, good, great, God, terrific," came the voice. "Now, if we work together and trust each other and don't panic, we'll be okay, we'll have plenty of time, we can do it by the letters. Okay, son. We can get it done, there's still time, okay?"

Walls could feel the panic flashing quick and bright under the man's voice as it fought through his Adam's apple and throat full of gunk.

"Yes, suh," he said, yassing the man to death, giving him what he wanted to get him smiling, like he was five again, just yassing and yassing him to death, all smiles and charm and secret shame. "We do it real slow, don't panic, we be okay, fine, yes, suh."

"Okay," said the voice, "now, if you're at the phone, you're sitting in the chair, right?"

"Yes, suh," said Walls, sliding obediently in the chair.

"Now, start at the phone jack, where the cord fits into the wall. Look at it, okay?"

"Yes, suh." He fixed his eyes on the plug where the cord went into the wall.

"Now lift your eyes about two inches. To the left is a little handle. Then there's a ridge. And at the ridge the control console sort of leans away from you. It's not a straight angle, but it's leaning away, right?"

"Yes, suh."

"Okay, now, on that leaning part—you're looking at its extreme left-hand side now—on the leaning part there are all kinds of switches. There's five groupings of two columns, ten columns in all. The column groupings are broken down so that there's a group of six—three and three in two columns—then a group of eight, that's four in each column, then a group of four, two in each column. And there's five sets of them, right?"

Fuck you, Jack, thought Walls. Wrong. Wrong and wrong again, sucker. It was a maze, a gibberish of little white boxes, and switches and wires, a nightmare. He closed his eyes, hoping it would go away, or that it would become clear. When he opened them, he was still in the maze.

"Do you see?" demanded the voice.

"I don't see nothing," he said.

"Look at it! Goddamn you, bastard, *look at it!*"

He could hear sobbing on the other end, hysteria, panic, terror.

Walls looked back, tried to see—the switches dazzled and flickered before him, seeming to squiggle into shapes like some kind of strange animal, a shape changer, a germy thing in some movie where people got whacked and cut.

"Terminal countdown has commenced," came the voice of the white bitch, sweet as sugar. "Terminal countdown has commenced."

Then, yes, he had it! Goddamn motherfuck yes*yesyes*! he had it. The columns, two of them twinned, and each of them broken down into little groupings, five of them, each to its board.

"Goddamn, motherfuck!" he shouted. "Hey, man, I got the bitch, I got the motherfucker!"

"Great! Great, great, *great!*" shouted the voice. "Terrific. Now, it's—"

And the line went dead.

      *   *   *

"It's dead, it's dead, it's dead," Peter screeched. "Jesus, it's dead."

"Terminal countdown has commenced," came Betty's voice on the loudspeaker.

Someone grabbed him, a sergeant, to calm him down.

"Just take it easy," he said.

Peter looked into the dead military eyes. Don't you understand, he thought, don't you see what's happening? Do you realize what's at stake here. It's—

"They hit the phone juncture, Doctor. Look."

It was the officer, pointing to a box high up on the wall exposed to Soviet fire. It had been mutilated by a burst, hinges blown off, the mechanical guts of the switching mechanisms shredded so that they hung out like entrails.

"Is there another phone?" the officer asked. "A phone inside that connector. Anything outside of it's dead. But maybe there's something inside."

Phones! Who remembered phones! Peter, who'd once lived his life in the maze of the blueprints of the South Mountain installation, tried to sort out his phone memories, something he'd never looked at. But it was there! He remembered, it was there!

"Down the hall," he said. "About twenty feet. There's another phone. It's just a little ways."

Their unbelieving eyes looked at him.

"You're wide open to the Soviet guns there, Doc."

"The bird is going to fly, goddammit!" Peter said.

"Man, they'll cut you apart."

"I just need a minute on the damn phone."

"We'll give you covering fire," said the officer. "We'll give you all we've got."

"I'll go with him," somebody said. "He's going to need somebody up with him firing too."

Peter looked. The soldier had a sheepish look under his filthy face, and some semblance of familiarity. Then Peter realized: he wasn't a soldier at all, he was that young FBI agent Uckley. Now, what the hell was he doing down here?

"Let's go," said Peter.

He ran to the corner; around it was the Soviet gun position and the telephone. Across the way Delta operators were firing on the Soviets. The noise of the fire was loud and percussive and frightening. Peter hated it, hated it all: the guns, the loudness, the sense of danger heavy in the air, and most of all he hated his own fear, which was like a living presence within him. And he hated her, Betty who was Megan, who loved him and hated him and whom he could never please.

"Terminal countdown has commenced," Megan said.

Uckley was next to him. He had two of the little German machine pistols with long clips, one for each hand. He looked scared too.

The Delta troopers on this side of the hall were busy clicking their bolts or whatever they had to do to fire.

"You ready, Doc?" came the call.

Peter could hardly find his voice. "Uh-huh," he squeaked.

"Okay, Delta, on my mark," said the young officer. "Go!"

The Delta operators jumped into the hall and began to fire down it. The noise rose and to Peter it sounded like someone rolling an oil drum half full of nuts and bolts down a metal stairwell. He had the impression, further, of dust gushing and roiling. He ran in panic, splashing through the water. The air was full of streaks and flashes. Clouds of mist rose. The corridor filled with screams. None of this made the slightest sense. He reached the niche in the wall where the phone was mounted, and attempted to squeeze into it. A bullet hit close by, evicting a plug of cement from the wall, which stung him. Bullets were striking all over the place. There was something freakish, almost paranormal, in their rapidity. They flittered like insects, popping off the walls and kicking up gouts of water on the floor. Next to him the man Uckley was firing bursts from both guns simultaneously, and squeezing in on him, putting his body between the Russian fire and himself. He was squished into the darkness of the wall by Uckley's warmth.

He picked up the phone.

It was dead.

He panicked, then thought to look at the receiver, saw that it was on a different line, punched the button, and the dial tone leapt into his ear.

"Hurry," screamed Uckley firing.

"Terminal countdown has commenced," said Megan.

Shut up, Megan!

Peter dialed.

           *   *   *

Somehow, Gregor made it to the table itself. It surprised him not to be dead. Now, however, he had the problem of rising to it. His two wounds bled profusely. He'd left a liquid trail upon the floor, and his pants were damp and baggy with blood. An odd noise rose to his ears, in syncopation with the diminishing raggedness of his breathing. It sounded like an accordionist whose instrument had been perforated. Then he realized it was his own body that issued the groaning sound: he had a sucking chest wound, and the air was leaking out of the ruptured bladder of his lungs with a pitiful squeak. He tasted blood in the base of his throat, swallowed it.

Then he rose. Where the strength came he could not fathom. It was just there, in his fat, chalky, clumsy body. He fought through oceans of pain to get up off the floor until he tottered shakily over the infernal machine. He breathed in sobs, his chest bubbling greedily. His head ached and pounded. Most of his body was numb. His fingers were clumsy. He didn't trust them to do what he ordered. His tongue felt like a dry lizard in his mouth. His lips had turned to limestone.

He put a paw on the machine. It simply lay there, though he fancied he could feel just the faintest thrum of vibration.

2358:35
2358:36
2358:37

The numbers flickered by. No power on earth could stop them. He stared, almost mesmerized as they dove toward the ultimate, the 2400, when the bomb would detonate and the world would become midnight.

Gregor started to weep.

What chance had a mere man against such magic?

His thick and sad fingers made an awkward stab at the gibberish of buttons atop the machine, but he couldn't even coordinate their movements and get them to touch where he directed them, not that he really understood where they belonged. He almost passed out.

A tear fell upon the black, blank surface of the bomb console. It lay there, picking up the flicking red of the rushing numbers. Other than the timing device, there was only the arming button, its safety pin long since removed. It had been pushed, and sat, recessed, in its little receptacle.

He imagined what would happen. It was an implosion device. A sphere of high explosive packed around a sphere of plutonium around a core of beryllium as its neutron source. The explosive would detonate, all its force impelling the plutonium onto the beryllium in the crucible of the nanosecond, achieving critical mass and chain reaction.

What can I fight it with?

2358:56

2358:57

2358:58

The phone rang.

Walls looked at it in shock, then picked it up.

"Yo?"

"Walls," it was a shriek, "you there?"

"Shit, yes."

"We've only got a few, oh—ah! Oh, sorry, I just—oh, shit, that hurts, my leg, oh, Christ, look out, get—okay, you okay? It's kind of hairy here."

"Go on, man," said Walls.

"Okay, listen to me. You find the columns yet?"

"No sweat, man."

"Great, okay, great. From the left, count over to the third one, okay."

Walls did it.

"Got that motherfucker."

"Okay, now lean forward, I want you to look at the first letter on each label, okay. Just the letter."

"No sweat."

"Find the one that starts with a P."

Walls fingered each one until he came on P, for Practical Electrical Guidance Check.

"Yo."

"Press it."

Walls pushed it.

"Now find the one for A."

Walls's eyes passed over the letters.

A. For Advanced Circuitry Mechanics.

"Yo."

"Punch it—oh, shit. Oh, Lord, punch it, God, they just hit this guy. Christ, punch it!"

Walls hit it.

"Now an I."

Walls found an I, for Inertial Navigation Circuitry Check.

He pushed it.

"God, great, almost there. Oh! Oh, fuck, God, that was close."

Walls could hear noises and screams in the background.

"The M. Find the M, man."

Walls found it easy. M. M, for Manual Recharge Override.

He pushed it.

"Done!"

"Great, now a B. Find the B and we're done."

Walls read the letters on the labels. His eyes flew down the column, panicked. He felt a stab of pain. His eyes flooded with tears, blurring and spangling what he saw.

"Find it? Find it, goddammit, you've just got that one button, come on now, it's about a halfway down."

Walls was sobbing.

"Ain't no fucking B here."

"Goddamn, find it. *Find it!* A B, *goddamn you, find it!*"

Walls went over it again.

"Ain't no B here," he cried, hating himself for his inability to change the hulking reality of the actual, "ain't no B here."

"Final launch sequence commencing," said Betty reasonably.

Puller was hunched up near the shaft doors, listening as one of the Delta men narrated the events. He could hear the rush of the gunfire as it filtered up the long tunnel. It sounded like the surf.

"Okay, Delta Six, the doc is on the phone, he seems to have made contact, the Soviet fire is picking up around them. Oh, Jesus, he just hit that guy near him."

"Give them covering fire!" Puller snapped.

"We're giving it everything we've got, Delta Six, I can see the doc on the phone, he's yelling and—oh, shit—"

"Hit?"

"No, it's the voice, she's saying they're going into terminal count-down, oh, shit, I don't think—"

Puller could hardly breathe. His chest felt as if he were about to have a heart attack, stony and constricted. He looked away, into the cold darkness, and suddenly there was an explosion off to the left. Its force, even from here, was considerable. Puller fell back, momentarily stunned, and the men around him recoiled against the sudden pressure of the blast. But it wasn't a bomb.

"The silo door just blew," someone said. "The bird is going to fly."

Indeed, the heavy silo door had just detonated itself into a shower of rubble. That meant thirty seconds until launch.

From the silo itself there now issued a shaft of light, high and straight, like a sword blade, narrowing as it climbed in the dark night sky, laying out the course of the missile that would follow.

"Shit," somebody said. "We didn't make it."

Men were running from the light, scurrying over the ragged face of the mountain. Now came the roar as primary ignition began; from the exhaust vanes, four plumes of boiling white smoke billowed out into the night.

"She's going, she's going, she's going," rose the cry.

Puller wondered what it would look like, saw in his deepest brain's eye the thing emerge, driven skyward by the bright flare at the tail, knew that it would first be majestic, stately almost, and then would gather speed and climb skyward with psychotic urgency, rising, its brightness diminished, until it was gone and the sky was black again.

"We didn't make it," said someone with a ludicrous giggle that Puller realized was a sob. "We didn't make it. They beat us, the motherfuckers."

"All right," yelled Peter, squashed in darkness under the body of Uckley, Uckley's blood dripping down into his face, "now I want you to read me the first letters on the column. We can make it, Walls, read them."

"S," came the voice.

Software Integrating Interface Check.

"Yes."

"P."

A bullet hit near Peter's arm.

Practical Electrical Guidance Check.

"Yes."

"A."

Advanced Circuitry Mechanics.

"Yes."

"I."

He could hear the Delta automatic weapons rattling away. Guns were so loud. When they fired, he felt the hot push of the exploding gases. And they were firing all around him. Another Delta team had worked its way down the hall and clustered about him. Their spent brass shells cascaded down upon him and he thought they looked like raindrops as they bounced on the floor.

"No, I think that's an L. Look closely."

"Fuck. An L, yeah."

Launch Gantry Retraction Mechanism.

"Yes."

"I."

Inertial Navigational Circuitry Check.

"Yes."

"S."

One of the Delta team was hit and fell with a thud in front of Peter. Shroud Ejection Mechanism Check.

"Yes."

"A."

Peter tried to think of the next A.

A?

A bullet hit two inches from his head, its spray lacerating his face. The pain was sharp. Jesus! He winced.

What the fuck was this A?

"Read me the letters."

He heard the voice move so slowly through them.

A-N. D-H-E-E. E-E-R-R. E-S-M. I-R-V."

Now, what the fuck was that?

Gregor felt like a fool. He was fighting an atom bomb with a Swiss Army knife. His mind wandered in and out. He looked at the rushing numbers. He wondered if he'd feel a thing when the bomb detonated.

He'd had some trouble with his thick fingers getting the blade opened. He remembered how just a few hours ago he'd used it to spring the car window! How different a world that was! He began to grow woozy with blood loss. The blade probed stupidly at the arming button. It didn't seem to make any difference. Yet there came a second when the blade seem to lock under something, seemed to hold steady, and Gregor leaned against it.

There was a pop, and the button itself flashed out of its receptacle and disappeared. He'd pried it loose! He bent, saw nothing, only a wire lead headed through a hole down through the armored case.

He stared at it.

His lungs issued the moan of a leaking organ, a last long grace note falling out of the riddled apparatus. He felt like a fool, an oaf. What could a man do in the face of such madness?

The numbers flashed ever onward, pulling the world toward fire and nothingness. He heard himself screaming at the insanity of it. His rage grew until it was animal, and from all that he had left he screamed again and again, as if the volume of his voice could somehow halt the rush of the numbers.

The numbers fell out of focus.

He blinked and they were back.

2359:18

2359:19

2359:20

He screamed again.

Then he lifted the pistol and set its barrel into the receptacle out of which he'd plucked the button.

He fired.

The gun bucked in his hand and flew free, out into space. The smell of powder rose to his nose.

Gregor laughed.

He'd tried to stab, and now shoot, an atom bomb!

At least he had his wit at the end of the world.

It was all sliding away in the foolish flutter of the numbers. His focus wobbled, then quit altogether. He was lost in blindness. The pain inside had become awful. A dog was loose in his guts, eating them.

Vodka! Vodka!

He reached into his jacket pocket. It was still there! He pulled the thing out and, not risking losing his grip on the bomb, he simply smashed the bottle neck against the table, shattering it, and brought the jagged nozzle to his mouth.

Hot fire raced down, its taste a century's worth of mercy. Here's to vodka, I drink to vodka!

He lifted the bottle in toast as the seconds rushed toward the last, the final, the midnight that was forever.

"I drink to the bomb!" he shouted.

"I drink to the motherland!" he shouted.

"I drink to Comrade General Arkady Pashin!" he shouted.

And he allowed the bomb to drink.

Into the hole blown through the button channel by the bullet he poured what was left of the vodka.

"Drink, you motherfucker," he shouted. "Drown your sorrows in vodka as better men before you have, you goat-fucking son of a bitch."

The bomb drank the liquid hungrily.

2359:52

2359:53

2359:54

Gregor watched the numbers slide away with growing, hazy disinterest. They were like a red tide of blood, come to choke the world in its own rotten evil. A laugh bubbled from Gregor's lips. He watched the numbers reach toward midnight. . . .

2359:55

2359:56

2359:57

2359:58

2359:58

    :58

    :58

Gregor stared at the number: forever and ever, it would read :58.

Then the light blinked off.

Gregor's head fell forward and he slid to the floor, where he quietly bled to death.

It was a joke!

It was a fucking joke!

And heeeere's MIRV.

"What's it on? Is it on a piece of paper or something?"

"It's on a card, taped to the—"

"*Tear it off! Tear it off!*" Peter yelled.

He waited a second.

"*What's the letter?*"

"B."

B!

Bypass Primary Separation Mode Check!

"Final launch commencing," Megan was saying.

"Punch it."

There was a second in which the universe seemed suspended.

"Punch it! Punch it! Punch it!" Peter was screaming.

"We have an abort," said Megan. "We have a launch abort."

The cheers from Delta rose, filling the corridor.

"You did it, Walls!" yelled Peter, lurching on the sheer joy of it, the sheer pleasure, looking at his watch to note this moment, to see that it was ten seconds after midnight, and they'd made it, they'd made it!

I beat you, Megan.

He sobbed the truth.

I love you, Megan, Jesus how I lo—

After Midnight

T he call came at 1:30 A.M. It awak-
ened Megan on the cot in the small room off the studio. She shook the
confusion out of her head, blinked, and thought for just a moment it
was Peter again, and the sound of his voice, twisted but recognizable
over the wires, came to her in memory. Her heart quickened. She saw
his face. She smelled him. In her heart she touched him. But then she
heard the yelling, the screaming, the pounding. The agents were acting
like boys at some Fourth of July celebration. It was juvenile, party time,
and it felt all wrong to her, somebody else's party. She was frightened.

She got up and went into the studio. They were still pounding each
other on the backs and shaking hands and hugging and she had a terrible
feeling of isolation from them. Then she looked and saw that the older
one, the one called Leo, wasn't part of it.

He walked over to her. Duty, that bitch, shone on his constricted
face. There was triumph in him, but no pleasure and actually a good
deal of pain.

"Mrs. Thiokol, at about midnight tonight our Delta force unit fought
its way into the installation at South Mountain and managed to disable
the Peacekeeper missile just prior to launch."

"So there's not going to be a World War Three?" she asked hollowly,
as if she cared.

"Not tonight," he said, but there was something else on his face. She
knew, of course.

"Peter didn't make it, did he?"

"No, ma'am, I'm sorry to say, he didn't. He was hit in the head at the
last second after Delta broke in and stopped the launch."

"I see."

She took a deep breath. She thought of her squashed tins, crumpled
and lurid on the floor. His head, smashed by the bullet. Peter limp on

the floor of some hard governmental site, among lean soldiers busy with the drama of their own existence. It was so imbecilic, she almost laughed.

"If it means anything, they say he was a hero. An incredible hero."

Oh, this was rich. "A hero." Oh, Jesus, spare me, you asshole. I mean, who gives a fuck? Am I on your team now? Am I supposed to sleep with some hideous little medal?

"No, no, it doesn't mean anything," she said, and went back to her room so that they could not see her grief.

Walls sat mute in the chair, facing the dead board of switches. He felt absolutely wrung out. He felt like he was back in solitary, in the little cell with FUCK NIGGERS scratched into the door.

Then he smiled.

Come through some doors today, yes, sir.

Walls waited in the launch control center for another hour, just like that, sitting there, trying to feel something. The only thing he felt was hunger. He was ravenous. He noticed a brown paper sack lying on the console, spotted with grease. He opened it, and discovered a peanut butter sandwich in a Baggie, a bag of Fritos, and an apple. He gobbled down the sandwich but was still hungry. But he didn't feel as if he had the energy left to open the Fritos.

Finally, the phone rang again. He picked it up.

"Yo?"

"Walls, this is Delta Six. We've mopped up the Soviet resistance now. You can come out."

"Yes, suh. You best get some medics here. Man in here, hurt bad."

"Yes, we have medics now."

Walls picked up his shotgun, went to the door and threw the heavy lock, and stepped out. He didn't understand then, though he did shortly afterward, that he was not only stepping out of the capsule, but also stepping into history.

As he put his foot out, a flash went off. He paid it no mind. It was a picture, taken by a Ranger who'd thought to bring his Nikon along, and the picture ended up four days later on the covers of *Time* and *Newsweek*, as the story of the Day Before Midnight, as the press took to calling it, became the story of the decade, or maybe the second half of the century. The picture showed a handsome black man with a red bandanna around his head. His face was dirty and drawn, glistening with sweat, somehow very sexy. He looked tough and beautiful and quite dangerous, all of which he was, and very, very brave. His eyes were the eyes of a battle-weary soldier: They showed wariness and fatigue, and something else as well, a profound humanity. He carried his shotgun with him, and had it at a jaunty angle; his camouflage fatigues were sodden with sweat and his hips were narrow, his shoulders broad. The veins and muscles on his arms stood out.

He became the icon of all of them, all the men who'd died or fought at South Mountain. The newsmagazines developed charts to show how he'd gotten in, where he'd hit people, the chances he'd taken, the luck he'd had, the brains and cool he'd shown. That he was functionally illiterate, and an authentic criminal, by the perverse currents loose in American culture in the late 80s, helped him. It made him a man of massive flaws, no Occidental superman of bland personality. His courage, however, was incontrovertible: A general was quoted in *Time* saying that he'd give up all his medals to have fought Walls's fight into the mountain, one of the great feats of arms in history. Of course Walls never served another day in jail: he was a hero; he had defined a new life out of the old one, on his guts and talent.

But all that was in the future. For now Walls simply stepped out, blinked at the flashbulb, and walked forward, unsure where to go. The soldiers, most of them from the Ranger battalion who'd come down to relieve Delta, stood a little in awe of him.

Then someone said, "Way to go, Delta."

"Delta did it," someone else said.

"Delta got it done," another said.

"That's Delta. That's the best."

"Goddamn, Delta kicked ass."

Then someone clapped and then someone else, and in seconds it was an ovation, and Walls just stood there, a little unsure what to do, whom to report to, grinning modestly.

Then the man who saved the world uttered the sentence that made him a global sensation.

"What's for breakfast?"

The truck with the three hearses left the Soviet Embassy at six A.M., went out Constitution to the Roosevelt Bridge, and picked up the

George Washington Parkway. It was followed the whole way to the Beltway by the FBI van.

"They're going to Dulles," said the driver.

"I know," said Nick Mahoney.

The Soviet truck turned off the Dulles access road, shot by the huge gull-shaped terminal, and turned down a road marked Cargo Access Only. The FBI vehicle did not bother to mask its surveillance, which extended only to the point of a huge Cyclone fence marked AEROFLOT. Beyond, Virginia technically became Russia; the truck sped through the gate and disappeared into the hangar.

"Wanna go back?" asked the driver.

"No," said Mahoney. "Just park here, right out in the open. I want the bastards to see us good. To know that we're watching."

Mahoney got out of the van, leaned against it, lit a cigarette, and peered nakedly through the fence. It was chilly; the sun was beginning to rise. Mahoney looked at it.

Hello, sun, he thought. Nice to see you.

In time, a single figure emerged from the hangar and walked across the tarmac to the gate.

"Mahoney, what do you want?" he said tiredly. "Do you want me to officially complain again? We've all had a difficult night."

"I'll say. So how close did it go before he stopped it, Max?"

Max Stretov was senior KGB, in charge of embassy security. He and Mahoney were old antagonists.

"You tell me, Mahoney."

"You know our mikes aren't that good. But just after midnight all hell broke loose in your place, I'll tell you that. You had your doctors in there, all your security personnel, senior KGB and GRU *Rezidents*, the whole staff, the works. You think we don't know how close it came?"

Stretov just looked at him. Then he said, "He was yours all along, I suppose. Poor Gregor, we never had him fixed for a double."

"That's the joke. We had him spotted but never turned him. We were using him for low-level disinformation. He wasn't big enough for anything else. I guess he was big enough last night, huh?"

"This fellow Pashin—"

"The late Arkady Pashin."

"Yes. He was a madman, you understand. Part of an insane group called Pamyat that pines for the old ways. What he did he did on his own."

"Yeah, sure. That's the line, huh? We'll let the smart guys figure that one out. By the way, Max, I got something for you."

"You know I can't take anything from you."

"Bend the rules a little, buddy."

Mahoney reached in his coat pocket and pulled out a small military ribbon, blue and white.

"One of the guys in the outfit had it," he said. "It's nothing, just a little trinket. You do me a favor, you give it to Gregor's widow, okay?"

The Russian looked at it, recognized it as the ribbon signifying the Silver Star, and knew that Mahoney had won it as a Marine captain outside Ap Hung Nghia in 1966.

"I can't take it, Mahoney. But it's a nice thought. He deserved it, I'll say that. The Goshgarian bitch put two bullets into him, and he lived long enough to stop the world from ending. Fortunately, he was an alcoholic. He shorted out the detonator mechanism with vodka. Such an absurd victory. Anyway, I wish I could take it from you."

"Yeah, well, I wish you could too. I'll say one thing: for a little fat fuck, he was a prince."

"A prince," agreed the Russian, turning back to the hangar.

It was dawn now, and looked to be another fine, bright cold Maryland day. Dick Puller was by himself, outside the command center. Actually, he'd wandered away in the night, and let other experts take over. It was for the medical people to handle now, because there were so many wounded and there was the terrible task of extracting the badly hit up the elevator shaft to the mountaintop and then to the medevac choppers.

So from where he sat it looked like the site of some civil disaster. Choppers were ferrying the wounded down from the mountain to the field hospital, where a shock trauma unit had been set up under a large tent with a red cross emblazoned upon it. At the same time, all the world's ambulances had collected at the tent, too, to transport the less severely wounded to regional facilities. Red lights blinked furiously and the intense commotion generated a sense of blur, of frenzy without direction. Puller just stared at it, barely conscious. He couldn't find the energy just now to sort it out.

Instead, he had a sense of grief. Yet it was not for himself, though he also had a presentiment of failure, of all the grounds on which he was vulnerable. Without thinking about it much, he knew, in the way these things worked, that he'd be destroyed again. He'd have to answer for Bravo, and why he'd sent it to die twice, the butcher, the baker, the candlestick maker. But the grief he felt at this time was not for himself.

Jesus, a lot of men, good ones, gone forever. That was what left you feeling so degraded and debauched afterward. You just wanted to go off somewhere and lie down and sleep and somehow will them back into their bodies and will them whole and healthy again. But you never could. You wondered if you'd ever look at a hill again and not see its slopes full of dying boys begging for their mothers and asking why it had to be them and not some other guys. It was the one question he'd never found an answer for in all his years and on all his hills.

He was sitting on a swing, gently rocking back and forth. He looked at his watch—0700. Morning of the new day. The early light was pale, almost incandescent. It played off the snow in peculiar textures, almost turning blue. The sky above the mountain also looked to be blue, blue and pure, without a cloud to mar it anywhere. He shivered, drawing his coat around him; it was very cold. He had a headache and felt older than the blue mountain that humped up before him, benign now, and remote. If there was a lesson in this, he didn't know it. It was no parable; it was just a battle.

He watched now as a young man left the command center and shuffled across the snowy field toward him. No, it wasn't Skazy, or poor Uckley, or Dill, or God help him, Peter Thiokol—all his boys who had not made it through the night. Poor Peter, he might even have been the bravest, braver than any soldier. He certainly was smart. Or Uckley, down where he shouldn't have been, standing out there, drawing the fire that came for Peter. And Frank. Frank, you were a prick and a hothead, and maybe even a psycho, but we needed a man to lead the assault, to go down first, knowing exactly the consequences, and you went without a second thought.

Puller saw that it was the junior Delta officer McKenzie, commander of the last attack on the Soviet strongpoint. He'd be the inheritor of it all.

"Sir, I thought you'd like to know the President is on his way. He'll be arriving shortly."

"Umm," was all Puller could think to say. The news filled him with terrible weariness. He hated that part of it the worst, where the bigshots came by after the battle and asked the kids who'd survived where they were from and told them their folks would be proud of them. Well, he supposed it would mean something to the kids.

"Do you have final casualty figures, Captain?"

"It's pretty bad, sir. Bravo lost seventy-six killed, maybe another hundred to hundred twenty hit. Delta lost twelve men in the initial assault; then, of the one hundred five we got into the tunnel, we lost sixty-five dead, the rest hit. Only seven guys in Delta came out without a scratch. Of the first squadron, twenty-two guys, you got one hundred percent fatals. The Rangers lost fifty-one KIA in the assault, maybe another seventy-five wounded. Third Infantry came out with only some mussed hair. Eleven KIA, thirty-one wounded. We lost six helicopter aircrew from the two crashed birds. Then there was that FBI agent Uckley. Also sixteen state troopers went along on the final assault. Seven of them were killed, most of the rest hit. Brave guys, those country cops. They grow 'em tough in this state, I'll say that. Three of the four people we sent into the tunnels, including that poor Vietnamese woman. Jesus, we found her back in the tunnel by the silo access hatch with an empty automatic and seven Russians around her. She did some kind of job, let me tell you. Without her, Walls doesn't get *close* to the LCC. Then the fourteen men on the mission to open the tunnel for the tunnel rat teams, we lost them all. Then there were three National Guard pilots. And the sixteen men in the installation security complement. And the two officers on silo duty. So we're looking at two hundred sixty-seven dead. Maybe four hundred wounded. I suppose it could be a lot worse. Hell, at Beirut the Marines lost—"

"All right, Captain. What about that poor welder? The one who burned Pashin?"

"They think he's going to make it, sir. He's stable. Lost a lot of blood, but he's looking good."

"I'm glad. What about the Soviets?"

"Well, we figure their strength to have been about seventy. We've got sixty-two body bags and eight badly wounded."

Then, absurdly chipper in the morning light, McKenzie suddenly smiled. His face was giddy with innocent enthusiasm.

"Sir, you did it. I mean, you really outfought that guy. You had him outsmarted at every step of the way. I have to tell you, in Delta we were pretty pissed off at you yesterday. But you knew what you were doing. You won. Goddamn, you kicked Aggressor-One's ass."

There was such indecent worship in the young man's voice, it filled
Puller with nausea. The stupid little prick. Puller snorted.

"Peter Thiokol did it, McKenzie. I just pointed the soldiers up the
hill."

But he was an argumentative little son of a bitch.

"No, sir. Respectfully, sir, you beat him. And Delta beat him, sir.
That's the lesson. You got a problem, you call the professionals. Your
professional, he'll get it done, sir, your elite soldier."

No, that was not the lesson. Puller saw that now. In the end it wasn't
Delta on the mountain. In the end it wasn't the professionals. It was the
regular people. A black convict. A Vietnamese refugee. A young federal
officer. A neurotic defense consultant. A welder. An Air National Guard
pilot. A gym teacher, an accountant, a housewife.

He looked at the huge mountain that sat atop the surface of the earth
and realized then what you had to do to get to the top of it and stop the
madness.

It wasn't the professionals. It was the regular people, the Rest of Us,
back in the world. It was our mountain, and we had to get up there. If
we didn't, who would?

Suddenly, the pulsing sound of helicopter engines rose above him.
Three huge Sea Stallions in green and white had appeared over it and
were beginning the descent. Even from the distance Puller could make
out the seal of the President of the United States.

"Sir, we ought to be down there. The Joint Chiefs will be along too.
And I bet the press will be here soon. They're going to be all over this
mountain by noon. It's going to turn into a carnival."

Puller rose, threw away his cigarette, and said yes, yes, the captain
was right, they had better go to meet the President.